THE BOMBMAKER

GAVIN REESE

LIQUID MIND PUBLISHING

Gavin Reese donates a portion of all his sales to non-profit organizations that benefit
law enforcement professionals and veterans, their families, and the heirs, survivors, and
memories of our Fallen Heroes. A portion of *The Debt Collectors* proceeds helps fund
law enforcement organizations that counter narcoterrorism. A portion *The Misery
Merchant* proceeds benefits organizations that improve the rescue, rehab, and recovery
of sex trafficking victims. A portion of proceeds from *The Kizazi Murders* goes to help
cold case homicide investigations in the Baltimore, Maryland, area.

More information is at gavinreese.com

MICHAEL THOMAS SERIES_

For Mrs. Reese, Mo Anam Cara, and everyone else who believed in me.

RELEVANT REALITIES_

Relevant Realities

"*The Church's Relationship with the Muslims:* The plan of salvation also includes those who acknowledge the Creator, in the first place among whom are the Muslims; these profess to hold the faith of Abraham, and together with us they adore the one, merciful God, mankind's judge on the last day." -- *841, Catechism of the Catholic Church, 2nd Edition.*

"Terrorism threatens, wounds, and kills indiscriminately and is gravely against justice and charity." -- *2297, Catechism of the Catholic Church, 2nd Edition.*

"If anger reaches the point of a deliberate desire to kill or seriously wound a neighbor, it is gravely against charity; it is a mortal sin. The Lord says, 'Everyone who is angry with his brother shall be liable to judgment.'" -- *2302, Catechism of the Catholic Church, 2nd Edition.*

"The symbolism of the burning of Notre Dame Cathedral, the most renowned building in Western civilization, the iconic symbol of

Western Christendom, is hard to miss...It is as if God Himself wanted to warn us in the most unmistakable way that Western Christianity is burning -- and with it, Western civilization." – *Dennis Prager, American columnist.*

"It is lawful to kill an evildoer in so far as it is directed to the welfare of the whole community, so that it belongs to him alone who has charge of the community's welfare. Thus it belongs to a physician to cut off a decaying limb, when he has been entrusted with the care of the health of the whole body. Now the care of common good is entrusted to persons of rank having public authority: wherefore they alone, and not private individuals, can lawfully put evildoers to death." — Saint Thomas Aquinas, Summa Theologica [II-II, Q-64, Art 3]

OATH OF THE ABSOLVERS_

Oath of the Absolvers

I, *Michael Andrew Thomas, swear my allegiance to Almighty God with eternal faith in His Church and Holy Scriptures.*

I affirm my obligation to equally care for the eternal welfare of all God's children.

I affirm that men infected with certain evils are bound for Hell without Final Absolution, which I willingly offer them as an act of eternal mercy.

I vow to never offer Final Absolution to a soul that may be rehabilitated by other means and other men, or without irrefutable knowledge of their grave mortal sins.

I vow to only offer Final Absolution to souls God has identified through His faithful servants placed over me, and to offer each identified soul Confession, Absolution, and Anointment.

I vow to endeavor to send God only souls fully absolved of their sins, prepared for His judgement and eternal entry into the Kingdom of Heaven.

I vow to willingly forfeit my mortal life or earthly freedom to vigor-

ously protect the identity, actions, and purpose of myself and my fellow Absolvers.

I vow never, under any circumstance or duress, to betray this oath, my fellow Absolvers, or those God has appointed over me.

I acknowledge that my betrayal would scandalously support and defend the very evils I've vowed to defeat. I swear these vows to Almighty God of my own free will, upon my mortal body, and with my eternal soul. Per Dominum nostrum (Through our Lord)...

MICHAEL STROLLED through a peaceful meadow filled with waist-high sunflowers. Surrounded by steep, glacial-cut and snowcapped mountains, bright, warm sunlight shone down on his face and arms. Merci walked by his side, and he reached out and grasped her hand. Her skin felt soft and warm as she gently squeezed back. Michael looked over at her, and she met his gaze and smiled.

"I knew I'd see you again someday," she explained. "I just never imagined it would be anything like this."

Father Michael Andrew Thomas woke from the unusual dream, blinked several times, and scanned the surrounding darkness. A thin, bright strip of light emanated from underneath the bathroom door and helped him recognize the luxurious hotel room he'd occupied for the last week. Michael oriented himself back in reality, took in a deep, calming breath, and laid back on the plush king featherbed.

He rubbed his face and tried to analyze the dream. *What the hell was that about? I miss Merci and her friendship, but, that dream felt like being in love with her.* He immediately realized the *faux pas* and shook his head. *She's only ever been 'Doctor Renard' to me. I didn't know her well or long enough to fall in love with her, but it'd be pretty damned easy to fall in love with the idea of her, or whatever I've made her out to be in my mind. Either way, Catholic priests don't get girl-friends or wives, so it's all wasted emotion.*

Michael laid still for several quiet minutes until he accepted he was awake. Like he imagined most people would do, he gave up on slumber and started the morning with his personal smartphone. He opened his email app, and the top item listed there was still the communication Doctor Renard sent yesterday, which he'd read just before falling asleep last night. He touched the screen to re-open it.

"Dear Father Michael—I pray that this finds you safe, warm, and happy. I understand, however, that you are happiest in the dangerous cold where the least of your parishioners have to live. Still, I pray that you are safe and well, no matter where you now find yourself.

I understand the boundaries of a friendship such as ours, and that you must maintain your professional distance. I take no offense, but it does my heart good to tell you about my life, even if you seldom respond. The benefit of such communication is that I can finally call myself only 'Merci' while respecting your station and title in this life. I can be 'Dr. Renard' to my colleagues. You, however, I count among my closest friends. Unless you ask me otherwise, I will continue writing to you. Just knowing you read my words and thoughts brings me comfort and reassurance, the very things you seek to dispense to the world around you.

I don't know where God has called you to serve, but I hope you're happy there. I know your parishioners are Blessed to have men such as yourself. I hope they realize how fortunate they are, and just how much God has smiled on their lives by bringing you into their presence.

My research has made unexpected advances in the last few weeks, which will delay my return to international aid work. For now, I must be home. It seems we will soon outgrow our present facility, so my partners and I travel to Lucerne soon to consider a larger laboratory space. Regardless of the outcome, I will let you know where to find me, if you ever wish to do so. Peace be with you, Father Michael.

Wishing you Love & Light, without agenda. — Merci"

Michael stared at the email for a long moment. *Monsignor was probably right. The only kinder words I've read were Catherine's love letters back in college. Mer—, Doctor Renard may say 'without agenda,' but that's not a letter you write to a platonic friend. I knew clerical work would lead to certain, temptations, along the way. Just not sure what to do about this one...*

The phone's digital clock proclaimed it was 3:42am. Michael calculated the time difference and shifted focus to a secured messaging app. He first texted his mentor and colleague, Monsignor Eduardo Hernandez.

H, everything alright back there? I can't come home yet, so I hoped you could check on my parents. How's Ira?

He sent the message, and a blue bubble appeared almost immediately to announce that Hernandez was typing a response.

Ira the Wonder Dog is fine. Your mom had a rough week, the new MS treatments have taken a toll. Your dad stops into the church every other day to talk and check on Ira. Be safe, and I'll worry about home until you get back.

Michael grimaced at the unpleasant reality that his family faced at the moment. *If I survive this job long enough, I can pay cash for mom's treatments in another year.*

He locked the phone, sat up to his left, turned on a bedside lamp, and set the device on the adjacent nightstand. A customized notepad from *The Oremus at Greenwich* sat next to the clock and displayed a handwritten address for his next destination. *John insists I take the hotel's shuttle service to a private airport. If he's so confident that no one will think twice about taking me out there, the hotel's registry must read like the Fortune 100 directory. Biggin Hill Airport's only really used for corporate jets and private aircraft. At least the Vatican's covert fleet can hide in plain sight among all the other multimillion-dollar planes.*

Michael took his official smartphone off its charger and checked for new emails and messages. *None, not even from Sergio. Hope he's wrong about the new phones John forced on us, but paranoid is safer than complacent.* He opened the last email his boss had sent yesterday evening, and Michael reread it to ensure he hadn't mistaken any of its details. *I can easily hear John's gruff baritone saying this.*

"Bonjour, shithead. Got your preliminary report on London and the request. Standby. Meantime, you're going straight back out. Meet your transport at Biggin Hill Airport no later than 0700. They depart for Paris at 0701, whether you're there or not. I made reservations for you at The Oremus there, as well. Keep up the good work and you ought to get a shitload of frequent flyer points this year, maybe even absolve your way to a nice set of steak knives for the rectory back home. 2297. — John"

Still seated on the edge of the luxurious bed, Michael stretched his neck and shoulders. He gave a reluctant sigh and accepted the urgent, unexpected request. *John normally sends us home between investigations, even the ones like London that refuse to pan out. I know it's not the same as saying 'no' to God, it's still hard to turn down a request from the Church, even if it does only come from the anonymous head of this clandestine sect. Might be His Holiness, Pope Cornelius II, or someone he's directed to actively combat evil in the shadows where it lives. Either way, it doesn't matter. John and the minders above him probably deserve more faith and trust than I've given. Especially with an investigation of this nature, I can't go out into the field questioning everything they send my way.*

Michael pondered the coded explanation of his next investigation, the numerical ending to John's email that referred to a specific paragraph of Catholic ideology. Although an obscure and lesser referenced section of the Catechism of the Catholic Church, Michael knew 2297's subject by heart. *Kidnapping, hostage taking, mutilation, terrorism, and torture. No idea which part of that I'm being sent to corroborate, but they're all among the most reprehensible aspects of human behavior. Most people will never understand that killing isn't the worst thing humans do to each other.* Michael considered some of the gruesome crimes he'd investigated when he still worked as a cop before he entered the priesthood all those years ago. *There's nothing on earth so cruel as a human who's inspired and motivated by evil. We routinely commit atrocities against our own species that even predatory animals would find immoral.*

Michael stood and refreshed a navigation page on the phone's browser. Last night's web search proclaimed the private international airport stood within a thirty-minute drive despite road construction on the A206 and the A21 highways. He confirmed a nearly identical commute this morning and returned his work cell to the nightstand.

Michael cycled through a slow deep breath to combat his rising apprehension. As he'd done for decades, he kneeled beside the bed to begin the first of his five daily prayer recitations. Unlike most days, he struggled this morning to first calm his mind and force anxiety from his heart. *The investigation here in London has been a recurring strikeout, so I haven't had to face this day. If my Paris assignment really involves terrorism or kidnapping, I need all the wisdom and fortitude God's willing to offer, and all the grace and divine guidance I can carry.* Another deep breath offered him no reprieve. *God willing, I'll officially become a serial killer today.*

Private Learjet. 20,504 feet above France.

Dressed in a black belt, slacks, and dress shoes to accompany a dark gray button-down dress shirt, Michael had chosen the mono-chromatic attire to better blend in with the Parisian population. *It's so ironic for the city to be one of the world's fashion capitals while most of its citizens dress in colors more befitting their morose national mood.*

When he felt it descend, Michael looked outside the lavishly appointed aircraft and scanned the northern French countryside below. The idyllic mix of farm fields, green forests, and small country roads reminded Michael of his childhood on his family's ranch outside Santa Fe. *All the alfalfa and grain crops should almost be ready for their first cut. The growing season might not be long enough here to give farmers all four cuts we're used to back home.* The cockpit door unexpectedly opened, and Michael nonchalantly unbuckled his seatbelt to defend himself.

The copilot emerged, apparently unaware of Michael's reflexive reaction. He closed the door and passed over a locked, black case that Michael had expected to receive earlier. Bright red paint displayed

"*Diplomatic Pouch—Internationally Protected Contents*" on both its sides.

"John sends his regards," the copilot explained in his thick Italian accent. "We normally give this when you first arrive, but John wanted a procedure change for this flight. I hope you understand."

"Of course." Michael accepted the hardened case and inspected its numerical locks. Just as the other times he'd flown on covert assignments for his anonymous hierarchy within the Vatican, Michael saw the case had a two-digit numerical combination lock near each side of its handle. *Seems legit.* He looked back up at the copilot. "Thank you for your help."

"*Prego,* Father Andrew. We will have you on the ground in a few minutes. Please tell us if you require anything else."

Michael nodded as the copilot retreated into the cockpit. *Father Andrew. I'm still not used to the pseudonym, even though Saint Andrew is one of my namesakes.* Once he was again alone, Michael retrieved a pair of medical exam gloves from his duffel bag and put them on. He input the combination John had specified in his email. 22-97. The case opened and revealed the usual sealed manila envelope. Michael removed it and scanned the familiar dark red letters printed on the envelope's exterior:

"*Diplomatic Pouch – Property of the Holy See Consulate – Internationally Protected Contents – Sachetto Diplomatico – Proprietá della nazione della Santa Sede*"

Michael smirked as he considered the reality that most people don't understand Vatican City was the primary municipality within the nation of the Holy See. *Almost everyone says, 'the Vatican,' so even the most famous structure in Vatican City takes blame and credit for all manner of things that involve the actions of its nation, the Church, the Pope, or Catholics at-large well outside its walls.*

Additional legalese appeared below the English and Italian language headings. Michael turned the envelope over and saw a two-inch, intricate red wax seal over each of its flaps. The Seal of the Holy See appeared in the upper half, with its cross centered beneath a large papal crown and between a sword and olive branch. Beneath that complex seal, a simple transverse cross, an X-like symbol, appeared in the wax. Together, they confirmed the envelope's origin within the Holy See and Michael as its intended recipient. Every time he authenticated one of these envelopes, the X reminded Michael what he risked on behalf of God and His Church. *The Greeks martyred Saint Andrew by crucifying him on such a cross. Ever since John assigned me to use 'Father Andrew' as my apostolic pseudonym, I've feared meeting such a fate. That kinda death makes third-world prison seem like recess.*

After the envelope passed his initial security confirmations, Michael retrieved a pocketknife and carefully cut into the wax seals. A concealed piece of parchment appeared, and he inspected the tiny numbers typed on it. 2297. 2302-8. 2268. *That matches what John sent over in the second email. Everything's authenticated and legitimate.* He opened the envelope and found only a single sheet of paper. Curious, Michael read its typed message:

"Welcome to Paris, shithead. Time to re-up your membership dues to The Merry Union of Snake Hunters & Gravediggers. This assignment's got different operational security protocols from what they usually do. Wait inside the aircraft until the crew tells you it's safe to proceed. You've got a room reserved at The Oremus hotel in central Paris. Check in with your Holy See passport. Further details await in your room. Safe opens with the same combo. This investigation's a damned sight more dangerous than all the others, so keep your wits about you. Stay frosty. – John"

Michael checked again to make sure the envelope was empty. *Nothing.* He put the paper back into the envelope, which he then carefully secured in a hidden flap at the bottom of the duffel bag. *Gotta preserve any latent prints that might still be there, just in case...*

Apprehension filled his heart and grew more intense as the plane approached its destination. *The only two things I truly hate are 'change' and 'the way things are.' I still don't implicitly trust John as I should, and any change he makes to our protocols makes me question why he's doing it. He could be isolating me because he knows the secrets I'm keeping from him, or some negative external force might have compromised me or one of the other Absolvers. Either way, I've lost my element of surprise and anonymity because John knows exactly where to find me and when I should arrive. Even worse, if he already knows the exact room I'm staying in, then, well, anything's possible. Anything or anyone could be waiting for me inside.*

Michael pondered what Paris held in store for him, along with his inability to avoid it. *Whether John and the anonymous, scared old men who give his orders are doing this for my safety or to isolate and eliminate me as a perceived threat, I probably won't know until it's too late to stop it. I wouldn't be the first priest they've made disappear in the past nine months. Regardless of their intentions or the reasons for them, I've gotta stay one step ahead.* His past successes buoyed his spirits, despite the difference in the risk he now felt. *I need creative solutions, just like I've found ever since I started John's training camp.*

The plane lightly *thumped* down on an asphalt runway as Michael formulated a plan. He knew one of his first priorities had to be contacting Sergio, his old clerical partner and clandestine ally within the Absolvers organization. *He might be somewhere out on assignment himself, but I have to let someone know where I'm going. If things go far enough sideways, I won't have that opportunity later.*

Michael's thoughts logically turned to "Thomas," the apostolic pseudonym for Father Shawn Moore, a former colleague who'd started the covert training camp with Michael and Sergio. *That guy ran himself so far off the rails they locked him up in a secret asylum. I haven't betrayed the Church and the Absolvers like he did, but that might not matter if they learn my secrets and lies.*

The in-cabin intercom speakers came on. "Welcome to *Le Bourget* Airport, Father, and to the north side of Paris. We will taxi for a little while and have you inside a hangar in just a few minutes. I will advise you when it is safe to depart the aircraft."

"Thank you." Michael never knew if the crew could hear him, but civility dictated his response. He watched the lush green fields and black runways and tarmac pass by the small window, all the while scanning for escape routes and nearby highways. *Not a large airport, must be a smaller, private operation.* The aircraft slowed and rolled to a stop inside an expansive hangar. Despite his internal turmoil, Michael patiently sat inside the unmarked Vatican jet. He hoped the directive to wait for the flight crew to release him had to do with their efforts to bypass a customs inspection, but no one had bothered to explain that. *This could work for or against me. If French customs has no record of my arrival, it helps me avoid being associated with any crime scenes later. However, if I've become a target or perceived liability, it also makes it easier for John and his minders to make me disappear now.*

20 Rue de Thorigny, #103. Paris, France.

GERARD ANTLÉ TRUDGED up the interior stairs to his expensive two-bedroom apartment in Paris' Third Arrondissement. *Well, it's now* her *apartment, even if my name remains on the lease.* Dressed in all black clothing and a black beret atop his head, Gerard had promised to join his daughter for breakfast, but he was late again. And, again, because of the job that his soon-to-be ex-wife hated so much.

His highly coveted assignment to the nation's elite counterterrorism task force, the Anti-Terrorism Sub-Directorate commonly known as "SDAT," dictated that he wore normal civilian clothes. Gerard had to blend in well with the rest of the population, at all times and in all places. This reality had made him something of a chameleon, and he commonly toted three or four very different outfits in the trunk of whatever undercover police vehicle he had. The investigations of late had compelled him to spend many of his days moving about in *Seine-Saint-Denis,* a predominantly Muslim immigrant and refugee enclave with a recent history of ethnic isolation, violence, and terrorism. Gerard and his Anglo partners struggled to blend into the homogenous environment, so he'd chosen to present himself as a taxi driver today.

He stopped at the front door to apartment 103 and reached for its doorknob. Only after a second thought did Gerard stop himself, knock, and wait. *It's bullshit to ask to enter my own doorway, but she's probably already changed the damned locks.*

Footsteps approached and the door opened to reveal Claudette, who looked as annoyed as Gerard had expected. "You're late, so all must be normal, yes?"

"Claudette." He only nodded to her and stepped into the compact living room. Even though it measured only 55 square meters, they paid an exorbitant monthly lease for the apartment's location. After Claudette accepted the position of *Conservateur Principal* at the nearby *Museé Picasso,* the apartment allowed her a short, two-block walk to work and greater presence for their daughter. Like Gerard, Claudette's work often demanded long hours, but allowed much greater flexibility to tend to Marie's needs. *There is no true emergency in the world of art museums, after all.* None of this had been a problem until Claudette doubted her happiness as Mrs. Antlé.

The front door *clicked* closed behind Gerard, and he looked about the living areas to his left and the hallway to his right. He neither heard nor saw his daughter. "Where's Marie?"

Gerard turned around and realized Claudette hadn't moved from behind the front door and now stood with her arms crossed. "She left when it became clear that you *again* did not have time for her."

"No one could call to tell me not to bother coming over?"

She shrugged. "You could not bother being on time, or, for that matter, calling to tell your daughter you were late? You want us to stand around waiting for the incomparable *Gerard The Great* to magically appear whenever it suits him?"

He raised his voice in response to her cutting sarcasm. "You know it's not like that, Claudette! You know what my job is like, and you know that I try damned hard to balance--"

"I know I haven't felt like the most important part of your life since you put on that goddamned badge, *that's* what I know, and I know, too, that Marie is starting to see and feel the same second-place treatment from you! All she wants is your time, and all you can deliver is disappointment! That's your specialty, you know!"

"You know what I do for work, how much my job matters to the city and to France, Claudette! I have *obligations,* liabilities you can never understand, and not just to you and Marie! I'm doing this job, sacrificing my time and parts of my relationships for you, so that--"

"Yes, I *know,* Gerard, you're *suffering* so we can be *safe,* but it's not that simple! That's not even the whole truth! You could take another assignment, you could be around at night and on normal days off, but you *choose* to keep doing what you do, and you never *once* asked what Marie or I thought--"

"I fight *terrorists,* Claudette, *monsters,* that wanna see people like you and Marie dead and bleeding out in the streets because of their perverted idea of God! I can't do that and work flexible hours like you can! There's no such thing as a crisis at your museum, right?"

"That's not fair, Gerard, you don't get to make yourself feel better for being a shitty husband and father by demeaning my life's work! I do what *I do* for me and my family, and *you* do what you do *in spite of us!*"

Gerard incredulously stared at his wife. "I don't understand how you know *so little* about me. I'm working a major case right now, and I *still* made time to come by to see my family, only to find you're working to make sure our daughter takes your lead and abandons me, as well."

"Well, congratulations, you'll get to be the hero again for all the other people of France. I keep hearing it's always lonely at the top."

He shook his head and stared at the floor in front of his unpolished dress shoes. "Actually, I'm likely being compelled to close the case. The politicians at the top of the agency forced a new supervisor into the unit, and he's been busy shuttering all our investigations into anything that even *smells* Muslim. I don't know what will happen if he does that, how high I can go to get to do my job--"

"Goddammit, Gerard! Your *job* is not to make waves! Keep your boss happy! *That's* what you're supposed to be doing, making certain you keep a paycheck that supports your family! But, no, that hasn't *ever* been good enough for you! You have to spend all your time pointing out everything that's wrong with everything and everyone else! To tell all the rest of us what we're fucking up! Just *once*, Gerard, *I beg you*, try to smile and be goddamned happy, even if only for a few hours!"

"But, I--"

Claudette waved a hand to cut him off. "You're going to give yourself a heart attack and your daughter will have to grow up without you, never mind what happens between us! *Grow up* and think about what you're doing to everyone around you! You always say principles are expensive things to own, well, you're *damned right* they are, *especially* yours, and I guess we're about to find out what you're willing to pay for them. So, go ahead, tell your boss' boss what he's doing wrong and then come back here to tell me what your next plan is to take care of your daughter."

"I have to do what's *right*, Claudette! What about Marie, do you think she wants a father who gives up his principles when they were no longer easy and convenient?"

"I think she won't give a damn when you lose your *job* and your *car*, and *our home*, and we're all living out on the *streets* because you had to 'do the right thing,' *again!* I think she would rather that you did what you had to do to provide for her and for us, to keep a roof over our heads and let us stay living indoors like people. When she lives in the gutter with the animals, no, I don't think she'll give a *damn* what your principles are!"

"Is that why you're seeing Alexandre?! You've already given up *your* principles?!" Gerard hadn't planned on confronting her about the affair, but he no longer cared about tact or timing.

Claudette showed her surprise for only a moment, but then shrugged and folded her arms across her chest. "No. I'm seeing him because he has his priorities right. I know that if the three of us ever find ourselves living in the gutter, he won't hesitate to *steal* food instead of wading through the dumpsters for thrown-out scraps. He puts us first, *always,* and I *love* that about him!"

Gerard felt his rage boiling up and walked toward the door before they broke anything. "Tell Marie--"

"No! I won't do your dirty work for you! *You* tell your daughter whatever you want her to know, but you should expect that she will believe your actions far more than your words." Claudette stepped in front of him and leaned back against the door. "Do you have your half of the rent money? The lease payment's going to be late again if you don't."

He stopped and shook his head in disbelief. "You know what my paydays are, and you know I'm always broke! I won't have the money until Friday! Does it make you feel good to do this to me?!"

She flashed a coy smile. "Do what, Gerard? You agreed to pay half the expenses when we moved here, and you agreed it was important because of my work and our daughter, and--"

"I've always respected your need to keep our affairs separate and not mix our money and finances, but you're bloodletting me, Claudette! We both agreed to the separation, but you've done nothing but demand *more and more* from me for the last nine months, and I see *no* effort from you to fix us so I can come home. If you don't intend for me to return with you and Marie, then just have the goddamned decency to tell me! I treat my terror suspects better than you're treating me right now, at least those assholes always know where they stand with me!"

His wife's demeanor became even calmer, and her words bit him all the harder. "I thought you would want to do the honorable thing and continue to meet your obligations."

Gerard balled up both fists up in front of his chest, the rage building up pressure there. "That was *before* you decided I had to move out, Claudette! You know how much I bring home, and you know what you take from me every month so that you and Marie can stay here in leisure and luxury while I eat dinner out of a fucking can in that shithole where I have to lay my head at night!" Gerard clenched his teeth and hissed at his wife. *"You're going to drive me mad before you find the decency to divorce me!"*

Claudette had gotten the exact reaction she'd hoped for, and her expression showed it. "How will that work for you and your *sacred* church, when you're divorced and can no longer accept communion? If I abandon you, the precious Roman Catholic Church will leave you, as well. Do you *finally* realize that's a *one-way* relationship? Just like your *goddamned job* with the police, the church *doesn't* love you ba--"

Gerard leapt at her, incensed by her venomous hatred and its partial truth. He jammed his left hand over the front of her throat, pinned her back against the door, and drew his right back in a fist, ready to make her suffer his wrath. The unexpected reaction brought immediate and genuine fear to Claudette's expression and gave Gerard pause. He held them both in place for a moment, and his voice returned as little more than a harsh whisper. "Go...*fuck*...yourself..."

"At least," she whimpered and swallowed hard against his hand, "*I* know how to do it right."

Their old inside joke caught Gerard off-guard, and he released her and stepped back. They looked at each other for a long moment. "We deeply loved each other once."

Claudette fumbled for the door handle and timidly stepped back as she pulled it open. "Young people make all manner of mistakes. It's what they do best."

Gerard inhaled, defiantly raised his head back up, and strode into the shared hallway. He didn't look back before tromping down the stairs. His footfalls almost covered the sound of the deadbolt locking behind him. *No sense putting effort into this. Our field has been scorched, plowed under, and salted. Nothing will ever grow here again. I almost pity the man who draws my attention today.*

MAY 6, 11:15PM (PDT) / 08:15AM
(ROME)_

Rural Training Compound. Esmerelda County, Nevada.

JOHN SAT in a plush Serta-branded professional rolling office chair and diligently typed at the laptop on the small writing desk before him. His usual, nightly efforts required absolute secrecy from the rest of the world.

The room he'd claimed at his most recent covert training compound in rural southwestern Nevada had just enough space for the desk and a matching dark wood bedroom set. The chair glided over the concrete floor, which he'd stained oxblood red and polished to a high shine, even though no one else would ever enjoy his handi-work. John had covered the room's two adjacent windows with blackout curtains, not that sunlight concerned him. He rose every day before dawn, stayed up late each night, and had to ensure no one else learned his schedule. Additional layers of weather stripping around his door and its frame prevented light from escaping into the hallway. A thick, dark brown towel laid across the minuscule gap at the floor.

John strove to keep his nightly efforts to coordinate the team's clandestine work a secret. His own cadres of instructors didn't rate such intel, even though he'd entrusted each of them with his life more than once during his forty-eight years of service to the United States government. Some he'd met during his long-ago stint in the Army, but most had been colleagues or contacts he'd developed over nearly four decades at CIA. *Still, they don't got a need or a right to know what me and my boys are up to, even if they are helpin' train the next class of operatives.*

John checked his watch and assumed his supervisor had to be awake. *Nine hours difference, so that weasel oughta be up and movin' about in search of some unwitting prey.* He sighed, picked up his cell phone, and considered the reality of this mandated interaction. *If only these things could just unscrew themselves...*

After ensuring the device's virtual private network showed his call originating from Bombay, India, John sent the call, held the phone to his ear, and absentmindedly rolled an old, spent bullet casing through the fingers on his right hand. A faded red *1* spanned the bottom and reminded him of that first deer hunt with his dad in eastern Wyoming all those years ago.

The call finally connected, and a European ringer sounded in John's ear and returned his focus to the present.

brrrrt brrrrt

brrrrt brrrrt

brr-

"Good morning, or, I suppose, more correctly, good *night*. How may I help you close out your day?"

"Good morning," John replied to his superior and stifled a suspicious frown at the man's friendly greeting. *Beware the predator that kills with kindness.* "I gotta couple issues we need to work out before I can sign off for the night. First one's the ongoing Nebraska problem."

"The Father Thomas fiasco. I'm still *outraged* he became an immediate threat to the secrecy of our organization."

"'Secret' wasn't *ever* gonna be an option. We can hope to stay 'covert,' at best. There ain't no organization in all of human history that stayed 'secret' once the second asshole found out about it. The problem he's causin' today is comin' from that same activist group. Ever since we stashed him away in our psych facility, they've been huntin' a court-a law with the jurisdiction to force us to hand him over. They wanna get him into a private facility where their own docs can prove he ain't schizophrenic and didn't make up all the allegations that came out in the press last fall."

"That's nothing new. It's my understanding they've been judge-shopping throughout Nebraska and the 10th Circuit to find friendly eyes and a bleeding heart. What concerns you about it now?"

John cleared his throat. "I got an email from an old colleague that's readin' *their* emails, don't ask how or why. They're gonna skip the legal process and kidnap Thomas. The group contacted a hacker syndicate to get into Church records and figure out where we're keepin' him."

"You're *serious?*"

John reflexively nodded. "As a goddamned heart attack. I think you oughta consider movin' him off-record, somewhere far and away from their expectations. Somewhere that he won't be included in a digital record, just in case they go through with it and the hackers get lucky, at least for a while."

"They really don't know who they're toying with, do they?"

His boss chuckled a few times, and the line fell silent long enough that John checked to ensure the call hadn't dropped. Instead of answering the rhetorical question, he silently awaited the man's decision on how to proceed. In the brief absence of conversation, John considered the irony of the man's statement. *They might not really know who we are, but I, for one, know a lot more than you think I do.*

Although he'd agreed to secretly work for Bishop Harold James Hoffaburr, Ph.D., almost two years ago, John had never met Hoffaburr's boss, Cardinal Paul Dylan. Through his old Agency contacts, John had easily pieced together the relationship between the two men, which had been confirmed when the cardinal accepted an assignment to serve in Vatican City as the Holy See's Undersecretariat of the Economy several months ago. *I'll be damned if they're gonna be the only ones that know a thing or two that they ain't supposed to.*

Hoffaburr had presented himself to John's first group of trainees at the Wyoming camp as a psychiatrist, and he knew just enough about the social science to pass muster with the men. John recalled that Jane, his only female instructor, had complained about the man and questioned his cover story. He assumed Hoffaburr had wanted to monitor the inaugural class for problems. Since the cardinal's assignment to Rome and Vatican City, John hadn't seen him a single time. *I hoped that becoming 'holy shit bigshots' over there would keep them from micromanaging me and my boys here. Neither of 'em know the first goddamned thing about training or workin' as a covert operative, but Hoffaburr sure likes to throw the lingo around like he does. Bet he's the kinda asshole that reads spy novels and then adds the fictional op-sec into his daily routine. To the man's credit, he ain't called me by name yet. Not that it really matters. The NSA can match my voice just as soon as I attract their attention.*

Hoffaburr finally cleared his throat and continued. "I think your proposal wise, John, and I'll see what we need to do to resolve it. What's the second dilemma on your radar?"

"Our man's feet-dry in France, and I expect to hear from him soon."

"Father Andrew, correct?"

"Yep."

"It's critical that he's secured and locked down in our hotel room, and that your man-on-the-ground is in place when he arrives. He's been toying with insubordination of late, and we, *err, I* have to know that he's onboard."

"Nothin' to worry about there, Andrew'll toe the line, one way or another. I got a program for that." John redirected the conversation without entirely changing their subject. "This specific problem he's there for, it's gonna present some, uh, *unique* challenges for a one-man-band. Just like we discussed a while back, it'd be prudent for us to send in another, maybe even two or three more, and let 'em run this op as a team. There's too much work and, quite frankly, it's just too dangerous for one man to do on his own."

"How many operations did you run by yourself over the years, in places far worse than Paris?"

John begrudgingly nodded. "Dozens, at least, but that--"

"But *nothing*. I'll give you that our rules of engagement are different than yours were, especially at the time you were busy running around the shadows of the world, but our men are busy combatting *unorganized* evil, not the massive espionage organizations you had to wake up and fight every day. Their greatest enemy is a competent police investigator who can place them at the homicide scene and identify them. Beyond that, our men should be uncon-cerned about anything more dangerous or malicious than a bus acci-dent. They're at greater risk of being killed by coincidence than felonious assault. We *both* know that."

"Listen, I--"

"Save your breath and your self-righteous speech, John. The answer's still 'no.' No teams. Not now, not for any reason, not ever. When our men swore their oath, each of them voluntarily accepted substantial risk to their life and liberty. Nothing's changed. Even if they are apprehended, God needs priests in the prisons, too, and that may be their true calling. Do you have anything else for me? I have a meeting."

"No. That's it." John disconnected the call without any normal social pleasantries and set the cell phone down on the dark wood desk. He hated pleading for help from his boss, a bureaucrat assistant who pretended to play spy games. *That asshole's got nothing but an entitled position and rank in our covert organization with absolutely zero minutes of real-world experience. My trainees know more about clandestine operations at the end of Hour One than the man that's in charge of us.*

John had spent decades in the Army and CIA and had grown accustomed to convincing and coercing ignorant men to do right by those beneath them. What he detested most about Hoffaburr was that he'd never risked his own life and had no idea how his directives impacted the individual operative. *If we're sending good men all over the world and puttin' them in direct danger to combat the greatest damned evils that walk the face of the earth, the* very, fucking, least *we can do is give 'em the tools to succeed and survive. Pretty simple shit, really, but it's a damned foreign concept to men that's never known the danger of stepping into the arena themselves.*

John woke up his laptop, opened a new document in a heavily encrypted subfolder and titled it "2x2." *I'll eventually have to disobey Hoffaburr, and I want everything in place when I do. He might see 'em as nothing more than a buncha gravediggers, but they're* my *gravediggers and I ain't never gonna let 'em swing in the wind on the order of a self-appointed emperor. Even with what we're paying these guys, it won't ever be enough to get killed over.*

His cell phone vibrated and skittered on the wood desk's surface with a new text message notification. John opened the encrypted app and saw Andrew claimed to be delayed getting to The Oremus. *He's stalling, and I don't blame him. I wouldn't trust us, either, if I were in his shoes.*

Vatican Housing Complex. Rome, Italy.

STILL DRESSED in a plush dark red bathrobe and slippers, Cardinal Paul Dylan opened the front door of his luxury apartment so his assistant, Bishop Harold Hoffaburr, could join him for their daily breakfast meeting. As was typical of his position, Hoffaburr wore a black cassock that those unfamiliar with the faith might confuse with a parish monsignor or priest. Only his color-matched purple sash, *zucchetto* skullcap, and cloth-covered buttons down the front of the garment identified his place in the hierarchy.

After Hoffaburr nodded and stepped inside, Paul closed the door and led his man across the deep white Berber carpeting to a zebra-wood dining table and white leather-wrapped chairs. Paul returned to his chair at the head of the table, sipped at his drink, and looked out the dining room's wide window while Hoffaburr continued on to the kitchen. He never tired of his glimpse over the Vatican City wall and the life that awaited his rise to the most powerful position on Earth. His high-end espresso machine *whirred* and *bubbled* as his assistant put its grind, brew, and froth functions to work. Paul took another sip and savored the moment. *I can see my future from here, and all the fated dominoes are even now falling into line to assure my ascension.*

Hoffaburr joined him at the dining room table and opened a rich, black leather binder with red trim. Paul had long feared his assistant's need for documentation, and so he kept his most damning secrets to himself. The subordinate cleared his throat and read the first item from his agenda. "The Italian Treasury Secretary wishes to meet with Your Eminence--"

"Can we start with the continued fallout from Vienna?"

With only an accepting nod, the bishop turned to the pages at the back of his binder, where he kept his *other* notes. "The incident and its subsequent murder investigation seem to have fallen from the international conscience. Even the local and regional news outlets have moved on and no longer pine for updates and new leads. The Austrian government and Interpol maintain the unidentified African refugee remains their only suspect. They've reached the predictable conclusion that Herr Alfred König was tortured and killed as part of a drug-deal-gone-bad."

"What became of him, the suspect, I mean?"

"He's 'gone to ground,' as John might say. Our priest and the intel staff identified him early in their investigation before everything went sideways, but he hasn't yet reappeared. As you directed in the immediate aftermath of that incident, we'll keep watch for him. He remains the only witness who can identify our priest and alter the accepted narrative. Our intel and analysis teams have uploaded his known surveillance photographs to our network, so facial recognition will eventually find him, unless he's returned to his home country. Should he reappear, we can decide what, if anything, to do about him then."

"Have our analysts made any progress on identifying the Mexican drug trafficker who'd been working with König?"

"Not yet. Interpol and the D-E-A know him only as 'Santa Lena

Cartel Leader Number 30,' and he remains a ghost. I'm told we may not have him identified for years."

Paul leaned back against his chair and held the coffee cup in both hands in front of his chest. "Ensure that the *entire* organization remains vigilant in these efforts. We may have removed *one* source of evil with König's death, but our aim must remain on absolving the world of *all* such sources. The men who trafficked their narcotic death through König's corporation, as well as the refugee who dispensed it to addicts on the street, they must *all* be held to account for their actions." He leaned forward, closer to Hoffaburr, to emphasize his point. "There is no other way for our little eradication project to succeed. The demise of a man like König is but a drop in the ocean."

"Of course, Your Eminence." His assistant drew a small star on his notepad next to several other notes. "What else concerns you, sir?"

"Have you determined our risk exposure, from *within* our ranks, I mean?"

"No, but that doesn't mean we don't face any. The absence of evidence--"

Paul waved his hand and interrupted. "Harold, I understand that we can't prove a negative! Did our priest, *Father Andrew,* did he betray our trust and confidence, or not?"

The assistant shifted in his seat. "I don't know, sir, and we may *never* know for certain. We never located the owner of the black Audi that dropped him at the airfield that night. That's too common a vehicle for car services in and around Vienna, so the vehicle itself has offered no investigative leads for our analysts."

Paul delicately stirred the little remaining milk froth into his coffee. "And what of the new phones we gave our priests, and the software your people installed on them?"

Hoffaburr shook his head. "Nothing, Your Eminence. The data hasn't yet turned up any evidence of a betrayal or compromise to our operational security protocols. I ensured we turned an especially intense light on data from Father Andrew's phone."

"And what of his funding sources, the anonymous, online Estonian bank accounts we set up for Andrew and the other priests?"

"We found nothing there, either. No suspicious transactions, and nothing that could associate him with the Vienna incident or our organization."

Paul scowled and his stomach turned acidic at the thought of their covert payroll. The princely sum felt like a monthly extortion. "Do you know the balance of his personal account, the one into which we pay John's ransom?"

The assistant nodded and flipped to another page. Paul knew Hoffaburr had agreed with John on this point, and he'd acquiesced only to gain the spymaster's cooperation. *If our Assassins of Evil suffer a paradigm shift that causes them to leave the Church and seek clandestine employment elsewhere, the veritable lode we've handed over won't stop them. If anything, we've given them the means by which to sever their need of us. Parishioners and priests leave the Church every day, but I cannot risk allowing these men to make it out wealthy and alive.*

"Andrew's account, as of three days ago, was just over $67,000. It's been open eight months with no withdrawals, and he still lives entirely on his priest salary. It seems that he's saving for something, but I'll continue to watch it, along with all the others, of course."

Paul sipped at his coffee, which gave him a moment to consider his own impression of his bishop's efforts and lack of new information. "My thoughts remain unchanged from our initial conversation. Let our analysts keep chewing on this mysterious Audi. They will eventually find something that allows us to dismiss or confirm the alleged problem." Paul darkened his tone. "You'll tell me right away if you find Father Andrew, or any of them, has lied to us."

"Of course, Your Eminence, it would only be a further betrayal to keep such information from you." Harold waited patiently for direction.

"So, it appears the matter in Vienna is concluded, at least for the moment." Paul set his coffee cup back on its saucer and brushed a lint speck from the front of his plush robe. "Whole sweaters can be unraveled by tugging only a few threads, Harold. If we find such problems, we must outsource a competent tailor capable of salvaging what remains of the garment. Speaking of loose ends," he offered, looked up, and stopped brushing the robe. "Has Thomas been moved?"

"Yes, he has, soon after my discussion with John. The details of the failed rescue plot are moot now that the traitor remains firmly within our control and influence."

Paul again looked out the window, distracted by the promise of tomorrow. He noticed that Harold followed his gaze.

The assistant spoke but maintained focus on Vatican City. "It's all working as you foresaw, Your Eminence. God has sequentially opened and shut all the doors necessary for us to draw ever closer to the precipice of your appointment. All is now within reach, just over that wall."

"I hope you took my advice and kept your bags packed. Provided that we tread delicately among the cassocked vipers, we won't live outside Vatican City for much longer now."

Hoffaburr looked back at him with a curious expression on his face. "Am I to understand that you know something more than Your Eminence has shared?"

Paul couldn't help but flash a knowing, Cheshire-cat smile. "All in due time, Harold. For now, I can only say there is a substantial play afoot on our behalf. God's hand is truly at work in our lives."

The subordinate smirked as a humorous epiphany struck him. "Well, you know the ironic consequence of your ascension being God's intended plan is, of course, that our failure to fulfill His objectives may risk our very damnation."

"Salvation and damnation each require the other. Neither exists on its own, Harold. Failure and damnation don't concern me, though, not with the new and clear understanding to His mysteries that God has revealed to us." The sun broke through some high, unseen cloud and shone down on Saint Peter's Basilica. *If the desire to become the American President is only cured with formaldehyde, what must it take to relieve a man of his want to succeed Saint Peter as the head of a nation-state and spiritual leader of all the faithful millions across the globe? Presidents are remembered and praised in history books, but popes are remembered and praised in prayer for all eternity.*

"No, Harold, we need concern ourselves only with being ready when the moment is upon us. That will assure our ascension, both to the papacy and God's eternal kingdom."

MAY 6, 08:43AM_

36 Quai des Orfèvres. Paris, France.

ON HIS WAY to a safehouse rented for his current investigation, Gerard had to stop into the main Task Force office to sign paperwork from a previous case. Located within the municipal administration buildings near the west end of a natural island in the *Seine*, known as the *Ilé de la Cité*, Gerard's Task Force held a sizeable and secure portion of the fifth floor. The beloved *Cathédrale Notre-Dame de Paris* occupied the east end of the small island. Even though it doubled his drive time, Gerard chose a convoluted route necessary to drive past the famed and fire-damaged cathedral.

Just as he'd done every day since the heartbreaking April 15th fire, Gerard slowed as he approached the cathedral and its surrounding cordons. Select members of the military and his counterterror unit stood in camouflaged uniforms with slung rifles to protect the vulnerable site from looters and opportunists who wished to denigrate the cathedral or steal its remaining relics and property. A pair of guards recognized his sedan and swung two stanchions open for Gerard to pass directly in front of the main entrance.

He waved at the men, further slowed, and wished he had time to stop. Despite the constant and sometimes loud throngs of disrespectful tourists, Gerard had always found tremendous peace inside. *I prayed inside Notre Dame for the last time on April 14th, and I doubt I'll experience its tranquility again for another decade.* After passing through an open stanchion on the other side of the cathedral, Gerard sped up and continued on his detour. The *Ilé de la Cité* had been the center of Paris since its founding and held many of its most iconic structures. While hunting a parking spot for his undercover police sedan, Gerard remembered how he'd been so awed by the island and its history when first assigned to SDAT. After years of fighting endless traffic, rude visitors ignorant of his people's history and culture, and politically appointed administrators, he'd grown cynical about his work in the National Police and the monument that held his office. Gerard entered the building unimpressed by his surroundings and longed only for a productive day.

He climbed the stairs, two at a time, up to the fifth floor and placed his RFID access card against a scanner outside the Task Force office's heavy steel doorway. A quiet, simultaneous *thunk* and *hiss* announced the multiple locks had retracted into the surrounding steel frame, and Gerard pushed his way into the private working area. Assigned to individual inspectors, thirty-two desks arranged in four columns of eight extended down the length of the room, each of them in some manner of disarray. The unit's various supervisors had private offices around the outside of the desks. Two conference rooms and a small kitchen stood at the far end of the room.

One of the only officials present in the room stood at a desk just ahead of Gerard, his hands rifling through a stack of file folders that didn't belong to him. Lieutenant Mahmoud Algeri wore a dark gray suit, creme silk shirt, and bright blue tie, as well as a matching blue *taqiyah,* a traditional skullcap worn by Muslim men. He looked up at

Gerard when he heard the door open, and a slight smile broke across his face. Most of the other desks sat abandoned, the inspectors assigned to them out on investigations. *And, since Algeri's assignment, most have decided it's best to be out of the building and out of sight.*

Gerard had learned blue was a color of protection in the Muslim world, which explained why his boss always wore something blue to work. *Is he trying to protect himself from us, or the criminals and terrorists we're appointed to pursue?* He nodded at the man and tried to walk past without a conversation, but his superior stepped across the walkway to block his path.

"I'm glad you're here, Inspector Antlé. Your case, it is now closed."

Gerard couldn't stop his outrage. "Closed? *How?!* Did the suspect detonate himself overnight?" This wasn't the first righteous investigation the political appointee had shuttered in the past months.

The callous lieutenant smirked at him. "No, thankfully he did not. I reviewed the reports and determined that we have insufficient cause to continue."

"*Insufficient cause?* Are you certain you read *my* case file, Lieutenant?"

The humorless man's smirk devolved into a disdainful glare. "I am quite certain of it. Our agency and government have long used these terrorism investigations to harass peaceful citizens, immigrants, and refugees who've committed no offenses. I took over this unit to stop this practice, and that's what I'm doing."

Gerard quelled his anger, and he worked to differentiate his supervisor from the man's faith. *His policy in one-way 'tolerance' and subjugation is NOT the way of the rational, moderate Muslim world.* He took a deep, calming breath and gave himself one last reminder before he spoke. *This maniac's an anomaly.*

"Sir, with respect, I must protest! All the signs are there, and the suspected bomber could be operational only days or weeks from now! We don't have time to wait for new evidence that allows us to begin the investigation all over again! The next complaint in this matter will follow his detonation!"

Algeri set his jaw. "There is no other way, well, at least, no other *legal* way. You do not advocate we violate this man's constitutional rights, do you?"

Gerard understood the position Algeri had forced him into, and his limited ability to change it. *I have few options to keep the suspect from killing while I'm still on the Task Force. I can do far less from the soup line.*

Algeri stared at him, still awaiting a response.

"No, sir. Of course, I do not wish such a thing."

"Then report to Sergeant Le'roux. He is heading up efforts to apprehend unlicensed taxis in the tourist districts." He looked up and down at Gerard's taxi driver outfit before stepping in closer so that no one else overheard him. "It appears that Allah selected your costume this morning. Le'roux's investigation *must* be where you're most needed."

Gerard watched his arrogant boss walk away. He exhaled, strode toward his desk, and prepared a list of his most urgent necessities. *I'll do what I must to protect my assignment and access to Task Force resources, but I'll be damned if I stop investigating a suspected terrorist to chase unpermitted cabs.*

Only two minutes later, Gerard exited a heavy, metal exterior door and stepped out onto the street beside the government building. He checked his watch. *No time to eat or to be a father, but I do have time for a smoke.* Even though French and Parisian law didn't forbid cabbies from smoking inside the taxis, the hazy smoke and residue damaged the audio-video equipment concealed inside the undercover police car. Gerard had intended to report to the safehouse by 9:30, but that no longer mattered. Even without a specific deadline or destination, he decided to burn only a single *Gauloises*. Gerard retrieved the red pack and lighter from a pants pocket, lit up, and examined the useless warning label.

The last four generations of Antlé men had smoked the same brand since World War II when *Gauloises* had become patriotic. The French cigarette had been associated with the underground resistance while his great-grandfather and his compatriots took subversive and overt action against the Nazis. More recently, larger-than-life figures such as Pablo Picasso, Jean-Paul Sartre, even the author Albert Camus had smoked or endorsed *Gauloises*. Gerard inhaled a multigenerational symbol of his second, closely held religion of devout nationalism.

He used the quiet moment to calm himself and consider how to proceed. *This little island has been the seat of power in Paris since the Romans defeated the Celts and housed their governor here in 52 AD, right where the Palais of Justice now stands. That Roman governor ruled this entire region, and now, another political appointee seeks to protect his own minority of people by persecuting and manipulating everyone else. I suppose nothing's changed then.*

After holding the tobacco smoke in his lungs, Gerard glanced across the street as he exhaled. A flyer for a band called *Coup D'avertissement* clung to a nearby light pole and rustled in the light morning breeze. *Warning Shot, that's a great name for a band.* Typical of almost every building throughout the city, spray paint graffiti adorned the brown plaster across the street. Gerard read the fresh silver and black paint like a "street newspaper" and spat toward it. *If I could catch one of those little shits in the act, just one, I'd make an example that would forever stop graffiti all across the city.* The band flyer and its surrounding graffiti monopolized Gerard's attention until his *Gauloises* gave up its last draw. He dropped the tobacco roach to the sidewalk and crushed it beneath his shoe. *Maybe they need a backup drummer. I could use a side-job to keep my lights turned on, at least until I'm lucky enough to have a benefactor like Claudette.*

He rechecked his watch and decided he had time for a quick,

second cigarette. *Where the hell do I have to be anyway?* After Gerard lit up, he looked over the white Peugeot four-door model that pretended to be his cab today. *Last chance to make certain everything's in order before I step 'outside the wire,' as the Americans say.* A white sign sat on the roof, which read "Taxi Parisien" and helped make him indistinguishable from the other fifteen-thousand cabs in the City of Lights. A fake cab company name, *"Le Trajet,"* appeared in yellow-and-black decals on both front doors, and bright yellow decals across the top of the windshield and back window displayed the company phone number.

Gerard smiled in pity at the thought of the long-suffering administrative cop who caught that assignment. Besides submitting the licensing and permit paperwork necessary to make the company appear legitimate in public records searches, that particular cop also provided the first convincing layer of deceit by pretending to be the company's dispatcher. Anyone investigating the veracity of the cab could call the phone number, talk to a live person, even confirm the individual cab number, its current driver, and arrange for a pickup. Common criminals are lazy, and they rarely made greater efforts than that. *The ruthless men I pursue, though, are both thorough and tireless.*

The Task Force administrators had long-established protocols that constituted the most effective and proven methods to defeat countersurveillance. Every member of their unit, even those who weren't strictly operational field agents had acquired taxi permits and a driver's license in their respective cover identity. The unit enjoyed greater flexibility to keep changing out drivers and cars as needed, especially during high profile operations and the month of August when most of the nation went on vacation. *None of it matters when Algeri shutters our investigations, though...*

As he finished his smoke and cast it aside, Gerard stepped over and entered the undercover Peugeot. After moving from the parking spot, he spied Lieutenant Algeri's assigned vehicle, a white Citroën, parked just ahead and rolled down his window. Gerard spat phlegm onto it as he passed. *Screw him. I'll do the right thing regardless of what that imposter orders, and I'm sure two or three teammates feel the same way.* As he considered his next steps, Gerard thought of the words inscribed on one of the personal seals Thomas Jefferson used while serving as the US Commissioner and Minister to France: *Rebellion to tyrants is obedience to God.*

PSSHH

Michael turned toward the impact in time to see shards of a thick water glass careening across the white marble patio behind him. A waiter in a black long-sleeved dress uniform and starched white apron apologized profusely to an elderly couple, so Michael returned his focus to the next objective.

He'd positioned himself at an umbrella-shaded bistro table in the back corner of an upscale hotel's sundrenched patio. Facing southwest, he held a commanding view of the *Seine* and the *Place de la Concorde,* both ahead and to his left, as well as Avenue Gabriel to his right. An open hardbacked novel laid on the cozy table in front of him. In concert with his dark sunglasses, the table's oversized blue canvas umbrella helped him linger there while obscuring his appearance from any potential onlookers.

To better blend in with the crowds of pedestrians and tourists, Michael had acquired a few items after landing in Paris that morning. He now wore a dark blue camp shirt popular with both hikers and tourists, but the dark hue helped him hide among the native population and its notorious dark attire. Gray travel pants provided hidden pockets to conceal the items he might need today, and a new pair of

Rockports offered stability and speed across uneven terrain without a tactical appearance. Michael had also bought a dark gray backpack that now held his smaller black duffel bag and its contents. He'd placed the backpack in the wrought iron bistro chair opposite him and pulled it under the table to discourage opportunistic thieves.

Michael occasionally sipped at a cappuccino, but he hadn't touched his chocolate croissant for the last half-hour. The Oremus, the hotel where he was ordered to check-in today, sat a half-block up Avenue Gabriel to his right and across a one-way residential street from his present location. A white Peugeot sedan drove by the hotel patio, ambled up *Avenue Gabriel,* and again stopped in front of The Oremus. *Same license plate. That's three times since I sat down. If he's not a cabbie or an Uber driver, something's wrong.*

Picking up a pen from the table, Michael made a few coded notes about the sedan on his novel's off-white paper and turned the page before setting the pen back along the novel's spine. He gazed at the building to his right, a massive, neoclassical pastiche structure. *Why would John order me to stay in a hotel across the goddamned street from the U-S Embassy? Everything that moves within a hundred yards of that place is under surveillance. Stupid.*

A police whistle commanded his attention, and Michael glanced to the massive *Place de la Concorde* in front of him. A traffic cop waved his arms to encourage traffic flow. *When I became a cop, I thought I could have done so much more to protect my neighbors from the dangers in society. Turned out there's a lot of opportunity to serve, but not so many to protect. I spent five years as just another cog in the criminal justice meatgrinder and envied the local parish priest for his manner of service. After becoming a priest, I realized how I missed the badge and gun, and my ability to directly confront evil. That led here, to this assignment, so I have to believe I lived through all that for a very specific reason and purpose.*

Michael nonchalantly glanced around and, finding that nothing else caught his suspicion at the moment, he casually flipped to the last few pages of his book. With pen in hand, he considered the list of numbers he'd already begun there: *1075, 1178, 1450, 1460, 1523, 2265, 2269, 2280, 2284, 2307.* He softly tapped his pen against the page to call forth further inspiration.

Each number Michael had included in his list represented a section of the Catechism of the Catholic Church that justified his actions to defend mankind by directly combating evil. *If I ever write that letter to Merci, I need to explain every possible reason I'm not stepping outside the scriptures and our understanding of God's word. It's so important that she has a chance to accept and understand this, but, in the meantime, I can also use the occasional reminder that I'm not just some maniac killing in the name of religion.*

Michael mentally reviewed the list and its corresponding topics: *Contrition. Penance. Sacramentum exeunitium, commonly known as Last Rites. Duty to Defend Others. Intentional Homicide and its loophole to kill to save others and defend against unjust aggression. Suicide and God's forgiveness for it. Just War doctrine.* He tapped the pen several more times. *These are among the foundations of our understanding that allow me to target, investigate, and kill the greatest evils that walk the earth. Once such men have proven themselves beyond voluntary rehabilitation, there is no other way for us to remove them from society and protect the dignity of their future victims. I'll never stop seeing the irony in saving their souls by killing them, but without the crushing weight of an imminent death penalty, such men never humble themselves before God and are destined to an eternity in hell. I offer their only chance to meet God with a clear, fully absolved conscience. Their soul has no other opportunity to enter the kingdom of heaven.*

Several more taps of his pen. *What else will I want her to understand?* Michael scanned his surroundings again as his mind mulled over the question at hand. Inspiration struck, and he added *2330* to the list. *Blessed are the peacemakers.* Setting the pen aside, he sipped at the cappuccino and returned to selling his appearance. *Just another tourist enjoying a warm spring morning in Paris.*

Michael leaned back in his chair, stretched his arms, and looked away to scan the expansive *Place de la Concorde* before him. He imagined what the eighteen-acre public square must have looked like in the 1790s when the French were busy guillotining King Louis XVI, Marie Antionette, and anyone else who just smelled too aristocratic. *I'd love being surrounded by this much history when I don't have to worry so much about getting caught or killed. I bet the city feels very different on vacation.*

Michael sat forward in his chair and went back to work. He held the unread book up off the table and, looking over it, surveyed The Oremus and his adjacent environs. Only then did he notice a driver seated in a new, pale blue Renault Clio, a four-door sedan about the size of a Toyota Yaris.

The subject vehicle was parked across Avenue Gabriel facing away from Michael, but with an excellent view of the area and, in particular, the front entrance of The Oremus. *If there weren't three of the same cars parked on this street, and one close enough to read the name, I'd have no idea what the hell kind of car it is.* Michael nonchalantly skimmed back through his novel to the places he'd made notes throughout the last hour. *There.* He read the license plate and time he'd recorded it. *GR-919-JL, 0903.* A quick glance up matched the plate to his notes. *The car was in place when I landed here an hour ago. No one's entered or left it since, so he's been holed up in that blue tuna can this whole time.* Despite his certainty that the driver was part of a stakeout, Michael didn't know if he was the intended prey. *Can't take that chance. Complacency kills quick. Paranoia lets you live all the way to the heart attack.*

In light of the potential opposition force staged outside his hotel, Michael went back to the novel and made a quick, coded shorthand list of his efforts to protect himself, something akin to a combine "to do" and "have done" list. *New burner phone for contacting Sergio. Discarded the luggage and clothing from the flight. Bought all new possessions. The cellphone John gave me is in airplane mode and turned off. No possible trackers. Multiple heat runs to get here from the airport, so no tails.* He looked up and glared at the back of the distant driver's head. *No one's followed me, no one can possibly know where I am right now. John altered both of my digital passport photos, so facial recognition software can't tie my real picture to either government image. I'm as off the grid as I can get so, effectively, I'm invisible until I mess up or let them find me again.*

Having restored a measure of confidence in his current position, Michael retrieved a prepaid burner cellphone from his pants pocket and dialed 17, the Parisian equivalent of 911. *I'd rather pay some smartass kid to walk up and confront the guy, but there's never preteen brats around when you need them.*

"Police," a female voice announced on the second beep. *"Quel est le lieu de votre urgence?"*

"I am *so* sorry, *parlez vous anglais?"*

She audibly sighed into the phone. "Yes. What is the location of your emergency?"

"My family and I just left the Place de la Concorde, and a strange man in a light blue Renault Clio stopped and tried to talk to my daughter."

"Is there an emergency, sir?"

"Well, yes, I think there is. My daughter's eight, and he asked her to follow him to his car. He offered to take her to see his puppy, but I think he wanted to kidnap her."

"Do you know where he is now, or where his car may be found?" Michael watched the Clio's driver while he slandered the man to the Parisian police. "He drove north on Avenue Gabriel, and I got his license plate. It's G-R-9-1-9-J-L. The car's light blue, like I said, and I think it was pretty new." Despite the call taker's apathy, Michael felt certain they'd have to dispatch a few cops to look for the car, just in case the allegation was legitimate. He gave the woman a generic, fake name and contact information to a hotel across town and ended the call. *Now we wait for the local patrol cops to shake the guy loose and see what happens.*

Michael checked his watch and tried to estimate how long until—

The blue Clio started up, and its tires squealed for a moment while the driver hurried away from the parking space. The tiny car merged into traffic on *Avenue Gabriel* and accelerated toward the *Arc de Triomphe.*

Michael calmly looked around for anything else that could have motivated the driver's sudden and urgent departure. *Nothing. Lots of pedestrians around, but nothing else stands out. He might have a police scanner, or it could be totally unrelated. Might be nothing, might be everything. If the driver's an undercover cop who doesn't want to blow his cover, that might be really bad for me. The police could bring about life-in-prison kinda problems. No way John would've turned me over to the cops, not even if he found out everything I'm hiding from him. Right?*

Michael considered all the omissions, half-truths, and blatant lies he'd offered since his recruitment to the Vatican's clandestine organization. Each violated the group's operational security protocols, at minimum, or defied direct orders and betrayed their absolute dedication to secrecy, at worst. *If John learns my secrets and gets me alone, he'd just handle it himself.* Michael grimaced at his own dark humor. *On the plus side, if I ever lose John's trust, I won't have to worry about him turning the cops or Interpol onto me, even with a hemisphere between us. The man's got a lifetime of secret agent contacts and cutouts for that kind of wet work.*

Michael gazed up *Avenue Gabriel* to The Oremus Hotel and the myriad of answers that awaited him inside. *I can't run or fight this until I know more about my opponent. If I have to risk my freedom and my life, I'd rather get on with it. Suspense is the only thing killing me from here.* Michael pocketed the burner phone, stuffed the novel in one of the backpack's external compartments, and stood. He gulped down the cappuccino, donned his dark gray backpack, and stepped from the upscale patio. As he blended into the pedestrian crowds on the adjacent sidewalk, John's words rang through his mind. *Burnin' daylight, shithead.*

MAY 6, 10:32AM_

Hotel Grimod de la Reynière. Paris, France.

MICHAEL STOOD on the sidewalk at the northwest corner of the *Place de la Concorde* and scanned the crowds moving around him. Somewhere nearby, among the vacationing families, couples, and strolling lovers, he feared a malicious adversary watched and awaited his arrival. Known to professionals as an "opposing force" or "op-for," Michael kept a vigilant watch for people too interested in him. *Just because I don't see threats doesn't mean they don't exist. John's told us a hundred times that we aren't as skilled as secular government operatives, but I've never felt that shortcoming until now. I have to presume their presence until I prove otherwise.*

Inspired by several young twenty-somethings to his left, he retrieved his personal cell phone, turned his back to the famous square, and assumed the familiar pose. Instead of documenting his narcissism, he shot a dozen quick photos of the cars and pedestrians around him. Across the sidewalk and next to the *Hotel Grimod de la Reynière*, a large blue street sign identified *Avenue Gabriel* and a semicircular blue topper above that specified the neighborhood: *8th Arrondissement.* Michael moved over and stood next to the prop to complete his intel gathering and surreptitiously photograph the rest of the crowd. *Now I have a better chance to spot any tails over the next few days, assuming I'm not arrested or dead by then.*

Another nonchalant scan didn't expose any threats, so Michael proceeded northwest along the tree-lined *Avenue Gabriel* to press his momentary advantage. Despite the meandering pace dictated by the pedestrian collective, he had to enter The Oremus before any security or surveillance personnel shifted to compensate for the driver's absence. *If the banished Clio and its driver are even involved. I don't believe in coincidence, but that doesn't exclude it from reality.*

In stark contrast to his outward appearance, Michael's eyes stayed active behind his dark sunglasses. Just as he'd found in major American cities, the tourists wore fun, bright, and comfortable clothing, chatted with friends, and smiled. The locals wore darker attire, earbuds to isolate themselves from the ever-present crowds, and dispassionate faces that appeared incapable of happiness. *New York, Boston, Paris. Change the local accent and it's all the same behaviors.*

While his target destination stood more than a half-block away, the US Embassy loomed large on Michael's right. *Someone's always watching and photographing everything near that place, and John's intel staff has proven access to US databases. I don't want to find out they've hacked into the real-time camera feeds, too.* Turning his back to the embassy building and the threat it represented, Michael waited for a yellow Citroën to drive up the slow, one-way residential street. As it passed, he casually crossed *Avenue Gabriel* to obfuscate his government's surveillance efforts.

No one in the nearby crowds mimicked his path. Michael looked across the street at the massive American flag that hung from the roofline of the US Embassy. Several groups of college-aged tourists posed for selfies in its foreground, so he used the brief opportunity to memorize the grounds' general layout and look for watchers. Rows of connected metal crowd-control stanchions stood inside the property's outer edge with dozens of subtle, waist-high concrete pillars placed behind them that supported the embassy's strategy and tactics to counter personnel- and vehicle-borne IEDs. The stanchions forced queueing visitors to climb over or zigzag through their entirety. Either entry method identified potential suspects and slowed their progress. *Crime prevention through environmental design. Gotta keep that in mind in case I have to escape whatever's in the hotel.* Michael grimaced. *There's no way the movies have it right and I get to run away from local authorities just by stepping onto American soil like it's some kinda ollie-ollie-oxen-free. Can't be that easy.*

Michael pressed on toward The Oremus and whatever fate awaited him there. Despite being located only one block from the famed *Champs-Élysées* between the *Place de la Concorde* and the *Arc de Triomphe,* Michael found himself increasingly isolated as people disappeared into businesses, rented residences, and small boutique hotels. He sped up to catch and tailgate a large tourist group.

As he drew closer to The Oremus, the street's shaded tree canopy fell away, and Michael studied the five-story hotel and its grounds for intel. An open, grand lawn with a lush, landscaped border covered the thirty-yard space behind the sidewalk. Matching most of the historic city, the hotel had a tan granite or marble exterior. Two-toned, light gray stone lined the balconies, windows, and dormers, and dark gray slate tiles covered the steep roof. Black-and-gold iron railing adorned the balconies to protect the hotel guests from gravity and poor choices. *No concealment between the sidewalk and the entrance, nothing I can hide behind that'll stop a bullet.* A scene from an old Peter Faulk movie played in his head, and he reminded himself to serpentine when the shooting started. Michael shook his head and refocused. *Small rooms on the two lower floors with tiny balconies. Floors three and four have larger rooms with long, shared balconies. Top floor's probably penthouse suites. The dormers and small balconies likely mean larger, private outdoor space on the other side of the hotel that faces the Champs-Élysées.*

Despite the extensive parkour routines John had forced him and the other recruits to endure in training camp, Michael knew he'd have trouble scaling the exterior walls of The Oremus. He glanced around at the adjacent buildings, which confirmed he could put himself on any other roof along the avenue. *I wonder if that was an intentional part of the hotel's security plan?*

When he reached the wide walking path to the hotel's entrance, Michael alone turned from the sidewalk. *For all my efforts to the contrary, I'm now singled out.* He walked as fast as possible without drawing added attention to himself. A tall, athletic doorman stood next to the hotel's oversized metal-and-glass French door entrance and watched Michael's approach. Despite the late spring warmth, the man wore riding boots polished to a high shine, tight white riding pants, a black suit jacket with blood-red accents and tails that fell behind his knees, and a black pelt top hat. His face showed no emotion, even when he stepped over to open the wide, heavy door for Michael.

Striding past the doorman, Michael barely noticed the luxurious lobby as he visually searched for an op-for. Ornate black, white, and gray marble floor tiles lay beneath occasional, large Persian rugs. Open to the lower three floors, the lobby comprised a tall, open sixty-by-sixty three-dimensional rectangle in the center of the hotel. Just inside the wide entrance and to his right, a bellhop waited to retrieve luggage from arriving guests and a concierge desk sat just beyond him. Michael considered finding an out-of-the-way seat to watch the employees and guests before identifying himself to anyone, but again decided speed remained his greatest asset.

He walked straight to the registration desk across the lobby, where a clerk in a dark blue suit stood behind the desk and passively watched him. As Michael drew near, a gold Oremus-logoed nametag on the man's left lapel identified him as "Adam."

"*Bonjour,* how may I serve you today?"

Michael smiled despite his anxiety. The interaction reminded him of the desk clerk at the Hotel Sacher in Vienna, and he realized that all such employees likely spoke to guests in two languages until they knew how best to communicate with them. *"Bonjour.* I need to check-in for my reservation." He dug out his Holy See passport from a concealed pocket in his travel pants.

"Name, please?"

"Andrés Bethsaida." Michael handed over his identification. The Holy See nation-state had printed and issued the forged passport in his apostolic pseudonym, so Michael never thought of it as a fake ID. *One less thing to make me nervous, never mind how I feel about everything else right now.*

The man clicked at a hidden keyboard and glanced at a monitor concealed from guests. "Yes, I have it here. The notes explain that you don't yet know how long you'll be with us, does that remain the circumstance?"

"Yes, I'm afraid it does."

"The room and our grateful hospitality are yours for as long as you'll have them, sir." A light *whirring* sound emanated from somewhere behind the desk, and Adam stepped away, reached down out of Michael's sight, and retrieved two credit card-style room keys. He placed them inside a slotted brochure, wrote on the interior flap opposite the cards, and passed the closed brochure and passport over the desk to Michael. "You're assigned room 144, which is on the floor above us, just down the hall from the elevators. *Jacques,* our concierge, will show you the way." Adam gently waved his hand toward Michael's right, and he turned to see another blued-suited man approaching them.

Michael retrieved the documents in his left hand and then moved both hands up to lightly grip the front of his backpack's shoulder straps. By keeping his hands there, he appeared non-threatening, but stayed better prepared to defend himself from a spontaneous attack. He glanced back to Adam and nodded. *"Merci."* Michael stepped closer to the inbound concierge and the elevators. *If things go south, I don't want to place myself squarely between two opponents.*

"Bonjour, Monsieur Bethsaida," Jacques announced as he drew close to Michael and extended his right hand. "I am Jacques. Please

allow me the privilege of showing you the way to your room." After they shook hands, he motioned toward the bank of three elevators before stepping off in the lead. Jacques swiped a hotel room key across a small gray sensor next to the buttons and pressed *UP*. A light *ding* sounded to identify the available car at the far end of the bank. Jacques hurried over, stepped inside, and held the doors open. He waited to press *1* until Michael joined him.

Keeping his hands up on the straps, Michael leaned his backpack against the front corner opposite Jacques while the well-oiled doors closed behind him. He watched the man much closer now that they were locked in a small metal box together. Although Jacques maintained a pleasant smile, his eyes offered something darker.

The concierge cleared his throat, clasped his hands over the front of his belt buckle, and held Michael's eye contact. "We've been expecting your arrival for several hours, Father Andrew. John asked me to convey his regards."

MAY 6, 11:17AM_

The Oremus. Paris, France.

MICHAEL KEPT his hands up but loosened his grip on the backpack's shoulder straps. He took a small, reflexive step back against the corner and narrowed his eyes to focus on Jacques, the concierge who'd just identified himself as a potential threat. *He knows my apostolic codename!* No sooner than the time required to prepare himself to react, a light *ding* announced their arrival at Michael's floor.

As much as he hated moving backward into an unknown space, he wanted to fight in a small elevator even less, so Michael stole a quick glance through the opening doors to ensure he wasn't stepping into greater danger. The lush red-and-creme hallway looked empty, so he walked out and put his back close to the nearest wall. Jacques stepped from the elevator and strode to his right, away from Michael. After another glance around, Michael followed at a reasonable distance and kept watch for movement as they approached and passed the recessed doorways that led to the adjacent hotel rooms.

Above each doorway, a metal plate displayed the corresponding room number. The plate's light crème background contrasted with its ornate border and the number, both of which were painted a dark, oxblood red. As they continued down the long hallway, Michael tracked the individual room numbers to anticipate their arrival. The even-numbered rooms were to his right. *168. 166. 164.*

Jacques stopped at the doorway to *162.* "Your room, Father." He motioned toward the unseen entrance and stepped back to block the hallway.

With his renewed suspicions raised even further, Michael stepped slightly left to allow himself the widest angle to spot emerging threats. A dark, oxblood red wood door faced him with its hinges on the left side, toward Jacques, and the handle closer to Michael. He held his ground for the moment. "I believe there's been a mistake. Adam said I'm to stay in *144*."

Jacques lowered his voice just above a hushed whisper. "Yes, that's right. This is it." The concierge nodded up toward the doorframe. "If you'll kindly buzz yourself in, I'll explain everything once we're inside."

Michael glanced up above the door. Where he expected to see *162*, he read *144* on the ornate plate. The check-in brochure, passport, and key cards remained in his left hand. Deciding to continue toward a resolution, whatever that was, he slipped one out and swiped it through the magnetic strip reader on the door.

whirrrrrr

As the deadbolt released, Michael stepped back and pocketed the key. He looked to Jacques and motioned toward the door. "After you, sir. I insist."

The concierge demurely bowed his head and stepped to the door. Michael stayed in place for a few ticks as Jacques pushed the door open and revealed a short hallway that led into a room filled with bright daylight from windows and French doors at the opposite end. Michael strode to the hinge-side of the doorframe, which offered a better view into the room. He paused only long enough to see a bathroom stood to his right, just inside the room, and that two beds, a dresser, and desk lay ahead. *Only a couple decent hiding places left inside. Doesn't mean it's safe, but there can't be more than two or three of them now. I can probably handle that.*

Michael stayed to his left as he entered the room. A quick glance showed him that no one hid inside the bathroom, and a few more steps confirmed he and Jacques were probably alone. Michael checked the closet before allowing the hallway door to close behind him.

The concierge stepped to the windows and pulled back the sheer white curtains, which further brightened the room. Michael withdrew to the doorway and the relative darkness there. *The light helps me confirm we're alone, but it also alerts anyone outside with a rifle that they've now got a target and a clear line of fire.*

Jacques held up a finger, which Michael understood as a sign to wait. He retrieved a small black cube from an interior jacket pocket, *clicked* a button on one side, and set it down on the dresser. A small blue light slowly flashed from the top of the device. "We can speak freely now. I apologize if I made you nervous, Father, but John gave me *very* specific instructions about how and when to address you today. Surprising a man locked with me in a small space is not a good strategy for me to see a long and healthy retirement."

Michael wasn't ready to make incriminating statements to the stranger. "I'm sorry, Jacques, but what are you talking about, and," he pointed to the cube, "what the hell is that?"

Jacques smiled and nodded. "Yes, John said you would not immediately trust me. There is a safe, well, actually, there are *two* in here, but the one the public can find is secured to a shelf inside the closet. Look inside, and you will find you already have the code to open it."

Michael didn't remember seeing a safe, but he'd only scanned the closet for people and threats, not a safe bolted to a shelf. He cautiously stepped backward, opened the closet door, and saw the black metal safe rested near chest height and had a ten-number keypad, along with # and * keys. *John's note from the diplomatic pouch this morning said the same combo would open the safe in my* *room.* He input 2-2-9-7, and the keypad *beeped* as he pushed each button.

Nothing.

Michael pulled on the door, but it hadn't released. *What the hell....* He turned back to Jacques and expected an imminent fight as his mind raced to decide whether to escape out the door or charge the only immediate threat. *The unobstructed windows are still dangerous--*

"*Pound,*" Jacques quickly offered as he slowly raised his hands up in front of his chest and took a step back closer to the windows. "Try your *code*, then press *pound.*"

Michael struggled to decide if he was being set-up, but he decided the few-second delay was worth avoiding unnecessary violence. He stepped closer to the keypad, but partially shielded himself behind the closet door and kept watch on Jacques as he entered the code with his left hand.

beepbeep beep beep

Michael risked a quick glance back at the keypad for the last button.

beep

click

While keeping his eyes on the concierge, Michael pulled on the front of the safe and it swung open.

Jacques breathed a visible sigh of relief that Michael felt also. "Okay," he smiled and lowered his hands. "Can you trust me now, just a small amount?"

"I still don't know what that is," Michael nodded toward the unidentified device. He gave a quick glance inside the safe and saw the much thicker manila envelope he'd expected on the flight over from London. From an abundance of caution, he closed the safe and pressed the # key again.

click

A quick pull confirmed it re-locked. Michael closed the closet, but he stayed away from the windows.

"The device emits a high-frequency tone that should help defeat eavesdropping efforts. Someone might still hear us, if they could get a recorder inside the room, but anyone listening from outside that relies on long-distance microphones will get nothing but static. The device is yours for the time you're here. Use it, don't use it, the choice is yours."

"Do you mind pulling the curtains back?"

"Oh, yes, sorry. I presumed too much." Jacques hurried over to the corner of the room and drew both the sheers and darkening curtains closed. As the curtains obscured the view into the room, Michael stepped farther inside, found a light switch, and ensured the room didn't fall into total darkness around them. He glanced around at the two twin beds near him, and the dresser/TV stand and desk on opposing walls near Jacques and the windows. *Nothing looks unusual, but I've been wrong before.*

His task complete, Jacques turned to face Michael. "Like yourself, I am employed by John and his, uh, *organization.* I provide men such as yourself with whatever they need to carry out, well, *whatever* they believe is necessary. There is nothing too big or too small for me to acquire, and the only obstacle I cannot defeat or overcome is time."

Michael crossed his arms and stood firm with his feet shoulder-width apart. "What kinds of *provisions* are you talking about?"

"Just about anything," Jacques held both hands out, palms up, to emphasize his words before loosely crossing both arms over his chest. Unlike Michael, his body language conveyed ambivalence, not distrust and potential hostility. "Most requests are for communications equipment, but occasionally--"

"Knives?"

"Several types are already in your safe, and that is sim--"

"Guns?"

"Also simple, unless you demand something exotic or automated."

"Suppressors? Subsonic ammunition?"

"Yes, both, but that is one area where time becomes a problem. If you need them next week, *absolument,* tomorrow, *c'est posible,* but *today?* Most likely not. Such things are too tightly controlled and regulated. However, just a functioning firearm that will kill without detonating in your hand? Pick your make and model over breakfast, and you'll have it before dinner."

"Back-up?"

"Back...up...you mean added personnel?"

"Yes."

"No, generally not. Under extreme circumstances, perhaps a man or two willing to risk dying for money without answers to their questions, but nothing more reliable than that."

"Mercenaries."

"More as you Americans might say, 'useful idiots.' They might help save your life in the moment, but they can only be trusted if you remain the highest bidder. Today's savior becomes tomorrow's nemesis." Jacques lightly shook his head. "I do not recommend submitting that particular request."

Michael snickered at the man's understated humor. "Anything else?"

"That is up to you. I'll leave my direct contact information." Jacques dropped a business card on the desk next to the black device. "My involvement is only at your discretion and need. Once I leave your room, I will never again acknowledge or speak with you unless you approach me. Even then, it will seem to anyone else as though we've never met. Godspeed, Father Andrew. I hope you enjoy your stay in Paris, and that you find success in everything you're called to resolve in our, uh, *complicated* city. Peace be with you."

Michael nodded and offered the ritualistic response. "And also with your spirit." Jacques strode toward the exit, and Michael followed the man once he passed. Finally alone, he locked the door and threw the interior latch closed, even though it would do little to slow or stop a determined and prepared adversary. Michael took in a deep, calming breath. *The departure from our op-sec protocols hadn't brought about my injury, death, or persecution...yet.*

Michael returned to the safe, entered his code, and retrieved the envelope concealed inside. He saw it displayed the same *Diplomatic Pouch* warnings, which further assured him of its authenticity. Red, two-inch wax seals overlapped each flap, and their interior detail displayed both the Seal of the Holy See and Saint Andrew's transverse cross. *Origin and intended recipient confirmed.* Michael briefly recalled his first day at John's covert training camp, when his boss explained the significant details within the former seal. *I never thought a large papal crown centered over an olive branch, cross, and sword was hard to understand, but I have always thought the cross should be bigger than the 'pope hat.'*

After cutting into the wax seals and inspecting their hidden parchments, Michael emptied the envelope and found another note from John on top of the other documents.

"Bonjour, shithead. If you're reading this, you and Jacques must have gotten off to a decent start. The short story is that I'm tightening up our op-sec protocols to mitigate risk to the field personnel. The hotel you're in, The Oremus, is owned outright by the Holy See, regardless of what the public records show. I'll cover this in more detail later.

Along with increased security, The Oremus lets us pre-position your intel packets, equipment, and any weaponry or specialized tools your investigation demands. This assignment is the most dangerous you've undertaken so far, and that's saying something. You'll find a second safe inside the closet. Its interior wall closest to the outer door has a magnetic push-spring that keeps it hidden. It'll open with the same code.

Your concierge is codenamed 'James the Lesser,' or 'Jacques la Petit' in his native tongue. Trust him as completely as you can ever trust anyone, including me.

The rest of the packet is what you've been getting from your contacts. Read through it before your meet so you got informed questions for a change. Start with the other safe.

You're welcome. Now quit burning daylight. -- John"

His curiosity piqued, Michael set the packet on the nearest bed and stepped back to the closet. After he pushed against the framed drywall façade, its magnetic lock released and opened to expose a black medium-sized rifle safe. The upper center of the door displayed a keypad and five-spoke wheel, so Michael entered the same five button code and turned the wheel to the right. The door glided open and revealed its unexpected contents.

Michael nodded in approval as a broad, relieved smile spread across his face. "I guess John's not ready to send me to prison, yet."

MAY 6, 11:30AM_

The Oremus, Paris, France.

MICHAEL STOOD inside his hotel room and stared in jubilant disbelief at the hidden rifle safe's contents. He immediately recognized the bolt gun. Its expensive high-power sniper scope, Multicam chassis and stock, and unique patinaed barrel could only be the .308 Browning John had assigned to him during his training camp last year. A small spiral-bound notebook leaned against the rifle. Michael first retrieved the notebook, and a quick flip through the initial pages confirmed his expectations. In order to make a truly precise and accurate shot in the environmental conditions and elevation of Paris, Michael had only two options: access a range where he could secretly calibrate the weapon system's settings, or make adjustments based on the specific data he'd documented in his "data book" from using that exact rifle, scope, and ammunition in the temperature, humidity, wind, and elevation in Wyoming. *John smuggled my rifle and data book all the way to Paris. What am I walking into?*

Michael set the book on the safe's internal shelf, hefted the precision rifle up to his right shoulder, and pulled the bolt open as he did so. To his surprise, a spent bullet casing ejected onto the closet floor just to the right of his feet. *Curious.* He confirmed the rifle's internal magazine matched the chamber. *Empty.*

Michael recovered the brass Gold Match jacket and realized something was written on it. He turned it around in his fingers until he could read the inscription:

From Wyoming, With Love.

He shook his head and pondered the bipolar, maniacal puzzle that was his supervisor. *John is the best and worst boss I've ever had. Supervisors like him are the reason cops go to work every day, retire at fifty-two, and drop dead from widow makers at fifty-five.* Michael dropped the brass casing in the pocket of his gray travel pants, stepped out of the closet, and brought the rifle back up to his right shoulder. Pointing it at a speck on the drawn curtain, he adjusted the scope settings with his left hand until the magnified image became crisp.

As excited as a kid on Christmas morning, Michael turned off the room's interior lights and opened the blackout curtain and sheer only two feet. Keeping the rifle concealed, he walked to the entryway and laid down behind the door and faced the windows. Michael immediately felt at home in the familiar position with the old friend at his shoulder. He scanned the building across the street and found a damaged brick between two balconies. Michael exhaled slowly, held the crosshairs on the center of the brick, and zoomed in until that brick filled his scope. He then picked a smaller spot among the damage, a discolored abrasion he thought no bigger than a dime and focused on that.

Michael reflexively fell into a slow, steady breathing cycle that allowed him to stay on target. He maintained the position for four slow breath cycles and kept the reticle's crosshairs tightly centered on that dime. *Like riding a bike.*

Michael stood up without ever dropping trigger on the dime, despite his absolute confidence that the rifle was safe and unloaded.

No benefit to that part of the exercise, at least not in proportion to the risk. I'm taking a big enough chance just having a rifle in France. He rose and returned the cherished weapon to its spot in the safe. Only then did he see the other firearms inside the reinforced black box.

Michael set the .308 to the back of the safe and retrieved an AR-style rifle designed for much dicier circumstances. Although he'd never touched this exact firearm, he had experience with many like it. This one, though, featured a collapsible folding stock, shortened barrel, and an internal suppressor. Despite its lack of manufacturer stamping and serial or model numbers, a high-end forge and gunsmith had obviously made it. The only mark on the weapon's barrel was a simple 5.56 *NATO,* which told him nothing more than the ammunition it required. Just as he'd done with the bolt-action rifle, Michael ensured the chamber and both drop-out high-capacity magazines were empty and then folded the stock. The weapon system was now less than eighteen inches. *This one's gonna be easy to hide in my backpack or under a jacket.*

Returning that to the safe, he checked a felt-covered shelf above the rifles and found the familiar and expected three-dart tranquilizer gun. A small hard plastic case next to it contained six more sedative darts.

Moving that aside, Michael removed a high-end integrally suppressed Ruger MK .22-caliber pistol. He'd once fired the original model of that handgun, which was designed after the German World War II Luger and remained among the most sought-after precision pistols. *This might almost earn the 'silencer' misnomer. With the right ammo, I bet the gun's no louder than snapping fingers.* Michael held the assassin's pistol in each hand, and its comfort, balance, and fit pleasantly surprised him. Ejecting the magazine, he realized it had aftermarket improvements to carry twelve rounds, plus one in the chamber. He replaced the mag, returned the pistol to the shelf, and saw several boxes of high-end precision ammunition for each weapon.

The excitement and novelty of having such an array of weapons in Europe disappeared as Michael considered their necessity. He secured the safe and its contents behind its drywall facade, strode out to the desk, and focused on the intel packet. *What the hell is John getting me into?*

With the lessening threat of an attack from inside the organization, Michael pulled the dark curtains open halfway to brighten the room, but still avoided presenting a stationary target to anyone positioned outside. *John wouldn't get these weapons into the room if he knew I'd be killed. He'd try to avoid blowback on the Church or Rome, and cops finding a dead priest with a stash of illegal guns does the opposite. I'm back to being in more danger from outside the Absolvers than from within, I think...*

Michael looked at the card Jacques had dropped on the desk and realized the concierge had provided his encoded contact information: *Jacques le Petit &q2e4t6u8oo.* That single code provided Michael the most confident authentication he could have requested. He retrieved his work cell, opened an app from within its encrypted Secured Items folder, and completed the required three-factor authentication to proceed.

Michael began by entering Jacques' username into his contact list. Once he entered the last digit, the app brought up the concierge's available contact information. He now had Jacques' work and home addresses, three phone numbers, two email addresses, and the most relevant, a direct message connection through the app. *That's one good thing to come out of these new phones.* His gratitude ironically reminded him of Sergio, a former clerical colleague of Michael's from Ecuador and, at present, another Absolver. *He's still confident we got the upgraded phones so John and the intel staff can keep closer tabs on our movement and communications, but at least they gave us a digital, secret-squirrel Rolodex as a trade-off.* Jacques wouldn't have access to Michael's clandestine contact information until he initiated a conversation, so Michael sent a simple message of "Thank you." *There. Now the quartermaster has my digits.*

Michael set the phone aside and dove headlong into the front of the intel packet. He skimmed John's page-one note again to make sure he hadn't missed anything, and then moved on to the pages behind it:

"*Updated Protocols regarding The Oremus hotels:*

Roughly translated, the name means, 'let us pray.' We used a series of shell companies to buy a failing global hotel chain three years ago and began extensive renovations at most locations. We expect the investment to become a significant source of profit in about two years. Most of the proceeds will fund our own operations and support other DICE assets. Our worldwide locations in major cities and tourist areas allow us to move men and equipment to safe locations, and to place men like Jacques in each of them. He can help provide whatever our operatives require to do God's work and come back inside the wire.

Your room number at any Oremus location will always be 144, and it will always supplant room 162. Any deviation indicates danger. Both are associated with those respective sections of the Catechism, which reveal Obedience in Faith and Perseverance of Faith. This subterfuge will help you avoid countersurveillance efforts.

The concierge at each Oremus will be one of our operatives who's permanently assigned there, and he will always be called James or the local variant. You can make requests to him in person, by encrypted app messaging, or by merely leaving your request inside the room safe. Among his other duties, James will check your safe for communications and supply requests each time you leave to try fulfilling them before you come back.

To further improve our operational security, you will leave sensitive documents in the safe whenever you vacate the room. The concierge accounts for all the pages and destroys them when your investigation's done."

Despite the relief Michael felt in knowing he could now get help from someone in the same city, the logistics required for Jacques to fulfill his duties gave serious pause. *The trade-off is that my own organization's now surveilling and tracking me. If they dedicate this room to Absolvers and covert Vatican operatives, the odds of it being bugged 'for safety' is almost certain. The hierarchy could justify keeping an eye on us for any number of reasons, including to protect us from outsiders and safeguard our secrets.* Michael scanned the room and struggled to find a way to search it without broadcasting his efforts to do so. *'Those who would give up essential liberty to purchase a little temporary safety deserve neither.' I fear that ole Ben's still right on that one...*

Michael decided he could best mitigate the risk of his new "safe-house" by spending the least amount of time there. He returned to the bulky intel packet and skimmed the next few pages, which provided boredom-level detail on the operations, logistics, and duties of the concierge at each location. The first page specific to his current investigation renewed his focus.

"Meet with Father Luc Devoux at Cathedral of Saint Denis on 6-May prior to 1400 hours. Do not delay. Time is of the essence."

He checked his watch and realized he'd have to hustle across town to meet his contact. *I lost three hours to my own paranoia, and now I'm pressed for time. Every other investigation's first pitted me against the clock, so why should this one be any different?*

Michael returned the intel packet to the safe and used a map on his phone to find an address a half-mile from the Saint Denis cathedral. *I'll have a cab drop me there and work back to the cathedral after I run a clean detection route.* He donned his gray backpack, which still held his few personal items, and decided against retrieving the pistol from the hidden safe. *There must be a reason it's here, but millions of Parisians and tourists walk the streets and major cathedrals every day without needing a gun. I'm sure I can make it in and out of a church without having to shoot back.*

Michael pocketed one of his keycards, secured the hotel room, and exited out the other side of the building, which avoided the concierge desk. Within three minutes, he stood on the wide sidewalk of the *Champs Élysées* and hailed a taxi. After the driver seemed to understand his intended destination, Michael dug into his backpack and scanned the vehicles moving through traffic with them.

Retrieving his worn copy of the Catechism of the Catholic Church, Michael turned to read 144:

Obedience and Faith: to obey in terms of faithfulness indicates a voluntary submission and adherence to what is taught because its truthfulness is assured by God, the very eternal origin of Truth itself. Abraham modeled a life of faith, obedience, and adherence, and the Virgin Mary is the perfect personified embodiment of this virtue.

Michael flipped the pages to section 162:

Perseverance of Faith: faith was bestowed by God unto mankind, and may be lost or abandoned just as any other priceless gift. Saint Paul advised Saint Timothy to 'wage the good warfare, holding faith and a good conscience. By rejecting conscience, some have made ship-wreck of their faith.'

Michael looked out the cab's back passenger-side window and sighed. *So, we need to have the faith to willingly kill our own like Abraham, and the conscience to wage the good warfare. Seems like the mentality of a legit shadow organization.*

He set the book aside, retrieved his work cell, and opened its encrypted messaging app. Michael found the open dialogue with John and gave him an update:

Checked in. Met Jacques. En route to contact.

Michael locked the phone, returned everything to his backpack, and watched the two-thousand-year-old city pass by as he considered his present reality in it. *What's out there waiting for me that demands that kind of firepower?*

MAY 6, 12:46PM_
ARRONDISSEMENT SAINT-DENIS. PARIS,
FRANCE.

AFTER A FORTY-FIVE-MINUTE CAB RIDE, Michael started his surveillance detection route at *Hospital Casanova*. He entered the lobby, walked to the opposite side of the structure, and exited through the kitchen. *If you act like you belong, people tend to believe you.*

Michael continued on to the *St. Denis/Porte de Paris* Metro station. Bypassing the above-ground tram lines, he descended to the subway platforms and caught the westbound number 13 train. Although not rush hour, the platforms and train cars were busy. *The locals have earbuds, novels, and newspapers, and the tourists have backpacks, maps, and guidebooks.* He scanned the car's occupants several times for anyone familiar or interested in him, but no one drew his attention.

After the needless and recurring stress, anxiety, and fear that he had been walking into a trap all day, Michael both wanted to allay his concerns and use that same hypervigilance to protect himself. *Can't have it both ways. I can either walk around with my 'head up my ass' and the risk that entails, or I can stay paranoid and let my stomach chew an ulcer in itself. The HUMA method gets people killed a helluva lot quicker.*

At the third stop, Michael departed the train at the *Garibaldi*

Station, walked up and over the tracks, and descended onto the east-bound platform for the same line. *If I thought someone was tailing me, I'd need a few hours to do this right. Given the lack of time and threats, I'm going with a 'good enough' effort today.* He grinned at how his decision brought forth one of his father's favorite expressions: *There's never time to do it right, but there's always time to do it twice. Dad would be disappointed, but I'm out of time, just like always.*

While awaiting the next train, Michael casually scanned the crowds on both sides of the platform. He recognized no one. *Any team that's still following me would need at least six players and several vehicles. The odds of that round down to zero. You can't ever be certain you haven't grown a tail, but you can reduce the chances.* Michael rode the train past his original stop to its terminus at the *St. Denis-Université Station.*

Because the train went out of service for a cleaning each time it returned to that station, the entire car emptied onto the platform and Michael's chest tightened. *There. Green backpack, blue sweater, white skullcap.* He recognized the man, or more precisely, his specific, bright clothing, and urgently memorized his details. *Middle Eastern male, early-to-mid-forties, five-nine, five-ten, heavy pear-shaped build.* The man stood out from the crowd and Michael churned through his memories to recall where and when he'd first seen him. *Oh my God. He was on the westbound line with me! That means he also got off and switched trains at Garibaldi! How did I miss that?*

He chastised himself for not being more careful and diligent in his countermeasures. Despite his ominous, internal dread, Michael casually scanned the crowd for an accomplice. His fear escalated as he realized he still hadn't seen the man's face. *He's either skilled or this is coincidence. I can imagine numerous reasons for him to have made the same switch, but the most probable involve malice.*

Michael could no longer just watch for familiar faces moving in the same direction, but he could blend into the back of the crowd and force any followers to slow and let him retake the lead. *Just like when*

I drove a patrol car. The guy I need to pay attention to is the one who won't pass me no matter how slow I'm going.

By the time he reached the escalator, Michael stood near the back of the crowd and watched ahead for anyone who turned around or looked back. No one else raised his suspicion and the green backpack had moved out of his sight, which presented another set of problems. Michael rechecked his watch. *Thirty-two minutes to meet the contact and a twenty-minute walk to get there. No time for surprises.*

As Michael ascended to the street, he stayed to the far-right side of the walkways and escalator to force any attack to come from his left side. He scanned everything and everyone around him, and his pulse pounded in his neck. A few deep, calming breaths helped, but didn't alleviate the early stages of his fight-or-flight response.

He again spied the green backpack and slowed his pace. The target stood across the street facing away and focused on a phone in his hands. Michael's destination compelled him to go right, so, instead, he turned left to stay behind the man. A newspaper and tourist-trap kiosk stood nearby, so he walked over and shuffled through a stack of *I ♥ PARIS* t-shirts. The Muslim man turned around and scanned the area, but he didn't focus on Michael or the kiosk where he stood.

Michael scowled as the probability shifted toward coincidence. *He's not in shape to fight anything more dangerous than falafel and crepes, but it doesn't take much effort or stamina to drop a trigger or detonation switch. Could just be a lookout doing his part for the cause, too.*

Elation spread across the man's face as another Middle Eastern male approached him, probably his son based on their age difference and similar features. The two embraced for a moment and began a boisterous conversation. They strode away on a side street perpendicular to Michael's intended direction of travel, so he scanned the area once more before walking away from the kiosk. *Looks like his boy's home from college and he missed the right Metro stop. Could happen to anybody, right?*

Michael breathed a sigh of relief and hurried away from the Metro station. Despite his time constraint, he chose a slightly longer route and hoped the apparent father and son didn't reappear. By the time Michael reached the Cathedral of Saint Denis, he'd regained confidence that he hadn't been followed or watched. *Never mind the digital watchers. John probably knows every step I take with this new phone.*

Michael entered the cathedral through its main doors, which stood at the structure's west end. In the sparse moments his cab ride had allowed for research, Michael learned *Saint Denis Cathédral* was also the Royal Necropolis of France with seventy-five monarchs and ten royal servants entombed there. Ignoring the opulent and historical beauty of its interior for the moment, Michael blended into the tourist crowds and scanned the new environment. *Still no threats.*

Unlike the cathedrals he'd visited in the American Southwest and the *Catedral Primada de Bogota,* near where he'd served in Columbia, the interior of Saint Denis was bright and open. Tall, light gray carved stone walls rose into pointed Gothic arches and held beautifully detailed stained-glass windows on three of its four primary sides. Michael breathed in the familiar, reassuring aroma. *It may look different, but all of God's houses feel and smell the same to me. Comforting, permanent, history.*

He joined tourists in the back of the church, known as the narthex. Unlike the rest of the Catholic faithful among them, Michael didn't dab himself with the blessed holy water or genuflect in the aisle before taking a seat in a pew to the far back, right side of the cathedral. *It's best I present a non-Catholic persona to anyone who might remember me here.* He stayed alert and wary of those nearby and looked around the nave, the main body of the cathedral, for one of the parish priests who served the Saint Denis community.

There. A young priest in the expected black cassock strode toward Michael from somewhere near the altar, which seemed to be seventy or eighty yards away. Michael nonchalantly rose, donned his backpack, and strolled toward the priest. Just as he'd done in The

Oremus, he kept a hold high on the shoulder straps to protect himself without advertising his preparedness to do so. *John always talked about how meeting your contact was one of the most dangerous aspects in any field operation. There's so much political and ideological division in the Church that it might only be a matter of time before I'm staring at a gun or handcuffs at one of these meetings. All it takes is one snitch and an undercover cop or operative to pretend to be my contact, and then it's all over but the prison sentence.*

The priest looked up as they approached one another, and Michael gave him a slight, disarming wave to draw the man's attention. *"Bonjour, parlez vous anglais?"*

"Yes, of course, and, *bonjour,* a good day to you, as well. How may I help you serve God today?"

Michael smiled at the unusual greeting. *The man's devout and direct. I like his style.* "I'm here to see Father Luc Devoux. Is he available?" The priest's eyes registered an internal apprehension, fear maybe, but the rest of his expression remained passive.

"I'm Father Luc, and, yes, I suppose I am available at this moment."

"Father *Devoux,* I'm *Father Andrew.*" Michael let the specific phrasing pique the priest's attention. *We're never called by our last name.* "I need to hear your confession."

Saint Denis Cathedral. Paris, France.

THE FRENCH PRIEST stepped closer to Michael and uttered his words as though he feared someone might overhear the exchange. "I can't *imagine* what I would need to confess."

Michael adopted a confident, reassuring tone. "I can't either. I won't know until you tell me. I'm here to offer absolution." After meeting almost a dozen priests like Father Luc, Michael appreciated the man's extraordinary position. They had vital intelligence that could help save the dignity of innocents, but none of the training and little of the intestinal fortitude required on his side of the conversation. *Much like my mentor, H, they appreciate the necessity of my work but can't take it up themselves.*

Father Luc looked around, having used up his intrinsic stoicism for their coded exchange. "There are many onlookers here now, along with teams of engineers that wander about. They are examining how to quickly erect a fire suppression system in our cathedral to prevent the *Notre Dame* tragedy from repeating itself here, so the once-lonely alcoves are not so today. Perhaps we can speak elsewhere?"

Michael tried not to show his own apprehension at the man's reluctance. "How about the rectory, even the sacristy?"

"Oh, yes, of course," the priest stammered out and blushed. "Your laity clothing confused me. Follow me, Father Andrew."

Michael covertly watched the nearby clusters of tourists and faithful and hoped the priest didn't draw their attention by glancing around like a lookout at a bank robbery. They approached the right side of the altar and the south transept, the right "arm" of the cross-shaped building. Looking past the altar for a moment, Michael appreciated the grandeur of its innovative and historic open ambulatory, the walkway that allowed pilgrims, parishioners, and tourists to circumnavigate the altar and enter the small side chapels behind it. He longed for the time to visit those smaller chapels and take in the ancient relics on display there. *Another visit, maybe, when I'm not working.*

Michael followed Father Luc through a partially concealed doorway at the far, east side of the south transept. They passed through the short, narrow marble doorway, which reminded Michael how much modern man benefitted from diet, exercise, and thousands of years of ever-improving medical technology. Early construction of the modern structure ended in the mid-1100s, the location having been the burial site of Saint Denis, who was martyred in 250 AD. *Either twelfth century men didn't stand very tall or wide, or they just relished banging their heads and hips all the damned time.*

Their footfalls lightly echoed in the narrow stone corridor, and Father Luc turned back and spoke to ease his anxiety. "Have you ever been to our cathedral?"

Michael cleared his throat, still unsure of where to balance his need for operational security and anonymity against trusting his fellow clerics with the most benign information. "No, I have not." *I can't be an emotionless asshole to this guy, especially when he's volunteered helpful information.*

"You should return for one of our tours, but we offer only two in English each month. I imagine we'll soon offer many more now that tourists and pilgrims may no longer choose to visit *Notre Dame* over us." The local priest opened another door that took them into the private rectory where the parish priests lived. "Please, sit," he offered and motioned to a tired set of worn furniture.

"Thank you." Michael had grown accustomed to spending time on chairs and couches that should have been replaced decades ago. *For the vast wealth and power of the Church, its most ardent and important supporters see little such benefit. They enjoy only a reasonably functional roof and living inside a monument to God and His people for a short time.* He stepped across the small room and sat on a short couch, while Father Luc took up one of the unstable dining chairs nearby.

"How shall I begin?"

"With reconciliations, Father Luc, I find it often best to begin at the beginning."

"Oh, yes," the younger man blushed and crossed himself, so Michael repeated the ritual. "Forgive me, Father, for I have sinned. It has been eight or nine hours since my last confession, and I'm still failing to safeguard peace in my heart."

Without the intel packet he normally acquired and read at these contacts, Michael had nothing to do but listen. He leaned forward, put his elbows on his knees, and focused on remembering everything he heard. *It'd be silly and dangerous to take notes.* "Go ahead, I'm listening."

"I hold anger and hatred in my heart, and I wish vengeance to befall a brother."

"God commands us to not to act against charity," Michael confirmed. "What caused your anger and hatred?"

Father Luc explained in surprising detail that an unnamed, life-long friend worked as a counter-terrorism investigator and operative for the French National Police. The unit's new supervisor seemed to fulfill early allegations that his appointment was a political appeasement to France's Muslim community and its long-alleged grievances of discrimination and prejudice within the police and military antiterrorism units. The supervisor had forced a growing number of legitimate investigations closed after declaring their basis in Islamophobia and racism, rather than reasonable suspicion, evidence, or probable cause. He had even accused his subordinates of attempting to subject the nation's Muslims and refugees to the baseless beheadings and murderous hysteria that followed the French Revolution.

Within the last few hours, the supervisor closed out an investigation into an alleged bomb maker who lived nearby in *Seine-Saint-Denis*, a strong Muslim enclave in Paris, and the investigation needed only days or hours to determine the man's involvement.

"What was this missing piece," Michael asked.

"They knew what building he lived in, but still, not which apartment. It is narrowed to only four or five dwellings, and the investigators expected to soon identify the exact flat. Their other efforts kept getting them closer, but Ger--, *err, my friend*, expected they would locate the exact apartment at any moment. As worried as I am with *my* anger at this man, who is so willing to endanger the public because of his religion, my friend is having a far tougher moment."

"What do you mean?"

Father Luc cleared his throat. "He left only a few minutes ago. I don't think he's ever visited during a workday, and I feared something terrible had happened in his personal life. He confessed his ceaseless anger, which even he admits is growing to open hostility. My friend feels betrayed and powerless, which is never good for a man with his training and responsibility, and knowing his suffering and temperament, in turn, anger me for him and his circumstance. The distrusted supervisor reassigned him to a trivial case well beneath his skills and training. If the police are correct, and this alleged bomb maker is just that, I fear my friend will soon act outside the legal and moral laws to prevent those detonations."

Michael cocked his head. "You mean..."

"I believe he will kill the suspect, and perhaps, his supervisor. He may even think himself justified in doing so. Even now, he is risking everything that matters in his life. Despite his orders, he refuses to accept the new assignment and is instead continuing the unauthorized investigation of a guest of the nation of France, and maybe even a French citizen. He stands to lose everything, even if he is later found to be right."

"Did he say that to you?"

"Not in so many words," the priest explained while the aging wood chair *creaked* beneath his shifting weight. "But I understood his tone and intent just the same."

"Do you think it curious that he's provided you with all this detailed information?"

"Yes, and no. I should have better explained our relationship. We are friends, that is true, but we've grown up together our whole lives. We trust each other absolutely, and it helped him to unburden even the smallest details from his conscience. I asked few questions and have let him say whatever he needed to me.

"He is afraid," the priest continued, "that his Muslim superior is either aiding such men, or he's so blinded by his own belief system that he can't accept that some among his own faith wish to commit grievous harm, violence, and evil."

"You've now twice avoided saying 'innocent.'"

"I believe in original sin, Father Andrew. None of us is truly innocent. Even the secular court systems are only willing to find us 'not guilty' or 'acquitted,' but they never say 'innocent.'"

"Fair enough."

"May I presume that you're armed and prepared to defend yourself?"

Michael couldn't hide his immediate concern. "Why is that important?"

"*Saint-Denis* is a Muslim enclave well on its way to becoming our seven-hundred-and-fifty-third 'no-go' zone. We still enjoy some police, fire fighting, and medical services in this area, but not for much longer. The police won't enter with less than four officers, and this historic cathedral is near the top of the terrorist wish list. In the eyes of our aspiring oppressors, destroying this site and its faithful would prove Mohammed's supremacy over both the French nation *and* Christianity. My fellow priests and I live under constant fear of assault and attack. I cannot wear clerical clothes outside the cathedral, and no one but the local rabbi will shake my hand. Anyone else I meet will, at best, offer me their wrist."

Michael sat back on the couch, shocked by the priest's testimony of his personal experiences inside the French capital. *Goddammit, that's why John had the weapons dropped to me, why he keeps talking about this being such a dangerous assignment. It's gonna be pretty damned ironic if I get killed because I wasted so many hours today preparing for a threat from John. Dammit.*

"If not for this cathedral and its associated university, I believe the police and emergency services would have already turned it over to the Salafists."

"What makes you say that?"

"My friend. His colleagues in the uniformed police services lament *not* having yet abandoned it. They risk their lives to serve the needs of people who wish them and their children dead and damned to hell." A weak smile appeared on his face. "Who can blame them? Even their employer, the French Republic, refuses to acknowledge or address the problem."

The priest grew silent and stared at the floor. Michael sensed he held something back. "What is it, Father Luc?"

The man inhaled a deep breath, held it, and exhaled before he looked back up and met Michael's gaze. "My friend, a brother in all but blood, believes in his heart and in his head that a violent terrorist attack is underway. If he's correct, at an unknown but imminent moment, a bomb will destroy the lives of dozens, perhaps hundreds of my countrymen and our guests. There is little time to stop whatever is to come, few chances to do so, and almost no option absent violent, uncompromising intervention.

"I quietly notified my monsignor and hoped that he knew how to help, how we could avert this without breaking our vows and endangering our very souls. I took that risk, and now, you are here. Just you. One man. And, apparently, a fellow priest who suffers the same limitations as I."

Michael held the man's intense gaze, unsure where the sadness in his eyes and the angry tone in his voice would lead.

"So. Father Andrew. I asked for help to save my brother's life, and to save him from himself. And, if possible, to save the unknown innocents from injury, suffering, and death. What can one man do to stop a flood? I hope that you're capable of more than prayer. That hasn't yet proven effective against this particular ailment."

Michael did his best to offer the resolute confidence this man needed to hear, regardless of what he knew and felt. "You're right. I am but one man, but I'm never alone. I can't yet tell how this will go, but my skillset extends well beyond reconciliation and prayer."

"I'm glad to hear you say that, Father," Luc offered, although with no change in his expression or voice. "I could never admit this to one of my parishioners, but you're walking into a lion's den. Even if you are *not* alone, your destination, *in my experience,* demands far more swift and lethal tools than prayer."

GERARD SAT in a dim office suite before a long folding table and watched a bank of ten large computer monitors arranged in two rows of five. Because the suite had no windows, a bare overhead bulb and the monitors offered his only lighting and view of the outside world. At the array's far left two monitors for cameras 9 and 10 remained black, but Gerard intended to resolve that in the immediate future. A small reception area stood just beyond the door to his right, but that space only had room for a few chairs and a water cooler. Peeling paint, furniture scuffs, and water damage alternately covered the walls, and dozens of water marks on the threadbare carpeting confirmed the extent and history of the recurring problem. A plastic bucket stood in the corner to his left that Gerard planned to use instead of risking interaction with neighborhood residents every hour or two. *It's best I'm running solo. The second guy would have little room to work, and I don't know many who would share my fifteen-liter water closet.*

Three of the Task Force's IT techs had finished the install only half an hour ago, and Gerard had just completed his diagnostic and operational checks. The original seven cameras still worked, and the tenants haven't yet found or destroyed the replacement at number 8.

83

He smiled at his good fortune, despite the recent setbacks. *Perhaps in spite of Lieutenant Algeri, God is smiling on me for the moment.*

Instead of following his lieutenant's dangerous and misguided order, Gerard found and leased a vacant office inside a three-story parking garage across *Rue de Corbillon* from their target. Although he preferred a greater stand-off from his suspects, Gerard's sudden lack of personnel demanded he position himself as close as possible. In addition to the suite's proximity to his target, its metal exterior door and surrounding frame provided absolute privacy after he changed both its locks to high-end Medeco deadbolts that couldn't be copied or picked. *Without getting a flat in the same building, this is the best we can do. 'We,' as if I'm not swinging on these gallows alone. Thank God Lucas's men moved the monitors and set them back up without losing the video-audio feed from a single camera.*

His cellphone vibrated on the desk's surface, and his current ringtone, a rock song from the recent American remake of *A Star Is Born* filled the small space.

"Black eyes open wide,
It's time to testify.
There's no room for lies,
and everyone's waiting for you!"

Gerard saw the call came from Task Force Headquarters and considered not taking it. *My chance of success is greater, though, if I don't yet have to go to ground. Maybe it's best I keep up communications with Algeri and his cronies.* He sighed and accepted the call. *"Antlé."*

"Gerard, it's Lucas," his friend and longtime colleague announced in French. "I understand you're keeping close watch on some of my equipment. That's very gracious of you, especially when you know how few functioning camera systems I have."

He ignored the man's sarcasm. "I like the way you're seeing this. I expected your call, but I hoped your men could keep their mouths shut for at least a day or two."

"Fuck that, they know better than to bullshit me. You're damned lucky I don't have to deploy them on another investigation right now."

"*What investigations?* Algeri's closed everything but his goddamned meter maid projects! Perhaps I should thank him myself for leaving your equipment unused, what do you think?"

"How did you set this up, Gerard? I heard Algeri killed your case."

"That might have been his intent, but he made the mistake of not using those exact words." Gerard cleared his throat of the lie. "The orders he sent to me and your technical crews commanded us to close the old safehouse. He didn't order me to return the equipment to you, or specify that I could not open a *new* safehouse."

Lucas scoffed through the phone. "How long can you keep this up?"

"If all goes very well, *or very badly*, only a few more days. I rented the office suite with an undercover credit card, so Finance won't question it for a month, maybe six weeks, when the itemized bill shows up. If I'm still here by then, I will have converted and begun attending the mosque across the street."

His friend chuckled at the notion. "I can let you watch my gear for now, but, if we get orders to set up a new operation, I'll have to come for it. I don't have spares lying around."

"Thank you, Lucas." Now confident in the lack of resistance or confrontation from his friend, his Gerard focused his attention back on the cameras. *He should come out soon, and I probably won't get another chance for another three days if I screw this up.*

"I get it, Gerard. Algeri won't hear it from me or any of my men, but they've already put our necks out if the lieutenant realizes it."

"*Hmmph.*" Gerard manipulated the cameras with a mouse to set each at its optimal focus for the current lighting conditions.

"Gerard? Did you hear what I said?"

"*Yes, of course.*" He looked down and tended to the conversation for a moment. "If he looks into this, I'll be out on the street, so, as far as it concerns your men, *I* ordered them to follow my directives as the lead investigator." Gerard looked back at the monitors, but only scanned for his target. "They never knew I *wasn't* acting with the lieutenant's direct orders and approval. No sense in putting anyone else in the soup line." *Every three days, just like clockwork, he comes out, and today's the day. Unless he comes back with an extraordinary amount of groceries, it confirms the number of stomachs in his apartment hasn't changed. That alone should mean no new players have stepped onto the field with us. He's unlikely to let any partners stay elsewhere, there's too much risk in doing so.*

"I'm sorry to hear about you and Claudette. I only just found out this morning, Gerard, honest, or I would've said something sooner. You two were always a great couple."

Movement. "Have to go, Lucas, my guy's coming out." Gerard started a timer on his watch and ignored his friend's condolences.

00:15:00

00:14:59

"Be safe, Gerard. We're cheering for you, even if you can't hear us doing so."

Gerard ended the call. *The silence of their cheers is deafening.* He put away his discontent about having stepped out into the arena alone and hoped that would last only until word of his efforts spread. *If I prove Algeri's dangerously misguided, not even the politicians running the police service can support his position. Let them relegate that asshole to investigating unlicensed cabs in the tourist districts.* As expected, he watched the suspect descend through the interior stairwells of his apartment building and move toward the street.

After locking both office doors behind him, Gerard walked through an interior hallway and then out onto the ground floor of the parking garage. Located just a block away from his target, only the top parking level offered a line of sight to 8 *Rue du Corbillon,* but the lack of cover and concealment up there made the perch useless. Gerard began his counter-surveillance routine by hurrying across the entire floor and checking on both vehicles he had stored there, a blue Fiat hatchback and the white Peugeot that had posed as his taxi earlier that morning. A casual look over each showed no evidence of new damage or tampering.

Among the reasons he'd chosen the vacant office suite had been the building's close parking access and lack of interior cameras. Although one device tried to record the vehicle, face, and license plate of everything that drove out of the garage, Gerard could maneuver around the floors and pedestrian entrances without creating a digital log.

Gerard looped back to the blue Fiat, opened his rear hatch, and removed two large door-sized magnets that displayed the name and logo of a fake grocery delivery service called *Ferme A Table*. The Task Force had also backstopped this business to ensure it passed an initial inspection by any countersurveillance team. *Maybe I should go out for my own groceries later, just to show the same logos on a different car in the neighborhood?*

With his subterfuge in place, Gerard drove out of the garage, hid his face from the lone camera, and checked his timer as he drove toward his target. 00:12:13.

MAY 6, 3:58PM_

8 Rue du Corbillon. Saint-Denis, France.

DRESSED in the skullcap and flowing linen gown more common for Saudi Muslims, he stepped out onto the street in front of his apartment building and checked his digital wristwatch. *Two hours until the evening prayers.* He pushed a button to activate its preset timer.

00:04:00

00:03:59

Having abandoned his family name and devoted whatever remained of his life to absolute service to God, he now called himself something more befitting his few remaining days: Abdel Abdullah Abrini. *Servant and slave to God. My agnostic identity died with my escape from Syria. Allah allowed me to learn electrical engineering at university and then brought me here to serve Him. That will remain the sole focus of the rest of my days.*

He had been mere months from gradation when the Assad regime fell apart and his nation collapsed into civil war. Although grateful to have been part of the rising tide there, Abdel wished he could have been born earlier. *What a difference I could have made with my skills and determination, I have everything to offer Allah but time. Humanity is forever out of time, although God and nature seem unconcerned with such things.*

Abdel strode toward the small local market and the first meeting with his brother. Not a relative by blood, but by the more important shared struggle against the nonbelieving world. Having never met the man, Abdel had integrated the meeting into his normal patterns. *Straying from the rigidity of my routine is far more dangerous than being seen speaking with another man in a neighborhood market.*

He walked north on his street and monitored the movement around him. Most of residents attended the mosque housed on the ground floor of his apartment building, and many of them celebrated the imminent Ramadan holiday by adopting a nocturnal lifestyle during the monthlong fast. *It's easier for the less dedicated to fast from sunrise to sunset if they're asleep for much of that time. Their softness insults Allah, but at least they expose their shallow faith to the world.*

Abdel despised Muslims who searched for loopholes in God's directives. *The point of the fast is to prove your faith and obedience through deliberate suffering.* With Ramadan upon them in a few hours, he'd already noticed an absence of the "faithful" in much of the neighborhood. Because of their command to fast and practice abstinence from sunrise to sunset for the full month of Ramadan, many of the heretics slept during the day and stayed up at night. *They consume all the food and water they want, and they enjoy all the sexual relations possible during the darkness. How fitting. They sacrifice nothing, but continue to proclaim themselves as faithful, obedient servants.* Abdel recalled a part of the Hadith: *Veerily, the smell of the mouth of a fasting person is better to Allah than the smell of musk.* The truly obedient, however, didn't cheapen their faith and its glorious burden to make their holy obligations more comfortable for themselves and their children.

Abdel slowed his pace at the next intersection, glanced along *Boulevard Carnot*, and then turned right only after finding no obvious threats. He walked past the *Mak D'Hal* restaurant, looked at his timer, and confirmed 2:15 remained until his appointed arrival time. Having reached his short walk's midpoint early, he measured his pace and continued two streets east to *Rue Gabriel Péri*. Abdel again slowed, scanned the intersection for anyone who watched him regardless of their ethnicity, and turned right.

The small, discreet sign hanging above the doorway of his destination caught Abdel's eyes: سوق عدن. The familiar and beloved Arabic amid this foreign land brought a smile to his face. *Marché d'Eden, the locals would say, the few who can read God's language. The ignorant tourists would call it Eden's Market and expect to find only their condemned apples offered for sale.*

Abdel pushed the metal-framed glass door open and stepped inside the shop. The door's upper corner collided with a tiny shop bell, which *dinged* several times. Luxurious scents of the spices and aromas of his childhood enveloped him, and Abdel breathed deep, allowing the intoxicating fragrance to be a natural and momentary distraction. His watch *beeped* twice. Exhaling, he nodded and smiled at the shop owner and walked around the shop's exterior aisles in search of any sign of trouble. At the back of the store, Abdel passed an employee-only door and reminded himself that it led to his preplanned escape path through a series of shared neighborhood courtyards.

Seeing nothing that concerned him, Abdel picked up a metal hand basket and conducted his normal shopping. Next to the produce, a small display of handmade scented candles caught his attention. He picked up a tall, light sand-colored cylinder and smelled it. The fragrance at once transported him back to his memories of his worship at *Al-Haram Mosque,* the Great Mosque of Mecca. Pride and honor swelled inside him, for he had completed his mandated pilgrimage to that very site and would soon have finished everything Allah required for ascension to Paradise. *I will send my last almsgiving tomorrow, which fulfills my commandments.* Modern technology allowed Abdel to support his choice of causes by delivering small, anonymous, and repeated donations to imams around the world. Despite international banking laws, like-minded activists were no longer restricted to paying hard currency to the local mosque and relying upon that one imam to advance Allah's will.

Abdel read the candle's label, which declared the scent was called, simply, *Obedience.* He laid the tall candle in his basket, careful to protect it.

dingding ding

Abdel looked at the front door and saw another Arab stepping inside. He wore jeans and a black leather jacket, along with the traditional white skullcap, a *taqiyah*. His attire was consistent with many of the Muslims who tried in vain to blend into French society. *Fruitless effort. They'll never accept our people, and we don't want to be known as French, but, still, some of us seek appeasement.*

The stranger made brief but polite eye contact with the shop owner, scanned the small market, and stepped inside as though looking for someone.

Abdel lowered his gaze back to the produce in front of him and watched the man with his peripheral vision. *He's too focused, and he's not here for groceries.* He tried to conceal his displeasure and debated whether the man could be a police informant or his contact. *What a terrible lack of subtlety.*

The stranger walked around the store, picking up and replacing random items without examining them. Abdel stood in place and picked through the store's bin of lemons to force the stranger to come to him.

As expected, the leather-clad man stepped to the opposite side of the fruit bin and stopped. Abdel replaced and retrieved another pair of lemons; in his peripheral, he saw the man stared straight at him like the amateur he obviously was. He quietly cleared his throat before speaking. "Do you know where I may find zaatar here?" His voice trembled and conveyed nervousness.

Abdel stayed focused on the fruit in his hand for a moment before responding to that first line of their coded phrases. "The shopkeeper may sell such spices, but it will not be as good as that from the homeland."

"Isn't that true of everything else in this nation?"

Abdel glanced up at him. The words had been exact and precise, but too loud and fast. He shifted his gaze to the shopkeeper who focused on a newspaper and paid them no attention. Abdel stepped left to position himself closer to his contact. "You're new at this, and too nervous. Are you capable of carrying out the work at hand?"

The younger man leaned forward and spoke in a coarse whisper. "I long for nothing else, and I will not fail, not for any reason."

"Did you do everything as I demanded?"

"Yes, precisely. No one followed me, and no one could have escaped my notice. Your map and guidance ensured my safe passage."

Abdel recalled the extensive routing he'd prescribed, which sent the contact through several choke points, U-turns, and isolated areas. *If anyone had been following him, even this simpleton could have identified him.* "Are you prepared? We are but days away from the end of our personal struggles."

"I've completed my appointed tasks, and my soul is ready. More than that, I am willing."

Abdel stepped over to an adjacent bin of squashes and his contact moved with him. The owner took no notice, but Abdel now believed that was intentional. "We cannot meet here again, it isn't safe. You will stay in here at least five minutes after I leave. Buy several items, I do not care what they are. I will email further instructions. Expect to meet me only once, perhaps twice more. The last time will be for the delivery on the day of our action." He glanced up and saw the man grinned too widely. *At least the shopkeeper can't see this useful idiot's face.* "Do you understand?"

"Yes, yes, completely."

Abdel handed him a yellow squash. "This one is good. Look for the email and draw no further attention to yourself. Leave here and continue the two kilometers to *Stade de France*. Board the metro there and follow the rest of my directions." He stepped over to the shopkeeper and paid for the small assortment of food he required for the next few days. His strict compliance with Ramadan also allowed him to spend far less on food, his only real indulgence in this life. *Further confirmation to God of my absolute obedience.*

Abdel strode from the market and stuck to his normal route to foil any government assets watching him. The evening prayer began in less than an hour, and even though his chosen path took him by the local mosque, he refused to go there more than necessary. *Righteous congregations are under surveillance, and the nonbelievers are too ignorant to know the difference, so I must assume they are all under government watch. Only imposters worship in that mosque, for even the imam is not a believer. That's far worse, professing a faith and ideology you wish to destroy.*

A smile broke across his face, but Abdel regained his composure. *God willing, they will soon know the price of their betrayal.*

MAY 6, 3:58PM_
RUE DES CHAUMETTES. SAINT-DENIS,
FRANCE.

GERARD GRIMACED and sped away from the parking garage exit. *I have to plant the devices, vacate the building, and get off the street before my bad man comes back. My lack of time forces me to choose an inferior tactic.* Gerard turned left at the south end of the parking garage and drove east through a narrow alley. Seconds later, he turned left again on *Rue du Corbillon.* He passed two buildings, turned on the car's emergency flashers, and stopped in front of the entrance to building 8. Gerard leapt from the seat and hoped any watchers would assume he was late in making his delivery.

He retrieved a half-dozen purple canvas bags from the hatch, which also displayed the white *Ferme A Table* logo and held various produce and *halal*-compliant canned goods in case someone challenged him. Gerard covertly nudged the cameras in the concealed left pocket of his pants and the small Sig Sauer .380-caliber semi-auto holstered inside the right front of his waistline. *Everything's in place.*

Gerard slammed the hatch closed and rushed to the building entrance. He pulled on the handle and found it locked. Undiscouraged by the expected obstacle, he shifted most of the grocery bags to his left hand and swept his right across all the apartment door buzzers. He wasn't surprised that only half of them lit up as they should. *No one's in here forcing the owners to keep up the maintenance, the local patrol cops are seldom here to keep the occupants from murdering each other.*

"*Mar-habaan?*"

Gerard spoke enough Arabic to recognize *hello,* but hoped someone might blindly buzz him in.

"*Mar-habaan? Hal min'ahad hna?*"

The question surpassed his proficiency, and Gerard pleaded for a child to reach the access button in just one apartment.

bzzzz

Gerard sprung forward and yanked the door open as soon as he heard its lock release. *Thank God for blind trust, or perhaps mere laziness!* He stepped into the building and found himself in the familiar, dark hallway filled with the stink of stale grease and too many varieties of curry. When he reached the closest stairwell, he climbed up while balancing his needs for stealth, speed, and avoiding suspicion.

As he reached the third-floor landing, Gerard glanced at his watch. 00:08:56. A subtle scan of that window frame confirmed camera #8 remained hidden among the flyers, plaster damage, and spray paint graffiti. *The teenagers in this building could find or destroy that one at any moment with the reckless way they treat everything here.* That camera had given Gerard a critical success several days ago when it confirmed their target ascended past that landing, but the man hadn't returned until today. *After I hide cameras 9 and 10 on the top two floors, he'll lead me to his specific apartment.*

Surprisingly, no one had yet stepped out to investigate the visitor, but Gerard didn't expect his luck to last. He stopped on the landing halfway to the fourth floor, looked around, and retrieved camera 9 from his concealed pants pocket. Gerard peeled the cover from its adhesive backing and pressed the small covert camera into the stairwell corner that looked up to the fourth floor. Having placed it near his knee-level, he thought the slightly inferior images would be worth the trade-off for greater concealment among the damage and debris there. Gerard stepped back, ensured he remained alone, and risked another look at the device. *The paint match is perfect, and it only has to blend in long enough to tell me where this animal sleeps tonight.*

Encouraged by his success, Gerard pressed on and repeated the process on the landing just below the fifth floor. He rechecked his watch on his way back downstairs. 00:05:02. Despite running out of time, he stepped onto the fourth floor confident he could escape as long as nothing--

"Who are you looking for?"

The sound of accented French grabbed Gerard's attention more than the words themselves. He covered his surprise and nonchalantly turned to the sudden, confrontational voice behind him. A gaunt teenage boy, no more than thirteen or fourteen years old, stood in an open doorway with his arms crossed over his chest. He wore a traditional, off-white gown common to the Islamic cultures throughout the Middle East.

Man-jammies. Gerard's deployments with the French military in both Iraq and Afghanistan had ensured he understood how easily a weapon hid beneath those long, flowing cotton gowns. The boy's posture inside the open doorway made Gerard suspect he had a weapon just out of reach, and that he wanted to keep it close, accessible, and hidden from Gerard for the moment. He noted the apartment number, 315, certain he'd need to avoid its residents in the near future.

Gerard looked into his dark eyes and saw only negative emotions, a mix of suspicion and hatred. *Confidence beyond his actual capabilities. Many a dead man made the mistake of relying on nothing but a weapon system.* "I realized I drove to the wrong building," Gerard explained in French. "I am still a street away from my delivery, I think."

"Show me."

"What?" Gerard now feigned surprise, which he expected would be the natural reaction for a man in his position. This wasn't his first time in such environments, and he'd come prepared to backstop his presence and cover story.

"Show me. Now." The boy stepped over but stayed close to the doorway. Just as Gerard had expected, another gaunt man, probably the boy's father, took his place and crossed his arms to stand guard while the boy communicated with him.

I doubt he speaks French, so the kid has to be the front man. "I don't need help, I only came into the wrong building, and I've just learned that for myself."

The boy looked into the bags but didn't touch them. A *creak* from the stairs below him announced an additional presence, and Gerard looked down at the landing to see two more Arab men wearing similar gowns and expressions.

Gerard still expected to prevail if this devolved into a confrontation, but four-on-one was the limit of his optimism and the little Sig's effective round capacity. He put his hands up near his chest to show submission and held the bags in place while the boy rummaged through them. Nothing inside angered him. In the last bag, he found and removed the fake invoice Gerard had written up for the grocery order. After skimming it, the boy spoke a few words to the other men and jammed the invoice back into Gerard's sack.

The minor glared up at Gerard and held hard eye contact with him for a moment. "*Get out,* and never come back here. No one in this building will accept deliveries from your business." His spittle emphasized the juvenile's indignation and local authority to speak for the whole of his building's occupants. "You will regret it if you do."

"I, I understand," Gerard stammered. "Thank you."

The boy again crossed his arms, raised his chin, and disdainfully commanded Gerard. "Go, now!"

Gerard only nodded and cautiously stepped down toward the landing. He needed the two men below and above him to misread his hesitancy as fear, but, in reality, he wanted to place himself in a tactically superior position along the walls and force his aggressors to his left. His movement protected the concealed Sig and his draw, if the circumstances required it. Although no one yet posed a significant threat to his safety, Gerard breathed a sigh of relief when the men allowed him to step out of the building under his own power.

To stay in character and escape before the bomb maker returned, Gerard hustled out to the hatchback and leapt into the driver's seat with all the grocery bags still in his hands. He started the car, slammed its transmission into drive, and accelerated away while Italian squash and potatoes spilled onto the seat and floorboard around him.

beepbeep

beepbeep

His watch alarm announced his fifteen minutes had expired as he charged on to the next intersection. *Those cameras better work, because I won't get back inside that building without an army and a gunfight.*

MAY 6, 7:03PM_

The Oremus hotel. Paris, France.

BEFORE HE EVEN STEPPED ACROSS its threshold, Michael knew that Jacques had been inside his hotel room. The blinds, which he'd left several feet open, had been closed and several lights now repelled darkness from the living area. *Nice to have someone else looking after the details.* Sunset remained two hours away, but the added privacy hindered any exterior surveillance efforts. *That's a rookie oversight. Can't let myself get hurried again, these little details add up and become dangerous when you miss too many of them.*

After ensuring he was alone and safe, Michael locked the dead-bolt, threw the interior latch, and breathed a sigh of relief. After departing the Saint-Denis cathedral, he'd spent the last several hours running surveillance detection routes and giving his operational security the effort it required. *Now that I know the threat I'm facing, I have to make damned sure that no one follows me. The only way to survive this assignment as a single asset is to oscillate between hyper-vigilant and paranoid for the next week. I can't relax until the Holy*

See Express is wheels-up and taking me away from French soil, whatever the outcome of this thing is.

Despite the relative physical safety of being secured inside his room at The Oremus, the possibility that his own organization had rigged the hotel room to surveil him made Michael uneasy. *This room's a fishbowl. I have to worry about what my target and his organization might see and dislike, and when I come back here, worry about John and his minders doing the same. Unless I get lucky, I won't find any cameras or audio bugs before the watchers know what I'm after. The older cops back in Silver City used to talk about losing more sleep over the admin than the bad guys on the streets. I now understand what they meant.*

Michael considered his renewed fear that his anonymous superiors might again learn about his lies and deceit, and his stomach turned at the thought of those consequences coming to fruition. *This sucks. Hard to trust a hierarchy that refuses to answer questions or identify themselves. Talk about blind faith.*

At the long cabinet that supported the room's television, two rocks glasses sat next to a small coffee maker and a plastic organizer filled with coffee accoutrements. He stepped over and opened the cabinet's left door, where he found a mini-fridge that gave up two mini-bottles of single malt scotch whisky. Michael emptied the chilled singles into a rocks glass.

After first sipping the strong, earthy liquor, he downed the rest of the double, and it warmed his belly and soothed his soul. Michael licked the peat-infused remnants from his lips, sighed, and considered his present difficulties. *There's too many players on the field. French police, probably the military, too, maybe their national spy service. Then, there's always the opposing force to consider, the op-for. Even uninvolved bystanders who might have inherent suspicion of white men wandering around their Muslim neighborhoods. That's the greatest worry. The cops and agents might grab me up for a few hours or days, but they won't sneak up in a blind spot and murder me on mere suspicion. Can't say the same for the bad guys.*

Michael set the glass down on the cabinet and decided against having another. *Gotta stay sharp enough to fight, and I still have a lot of material to plow through.* Returning to the primary safe in the hotel closet, Michael retrieved the inch-thick intel packet, grabbed a bottle of water from the mini-fridge and settled in at the desk for several hours of reading.

He skipped the note from John introducing him to The Oremus and Jacques, and he instead focused on the pages that followed it. The first relevant document showed a full-page, full-color high-definition image of a Middle Eastern man in a traditional knitted skullcap and linen gown. The still image had obviously come from a video surveillance system, and it showed nothing but the man's head and shoulders from a slightly downward angle. The target's dark eyes gazed into the camera and looked cold and hard even in that format.

Michael set that aside and read through the pages that followed.

"EXECUTIVE SUMMARY: The subject of this investigation calls himself ABDEL ABDULLAH ABRINI. He is a man of Middle Eastern ethnicity, stands approximately 5'10" (175 cm), weighs 145-155 pounds (68 kilos), and is thought to be one of four men who entered from Tunisia as refugees in 2010. ABRINI is estimated to be 27-32 years old, which is consistent with all four subjects. The images taken by French authorities at the time of the refugees' entry are too poorly resolved to derive a confident identification through facial recognition. Although French officials quickly denied all four asylum applications, each potential suspect continued into France with some protective legal status and state benefits as commonly granted such persons.

It is important to note that no person with this name is known to French authorities and has never lawfully entered, resided, or held government-issued identification from any Euro zone nation. The subject's full name means "servant and slave to Allah, Cross Me," and, as such, intelligence analysis indicates this is likely a pseudonym taken to pay homage to several terrorists who perpetrated the 2015-November attacks in Paris. This lack of verifiable identity further complicates and limits the extent and effectiveness of our initial research and analysis efforts.

KNOWN BACKGROUND: *Our present lack of confirmed, verified identity limits extensive research here. It is important to note that of the four potential refugee matches known to the nation of France, two have since been investigated and arrested for minor crimes, and two have likely returned to Middle Eastern nations in support of ISIS/ISIL training and fighting. The extent of their involvement and training by such organizations is unknown and must be presumed to be significant and extensive."*

Michael re-read the last section in disbelief. *They've surely drummed up something better than uncorroborated allegations.*

"ILLICIT METHODOLOGY: Current practices and attempted efforts are derived from French police reports and correlations. French postal inspectors learned of suspicious parcels inbound to private postal offices that originated from Chinese chemical manufacturers. By the time inspectors followed up on the first reports, the parcels and their recipient could not be identified or contacted. A proactive inspector, once aware of the potential problem, identified the shipment and intended delivery of a third suspicious parcel. Inspectors intercepted the package and determined its contents to be benign. The shipment was allowed to proceed, and the subject now known to us as ABRINI accepted its delivery. Based on the consistencies with the two previous parcels, a subsequent investigation worked to identify the recipient and his background. Authorities learned the resident lived in the apartment building at 8 Rue du Corbillon, but not the apartment in which he lived or known associates, networking, etc.

French authorities investigated ABRINI for criminal offenses derived from terrorism and explosives manufacturing statutes, but their efforts proved too insufficient and slow to avoid the investigation's anticipated closure due to internal strife and political correctness. Despite the uncertainty of ABRINI's intent and actions, DICE analysts expect law enforcement to abandon the investigation without resolution.

The extent of Abrini's organization is unknown. Authorities have not yet established or identified his associates, if any, or his communications contacts. Our analysis is that such contacts and potential organization exist and should be expected.

OFFENSES AGAINST HUMANITY AND MORAL LAW:

2268: Intentional homicide. The actions and intent alleged against ABRINI and any potential conspirators or accomplices constitute grave moral offenses so grievous that heaven cries out for vengeance.

2297. Terrorism/Torture. ABRINI's alleged actions and intent to take part in and promote terror, indiscriminate injury, threats, and death are grave offenses against justice, charity, and morality. This is all contrary to the very principles of human dignity, respect for the person, and against God's moral law.

2302: Safeguarding Peace, Anger. ABRINI's alleged actions and intent demonstrate deliberate intent to kill, seriously wound, or murder another out of anger, which is a mortal sin gravely against the character of mankind.

2303: Safeguarding Peace, Hatred. ABRINI's alleged actions and intent, born of hatred, contradict the moral virtue of charity, and rise to a grave sin once he wishes grave harm upon another.

2304: Intrinsic Peace. ABRINI's alleged actions and intent degrade the further improvement of mankind, which may only be achieved through respect and peace. Although born intrinsically, peace is promoted by guarding individual property, freely exchanging ideas, protecting the individual and their communities, and loving one's neighbors as fraternal brothers. Peace is achieved through consistent justice, good will, and tranquility.

2305: Earthly Peace. ABRINI's alleged actions and intent counter the character demonstrated by our Messiah, who sacrificed and suffered for the reconciliation of all mankind. He explained, "Blessed are the peacemakers."

2306: Pacifism. ABRINI's alleged actions and intent threaten intentional violence, suffering, and indignity on his neighbors. He is *alleged to wish to visit grave physical and moral dangers, vengeance, destruction, and death upon mankind.*

2307: Avoiding War. ABRINI's alleged actions and intent counter God's command to pray for peace. His alleged actions invite further hostility, division, and indignity between God's children and encourage escalated warfare between nations and groups already at odds.

2308: Self-Defense. ABRINI's alleged actions and intent violate the self-defense allowed the individual and the nation-state when violence and injustice are visited upon them."

"CORROBORATION EFFORTS: Division of Intelligence and Counter-Espionage analysts and research personnel have examined French police databases, documents, investigative reports, which either corroborate or are consistent with parishioner statements made to the complainant. At this moment, we require first-hand confirmation from an objective source or the target himself. Absent further, more detailed information, we have nothing but allegations and consistencies that do not yet call for absolution."

Michael's growing skepticism eroded his confidence in the accuracy of the allegations and his potential for success as an individual operative. *How am I supposed to accomplish something an entire specialized investigative unit couldn't?* The unanswered questions remained at the forefront of Michael's thoughts when he continued reading.

"CAUTIONS: ABRINI, regardless of whatever danger he may or may not pose to the public and to our operatives, resides in a neighborhood known to public officials, police authorities, and, thanks to the 2015-November Paris terror attacks, to the literate world as a haven and protected enclave of violent, literal Islam. Outsiders, however that is subjectively defined, are not welcome and likely to face intimidation, threats, assaults, or worse. The successful closure of this investigation demands significant time in that environment to definitively confirm or dispel allegations from the parishioner and their employer, the French National Police. Use all reasonable precautions and

remain ever vigilant against perceived, potential, and realistic threats to yourself and those around you.

Numerous online communications, videos, and news reports confirm the communal establishment and endorsement of a local religion police in Seine-Saint-Denis that enforces violations of sharia law and the Hadith. To date, this enforcement is thought to have been limited to harassment, physical confrontations, and minor assaults, but the existing rift between the radical, literal followers of the religion and the moderate followers of the faith is increasing the frequency and severity of the encounters. Expectations are that coordinated, premeditated strikes against moderate Muslims and their mosques are currently planned and now fast approaching.

The successful isolation and self-segregation of that community (sharia enforcement, successful street prayers, ethnic/race-based crimes) demonstrates continued progression toward the official establishment of a local caliphate. The individuals and groups who feel responsible or called to fulfill this purpose will likely seek to protect the gains they have made toward creating permanent segregated enclaves within the greater city and nation. While assets within the Division of Intelligence and Counter-Espionage could not objectively identify a local communal authority or responsible hierarchy, coded communications and behavior among the most radical, known members in this vicinity are consistent with the establishment of an active, outward-focused social entity that proactively seeks to identify, target, and eliminate external threats to the community's growth and intensifying isolation. Members of this neighborhood in Seine-Saint-Denis have trained and fought with ISIS/ISIL in Iraq and Syria, and several have experience with minor counterintelligence operations.

Great, Michael thought. *This really is something for the I-M-F.* Shaking his head, he pressed on in search of a positive revelation.

DEVIL'S ADVOCATE: Much of the information DICE used to corroborate the parishioner's statements originated within that party's own police agency. The potential for confirmation bias here is obvious, and the lack of direct, objective identification of the target and his actions, motives, and intent is glaring and cannot be overlooked. Despite 'consistencies' noted throughout this document, we must not allow ourselves to elevate that lesser status as either factual corroboration or evidence of actual wrongdoing.

The operative(s) assigned this investigation should consider their presence in these areas a significant safety risk. DICE intel staff and risk managers believe it prudent to remain armed at all times and to avoid boxed-in streets and choke points whenever possible. Previous victims have reported to police and medical personnel their belief that Muslim attackers had been lying in wait for random victims of their chosen demographics."

The last section compelled Michael to chide himself again for his insufficient threat awareness. He rose from the desk, strode to the closet, and retrieved the suppressed assassin's pistol from the hidden rifle safe. After racking the slide to chamber the first round, Michael slid the magazine out and topped it off with another round from the ammunition boxes on the safe's internal shelf. He reinserted the magazine and slapped its bottom plate to ensure it fully seated into the pistol's frame. *There's almost no chance that anyone followed me back here, but if they did, I can greet them with a full combat load.* He dropped a second loaded mag into his left pants pocket, secured the safe and its facade, and closed the outer closet doors. Returning to the desk, he set the unholstered pistol at the back edge, and pointed it toward the solid block corner to his right. *Can't rely on luck. That shit expires without warning.*

Michael checked his watch and sighed. *Gonna be dark soon. It would damn near be suicide to go stumbling around the target neighborhood at night before I've established a few escape routes and identified at least one safe haven.* He leaned back in his chair and set the Executive Summary aside. *Into the weeds and raw intel that John's teams of anonymous 'desk-nerds' condensed into the Summary. Gotta be a map in here somewhere.*

The first paragraph on the following page relayed Abrini's possible ISIS/ISIL connections and travels. *If the man's a devout, literal follower of Islam, they've sent me here on a kill mission. He'll never submit to Catholic orthodoxy, and I'll just become an assassin for John and his nameless superiors within the Vatican.*

brrtbrrtbrrt

Michael's work phone announced that John had just sent an encrypted message. *Of course. Every time you speak of the devil...*

MAY 6, 7:14PM_

The Oremus hotel. Paris, France.

MICHAEL ANSWERED John's phone call. "Got your message."

"Well, *bonjour* to you, too, shithead."

"This is a kill mission."

John's voice seethed through the phone. "Before you say another *single goddamned word*, go in the bathroom, turn on the shower and the faucet, *full blast*, and close the damned door behind you."

Michael rose, complied with John's demands, and sat on the closed toilet lid. "What's this about?" He pressed the phone harder against his ear to hear over the running water.

"Hell, the place *might* be bugged. It'd be good tradecraft for you to assume that someone goes through your shit every time you leave a hotel room, and that it's somebody that wants to do you harm. Always assume somebody's listening, because they probably are, between the damned government surveillance of its own citizens and their fears about each other. Not sayin' that's the way it is, at least right there and now, but you'll live a helluva lot longer if you spend the rest of your life believin' it's always true, even if it ain't."

"Thanks for confirming my paranoia. I didn't have enough worries on this one."

"I mistook you for being smart enough to have figured that shit out on your own. Tellin' me I bet on the wrong horse here?"

"No. I hoped my fears weren't justified."

"I forget from time to time that y'all still gotta lot to learn." John paused and his tone bordered on 'apologetic.' "If that room's bugged, the water noise oughta keep anyone from hearing you. That's the good news. Bad news is that most people don't talk in the bathroom like that, so you're kinda tellin' anyone watchin' that ya know what the hell you're doin' and they're on the right track. You're protectin' and confirmin' yourself as a righteous target at the same time. Double-edged sword, like everything else you do. Now, what's your concern?"

Michael softened his tone to avoid antagonizing his boss. "Tell me I'm wrong, and that you haven't sent me to assassinate a man."

John scoffed in his ear. "Stop with the damned drama. World leaders and politicians are assassinated, this asshole might get killed, but he ain't never gonna have the distinct honor of being assassinated."

"I'm serious. I have no chance to absolve this guy of his sins, no matter what I find. A devout, literal Muslim won't *ever* submit to Reconciliation and humble himself before Christ or our Catholic rituals. You should've turned this over to your old contacts, the C-I-A or O-G-A, or whatever acronym they're using these days! Let them deal with it! I've proven my willingness to cleave a man's soul from its earthly shell, John, but I need a *chance* of saving them from hell in the process! I have *zero* probability of success here!"

"How do you think that differs from the serial rapist in Rome, or the overdose-death-dealer in Vienna? Did you think they were just gonna roll over and submit to your every damned wish, just 'cause you caught 'em, tied 'em up, and gave 'em their *one last chance* to meet God on good terms? We hunt monsters, Andrew. *Monsters.* Even leopards can't change their spots."

"If you don't think people can change, then this has always been about killing, not salvation."

John's tone changed and became conciliatory. "You're right, at least that I *don't* believe people change. I have *seen* it a couple times, though."

Michael shook his head and grimaced. "John, are we a group of priests who protect human dignity and give evil men a final opportunity to enter heaven, or are we a bunch of assassins using religious dogma and faith to justify murders and serial killings?"

John sighed through the digital connection. "Nothin's changed from Day One at the training camp, Andrew. We're selective gravediggers. That's it. Some kinds-a evil deserve our full and undivided attention, and we only act to defend past and future victims. If the target allows it, we can put in a good word for him with Saint Peter, but that ain't up to us. Never has been, never will be.

"For this particular investigation," John continued, "you oughta revisit section 841 in the Catechism. The Muslim population has a special and integral part to play in God's plans. You might be right, and maybe this asshole'll refuse to come around to our way-a thinkin'. But you might wanna make sure you know Christ's special status in his Qur'an, and about the Muslims' inclusion in Christ's plans." The aging spymaster paused. "You ready to get back to the strategy and tactics of your operation, or you wanna keep up this philosophy debate until the clock runs out to stop this thing?"

Michael shook his head and recognized how his internal struggles continued to plague his operational effectiveness. "No, let's get on with it."

"That's more like it, shithead. There's a lotta unknowns on this one, and I hate that shit, same as you. I didn't wanna send nobody out on this until we corroborated the allegations, but everyone's afraid that can't be done in time from afar. When we got word that the French police were gonna flush the investigation without knowing how this ends, we had to step in and fill that gap."

"I didn't realize you knew that ahead of time."

"Like I said, I don't enjoy puttin' you behind the eight-ball, either. Most of Europe's spent the last ten-to-fifteen waiting for their hug-a-thug social programs to convince radical Islamists to come around to secular liberalism. Their world is fallin' down around 'em right now.

"Even though they're one of the worst, Andrew, it ain't just France, it's the whole goddamned continent. Sweden just got done prosecutin' and convictin' a retiree for havin' *thought crimes.* This sweet little old lady had the audacity to post her opinion on social media about being fed up with how Muslim refugees and immigrants get away with all manner of crimes there. Biggest mistake she made that day was thinkin' she still lived in some form of democracy. England's doin' the same shit. Say anything you want about Christians and Catholics there, but nothing against Mohammed or Islam."

Michael leaned back against the tank. "That's a bipolar existence. Didn't the head of the Swedish Security Service just say violent Islamic extremism is the greatest threat to their national security, and that Sweden's likely to endure another terrorist attack?"

"Yep. Kinda hard for decent folks to live in a society that welcomes ISIS fighters back with open arms, sayin' we gotta respect the human rights of hardened terrorists."

Michael scoffed and shook his head. "A Russian invasion might save Sweden from itself. If my only choices are Putin or Sharia, Vladie wins every time."

"They're already livin' through another hell right now with the *perception* of safety and security. Nothing more dangerous than that, which is why you always hafta stay *intel-positive.* You won't live long if you're givin' away more intel than you're takin' in."

Both men fell silent before John continued. "Whenever y'all got sideways in training, I punished the *hell* outta you because pain and misery are damned good teachers. If you fuck up out there and give away intel to the enemy, you don't get another chance to do it right, and you don't get to learn from it. You get *dead*, Andrew, *D-R-T*. You don't getta learn from the mistake, you just get Dead Right There. The cops and coroners hafta try to make sense of it and your folks get a midnight phone call, maybe a visit from the local cops or feds, wantin' to know what the hell you were doin' in a foreign nation that got you killed. They'll figure out quick that Customs ain't got no record of your entry, so there's gonna be a shitload of questions for anyone that knew you. Your monsignor out there in Santa Fe, what's his name, *Hernandez?*"

"Yeah."

"How much does he know, even if it's just a hunch or suspicion? How well do you think he'd hold up to being interrogated by a couple pissed off feds in a small room that wanna leverage him into givin' them every little detail of your life and whatever he *thinks* you mighta been doin' that got you dead? Would he hold up long enough to protect all of us, or would your little op-sec fuck-up destroy the whole organization and everything we're tryin' to do here?"

Michael swallowed hard. *No matter how small the mistakes, their sum matters over time.* "I remember the lessons, and I didn't stay diligent about it."

"Well, then square yourself and get with the program. Every choice endangers or protects more lives than just yours. This assignment's no damned cakewalk. You're one-a my best, and you'll hafta be at *your* best to survive this thing with no more holes than you started with. If he is what we fear, the man you're investigating will kill you without a second thought, especially once he understands you wanna keep him from fulfillin' whatever he thinks God's tellin' him to do. *Accept* that, and act accordingly. Startin' right now."

The call disconnected. Michael rose and slipped the phone into his pants pocket. He shut off the faucets, stepped back into the hotel room's living area, and covertly scanned the room. *John's right. I have* to assume that someone's always watching. Just like he told me in training, it's only a matter of time until the suits upstairs wanna bring in new gravediggers with shorter memories of where all the bodies are buried.

MAY 7, 03:02AM_

The Oremus Hotel. Paris, France.

MICHAEL HURRIED to escape the attic of a three-story rowhouse, well aware he had only seconds to avoid detection. *I can't risk being identified, and he'd have every right to fight me, thinking I was a common burglar!* His heavy, careless steps thumped against aging wood stairs as Michael fled toward the ground floor. Keys rattled in the front deadbolt somewhere below him and echoed up the stair-well, compelling Michael to move even faster. As he reached the bottom floor, the figure of his short and dumpy target, Basil Wimberly, appeared through the opaque glass front door. Wimberly *banged* hard on the door and the glass shook as Michael ran out the back.

"*I know you're in there, Andrew!*" The man's meek English voice now boomed through the house.

Michael flung open the back door and sprinted outside into the man's back garden. After only a few steps, cold rain fell hard on Michael's face as he hurried across the one-way street next to the

Royal Opera House in Vienna. He had to get back upstairs before anyone else discovered the body. He pulled open a metal door, stepped into the commercial office building, and recognized Pietro Isadore's apartment building in Rome. Still desperate to avoid discovery, he ran through the hallway, up a flight of creaky wooden stairs, and through an unfamiliar doorway. *I have to escape, I can't be found!*

Michael tossed the door open and ran inside without regard to what awaited him. His shoes *splashed* through shallow puddles in a familiar, terrifying back alley in Bogotá. He slowed and tried to focus on the surroundings. *I can't bring anything into focus.* Fuzzy images of the lean-to's, shanties, and dark, ominous shadows shifted as he walked. Everything around him watched and followed his every step. Michael's fear escalated and his accelerating heartbeat *thumped* in his neck and temples. *He's right here somewhere, just out of sight, deep in the shadows--*

"*Alto,*" a malicious voice called out from the shadows to his right. "This time, I've got *you, serial killer!*" Sharp pain from an unseen blade plunging deep into his liver--

Michael awoke and abruptly sat up to defend himself. Finding the assassin's pistol on the nightstand just as he'd left it, he grabbed up the gun in both hands and swept it over the surrounding darkness. Michael recognized his hotel room, which subsided his irrational anxiety. With the pistol still in his right hand, he breathed a sigh of relief and flopped back onto the mattress. Sweat had soaked through his pillows and t-shirt, so Michael tossed back the comforter. *Goddamned anxiety dreams. These new ones make me miss the classic Universal Cop Dream where my gun won't fire back, or I can't punch the guy that's beating the shit of me. I'd gladly take those back, at least they didn't make me feel like I'd mucked up my life so badly that I'll end up in hell. Mucked.* He mocked himself. *Gonna kick that swearing habit one fuck at a time, I guess.*

Casting aside the damp pillow, Michael crawled to the other side of the king mattress and pulled a fresh pillow under his head. He laid on his back with his right arm cast over his sweaty forehead and considered what lay before him. *John's set me up for failure, whether it's intentional or not. My target lives in an unknown apartment in an ethnic neighborhood known to be suspicious and violent toward outsiders. We don't have any confirmed sins or crimes that warrant direct action. If I find irrefutable evidence he poses such a risk to the public and his own soul, then I'll have the equally impossible task of convincing a radical Islamist to place his salvation in the hands of Catholic orthodoxy. Even if I succeed at everything else, I expect to fail at reuniting his soul with God, and I'll answer for it one day.*

Feeling the weight of the pistol still in his right hand, Michael reached over and replaced it on the nightstand. He laid back in the darkness and tried to quiet his mind, but a nagging reality only grew louder. *If all this proves true, I might become a serial killer today. Won't mom and dad be proud to know that little tidbit?*

He cleared his mind, sat up, and *clicked* on a bedside lamp. *Still a few hours until I have to be in Seine-Saint-Denis at sunup. No reason to lay here and stew though, I've gotta go fight evil today.* Michael retrieved his personal, burner phone from the nightstand and considered calling Sergio. The nightstand's digital clock read 3:14. *No idea where he is, or what he's doing right now. Better not risk waking him up on an op, I don't need an ear that badly.*

Instead, he opened his personal email app and saw he had another note from Doctor Merci Renard, his friend from Columbia. *I think she'd understand my life and purpose even less than my parents.* Uncertain when he might read it later, Michael sat on the edge of his bed, opened the email, and read her words.

"Dearest Father Michael--I've found myself thinking of you over the past day, even more so than usual. Although initially concerned that you might be in danger, I've comforted myself with the understanding that wherever you are, you've landed exactly where God needs you to do whatever he requires in the service of His children. I know your righteousness and absolute morality will see you through whatever obstacles now stand in your way. I continue to pray for you and for those you seek to help.

It's already late here, and I've another early day of research ahead of me. Love & Light, Merci"

The doctor's ruminations calmed Michael's nerves and steeled his resolve. *Even priests can stand spiritual reinforcement every now and again. Maybe Merci would understand this, and I haven't given her enough credit. She expects me to do what's right and just, regardless of the opinions and perceptions around me.* The realization reminded Michael of an article he'd read from an Episcopal minister who became a Catholic priest despite being married and sexually active with his wife. He proclaimed that she made him a better priest when the phone rang at 3am and he considered sleeping through it. *Women often make us better men.*

Michael considered responding, but only for a moment. *I can't be distracted with more emails from her, not until this is over. Even then, I'm just not prepared to let the truth of my life destroy our friendship.*

Turning his focus back to the task at hand, Michael rose from the bed and dressed for the day. He donned dark gray slacks, a black dress shirt, and a black driver's cap to blend in with the general Parisian population. *I can't pretend to live in the Muslim neighborhoods, but I can try not to look like a foreigner. I'll be safer if they think I'm a French cop. The possibility of backup and a weapon should give even the worst men pause.*

He reviewed overhead maps of the target, the surrounding neighborhood, and the limited escapes and safe havens in the area. *Critical failures are always the result of multiple errors. One bad decision will never get you killed or hurt. My neck's going to be out far enough that I can't afford any more consecutive mistakes. One, maybe, two, probably not. Three? That'll get me D-R-T wherever I am.*

Michael packed a matte gray messenger bag with the day's essentials: combat first aid kit, protein bars and two bottles of water, a portable charger for his cell phones, binoculars he'd brought with him from London, and a notepad and pen. *It'd be nice to have an Audubon Society bird guide, but anyone willing to rummage through my bag wouldn't believe it, anyway.* He pulled the top flap closed and snapped it in place over his gear.

Michael set the bag aside, spread his cleaning equipment and Q-Tips on the desk, and then unloaded and disassembled the Ruger pistol. Although his normal cleaning efforts aligned with "good enough," he meticulously cleaned and oiled every contact surface inside the weapon. *First time I've felt my life really depends on this. 'Luck' is for the suckers unwilling to prepare for predictable problems.* The notion reminded him of an Army Ranger expression relayed to him by a former college buddy. *Prior planning prevents piss-poor performance.*

While removing miniscule grit from the pistol's inner workings, Michael considered his purpose. *Islamic radicals continue to hold that religion hostage and ruin the fate and lives of everyone within blast range or rifle shot of their insanity. I have this one chance to stop a potential villain who threatens to further plunge humanity into division, fear, hatred, and bloodshed.* He wiped a cotton patch over the weapon's interior surfaces to collect excess lubricant. *All that's required is the risk of my mortal life and the eternity of another. The death or failure of either of us will have implications far beyond ourselves.*

After reassembling the pistol and returning the cleaning kit to its small plastic container, Michael composed a list of equipment, data, and analysis he needed. *I can leave the gear list in the safe for Jacques and send John an encrypted message for the intel. Give his desk-nerds something to do today.*

That task complete, Michael stood, slid two extra pistol magazines into his left pants pocket, and secured a leather holster in the right side of his front waistline. The suppressed, nearly silent .22-caliber pistol slipped inside and disappeared under his untucked shirt. *May all my problems be so small.* He slung the messenger bag across his chest, tightened its strap so he could run with it, and stepped over to the closet. He opened the small safe, secured the intel packet there, and placed the folded handwritten note on top of it.

Michael turned the note so *Jacques* was visible without removing the paper. After locking the safe, he turned off the room's interior lights which confirmed no predawn sunlight poked in around the room's blackout curtains. Michael checked his watch. *4:51. The Metro will start running soon, and I still need time for an effective surveillance detection route to get on the first train.*

Michael inhaled a reassuring breath through his nose and kneeled next to the bed. He hated thinking of his daily prayer as "chores," but he still rushed through the recitation. At 4:59am, Michael stepped into the bright, quiet hallway. Finding it abandoned, he secured his hotel room door and strode toward the farthest exit. Each step better suppressed his doubts and renewed his sense of righteous purpose. He focused on the mission for that day and ignored the cumulative significance of the past few months. *If it's meant to be, at least one avenue of this investigation will pay off and make the others moot. With the right gear and intel, I can hedge my bets in a day or two. I wonder what the over-under is on this operation's success...*

MAY 7, 06:12AM_

Place de Clichy Metro Station. Paris, France.

MICHAEL ROSE from a blue plastic-and-vinyl bench seat and nonchalantly confirmed the suppressed pistol remained well-concealed beneath his untucked dress shirt. The messenger bag slung across his chest and over his left shoulder carried the tranquilizer gun and extra darts. As long as he retained control of the bag, those items didn't require the attention the lethal weapon demanded.

He scanned the few dozen early morning passengers scattered around the subway car with him. *No anomalies.* The westbound #2 train had sat open at the *Place de Clichy* station for five seconds, and the car's automated double-doors would soon close. Michael strode toward the platform, folded a Spanish language newspaper he'd found at a news kiosk several stops back, and timed his exit. *Five, four, three...*

Michael stepped out onto the concrete platform as he reached *one.*

bzzzzzz

On cue, a warning alarm sounded, and the doors slammed shut behind him. Michael stayed in place and scanned the remaining passengers once more as the train accelerated away. *No one's trying to force the doors open, and nobody gives a damn that I left.*

He ambled toward the stairs, now well behind the hurried crowds that had disembarked the train when it first stopped. *If I had a tail, they're well in front of me or they couldn't get off the train. I'm clean for the moment.* Keeping himself behind the rushing commuters, Michael followed the Metro signage to the platform for the northbound #13 line and reviewed the order of the upcoming stations. *Nine stops to the end of the line, but I need to get off one early to avoid the forced exodus.*

Michael strode to the far end of the platform to board the next train's lead car. A digital overhead sign announced the next arrival in four minutes. After finding an isolated bench, Michael sat, retrieved his work cell, and reviewed the intel list he'd sent to John several hours ago through their encrypted communication app:

--lease records and known building tenants

--vehicle registrations

--voter, census, visa, immigrant records tied to building

--income records for potential suspects

--shipping info from chemical supplier for building and local mailbox

--postal records of mail recipients in the building

--utility and power usage records

Michael read over the short list again, well aware it represented a mountain of work for its recipients. *What am I missing?* When nothing came to mind, he again glanced among the growing crowd around him. *No one's familiar.* Michael next opened a notepad app and revisited the equipment list he'd left in the hotel safe for Jacques:

--long distance mic, concealable if possible

--chemical sniffer for CBRNE operations and hazmat operations

--IR or thermal, FLIR if possible

--handheld digital translator

--govt ID or social welfare NGO documents

--triggerfish or similar

--covert Wi-Fi cams and extra batteries for balcony/windows attachment

Michael wondered if Jacques knew what a triggerfish was. *Should've just asked for a tech device that can mimic a cell tower to identify and record electronic communications in the immediate area.*

Trash strewn along the rail lines rustled for several seconds before a warm, humid breeze brushed Michael's face. Delivered by Doppler Effect and amplified by the subway tunnels, the *whine* and *squeaks* of an approaching train echoed onto the platform. Michael stood and inhaled. *The air inside every subway smells like steamed bums, mold, and machine oil. A few add stale urine, too, just for local flavor.* The breeze intensified and scattered litter along the tracks while the train's brakes *squealed* in a long metal-on-metal protest over every other sound on the platform. The aging Metro train emerged from the tunnel and ground to a hasty stop. Michael hadn't yet found any potential adversaries among the gathered passengers, so he dropped his phone back in his pants pocket and boarded the lead car.

brrtbrrt brrtbrrt

The phone vibrated against his leg, and Michael quickly retrieved it. He hurried to open the encrypted messaging app with his fingerprint before the train departed and his phone lost its signal. *John already responded.*

"*I'll try to work my magic, shithead, but don't hold your breath. I almost guarantee we can't get all this info for you. Proceed as if you'll never have any of it, and I'll push the desk nerds to do their best. Stay frosty. -- John*"

As the train departed *Place de Clichy Station*, Michael dropped the phone back in his pocket and scanned the other passengers again. Absent a potential threat, Michael reminded himself of his detailed plan for that morning's objectives. *Gotta keep the hospitals, landmarks, and safe havens in mind, along with the fastest route to them. John's devoted more time and effort to this investigation, and it re-iter-*

ates the danger I'm facing out here alone, and how much relies on my success. Just because John ran solitary, seat-of-the-pants operations all over the world doesn't mean that shit was ever a good idea or best-practice. More than anything, it means he needs to buy a lottery ticket. Michael looked out at the metal and concrete tunnel passing by just feet from the plastic windowpanes. I think my old life as a cop exhausted my dumb luck. I can't afford to tempt fate anymore.

Michael's cell phone again vibrated in his pocket, and he pulled it out just enough to read an automated calendar notification: Ramadan begins. He contemplated that unexpected reality, and whether it might impact the investigation. Replacing his phone, Michael scanned the other passengers again and noticed a group of three Muslim men clad in dark gowns and blue skullcaps alternately eyeing him and talking among themselves. Michael surveyed the rest of the car and realized many of its occupants were Muslim, Middle Eastern, or both. I should've noticed that. I'm too focused on finding familiar people I've seen somewhere else. Behavior matters more than anything else, but homogeny isn't insignificant, either.

Michael hoped the three were headed to a mosque for the sunrise prayers. I'm already drawing attention, and I can't risk running into the same three men for the next week. He shifted his focus back out the window and tried to appear docile and harmless. I need to find a perch near the apartment building. The overhead map showed a parking garage to the southwest, but there isn't any place to stay in there. No hide sites.

Michael risked a glance back at the three men who also remained interested in him. Please God, don't make me need Roscoe today. But, if I'm forced into such action, make my shots smooth, accurate, and few.

MAY 7, 06:14AM_
8 RUE DU CORBILLON. SEINE-SAINT-
DENIS, FRANCE.

ABDEL ABDULLAH ABRINI strode toward the neighborhood mosque and joined a growing crowd outside that waited their turn to enter. The call to prayer sounded through a tinny public address speaker hung above the only entrance, and Abdel forced a pleasant smile to conceal his emotions. *The Mu'athan who calls the imposter Muslims to pray in this mosque five times each day is a heretic of the highest order. His day of reckoning fast approaches and Allah will judge his obedience much sooner than he now expects.* Despite the animosity Abdel held for the imam and the unbelievers who followed him, he rejoiced at his purpose for visiting today.

The narrow doorway and interior hallway created a chokepoint that slowed the congregation's ingress and egress. While they pooled and shuffled forward, many around him caught up with friends and neighbors. Abdel had avoided personal interaction with everyone but the imam, and he'd still worked to limit his contact with Siddiqi. *I have no reason to know these pseudo-Muslims who seek appeasement with the West and threaten Islam's destruction. If they will not aid me, they are an enemy of Allah that works against me. They will soon realize their mistakes, but without time to avoid the consequences.*

Someone behind Abdel brought up news of the ongoing investigation into the cause of the 15-April fire at the Notre Dame Cathedral. A brief smile came to his face as he relished the memory of flames leaping high above the heretics' monument. Abdel regained control of his elation as a second man behind him responded to his friend's inquiry.

"It is shameful, a terrible loss if only an accident, but if proven to have been *arson?* What an *abomination* to God to target and persecute another people of faith. If someone intended to burn the *Notre Dame,* I *pray* it was not one of ours."

Abdel resisted his deep, heartfelt desire to berate the unknown man as the nonbeliever he was. *Today is too important, and Allah has used this imposter to remind me that our house requires the same cleaning He provided to the cathedral for its worship of a false god and prophet. Mankind may think it an accident, but nothing happens without His permission.*

None of the surrounding men engaged Abdel, and he feared they understood his demeanor better than he expected. After finally stepping over the threshold, he saw Imam Abdul Siddiqi at the end of the narrow hallway. The spiritual leader shook hands with each man and greeted the women as they filed inside. Dressed in a simple white *taqiyah* skullcap and brown linen robe, Siddiqi presented the requisite appearance of a man in his position. *He never wears gold or silk and shows pride in his presentation without arrogance. It is a shame he blasphemes Allah and leads his servants so far astray.*

Abdel had scheduled his meeting for today, a Tuesday, because attending mosque for prayers was optional until the *khutbah,* the mandated Friday prayer. Although larger *khutbah* crowds offered greater anonymity, Abdel feared various French authorities watched and tracked Friday's congregation, the *jamaa'ah,* at every mosque. *I can't risk bowing next to one government agent and being photographed and identified by another.*

Abdel smiled when the man before him walked away from Siddiqi. He stepped forward, extended his right hand, and awaited the man's greeting.

Siddiqi grasped him like a long-lost friend. *"Alsalam ealaykum,* Brother Abdel, Allah's blessings unto you."

"Walsalam ealaykum." He was too surprised and curious to match the imam's enthusiasm. The religious leader offered a warm smile, but his eyes showed the suspicion and uncertainty that Abdel feared. *He would be an agent of the West given the chance, and I cannot permit him the time and opportunity to aid their efforts.*

Abdel released the imam's grip, averted his gaze, and continued to the washroom, where he cleansed his hands, arms, feet, and genitals. With that ritual complete, Abdel entered the *musalla,* the small mosque's prayer hall, and casually scanned the congregation and spotted the clothing he'd required the contact to wear: a yellow short-sleeved shirt and green *taqiyah.* Abdel had needed him to stand out without drawing too much attention and he, of course, could not identify Abdel. Keeping to himself, Abdel watched the rest of the crowd until Siddiqi approached the pulpit. No one had shown interest in him or his contact, so he placed himself at the younger man's left side and tried to make their proximity appear circumstantial.

Abdel offered the customary greeting, which the man returned, but he maintained such a passive expression that Abdel glanced around in search of another man in similar clothing. Seeing no other yellow short-sleeved shirts, Abdel began their coded exchange. "Have you been here for *Jumu'ah khutbah?*"

Yellow Shirt offered a slight smile. "Once, many years ago, while visiting family nearby."

Abdel nodded. "I expect you will find none greater anywhere." *It is complete.*

The *mu'athan* ended his call to prayer at 6:24am, the appointed time for that morning's worship. Siddiqi began the prayer ritual and fulfilled his role as *Khateeb.*

After the fifteen-minute ritual concluded, Abdel remained next to his contact as the congregation rose and maneuvered back toward the single-file exit. He spoke in a hushed tone after ensuring that Siddiqi was not watching them. "You and your men are prepared?"

"Yes. Prepared and *eager.*"

Abdel allowed himself a smile. *Both teams are ready, and neither know of the other.* "Very good. Once you return to your quarters, discard this clothing. Do not wear it again. Do not keep it. Do not leave it in your trash for collection. Take it elsewhere, someplace that cannot be associated with you and your men. Do you understand?"

"Yes. I will make it so."

"You will not see me again until the day we proceed, but I will email you the delivery date, time, and location. Keep your men together and isolate yourselves as much as possible. Wait for my word but stay vigilant. Our ascension is imminent, my brother."

Abdel warmly clasped the man's shoulder and then turned and left the narrow hallway without another word. *I can't be seen outside the mosque with him. Neither of us can risk being placed under investigation. Our success now depends on their simultaneous seclusion from society and encouragement from one another.*

Abdel strode back into the main entrance to his apartment building. Confident he'd so far escaped detection by the French authorities, his thoughts remained focused on the two groups of five men who awaited his devices and permission to martyr themselves. *We must move before they falter from Allah's appointed path. A lonely mind has too much time and space to wander, so they must stay sequestered together to remain determined to advance closer toward that One Great Day.*

Rural Training Compound. Esmerelda County, Nevada.

AFTER FINISHING his nightly *Compline* prayer recitation, John stood and accepted the realization that he needed help managing the Absolver's recruitment, training, and ongoing field operations. *This is too much, and I'm gettin' too old to keep chuggin' along on four hours a night. It's a young man's game, and I've kept it up a decade longer than most.* He checked his watch, added nine hours, and dialed his superior's phone number. *If the bishop ain't up by now, he damned well oughta be.*

"*Bonjourno.*" Hoffaburr had been greeting John in Italian, and he didn't know if it was eccentricity or the man's futile efforts to blend into the local population.

"Morning. Need to get a hand with a couple things, if ya got a minute."

"I have a few moments before my next meeting. How may I serve you and our men today?"

John's indigestion bubbled up at the hypocrisy. *If they're 'yours,'*

131

you oughta put their needs first for a goddamned change. He reached for a bottle of antacids on his desk and ignored the question. "We got a massive intel request from Andrew on this Paris operation. If you'll recall, I told ya we sent him over there too soon without much to go on, and now that he's got his feet wet, he needs a lotta back-office support. I need priority allocation on enough analysts and intel resources to get the answers our man needs."

"What's he requested?"

His boss' tone conveyed disbelief, so John put his readers back on and summarized the list. "Let's see. He needs to know about utility records for every apartment in the building, power, water, and gas. Vehicles *registered* to that building, cross-referenced against the known tenants in each apartment. He'd like for us to look for vehicles and apartments registered only to women."

"Does he understand the target's a *man?*"

John closed his eyes, shook his head, and silently swore. *Hate havin' to explain the basics to my bosses, and it hasn't changed no matter where I've worked. The good operators hardly ever leave the field, and the ineffective ones get promoted.* "In literal Islamic cultures, women don't generally live on their own, so, apartments and vehicles registered only to women are good indicators a man's livin' there that don't wanna be known to authorities, for whatever reason."

Hoffaburr scoffed and John pressed on with the list. "He also wants us to get postal records of deliveries and known tenants, and, a-course, to compare 'em against the apartment lease info. We need to pull records from nearby private postal companies and see if anyone from the building rents a mailbox or gets deliveries somewhere else. Check police and civil records for noise complaints, suspicious odors, or anything consistent with a haz-mat issue. And he wants us to hack into the Chinese chemical manufacturer databases to look for shipping addresses near the target building, and for known or registered tenants."

"Isn't that beyond our reach?"

"The companies aren't under total government control, so, if their records are on a computer network, we can get 'em, just a matter of time. Lemme see, what else? Also needs to know income and employment records for anyone registered or known to the apartment building. But," John chuckled and pulled the cheaters off his face, "that's about the gist of it. Best part is that it's urgent. If Andrew can't get it yesterday, that's alright, as long as we can drum up the info right now."

Hoffaburr cleared his throat. "I'll call the on-duty analyst supervisor at DICE and get whatever you need. We have enough codeword-authorized analysts and researchers, and nothing we've done so far has raised suspicions. This should be no different, and they've always come through for us."

"I appreciate the urgency. I'm still worried we've set him up for real trouble over there. The other thing, and I'm afraid it's gonna keep comin' up, but I really wanna dedicate a team to this one. We're short on time, damned thin on corroborated knowledge, and the neighborhood's--"

"No." Hoffaburr's curt response stopped John's objection. "I don't understand where I've been unclear, or why you continually revisit the topic. No teams. Ever. Not for any reason, for any investigation, or for any Absolver. The risk to our operational security is too great if they're allowed to become too familiar with one another. You agreed--"

"*Yes,* Your Eminence, I *did* agree to the premise, but a few-a the threats are beyond the capability of a singleton asset, especially with how we've limited the training program. We're not workin' these men up to be full-on secret agents, so if you and the hierarchy wanna send 'em all over the world to every hotspot that pops up, with not a goddamned *ounce* of regard for their safety--"

"How many times did you find yourself in dire straits with your previous employer?"

John exhaled and shook his head. "That's different, these kids ain't no fuckin' *Jason Bourne,* we ain't givin' 'em that kinda training--"

"*Yet,* they continue to go out into the dangers in which we thrust them, and they come back every time. And, I might add, relatively unscathed, despite facing what you *perpetually* fear are far superior adversaries."

"If we ignore that Andrew damned-near died of a drug overdose in Vienna, or that Alpha contracted malaria, or that Jude--"

"And yet, all are *upright and operational* today." Hoffaburr sounded pleased to have used John's vernacular. "I'd offer that your quality as a trainer and instructor must far exceed that of your mentors. You should stop being so hard on your training program, and perhaps consider that God won't put anything before our men they're incapable of resolving."

John scoffed. "Well, not until He *does*." He shook his head and seethed in silence.

"No teams. Not ever. How can I make myself so clear that we never revisit this topic?"

"Consider it done." John disconnected the call and considered his options. *At some point, I'll have to betray either the men below or above me. I ain't there yet, but I think I can see it from here.*

MAY 7, 4:03PM_
13 RUE DE CORBILLON. SAINT-DENIS,
FRANCE.

GERARD SAT in the small parking garage office suite rented for his rogue operation. He'd watched the ten-monitor array for the last eight hours but gained no new information. *Most of the neighborhood's sleeping during the day and living a nightshift existence. Pretty smart thing for the parents, as I assume it's easier to put a two-year-old on that schedule than for them to understand why they can't eat or drink all day.*

The suspect had already deviated from his established behavior pattern by attending that morning's prayer in the downstairs mosque. Gerard hadn't expected him to emerge for another few days, which elevated the probability that his actions could be imminent. Despite the elevated risk and necessity of closely surveilling the suspect, Gerard struggled to fend off the typical stakeout boredom of watching nothing happen. He reviewed his handwritten drawings and notes from yesterday's venture into the apartment building. Within minutes of his departure, the newly hidden cameras had shown his target ascend to the fifth floor and enter #415, the upper-most northwest corner apartment. Gerard had since learned its only windows faced north, and several hours of scouting the neighborhood had failed to identify a safe hide sight that allowed him to see inside.

I'll try again tonight after I can better hide in the shadows and stair-wells. If he's switched his life around for Ramadan and his lights are on, I'll see farther into the apartment. Still need a better spot than the top of the madrasa, though.

Gerard rotated his chair and looked at a corkboard on the wall where he'd hung a map and overhead Google Earth images of the building. He smirked at the realization that his pinned-up intel resembled the conjecture of a madman. *I'm only missing the red yarn to connect the dots.*

"What's the next step," Gerard asked himself and scanned the images hanging before him. *Lucas will not allow his technicians to move the hardware and monitors again. A drone, perhaps?* He dismissed the notion as too likely to spread panic and outrage through the neighborhood once someone spotted it.

Gerard's cell phone vibrated in his pocket, and he retrieved and answered it without checking the caller ID. "Antlé."

"Inspector," Lieutenant Algeri hissed his title, "you didn't report in to Sergeant Le'roux. He claims not to have seen or heard from you since our conversation."

Gerard reflexively straightened in his chair and tried to predict the outcome of his available options. "Forgive me, Lieutenant, I had a family emergency after you and I spoke, and I have to call off work."

"Is everything all right?" His supervisor's tone had softened, and Gerard wondered if the concern was genuine. "Should I send someone by your apartment to check on you and your family?"

"No, thank you, sir, it's nothing like that, not an illness, exactly. I hope to return to work in the morning."

"I hope for that, as well. Sergeant Le'roux and I will be awaiting you."

"Thank you for your concern."

"It is no matter. Our families and personal lives must always come first, no? After all, we wear the badge for only a short while, but our blood and kin are forever."

"Yes, sir, they are. I'll see you tomorrow, then." *Is he talking about me, or did he just explain his motive for shutting down my investigation?*

"If we miss each other, ensure that Sergeant Le'roux calls me right away to confirm you're accounted for. I fear you're treading on thin ice, Inspector Antlé, and I dearly hope you haven't been foolish enough to have maintained an investigative presence in Seine-Saint-Denis."

"Of course not," Gerard lied.

"I'm glad to hear that." A tense, uncomfortable silence developed between them. "If I send someone to assist you, where may they find you? I understand you're separated from your wife, but it doesn't appear you've updated the residence listed on your employment records. Is my information invalid and you've returned home?"

Gerard's stomach dropped and his suppressed anger nearly boiled over. *How the fuck does he know that?! Claudette and I have told almost no one!* He cleared his throat and took a moment to compose himself before responding. *There's too much at stake to get fired today.* "I don't know where you learned the details of my personal life, but I'm staying with my brother, not that it matters to anyone but me and my family."

"I mean no intrusion, Inspector. I'm sure you can understand we must be ever-prepared to assist our employees in every manner, especially with the ongoing anti-government protests. I meant no offense. Good day."

Gerard disconnected the call, dropped the department's cell phone on the desk, and exhaled in frustration. He clasped his hands together behind his head and stared at the visual representation of his conspiracy theory. *How long can I keep this up? Le'roux's a good cop, but he's also got a family to worry about. How far am I willing to take this with no hard evidence that I'm right?*

MAY 7, 9:58PM_
RUE DE LA RÉPUBLIQUE. SAINT-DENIS,
FRANCE.

ABDUL SIDDIQI STROLLED among his neighbors and his congregation along *Rue de la République* and wore a satisfied smile. *My son is home from university for his summer internship, and Ramadan is upon us. God is great.*

He had served this segregated community for four years. As he wandered among the throngs of diners, revelers, and scampering children, Abdul shook hands, exchanged well-wishes, and checked on the welfare of his followers. *This neighborhood and its people had been infected for at least two decades, but it's finally shifting to a path more compliant with Allah's teachings.*

Abdul stopped and stood with his back against a building on the south side of the street. He crossed his arms and just people watched. The spirited and joyous atmosphere on this first night of Ramadan reminded him of the nightly celebrations on this very street that had emerged during the Arab Spring. *Our people have such a capacity for joy. It is good to see this, and to work toward making such contagious elation a more common occurrence here.*

The children were most swept up by the street-party atmosphere as they ran among the crowds, cars, and baby strollers, alternately giving chase and fleeing from their friends. Even the morose

139

teenagers smiled more than usual. Abdul quietly thanked God for allowing his followers to rejoice in the collective and individual sacrifices of their faith and service to the one merciful and loving God. *Ramadan remains my favorite celebration for many reasons, but this atmosphere is chief among them; this feeling, these moments, when we can celebrate and sacrifice together as a people united by servitude.*

Contrary to the logical assumption that his presence might convey, Abdul disagreed with much of his congregation and the Muslim public on common Ramadan protocols. *I understand why parents with young children switch their family to a night schedule. Comforting a hungry and thirsty two-year-old without food or drink is impossible without punishment. However, that effort contributes to their sacrifice and shows the sincerity of their faithful obedience. Those same parents then, in following the intended sacrifice, entitle themselves to the greatest blessings as a reward for their added burden.*

Abdul checked his watch, having already been awake for most of the last eighteen hours. *Afternoon naps between the prescribed prayers are rocket fuel for men in my position.* Still, his bedside alarm would wake him at 4am, just in time to walk to his converted mosque and lead the *fajr* prayer at 4:35. Abdul yawned and accepted he couldn't often stay out during the monthlong fast, but he thought it important for his congregation to see him this first night. *Islam is an individual faith, so the people don't need me to worship or obey God, but I hope that more of them grow to trust my worship, my word, and my counsel.*

As he stood upright, an unfamiliar Caucasian emerged from a small crowd of aspiring diners outside a restaurant on the other side of the street. The stranger wore a black driver's cap, dark gray slacks, and black dress shirt. A gray messenger bag slung across his chest. *Unusual for French men to wear a worker's hat at night. Is he returning to some nearby home?* Abdul searched his memory but found nothing familiar about the now-suspicious man.

Abdul considered the benign reasons such a man could be among them on this, the first night of one of their most sacred celebrations.

He's here either by pure accident or a specific purpose. Did he rent a room nearby unaware of the realities of the enclave, or perhaps departed the wrong Metro station? He could be lost, but, from this distance, he doesn't appear drunk or impaired. What if he has a sinister, ulterior motive?

Leaning back against the wall, Abdul scanned the jubilant crowd for anyone else who appeared out of place and considered what to do. *My people have been targeted and persecuted for fourteen-hundred years, ever since the Jews and Christians first denied Mohammed's legitimacy. Whether they conspired against him will never be proven, but the denial and global persecution are undisputed.*

A young couple, new parents in his congregation, stopped and engaged Abdul in a brief conversation about the mosque website. Abdul sought a reason to excuse himself, but they suddenly found other friends and strode off on their own. He required little time to reacquire the stranger.

The Caucasian smiled pleasantly enough, but he looked around as though worried about being discovered. *He behaves like a shark that struggles to smile and make friends with the surrounding fish.*

As the stranger passed by, Abdul followed him. *Not too close or too long, but only enough to determine why he's here.*

MAY 7, 10:04PM_
RUE DE LA RÉPUBLIQUE. SAINT-DENIS,
FRANCE.

NOT LONG AFTER NIGHTFALL, Michael had stepped from a city bus at the intersection of *Boulevard Carnot* and *Rue de Chaumettes*. He'd spent the entire day moving in and out of the *Seine-Saint-Denis* neighborhood, familiarizing himself with the area, and getting occasional and repeated looks at the target apartment building. He now risked a more extensive and intimate stroll for detailed intel that cabs and public transit couldn't offer. If the right opportunity presented itself, he would attempt entering Abrini's building. *I should have brought something bigger than this messenger bag. If I'm going to stay out for this long, I need to pack enough clothing to change my appearance a few times. The locals will notice seeing the same white face and clothing over and over again.*

As expected, most of the nearby residents and shop owners he'd encountered were Middle Eastern, Muslim, or both, with a small spattering of older residents who'd likely lived there for decades and university students who hadn't. Many of the signs displayed Arabic and French, although some left off the national dialect. *Not especially welcoming. Most of the world wouldn't know if they're walking into a restaurant, a bath house, or a mortuary.*

As Michael had walked south toward *Rue de la République,* the sounds of crowds and playing children echoed off the tall stone build-ings and the narrow, one-way residential street. Once he turned right onto that street, he saw the crowds he'd heard since leaving the bus stop, and the street fair atmosphere surprised him. The restaurants were filled, and many had lines spilling out onto the sidewalks. Competing Arabian music emanated from many of the establish-ments, and no one cared about the volume or the hour. The scene struck Michael like a Middle Eastern Mardi Gras without the booze and nudity.

Even without the draw of bars or dance clubs, throngs of people congregated on the sidewalks beyond those waiting for service in the restaurants. Celebration filled the air and reminded Michael of the Old Town Plaza from his childhood in Santa Fe on the first warm spring weekend. *Feels like a long, cold winter has finally passed and the whole neighborhood is enjoying the outdoors together for the first time in months.*

Michael's presence drew attention from many within the crowds as he moved toward his turn at the next intersection. Despite having been a racial minority for the five years he served parishes in Ecuador and Columbia, this was the first time he remembered making people nervous. *I wanna say it doesn't matter and that people are just people, but this feels like being a cop again, like when we had to go on late-night bar checks. Everyone in the place turns around to see why the hell you're there, the music stops, and you can feel the escalating tension. Then, the piano player switches to a minor key and shit gets Western.*

Michael kept a casual but deliberate watch on the crowd, which alternately parted to let him through or forced him into the street whenever the sidewalk exceeded its capacity. He couldn't tell if anyone followed him, and he couldn't risk appearing too attentive. *If I'm nervous and vigilant, they'll assume there's a reason for it. I can't get into the building tonight, but I still need to blend in long enough to escape.*

MAY 7, 10:15PM_
RUE DE LA RÉPUBLIQUE. SAINT-DENIS,
FRANCE.

Abdul Siddiqi strolled along the south sidewalk and mingled with the crowds there, while his target strode along the sidewalk across the street. He didn't mind that the man moved faster, but he wanted to keep him in sight to learn where he went and why he might be in their neighborhood.

He shook hands with a few men and exchanged greetings but excused himself and blamed his need for a few hours of rest. Ever gracious, his parishioners took no offense at his departure. *I now hope this man gives up his secrets before I reach my apartment building.*

The Caucasian stranger now led Abdul by forty or fifty meters, so he hastened his stride until he matched the stranger's pace. *I'm unlikely to make him nervous, not from this distance and among these crowds.* As the man drew closer to *Rue du Corbillon*, the street upon which Abdul's mosque stood, he grew more concerned about the stranger's dress and the bag slung tightly across his back.

Without a conscious understanding of what had changed, Abdul sped up and jogged toward the stranger. He saw the concerned looks from the surrounding crowds, but he had to stop the man from approaching his mosque.

Michael kept to the north side of the street and strode on toward *Rue de Corbillon.* Rather than restaurants, retail stores occupied most of the surrounding ground floors, and a small market stood on the south side of the street just ahead. Something between the size of a food cart and a small bodega, Michael imagined the place couldn't hold a dozen people at once. A group of four young men stepped out onto the sidewalk and noticed Michael as they did so. All four wore green or brown linen gowns and white skullcaps. Their jubilant conversation stopped, and they stared at him in silence. *They're the personification of MAM in army jargon. Military Age Male.*

Michael couldn't tell, at this lighting and distance, if surprise or animosity drove their behavior change. He continued walking east but veered to his left. *Whatever they think they're gonna do, I can't let them encircle me.*

The apparent leader glanced down the street, from where Michael had just come, and then moved to intercept him with the other three in tow. He glanced back and saw an older, middle-aged man rushing toward him. *There's my answer.* His potential escape routes and opportunities rapidly closed around him.

"*HE, toi!*" The leader pointed at him when Michael didn't

respond. *"Oui, toi!"* As he grew closer, the man's thick "unibrow" and a large mole on his left cheek became visible under the ambient streetlight.

Michael didn't understand the words themselves, but their collective intent was clear. He had only a moment to decide how to play this, and there was no outcome that allowed him to merely continue on his way. The hard, hastening *klops* of heavy sandals propelled him into action.

Michael cinched his messenger bag strap even tighter and sprinted off in the same direction he'd been walking. All five gave chase, but Michael hoped his sudden speed and their footwear would collectively allow his escape. Michael rushed past *Rue de Corbillon*, where he had wanted to turn back north, and didn't yet look back. He pumped his arms, leaned forward, and gave his legs every bit of steam and momentum he could muster.

Michael continued on at full bore until accumulating lactic acid burned his legs. He'd sprinted several hundred yards without any evasive movement. As he slowed, Michael glanced back and saw his pursuers scattered along several residential blocks, but none of them ran any longer and the closest adversary remained seventy yards away.

Although he slowed, Michael feared that walking might inspire them to try catching him. *Now I have distance and I need to get out of sight. Let them focus on something else, like talking up their bravery.* He turned left at the next intersection, ran north, and crossed to the darker side of the street where nearly bumper-to-bumper parked cars and the unlit east sidewalk would aid his escape.

As Michael reached the next intersection, he stopped in a dark, recessed doorway and looked back. He nudged the concealed pistol in the front of his waist, grateful it hadn't fallen out on the street in his wake. Three of the four men gathered beneath the streetlights a full block behind him. One bent at the waist just trying to breathe, one held his hands up on his head, and the third pointed farther up the street at the west sidewalk. None of them showed the interest or ability to pursue him farther.

Michael slipped around the corner and again moved from their line of sight. As he sped up to a light jog, he considered how much worse that could have gone. *I don't know how long I can fight four men without shooting them, and if one of them had caught me, I'd have had to hurt him badly enough to discourage the other three. Either result means the whole neighborhood would look for me and I couldn't come back. This way, everyone lives to fight another day.*

When Michael reached the next intersection, he glanced back, saw none of his pursuers, and returned to his intended stroll. Walking north again, he planned tomorrow's efforts. The brief success of his flight gave way to the dangerous reality of this assignment. *How am I going to pull this off if I can't even walk the goddamned street without attracting hate and violence?*

GERARD DROVE his fake taxi to a handicapped parking area, which was the closest lot to the Saint Denis Cathedral. He emerged from the sedan and joined the few early morning parishioners who struggled to practice their faith amidst the tourists and gawkers their cathedral hosted six days a week. *This place is rarely quiet and solemn.*

Gerard hurried inside, and just as the other regulars walking around him, he didn't pause to gawk at the cathedral's immense beauty and grandeur. He'd seen it far too many times to be impressed today. *The whole appeal of Saint Denis this morning lies within one man, not its structure.* As Gerard pressed on toward the confessional booths, he and Father Luc Devoux made eye contact. The priest's concern at the unexpected visit clearly registered on his face.

"I'd bid you a good morning," Luc offered when Gerard reached him, "but I fear it's pointless. What's wrong?"

"Do you have a few minutes for an old friend?" Gerard gestured toward the closest booth. Luc nodded and stepped toward his appointed side.

Gerard entered the confessional booth, closed the flimsy door behind him, and apprehensively sat on a thin, threadbare cushion atop its flat wood seat. *I can pretend that none of this is real until I say it aloud, but that's not accurate. It's happening with or without my involvement.* From his side, Luc slid open a narrow blind so that only a thin wood screen separated them. Intended to obscure the priest's vision and assure parishioners of their anonymity, its symmetric and repeated *fleur de lis* pattern had more effectively immortalized the anonymous carpenter's 18th-century craftsmanship.

"What's troubling you, brother?" Even ignoring their lifelong friendship, Luc had listened to Gerard's confessions long enough that neither pretended any potential anonymity existed between them.

Gerard crossed himself and bowed his head. "Forgive me, Father, for I have sinned. It's been one day since my last confession, and I'm carrying fear and anger in my heart." He paused to catch his breath and stymie the emotions threatening to swell beyond his control.

"I'm here to help. God loves you. Go on."

"So much has happened in the last day, and none of it for the better. I'm desperate, Luc, it's spinning so far out of control. It's all I can do to carry on. If I stop to think, everything overwhelms me. My marriage is over, and my daughter barely speaks to me because she thinks it's my fault." Closing his eyes, Gerard hung his head and inhaled a deep, calming breath. *Have to get it out...*

"The investigation I discussed with you," he continued, "the one here in Seine-Saint-Denis? It has been, *canceled,* by my superior, the esteemed and all-knowing Lieutenant Algeri."

"What? Why?"

Although surprised by Luc's reaction, his friend's harsh whisper conveyed the incredulousness Gerard still felt. "I know, I'm still asking those same questions. He claimed that we had no criminal basis for the investigation, not even *reasonable suspicion* of a crime. Without making an official accusation, he accused my team with acting from our own racial bias." Gerard inhaled and shook his head. "The worst part is, of course, that he's wrong. About everything, well *almost* everything. He actually could be right that the man's committed no crime, but Algeri's *absolutely* wrong about the basis of our investigation! The suspect might have no ill will to the people or the nation of France, but, if Algeri gets *his* way, we'll never know for sure unless his bombs detonate!"

"What does that mean for you, for your case, and the work you and the team--"

"Up in smoke," Gerard scoffed. "At least, it should be."

"*Should be?* Gerard, what are you withholding?"

He leaned against the uncomfortable, straight seat back and looked up at the booth's familiar ceiling above him. "I'm afraid that I'm risking everything right now, Luc. Everything. My job, my career. Claudette, although I fear she won't come back. Even Marie's safety hangs in the balance."

"What's happened that your wife and daughter are at risk? There's nothing so great that God and His angels cannot overcome it."

Gerard stayed focused on the ceiling. Somehow, it soothed him and eased his general discomfort with the whole confessional process. "I disobeyed Algeri's orders. As the agent in charge, it was my responsibility to dismantle the operation, return its equipment to the quartermasters, and move on to my next assignment. I did that, of course, because I needed Algeri to believe I had complied. Instead of following through, I used my official credentials to rent another safehouse and ordered the technology workers to move everything over there. Only a few hours passed between Algeri's order to shutter the investigation and the moment my surveillance equipment came back online. Even if he hasn't yet learned of it, I can't dispute the debt when it's billed to my expense account at the end of the month."

"Oh, Gerard. No."

"Oh, yes. Then, I got a phone call from Algeri just yesterday afternoon. He knew I never reported to my new bullshit assignment to find unlicensed cabs in the tourist areas." Gerard moved his gaze to the screen, even though Luc sat back beyond his sight. "I mean, really, what the *fuck* is that? He forces me to close a *terrorism* investigation to go write tickets to taxi drivers who can't afford the government permits and fees? I didn't go to the police academy to do chickenshit work, Luc, and I didn't come home from the Middle East to let my enemies there attack my people and my family on our own soil."

"How much do you think Algeri knows?"

"He knows I'm up to something, but he has nothing but suspicion for the moment. If he knew, I'd already be terminated. Algeri's not stupid, he's just misguided."

"So, how do you proceed from here?"

Gerard exhaled, leaned forward, and rested his elbows on his knees. "That's the most important question, isn't it? I don't know. No one else has come forward to help, I mean, not really. The tech supervisor knows what I'm doing, and he won't stop or report me, but he's not sending his men out to help, either. It's just me. Well, me, and about a dozen cameras that I'm getting to know well.

"I even got his apartment identified, Luc, just yesterday! Now that I know that, we can tighten the noose around him, but I need access to our databases for records checks. Algeri can see my database access and searches, though, so he'll uncover my betrayal as soon as I press 'enter' for the first search. I can't ask anyone else to look into it, because I'm certain he flagged the address, just to see if he can persecute me. If a French cop searches for anyone living at 8 Rue de Corbillon, Algeri will question if I asked them to do it. My hands are tied until I can get around this."

Gerard paused and breathed deep again. *Keep yourself together.* He spoke to himself as much as he did the priest. "Perhaps this is untenable. I'm risking every *thing* and every *one* I care about, and I might not be right, in the end. Won't that be a bitch. Throw it all away to prove the accusation's false."

"What if you had help? I mean, maybe, if one more person who understood the importance of being thorough and discreet in the face of adversity?"

Gerard shook his head. "That's sweet, Luc, it is. I appreciate where your heart is, but you don't have the experience that I need--"

"Not me, stupid, someone *else* with the expertise to help. You don't need to berate me, I'm well aware of the limitations to my effectiveness."

He blushed at his mistake, but still found the image darkly humorous and took the opportunity to rib his friend. "Forgive me, I thought you were finally emerging from the safety of your stone fortress to immerse yourself in God's *real* work."

"Eat shit, the arrogance of you and your army and police colleagues--"

"Yeah, yeah, Luc, I know the long history of your precious French Navy, but your skill with running an 18-century sail does no good for anyone today." Silence enveloped the booth and Gerard sensed his friend's impatience. "Truly, I meant no offense."

"Still, I wonder what the addition of one more person could do for your potential success?"

"What's the *point*, Luc? I've been ordered to report to the taxi sergeant this morning, so to keep my position and continue to feed my daughter, I'm forced to walk away from this at the very moment we've had a major break in the case! It's over, and I have to hide my efforts so Algeri doesn't ever discover them."

"Humor me. Please."

Gerard looked back at the ceiling and pondered the possibilities. "One more body, just one. It depends on what they could do. Another trigger puller is almost no use to me. I don't need more gunfighters, I need someone skilled in deception, intelligence, countersurveillance. Someone who can help me get around the current problems I have with getting the intel and database access I need to keep putting together this puzzle. If that were possible, if *that* could be done? Then, having one more man might make the difference I need."

"What are your plans, then, having the mandate from Algeri and still needing this one missing, specialized asset?"

Gerard sighed, still unsure himself. *I know what I want to do and what's demanded of me, but I don't know how to live with either deci-*

sion. "I could not be more torn. I have a duty, from my oath and my own need to protect my people from monsters, like no one protected *us* when we were growing up, you remember?"

"You know I do. Evil comes to every man at some point, Gerard. I hope that it's done with me in this life."

"I fear it is not yet done with me, friend. I want to do what's right for the public, but that means I have to risk whatever remains of my marriage, along with the health and security of my daughter. This is an important job, and it's the best one I've had since I left the army."

"Do you think your former work as a sniper in the Middle East has clouded your objectivity with this investigation?"

The unexpected question forced Gerard to pause and consider its possibility. "No. No, I do not. In the army, I got a target that others had identified. Sometimes, I developed targets on my own from their actions and behavior. I don't care that the subject here is Muslim, or Middle Eastern, if the allegations were against a fellow Frenchman, I'd have done nothing different up to now. That job was easier, even though I spent so much time hiding in adult diapers. From a place they could not see came a shot they would not hear. Simple. Effective."

"Are you confident that this one man, with the right skillset and capabilities, could make the substantial difference you need right now? Could you know for *certain*, one way or the other, in only another few days, and then walk away with a clear conscience, *if* you had the help you need?"

"It doesn't matter, it *just* doesn't matter! I don't *have* such a man who's stood up and volunteered to put himself in harm's way to join my fool's errand! *None* of my coworkers have the spine, or they'd have so by now. My efforts are no longer a well-kept secret, so Algeri will soon know *everything* I've done. He'll send me off as soon as he does, might even hold a press conference to take credit for culling Islamophobia from the S-DAT."

Gerard paused and both men let the silence stew around them. "I have to make the responsible decision to keep Marie from living in the basement of the goddamned Picasso museum when I lose my job and Claudette can no longer pay her bills."

With his priest uncharacteristically silent, Gerard leaned forward with his elbows on his knees and his head in his hands. "This is an impossible task, Luc, I have no way to succeed on my own, and I fear the only way to do so, if I'm wrong, is tantamount to murder. I can't risk that. I have to try convincing Algeri or his boss to allow me more time and resources, or, I guess... nothing. Just walk away and see if anything explodes later. There is no other option.

"We can clean up the mess and Algeri can assign blame afterwards, that's something we're very good at. It's even possible he'll help me collect the dead, as long as they're his fellow Muslims. Bastard won't even shake hands with a Christian." He looked through the screen. "Are you even *listening* to me anymore?"

Luc cleared his throat and spoke in a hushed tone that barely passed through the screen. "Maybe you're giving up, too soon. It *is* possible that another like-minded man, such as yourself, with similar skills and mindset may be afoot."

"Who? What are you talking about?"

Through the screen, Gerard saw Luc gazing down toward the floor. "The trouble, I fear, will be finding him in time."

"Luc!" Gerard waited until his friend snapped out of his thoughts and made eye contact with him. *"Who?!"*

"I'm, uhh, not *exactly* sure, but you have to understand the risk I'm taking is the same as you've incurred in recent days. I can be severely reprimanded, and I might even risk excomm--"

"Luc, if you don't explain yourself, right now, I'm going to beat you like the day we met!"

"Andrew! *That's* his name, Gerard, at least, I think it is. *Father Andrew."*

The Oremus Hotel. Paris, France.

MICHAEL STEPPED from The Oremus Hotel into a perfect spring morning in Paris. After checking the area for any obvious op-for, he strolled toward his first objective and allowed himself a few moments to breathe in the cool morning air, to let the low sunlight warm his face, and to enjoy the *Champs Élysées* without its typical hordes.

As he approached the first intersection, Michael brought his focus back to his dangerous reality. He nudged the back of the suppressed .22-caliber assassin's pistol concealed in the front of his waistline, scanned for threats, and reminded himself of this operation's potential dangers. *Too many players on the field, so I might attract attention from the French police, military, or intel services if they're watching Abrini, or any other target in the same area. That kind of op-for has enough time and resources to dedicate a team to finding out if I'm friend or foe.* He inhaled a deep breath and nonchalantly assessed the other pedestrians while waiting for a traffic light to change. *I don't have time to sit in lock-up for a few days until someone decides they have to release me.*

As he strode toward the second-closest Metro station, Michael considered his operational objectives and resources. *Jacques delivered the triggerfish and two covert Wi-Fi cameras, but I'm not ready to penetrate Abrini's building yet. The N-G-O docs Jacques produced will only get me in and out once, maybe, so I can't risk burning them on a walk-about.* Out of anxious habit, he rechecked his watch and used the movement to nudge his concealed pistol. *Jacques should drop off the haz-mat sniffer later today. I could get used to having this guy around.*

Michael perused the magazines and daily publications at a newspaper stand to cover his surveillance detection efforts. Once satisfied he hadn't yet grown a tail, he purchased a British paper and strode down the Metro station stairs. *A Spanish language paper would be more useful, but there's no point in pretending I'm French.* He waited to open the paper until he descended a long escalator. Standing to the right, he turned his body slightly left so that no one could approach without his notice. A below-the-fold headline caught his attention.

ISIS VIDEO DECRIES INVASION OF S. ARABIA

Michael skimmed the article and its summary of a recent YouTube post condemning the longstanding NATO military presence in Saudi Arabia. *That's upset literal Islamists for decades. The Qur'an forbids the practice of other religions in that nation, so the presence of foreign nonbelievers violates that sura.* Michael scoffed in frustration and risked another casual scan of the platform. *If that's so upsetting, why isn't ISIS protesting the Saudi government, or taking out their aggression on the monarchy that signed the treaties? Wouldn't that be more effective than bombing soft targets around the rest of the world?* He scoffed when the thought reminded him of an expression one of his former shift partners from Silver City offered in every such discussion: *Don't apply Western logic to Middle Eastern problems, son. That mistake's kept a dozen generations of the world's ancestors in a goddamned pickle barrel.*

brrtbrrt brrtbrrt

Michael folded the paper in half again, tucked it under his left arm, and retrieved his work cell. Its notifications alerted him to an encrypted message marked *Urgent*. Opening that app, he saw it had come from John.

Desk nerds are still working to confirm--ABRINI's imam might be on the US Terror Watchlist.

Michael typed a hurried response: *The mosque in ABRINI's building? Does ABRINI follow the imam's teachings?*

The blue cursor blinked patiently on Michael's screen while John typed.

Yes, same mosque. Cops have footage of ABRINI attending several Friday prayers over the past four months. Who else gives the sermons and guidance, if not the imam?

MAY 8, 06:45AM_

8 Rue du Corbillon #415. Saint-Denis, France.

ABDEL ABRINI FINISHED his sunrise prayer recitations, rose to his feet, and rolled his prayer rug. Placing it next to five large backpacks, he realized his behavior would soon change. *I must become even more cautious once they're loaded and prepared.* He walked to the apartment's open windows and inhaled the cool spring morning. *Two more days until I secure the apartment. I am at least six hours ahead of schedule, but I can further improve that.* Abdel held his breath for a long moment, exhaled, relaxed his shoulders, and physically expelled his stress. *This perfects our scheduled delivery and will lead other believers to the strict obedience that God demands of his servants.*

Abdel had devoted several days to the tedious soldering and wiring work required to assemble his improvised explosive devices. Having created their design and produced the triacetone-triperoxide explosive himself, Abdel held a satisfaction and pride unattainable with purchased components. *Even though common household goods may generate a lesser, impure version, I prefer to manufacture the much more lethal version derived from pharmaceutical-grade precursors.*

Inside a walled courtyard that stood just to the north of his building, a group of school children emerged from a screen door. They ran, laughed, and played, unaware of his presence. Sadness overwhelmed his heart, and he turned away from the scene. *I wish for another way, but the path and the mandates are clear. I will put the backpacks aside for today and pray for the obedience of Abraham. There is still much to be done.*

Despite the miniscule possibility he was under surveillance, Abdel left the windowpanes ajar and pulled the curtains closed, which let them occasionally sway in the light morning breeze. He assessed his preparedness for whatever the day might bring, and first focused on his defensive posture. His dark green two-cushion couch sat to his left and faced the door at the opposite corner of the apartment. A few square-meters of open space stood behind the couch, and he stepped over there to ensure the AK-47 smuggled into France from his Syrian homeland remained in place and ready. Abdel rapped his knuckles on two steel plates hidden behind the couch cushions that would defend him from inbound rifle fire and then turned toward the opposing doorway. Except for the writing desk at the far-right corner and the undersized kitchen appliances just inside the doorway, the living area offered an unobstructed battle space. *I can repel anyone, no matter how they try to enter my home.*

Abdel moved into the small bedroom where he hid the bulk of his offensive efforts. He retrieved his reading glasses from a makeshift nightstand, and his wife's adjacent blue scarf caught his eye. Picking up his cherished memento, Abdel deeply inhaled its aroma. Even though eight years had passed since Assad's goons had murdered his family, he deeply missed Sarah and their daughters every day. *Every hour of every day.* The garment no longer smelled of her musk, it hadn't for years. Sometimes, he caught a momentary, fleeting whiff of her scent. Sadly, this was not among them. Long accustomed to the recurring sadness, Abdel reverently folded the scarf, replaced it, and scooped up the reading glasses he'd first sought. *I will see them soon enough, once I have completed everything that Allah demands of me to join them in Paradise.*

merht merht merht

The antipersonnel alarm sounded from the computer on his writing desk and Abdel rushed toward it. As he swiped his finger across the mousepad to wake up the device, a second alarm sounded.

beebeebeep beebeebeep

The first alarm activated several times each day, but the second was much more infrequent. Abdel hurried to type his password and bring up the surveillance monitors.

wwwwhhhhrrrRRRRRRRRRR

A klaxon air-raid siren sounded from the computer. Even without the ability to see what approached his door, Abdel stood upright, retrieved a black semiautomatic pistol from the desk's belly drawer, and pointed it at the door to his left. He backed up to the north wall, which placed him near that corner of the apartment. *If they are now coming for me, I'm trapped here, but I can kill the first few, no matter how they enter!*

Dozens of rapid footfalls grew louder and echoed up from the stairwell behind the door, and Abdel imagined black-clad anti-terror police running up to storm into the apartment. Without conscious thought, Abdel repeatedly murmured *Allah Akbar* under his breath while the barrel and front sight shook under the strain of his tight, panicked death-grip. The steps only grew faster, louder, and more determined as they closed in on him. A familiar series of *thuds* announced they'd arrived at the landing just outside his threshold.

Laughter echoed from the hallway outside his door.

"I won again," a young girl shouted in Arabic.

"You always cheat," came a smaller response.

Abdel loosened his grip, lowered the gun, and sat back against the wall where he'd stood. Whether true or not, the girls' voices sounded so similar to his own lost daughters. Tears welled in his eyes while his elderly neighbors ushered their grandchildren inside their humble dwelling. *It's not long now, my angels, and your sweet voices will fall on my ears again.*

Distraught, Abdel set the pistol on the floor next to the desk and struggled to resume the day's work. *I must stay consumed in the work, on the tasks set before me, and the divine path they compel me to walk.* After several cycles of deep, restorative breathing, Abdel had steeled his resolve. *Before the day is out, I'll have assembled three devices to prevent entry into the apartment, and the first of the I-E-Ds will be ready. Once complete, the French authorities will have no way to stop my retribution. Not even my murder could prevent what is to come.*

AFTER DEVOTING MORE than two hours to his surveillance detection route, Michael ended the SDR by hiding in plain sight. He sat at a small table near the window of a Turkish coffee shop across *Rue du Corbillon* and just north of the target building. Three window seats allowed a better view through the large plate glass panes, but their location would have also highlighted his presence. *Too obvious, and too easy for anyone outside to take an interest in me.*

Michael kept to himself, skimmed the newspaper, checked his phone, and sipped dark, rich coffee. As one of the few patrons, he'd initially drawn inquisitive looks from both employees, but they forgot about him after he spread the paper out on the corner table. *This day-night Ramadan switch is no bullshit, there's only a few people moving around the neighborhood.*

Growing concerned that he couldn't risk staying in one place for very long without drawing unwanted attention, Michael retrieved his cell from the tabletop, opened its encrypted messaging app, and returned to his dialogue with John. *Not sure the old man's still up. Hell, I don't even know where he is now, just that the Wyoming facility is closed. This much uncertainty can't be normal in espionage work, can it?*

Michael briefly shook his head at all the unknowns in his life and texted his boss: *I'm static for the moment. Any updates on the intel requests?*

A blue cursor blinked on the screen when John began typing.

Some. More to follow tomorrow. No income or employment records under name ABRINI. No income or employment recs for ANY known resident of building; could be many reasons for that, most are benign. No suspicious returns from utility records. No hazmat/suspicious calls to police for the building.

The blinking cursor announced John's continued typing while Michael considered the lack of income and employment records for all the known tenants. *Resident lists could be wrong, and people are paid in cash all the time. The database might not include public aid, or refugees and foreign nationals. I need more info before the absence of documented income means anything.* The next message populated on his screen.

No vehs reg to ABRINI, that building address, or the known tenants. Two private POB services in the area, neither have digital records we can hack into. No help there on renters or shipping-receiving records. We might have two possible apartments for ABRINI though...

The blinking cursor returned, and Michael scanned the small shop and the immediate exterior. *No vehicle records, that's not a surprise. Only the dumbest bad guy uses a car registered to him or his address.* John's text appeared in his lower peripheral.

Two apartments are leased to a female that's supposed to live alone. Very unlikely in that culture and neighbhd. #105, 213. Remember those are 2 and 3 floor numbers in Europe.

Michael grimaced at the incomplete intel and typed his response: *Did the analysts check the utility usage in 105 and 213 to estimate their actual occupancy?*

No, I'll get that back to you.

Also ask them to ID males associated with those two women, especially family or anyone who entered France with them.

Good idea. I'll make the requests. Waiting for public asst recs and postal recs for the known tenants. Emailing the data and intel to you now...

Michael sat up, took another sip of coffee, and glanced around again while he waited for the blinking cursor to turn into another message.

How are you gonna confirm the apartment?

Michael leaned forward to protect the screen. *Not sure, need to enter the building first. Have a relief worker ID package now. Inbound tech and cams will help. Need another day or two for entry, I think.*

The blinking cursor briefly returned.

Is Jacques working out for you?

Yes. Very helpful, good & quick access to resources. Michael considered himself fortunate that the only rejected item on his list was a functional audio translation device. *I can use just Google Translate as an intermediary, but I hoped for something less overt.* The cursor returned as John typed.

I asked Jacques to drop a book called 'Inside Islam' to you. You need to understand ABRINI's mindset if you want a real chance to save his soul, as you say.

A moment of optimism washed over Michael that this might not be a kill mission, after all. Michael checked his watch and then prepared to leave. The cursor blinked while he nonchalantly folded up his paper and gathered the few items from the tabletop. He glanced down at the phone when John's message appeared.

Brush up on the basic IED render-safe protocols. It ain't as simple as that old red-wire, blue-wire BS. 1 chance and 1/1000th of a second to get it right. Good news: if you screw up, you'll never know it. The explosion is faster than your nerves register heat and pain. Your brain will never realize your death.

GERARD SAT on the cedar steamer trunk at the foot of his daughter's bed, just as he'd done for years whenever they had a private conversation. With his elbows resting on his knees and his hands clasped together in front of his face, he prayed for her to realize his sincerity and desperation. Marie, true to her current teenage priorities, sat a few feet away at her corner desk and pretended to ignore him.

"Marie, *please,* this is really important. I need you to understand, and I want your advice."

His daughter sat up straighter, tilted her head a bit, and slowly swiveled her chair around to face him. "It's about time, I've been trying to get you two assholes to listen to me for years."

"I am in trouble, Marie, *real* trouble, and I need your help."

Shock registered on her face at the idea that her father, an antiterror cop and former army sniper might have done something wrong. Gerard put his hands out to emphasize his words. "It's not like that, sweetheart, I've not done anything wrong, not against the law, at least, but I still might be in trouble."

"*Papa,* what's happening?"

His heart swelled. Gerard brought his hands back up and clasped them in front of his mouth but stopped himself from hiding his

171

emotions. *She hasn't called me 'papa' since grade school, before she joined the in-crowd and became too cool for me. Keep it together.* "There's something going on at work, and--"

"Something dangerous?!"

"Maybe, sweetie, I don't know yet, but probably. Not *yet.*"

"Well, *what?* Are we moving again, or..." Her eyes suddenly widened, and she inhaled a fearful breath. "Are you leaving us, like, for *real?!* Please, papa, *tell me what's wrong!!*"

Gerard swallowed hard. *There is so much that I wish were true at this moment, but my hopes are not my reality.* "I have to make a very difficult decision, and I fear the outcome will change life for all of us."

"Papa! Please--"

"Marie." Steeling his resolve to see this through, Gerard made empathetic eye contact with his only daughter and adopted a calm tone to quell her fears, just as he'd long done with people in all manner of crisis. *Her world has been falling apart for months, I can't be surprised, especially while I'm half of the problem.* "Please. Let me finish, there is much to explain, and I need you to hear all of it before giving me your decision."

"...okay..." The sixteen-year-old grabbed a stuffed bear from the desk, the one that had always comforted her as a child, and she clutched it against her chest.

"What I'm about to tell you, you cannot repeat to *anyone,* and I mean that, not a single person. Not even your mother knows everything I'm about to tell you."

Marie's eyes narrowed and revealed her apprehension. "...o-kay..."

"I have been investigating a man for several weeks now who might be a terrorist. I can't give you details, but I've worked *very* hard to prove he is guilty *or* innocent, and I will be happy with either result. I have a new supervisor, Lieutenant--"

"Algeri. The weasel."

"Yes, that is what I've said, perhaps too many times. But, yes, him.

He closed the investigation and ordered me to abandon it. He believes, right or wrong, that we have no reason to move forward."

"I don't understand. How does *he* know the man's innocent, but it's *your* case and *you* don't even know?"

Gerard shifted his weight on the trunk and searched for an answer that didn't reveal confidential aspects of the case. "That's the exact position I'm in, and, because of that question, I've disobeyed his order to stop."

Silence enveloped them for several moments. When Marie spoke, fear had crept into her voice. "What does that mean? Are you going to, *jail*, or some--"

"No, no, nothing like that. But I have kept on with the case, and I'm at a fork in the road, if you will. I *have* to make a choice, and I can't undo whatever action I take today. I must either *continue* the investigation and face whatever consequence comes of it, *or* I follow the lieutenant's orders and abandon it."

"And, whatever consequence comes of it," Marie parroted.

As he often did during interrogations, Gerard let the heavy silence grind on both of them.

"Where is the investigation, I mean, where does he live?"

Gerard inhaled and held his breath. *I feared she would ask.* "It doesn't matter."

"It's in Seine-Saint-Denis again, isn't it?"

Gerard wanted to lie and save Marie from the memories of her narrow escape from the 2015 attacks and his disappearance for the four days required to hunt and kill those responsible. However, he feared violating her trust even more. "Yes."

Tears welled in her eyes and her grip on the bear would have choked a living animal. "What *choice* do you have? You *can't* abandon it, papa, you *can't!* If you can stop the next attack, you must do it!"

"Marie, the problem is this." Gerard cleared his throat and pushed his own emotions back down into their box. *I can't ask this of her, but I can't lose her too, knowing I'm about to throw everything else away.* "If I continue, and this man turns out to be innocent, I'll probably lose my job. If that happens, I'll never work as a cop again. No one will *ever* hire me after I've disobeyed a direct order, especially one that proved to be justified."

The realization gave her pause. "Do you think you're wrong?"

No. The reflexive answer nearly leapt out. "I don't think so."

"Why can't you just get *another* job, if it comes to that?"

"I can, of course, if I must, but in the meantime, that might mean some very tough times for the three of us, whether I'm living with you and mama, or not. You mother cannot afford to stay here if I lose my income, and your school--"

"But, papa, none of that *matters!* I will live in our *car* and eat, I dunno, *donated scraps* if I must, I'll get a job, but, if you do *nothing*, people might *die!* My comfort, our *things!* I can't ever be happy knowing that people lost their lives, their *families,* for me to keep having *nice things!*" Marie's eyes plead with him, and tears finally fell onto her cheeks. "I *trust* you, papa, and I couldn't live with myself knowing that people might die so you could keep an income. Even if you're *wrong,* it's still the *right* thing to do. I know you couldn't live with yourself, either, just walking away--"

brrtbrrtbrrt

The imaginary scene disappeared. Gerard's cellphone skittered across the wood desk in the covert parking garage office he'd rented and brought him back to reality. He blinked hard, several times, and scanned the locked room. The monitor array still displayed live images from the ten covert cameras he'd placed around the target apartment. Nothing in the feeds immediately concerned him.

brrtbrrtbrrt

Picking up the phone, he saw Claudette had sent two text messages.

The rent is due.

Marie needs money for her drama classes.

Gerard locked the phone and set it down without responding. He rubbed his hands across his face and thought about the daydream.

Marie's sixteen. The conversation would never go like that, not until she knows something of sacrifice about a decade from now. Maybe then she will forgive me for whatever comes of this.

He pushed aside a stack of tickets Sergeant Le'roux had demanded he write that day. None of the driver, vehicle, or license plate information on the tickets were accurate, but Le'roux could only extend him so much help. Although the detective sergeant had agreed to leave him alone for a few days, he'd demanded in return that Gerard give him something each day he could use to prove they'd both followed orders. *I need to hand these forged citations to Le'roux in person, and that means leaving the monitors. I can't trust him like I have Lucas and his techs, so having him come here is out of the question, even if another white face could go unnoticed in the neighborhood.*

Gerard exhaled and accepted his need to trust the suspect not to deviate from his established patterns. Desperate and cornered, Gerard closed his eyes, bowed his head, and prayed for guidance. He breathed through four slow, calming cycles, but heard and felt no response. Not that he actually expected to, despite his hopes. *No answer is, in fact, an answer.*

Opening his eyes, Gerard looked back to the monitors and resigned himself to abandoning the case. Even after what Luc told him this morning about the foreigner, Gerard had no other viable option. *He can't reach this mystery man, his 'Father Andrew,' and I can't risk everything important in my life on the mere hope he'll materialize.*

Gerard exhaled and wondered how to salvage his career with Algeri. *I'm fucked. My life might not have to be over, but I'm about to endure the greatest schism I've ever known.*

Movement. *There.* A Caucasian man moved casually across the screen on camera #4, which faced north and covered the sidewalk across the street from the entrance to the apartment building. As the man walked toward the traffic stanchion that concealed that camera, he slowly grew larger on Gerard's monitor. *I've seen him before, but, where?*

Rifling through his memory, Gerard required only a few moments to place the outsider. *He has the same gate as that man from last night, well, at least,* before *he sprinted away from the imam and his small mob.*

The unidentified man strolled along the sidewalk, and then bent down to pick up a plastic wrapper near his path. He cast a sideways glance toward the target. Momentary, but obvious to Gerard's training and experience. *Time to meet the man I'll either arrest or die next to. Whatever the outcome, there's no reason for us to remain strangers.*

MICHAEL REACHED the south end of the target street, *Rue de Corbillon,* and turned right on *Rue de République,* which placed him in front of the small bodega his pursuers had patronized last night. Now devoid of the crowds and street-fair atmosphere, the area was almost abandoned. Bright restaurants that had boisterous mobs of diners spilling out their doors last night were silent, shuttered, and unwelcoming. Michael assumed the area catered to a late-night crowd, but pressed on and kept a covert, vigilant watch over his eerie surroundings. He needed to familiarize himself with the target environment and establish what defined its "normal," which he couldn't accomplish from a distant laptop with Google Maps. Once enough of his requested equipment, intel, and analysis came in, Michael intended to commence the heavier lifting of penetrating the apartment building and proving or dispelling the allegations.

He stopped into a small creperie along the north sidewalk, which he believed was a common thing to do on a sunny spring morning. A woman working behind the counter wore a beautifully detailed blue-and-green headscarf, and she beamed as Michael entered. He couldn't help but return the gesture.

"*Bonjour,*" she called out.

"Bonjour. Une crêpe au Nutella, s'il vous plaît."

"Bien sûr."

Michael scanned the neighborhood from inside the creperie. A white male dressed in dark gray slacks, a black long-sleeved dress shirt, and a floppy cap strode by on the sidewalk. At first glance, he looked like almost every other Parisian taxi driver, except for his striking resemblance to the actor Daniel Craig. The man walked next to the street and barely escaped colliding with the sideview mirrors of the small coupes and sedan tightly parked there. As he moved across the front of the shop from Michael's right, the man looked inside and made momentary eye contact. Although his clothing matched that of an ordinary cabbie, the stranger's eyes, scars, and tactical positioning announced that he was far more dangerous. A chill descended Michael's spine. Despite having never seen the man, he immediately and intimately recognized *what* he was. *He's a hunter, a wolf who's circling closer to drive his prey.*

Michael calmly looked to the clerk, realized she hadn't seen the exchange, and then glanced back to the sidewalk. The unknown predator passed out of sight to the left. Stepping closer to the doorway to widen his field of view, Michael watched him cross the street and angle toward the bodega. *No idea who he is or who he's after, but there's no mistaking that specific shade of darkness in a man's eyes.*

During his tenure as a patrol cop, even in the small town where he'd worked, Michael had developed into a benevolent predator himself. To survive the streets, he'd grown to recognize those same traits in people around him. While many of his colleagues strove to be sheepdogs, Michael tried to emulate the lion, the king of the jungle. *Every hunter must become comfortable with violence, and that irreversibly changes a man. Even the most righteous among us embrace and project a symbiotic darkness that comes from the repeated application of speed, surprise, and overwhelming violence of action to solve otherwise impossible problems.* The stranger disappeared into the small market without looking back. *Only a sociopath commits violence with smiling eyes.*

"*Monsieur?*"

Michael turned and stepped back to the counter, where the clerk handed him a parchment-wrapped crepe. "*Merci.*"

"*De rien.*" She gave him one last smile, wiped off the counter, and disappeared into the back.

Michael shuffled the hot crepe back and forth between his hands as it cooled and scanned the street. With no sign of the cabbie-hunter, he stepped outside and movement to his left arrested his attention.

The cabbie strolled so close to the buildings that Michael couldn't see his approach from inside the creperie. *God dammit.* He nudged the top of the concealed pistol to ensure it remained in place and ready. Although he'd planned on walking west, the same direction as the cabbie, he didn't want the stranger behind him. Michael stood in place, bit a small nibble off the crepe, and tried to appear natural and calm. *He'll walk past in about ten, twelve seconds. If I have to fight him, I want to see it coming. Letting it happen here might mean the clerk will call the cops or medics, depending on how it goes. Better than bleeding out in a back alley on the other side of the block.*

Michael casually scanned the street, listened for the man's steps, and counted off his estimated arrival. Another small nibble. *Five...four...* He took a half-step back until his right heel pressed against the shop's exterior wall. Michael wanted the additional leverage and the decreased probability of a ground fight in the street. When the stranger came within ten feet, Michael looked at him and adopted a polite smile. The man veered left to barely avoid Michael, and his predation signals had elevated despite both hands staying visible. Michael anticipated a lunge and braced himself for impact.

The cabbie held eye contact and shrugged, which naturally kept both his hands visible to Michael as he strolled only a few feet away. "If you're here to help, meet me at McDonald's in five minutes." He lowered his hands, resumed a normal stride, and walked past Michael as though nothing had happened.

Michael stood in place and glanced back inside the store. The clerk had stepped out of sight. He scanned the street and didn't find anyone interested in either of them, or their interaction. *Help what? Who? He knows I speak English, but does he know I'm a priest? Does he know more than that?* Michael took another bite before looking back at the cabbie, who continued on at the same pace. Only fifty yards ahead of the stranger, Michael spied the familiar golden arches. *How now, brown cow?*

He worked his way through the crepe and pondered his options. *No reasonable, alternate route to the meet. Probably not a second entrance into the place, anyway, buildings here aren't like the ones back home. It's a public place, almost guaranteed to be cameras. Not good for my anonymity, but it's a terrible place for him to try killing me for the same reason. A reasonable authority figure wouldn't invite a confrontation there, too many kids around at any given time. He's either an anti-terror cop or a rando who's nuttier than squirrel shit. Never gonna find out standing here.*

Michael crumpled the parchment, tossed it in a trash can just inside the creperie, and gave the immediate environment a long, last look. *Nothing obvious, no one's trying too hard to* not *be seen. What the hell...* Stepping off to follow the cabbie-hunter, Michael kept his guard up and ran through a constant mental string of "what-ifs" to keep potential flight paths and escape routes at the forefront of his conscious mind. *Those few critical seconds can be lifesavers if I get surprised and have to jackrabbit.*

The restaurant, unlike its American counterparts, was in a common storefront similar to a strip mall, except that the three-story stone structure had been built before the US became an independent nation. This prevented Michael from seeing into the building without standing in front of its windows. He sighed and accepted the additional risk.

A few dozen pedestrians moved about the vicinity, strolled in and out of various businesses, and engaged in the normal activities of daily life. *No one's nervous, attentive, or odd.* Even though most of the people he passed that morning had regarded Michael with discomfort, curiosity, or suspicion, he saw no sign of malice or fear. *The more powerful emotions are the hardest ones to hide, the easiest to see in others.*

His chest tightened as he closed in on the familiar sign, and Michael recognized the irony that the iconic arches had been so comforting throughout his childhood and college years. *Now I'm headed inside to risk my freedom and my life. Don't let me down, Ronald, I really don't wanna die in a goddamned fast-food joint.*

Michael slowed his pace a bit, discreetly nudged the hidden pistol again, and glanced through the tall front windows. His contact carried a green plastic food tray from the front counter toward the back of the dining room, and he selected a table deeper in the building just outside the restrooms. He sat against the sturdy back wall and faced the only entrance. *Exactly where every cop and operative wants to sit.* Michael pulled the door open, stepped inside, and scanned the few tables of patrons. Given that most of the neighborhood fasted during the day, the scant business seemed normal. Although not as helpful at detecting undercover cops, Michael's first instinct was to scan for military-age males. *A couple young families, pretty much who I'd expect to see here. The only single MAMs are me and the cabbie.*

Unsure what to do next, Michael strode toward his contact, who nodded and glanced toward the registers. Following the man's direction, Michael strolled to the counter, fumbled through enough Frenglish to order a combo meal, and patiently waited for its arrival. The few moments gave him another opportunity to examine everything around him for potential threats. Still seeing nothing of concern by the time his croissant sandwich and espresso arrived, Michael accepted the food tray and strode toward the contact. *He hasn't arrested or shot me yet, but he could just be waiting for the backup to arrive and take me off when he has numbers on his side. That's the prudent way tactic if you can leverage the resources.*

Michael imperceptibly took a deep breath in through his nose, and he held it for a moment as he passed the food counter and strolled left to approach the cabbie's table. As soon as they made eye contact, the target stood up and Michael instinctively nudged the pistol. In that instant, he pre-planned his threat response: drop the tray, pull the front of his shirt up with his left hand, and retrieve the pistol while stepping left and ducking to cover.

The cabbie had already eaten his food, but made a little show of crumpling a paper, which he abandoned on the table as he picked up the tray and walked toward Michael.

Confused by the events, Michael slowed his pace but continued on toward the same corner of the dining room. The cabbie met Michael's gaze as he departed and glanced back at the table and its crumpled paper. *Alright, so it's a kind of dead drop, not a meeting.*

Michael sat down at the table next to the cabbie's and unloaded his food tray. He set the empty tray on the cabbie's table and retrieved the paper by concealing it in his left palm. *Just paper, nothing hidden inside it.* Michael pocketed the note and again scanned his surroundings. Young parents sat at a few tables and their children played with crayons and shouted, but nothing stood out. *Still no obvious threats, no one interested in me or the paper.*

As he nibbled at his breakfast sandwich, Michael looked around for cameras and found two that watched the inbound traffic through the front door. A third focused on the food counter and cash registers. He retrieved the crumpled paper and saw rough handwriting in black ink.

"*Parking garage. West entrance.* 10:45. *Not late, not early.* 10:45."

Michael recrumpled the paper and wondered how to destroy it. *This shit's way outside my lane, so John never went over this in training.* He glanced at the balled-up paper. *Not gonna eat it like some stupid spy spoof...unless, maybe I should?*

Instead, he delicately dropped the paper ball into his espresso. Nothing magical happened that rendered the note illegible, but Michael felt confident he'd done enough, given the low probability that a second, additional op-for had been watching him during the last thirty minutes.

He sat back in the vinyl bench seat and considered the next move. *The more I follow this guy around, the more I confirm who and what I am. He might not know my employer or assignment, but he'll understand I'm an operative. There's only one parking garage nearby, and his team could be waiting to help, arrest, capture, or kill me. Decent tactical move, it's a much better place to accomplish any of those objectives. Whoever this guy is, he's forcing me to go all-in to see his hand.* Michael sighed, retrieved his work cell, and used its mapping software to examine the garage, which stood only a few hundred feet to the northeast. He checked the time. *Twenty-three minutes. I don't really have a choice about going, but that doesn't mean I have to walk straight into an ambush.*

MAY 8, 10:44AM_
RUE DE CHAUMETTES. SEINE-SAINT-
DENIS, FRANCE.

AFTER HUSTLING to cover a half-mile route and clandestinely approach the meeting from the north, Michael stood inside a small food market, sipped at a paper cup of dark, rich espresso, and watched the parking garage entrance. Although the McDonald's stood only a few hundred feet across the street to his southwest, Michael hoped the cabbie had wagered on him not taking the long way around the massive city block.

From the east side of the street and due north of the three-story garage, the market's three large southern windows allowed Michael to watch a small brick-paved courtyard between the buildings and see anyone who entered or left the target. With the sun already high enough overhead, the relative darkness inside the store assured Michael no one in the courtyard or garage could see him, not that he'd yet identified anyone there, anyway.

The late spring morning had warmed up and Michael wished he'd visited the famed city under different circumstances. *I'd like to take in the sights, listen to the birds chirp in the Eiffel Tower Park, and stop at every crepe stand I pass. Instead, I'm playing spy games way beyond my training and hoping for the best.* He rechecked his watch. 10:45.

Michael tossed the cup in a small trashcan and stepped out onto the sidewalk. A brief pause allowed him to scan the street one last time. He consciously felt the concealed pistol's weight at his front, right waistline and avoided nudging it again. As with much of Paris, the narrow residential street allowed only one-way traffic, southbound in this case, toward the garage. Lined with tightly parked cars on its west side, most of which showed repeated contact on the bumpers, quarter-panels, and doors. *A city of a few million shitty drivers from all over the world, narrow cobblestones streets, and not an ounce of elbow room.*

Seeing nothing that concerned him, he strode toward the garage's pedestrian entrance. *Immediate escape is back toward the McDonald's. Gotta cross the street and get on the other side of those parked cars if things really go south.* The closer he strode to his objective, the more he limited and prolonged his escape options.

Michael hoped he'd retained some element of surprise, but, as he stepped into the shade of the garage's ground floor, he realized his failure. The cabbie stood among the line of vehicles parked up against a vertical, north-south concrete support wall in the center of the floor. *He's no more than twenty yards away, an easy pistol shot for either of us.* Both the man's hands were visible, but he made a show of leaving the cover of the engine block and stepping over to the sedan's cab to place his hands in plain sight on its roof.

Michael stopped, scanned his surroundings, and cautiously approached the man only after he saw no one else around them. *Too easy for someone to pop out between these parked cars. Stay alert...*

"Thank you for coming," the cabbie offered in lightly accented English.

Michael didn't respond. Waiting until he stood just a few cars away, he dropped onto his stomach to look under the cars for anyone concealed among them. *Nothing. We're alone. Maybe.* He hurried up from the compromising position and found the man hadn't moved. Michael walked to the opposite side of the same blue sedan. Stepping between the parked cars, he turned around and leaned back against the concrete support wall, faced the stranger, and crossed his arms.

"I understand the position I've put you in."

Michal held the man's eye contact for a moment. "Can you explain it to me, then?"

"I suspect you are here to help. If not, then you are *very* lost and I must help *you*."

Michael shrugged. "I don't know what help you need."

"Of course, not, and that is why you, an obvious foreigner, followed a complete stranger into a restaurant and an isolated parking garage in a neighborhood known across the globe for increasing ethnic violence and segregation." He smiled at Michael and shook his head a few times. "You can say whatever you and your organization demand at this moment, but you've spent the last thirty-two minutes confirming my suspicions. We can continue this futile dance, if we must, but I fear we're both running out of time."

Michael realized the truth in the cabbie's statements and hated the intel disparity that existed between them. He inhaled and sighed, facing the only reasonable choice before him. *Have to divulge this in small pieces.* "I'm an investigator."

The cabbie showed no reaction and let silence press on Michael.

"I'm Andrew. What should I call you?" Michael saw recognition, maybe even relief, flash in the man's eyes.

"I am Gerard." The contact had regained his emotionless poker face. "What is it you hope to accomplish here, Andrew? You've been sent to a Muslim enclave to investigate the population during their holiest holiday? I fear you'll find no success, but plenty of danger for your effort."

Silence again hung between them, and Michael considered what else to reveal. "What about you, Gerard? I don't think you're here for a haircut."

The man smirked and then chuckled. "No, I suppose I am not. One of us has to go first, yes?"

Michael only nodded and offered a pleasant smile.

"I'm here to determine if a particular threat exists, and I hope to save a great number of people from harm."

"As do we all."

The cabbie stood up straighter and cocked his head to the side in surprise. "We *all*? Who is *we*?"

"You and me. Us. We."

"You're American, yes?"

Michael shrugged. "Something like that, but, mostly, I'm *skeptical*. You asked for this meeting, so you wanna tell me what you want, or do I need to walk away?"

Gerard hung his head in frustration and exhaled. He swore in French under his breath, something Michael understood only in context. The cabbie lifted his head and held strong eye contact with Michael. "I'm a counter-terror cop," he whispered. "I'm investigating a possible bomber, and I can use your help, *if* that's also why *you're* here."

Michael slowly nodded, grateful for the man's candor. "I think that's exactly the kind of thing I would like to help with. *Gerard*, right?"

"Yes."

"How did you learn about me?"

Gerard averted his gaze and shrugged. "One sees things while watching such a homogenous neighborhood. One learns things over time."

Michael chose not to challenge the lie. *Bullshit. I've got a leak, and I bet his name rhymes with 'Father Luc.'* "What now?"

"Now? I think we have to put ourselves at further risk and see if we may trust one another." Gerard walked around the car and nodded for Michael to follow. "I still don't know if I'll have to arrest you, kill you, or be buried next to you, but fate and God will tell us when the time is right."

Michael gave the parking garage another quick scan and then followed Gerard to a set of heavy metal double-doors that had been painted bright yellow. He opened the door on the right and led

Michael into a short hallway. A storage room door stood to their left, and Gerard unlocked the deadbolt and handle on a metal door to their right.

"My darkest secrets are not in here, but all my newest ones are." Gerard pushed the door open and motioned for Michael to step inside.

"After you."

"As you wish." Gerard nodded and stepped into the room and out of view. Michael hesitantly moved in behind him. Finding the room unoccupied, he focused on the other potential threat: cameras.

Gerard watched him scan the room. "There is no surveillance equipment in here. You may relax, as impossible as that may be for us both." He stepped into an inner, windowless room, and Michael stayed close enough to deny him the chance to take up an unseen weapon. A large array of ten television monitors stood on a desk to the right. Gerard shook a mouse on the desktop, and they turned on to display various feeds and angles.

Michael recognized his target building, as well as the same surveillance camera photograph of Abrini he'd seen in his intel packet. Several more photos hung next to it that Michael didn't have. Each showed the same man at different places, lighting, and clothing. *That confirms we're hunting the same man, even if for different outcomes.* "What is this?"

"I hope to God it's what you're here for," Gerard scoffed. He pointed to the apartment building Michael still needed to penetrate. "What can you tell me about this place?"

Michael cleared his throat. "Well, it stands at 8 *Rue du Corbillon*, and, as I understand it, a bad man might live there."

Gerard nodded and dropped his hand. "Yes, perhaps. Or, it is also possible there are many, or none." He turned to Michael and crossed his arms over his chest. "What are your intelligence and analysis capabilities? Not what you can get or find out weeks or months from now, but what can you find out in the next twenty-four to forty-eight hours?"

Michael shrugged and crossed *his* arms to mimic Gerard's body language. "It's easier to answer your question if I know what you're looking for."

Gerard's anger and frustration showed in his body language and tone. "I've just *lifted my skirt*, so to speak, and showed you everything you or my superiors need to ruin me and my family. I *have* to know something in return. It's now *your turn* to take the same risk. That's how these things work, Andrew."

MICHAEL INHALED THROUGH HIS NOSE. He took one last look around the small, windowless office and realized he wouldn't spot any recording equipment concealed in there. *Gerard better be who and what he says he is. Here goes.*

"Maybe this will help," he began. "I can't tell you my intel capabilities, but I will know more in the next day or two than I do right now. I expect to identify the known occupants of the building through postal records, employment records, vehicle registrations, and refugee databases. That information will be cross-referenced against itself, and then compared to utility records. I hope to narrow my investigation to one or two apartments by then."

Disbelief showed on Gerard's face. "He lives in 415, at the top northwest corner of building. You don't yet know that?"

"No."

Gerard stepped closer and pointed to one of the monitors. "I hid this camera in the stairwell just below his apartment. You can see his door here, and these stairs are the only avenue to his residence. He leaves once every few days, and always for less than an hour. A family, grandparents, I think, live across from him." The cop put his hands on his hips. "What *do* you know?"

"He received a series of suspicious packages thought to be chemical precursors for making the explosive part of a bomb, an I-E-D. The investigation has since stalled, and no one's been able to get a look into Abrini's apartment to confirm the allegations."

More disbelief. *"Abrini? You know his name? This man?"* Gerard pointed to the suspect photos pinned to the wall next to the monitors.

"Yes. *Abdel Abdullah Abrini.* Did you not?"

"No, not yet, I knew only the horseshit name from the parcels. How did you learn of 'Abrini?'"

"That was part of the original intel package." Michael shrugged and changed the subject. "Is Abrini associated with anyone in apartment 105 or 213?"

"No, why?"

Michael broke eye contact and scanned the monitor array to find the second and third floors that might show those doorways. "Just a lead we developed. Those apartments are leased to single women with no other identified tenants, which is consistent with someone who's hiding from the government, for whatever reason."

"How do you know this, *Abrini,* and the tenants in 105 and 213?"

Michael recognized the cop's growing suspicion and worked to allay the man's concerns. "I assumed it must have come from your government or someone like you."

"Wait. You have access to my unit's records, the *police* and *counterterror* databases?"

Michael's chest tightened. *Dammit.* "Maybe, maybe not. I just meant that, *in general,* I thought it came from various government records."

Silence ground on both men.

"I don't expect this will be comfortable for either of us," Gerard finally offered. "If we're to confirm or dispel the allegations, though, in this neighborhood where we can trust no others, we have to trust each other, if only for the task at hand. We will *both* fail if we cannot work together."

Michael had to risk exposing himself a little further. *He needs to see competency, in more than just my intel and analysis assets.* "What else do you need to know?"

"You can defend yourself, Andrew?"

"I've picked up a thing or two."

"Such as, what?"

"This and that."

"You train to fight in the ring, yes?"

Michael shook his head. "No. For me and those *like* me, fighting in the ring *is* training."

"I might need you to prove that before I trust my life to your combat skills."

"You should know that I don't spar, Gerard. I teach, *sometimes,* but I don't spar. I can't train my mind and muscle groups to go easy or merciful. If I have to put hands on someone, *Inspector,* I need to know I'm gonna give them everything I have."

The cop eyed him, as though using the man's title and the discreet warning had its intended result. "Do you understand what you're walking into here, in this place, this neighborhood?"

"Back home, we'd call it a hornet's nest. Lots of anger directed at innocents, not much discrimination, thought, or remorse in who and what they attack."

"A perfect description, but I wonder if your hornets, 'back home' as you say, do they strap on vests and detonate themselves for their God?"

"No, those assholes live to sting again."

The inspector looked at him quizzically. "Who do you work for, again?"

Michael smirked at the attempt. *Hell, he's a cop with his neck stretched out for the government's guillotine if this goes sideways.* "My current employer isn't really important, but 'O-G-A' will work if you need to blame someone. I *used* to be one of you, actually."

"A police?"

"For a time."

"What made you change careers? Tired of the continual disappointment in humanity?"

"Long story. Maybe I'll tell you sometime, if we survive this as free men who avoided both prison and the morgue."

"I hope to hear it. If, as you say, we escape either ending." Gerard turned to the monitors. "I expect these are my greatest contribution to our efforts. I may be wrong, but I assume you do not have surveillance installed yet?"

"No, I do not." Michael leaned over, put both hands on the desk, and studied the locations and angles of the various camera feeds. *Gotta stay out of their sight when I'm out on my own. Gerard and I can work together, fine, but there's no way he gets to know everything that John passes along, or every move I make.*

"As I'm sure you see, I have no view of the apartment windows. They face to the north, and they are four stories above the ground. I have nowhere close and tall enough to put my little cameras. They are quite good, and quite clear, with limited optical zoom, but they are not sufficient for that purpose."

Michael understood the inferred question but didn't want to answer. "Can you get FLIR?"

"FLIR? How do you say, what's the damned word--"

"Thermal?"

"*Yes,* thermal! In short, yes, but not for us. Because of the expense of those items, there's a massive stack of approvals to borrow them from the quartermaster, and that will require the signatures or forgery of my superiors. That, I cannot do."

Michael pointed to an area on one of the monitors near the southeast corner of the apartment building. "What's in this blind spot?"

Gerard chuckled. "That was fast, you're very good at finding the failures of those around you. Just part of the job, no? I kid. There is a small neighborhood mosque, a *majrid* in Arabic, of course. It is not built for that purpose, but that ground-level corner had once been a halal market. It closed after the last round of terror attacks in 2015, and a local imam took the space for his small neighborhood congregation."

"Is it possible to watch the entrance?"

"Oh, sure, if I had more cameras, but our focus was finding the one suspect up to this moment, so we allocated our resources there. The mosque hasn't been under surveillance for more than a year, and we didn't think it would help us find the bomber's apartment."

"Can you set something up now?"

"Now that Ramadan has started, the families will be out right after sundown, and they'll fall asleep only just before sunrise. It's too risky to plant them during that narrow timeframe. No reason for anyone but residents to be there, and especially not us Caucasians."

"What do *you* know of the imam?" Michael hoped to avoid revealing his uncorroborated watchlist intel.

"He's self-declared, we think, with no formal training, but he's called Abdul Siddiqi. We know nothing between his arrival in France from Morocco and his takeover of the market space. My team never got anyone inside the mosque to hear what he has to say. He is very attentive and suspicious of outsiders, though, and he's never looked at me as though glad to see my white, French-Catholic face in his neighborhood."

"Any access into the building from there?"

"No. The mosque has no interior doorway into the building. So, the only route between them requires your beloved Spiderman to climb the wall to his balcony windows or all the way up to the roof."

Michael smiled at the man's joke and tried not to show his elation. *That's what I was hoping you'd say.*

Gerard stood upright and again crossed his arms. "So, we know each other, enough, anyway. You've seen my video surveillance, and we now know that neither of us has a thermal camera ready to go. What, besides the bomber's name, do you intend to bring to this investigation?"

Michael continued to memorize the camera angles as he spoke.

"Do you know who he's talking to, or what he's saying and reading online?"

"No, we have none of that."

Michael stood and retrieved his work cell from a pants pocket. "You ever heard the term, 'triggerfish' or 'IMSI Catcher?'"

"No."

"I'm hoping to get a peek inside the building and see what's being *said* and *read* online, and who's talking to whom. No idea what we'll learn, but the data might reveal whether we're looking at a lone wolf or a conspiracy. Maybe even find out Abrini's real name."

Gerard tightened his arms. "How do you know it's a fraudulent name?"

"Sometimes, Gerard, we'll have to accept *information* without much *explanation*, but no one with that name ever legally entered France, and no one with that name and his approximate age is known to *any* European government for any reason."

"Okay, I'll trust that for now. How do you intend to enter the building?"

"I considered using an orange maintenance worker jumpsuit, but I have passable documents that identify me as a relief worker."

"A reflective orange uniform will get you behind most doors in Europe, but, not so much here." Gerard regarded Michael as though still sizing him up. "What's next, then?"

"Next, I have to make a few calls and find out the status of my intel and asset requests." Michael started for the door. "If I'm not back in a couple hours, you should send an ambulance."

Gerard winced. "A couple hours. Do not be early, do not be late."

Michael strode back out of the small office and waited until he reached the sidewalk along *Rue de Chaumettes* to access his phone apps. Before checking in with John, he first needed to find a second-hand clothing store. *I wonder what the French equivalent of Goodwill is? I need to look homeless and a little mental to carry out tonight's objectives.*

After skimming a few of the most recent online articles, Michael set a course for the *Canal Saint-Martin* and a large homeless tent encampment there. *I'll get to complete one kind of God's work on the way to another.*

MAY 8, 11:52AM_
8 RUE DU CORBILLON #415. SAINT-
DENIS, FRANCE.

ABDEL ABRINI OPENED HIS LAPTOP, logged in his password, and activated its virtual private network software. After confirming his data signal routed through several computers across the globe and emerged at a terminal in Oslo, Sweden, he logged into his preferred messaging site. Although the majority of its millions of customers used the open-source software for its reliability and convenience, Abdel and his second group of subordinates coveted its end-to-end encryption.

With the additional security provided by the VPN, Abdel had no concern that French authorities could identify and locate him in time to stop the imminent reckoning. *They would unlikely ever find me, but they will certainly not do so in the next three days.*

Abdel opened a dialogue with a contact called *Athnan,* the English sound for the Arabic word meaning "Two," and began typing his last series of communications in Arabic with the leader of his second team. *Peace be unto you.*

And peace be unto you, as well, came the immediate response.

"Good," Abdel murmured to himself, "he's ready and waiting for me." He typed the last of their sequenced authentication phrases, a series of numbers that identified specific suras from the Qur'an that reinforced that those killed fighting for Allah ascend to Paradise and justified their intended action.

47:4-6

3:157

Abdel smiled at the immediate reply. *One more, just to be sure.* This time, he typed out part of a sura that chided those who shrink from warfare and praised the servants who wished for death. *Did ye think that ye would enter heaven without Allah testing those of you who fought hard in His cause and remained steadfast?*

The cursor blinked for several seconds before a small blue bubble appeared in the dialogue to indicate *Two* was typing.

Ye did indeed wish for death before ye met him: Now ye have seen him with our own eyes!

Abdel typed furiously, his heart and mind energized by the obvious dedication of his men and the well-lit path they walked together.

My brothers. Be ready, be vigilant, be prepared in all ways. I will meet you at the predetermined location on Ramadan-6, no later than 1000. All of you must wear football jerseys, preferably those of the Paris-Saint-Germain Football Club. The crowds outside the contest that day will be your target.

Abdel paused and prayed the next directive wasn't necessary. *By 10:15, if I have not arrived, evacuate and flee according to the previous orders. You will not hear from me again. Prepare to ascend.*

The blue bubble again appeared.

We understand. God is great! Peace be unto you.

Peace be unto you, as well. Abdel closed the dialogue, deleted it from the account, and uninstalled the software from his laptop. He glanced to the right side of the writing desk, nearest his half-open windows, and beamed at the two flyers that had inspired his precise timing to conclude the operation. Although he had wanted the attacks to coincide with Friday prayers, the two public notices he'd found only an hour ago changed his mind. *This way,* all *the imposters will pay for their sins while this arrogant nation again recoils at the necrotic sting of God's true servants.*

Abdel stood from the desk, strode to the apartment's only door, and donned his slip-on sandals. *Now, the first team must be notified, as well. Time is short, and I have much to do in these final days and hours.*

AFTER SUCCESSFULLY PRESENTING himself as a local beggar, Michael had camped out atop the fire escape of a tall building due north of his target. Once he'd parted ways with Gerard last evening, he purchased a worn, mismatched ensemble at a used clothing store and proceeded to the encampment at *Canal Saint-Martin*. A homeless man living there accepted €100 for his faded, ripped, and threadbare military fatigue jacket. Although he'd thanked Michael profusely for the exchange and offered to sell more of his belongings, Michael had only thanked him and encouraged the man to buy food and another jacket. *The priest in me wants to believe that money will change the direction or temporary comfort of his life, but the cop in me knows better. I'd be a fool to bet against that cash going to drugs and alcohol, but I will always hope I'm wrong.*

Using an instant aging process he'd learned at his former police department, Michael scrubbed enough motor oil and dirt from an asphalt parking lot to make his clean second-hand clothes match the jacket's authenticity. After acquiring and preparing the rest of his homeless kit, he returned to The Oremus for a nap and the gear he needed that night. With the shift in activity during Ramadan, Michael had to remain cautious and prepared to have any chance of survival or success. *The homeless are a vulnerable segment of society commonly targeted for harassment, random violence, and deliberate, premeditated assaults from within their own population. I'm offering myself up for an unknown portion of that whole experience by stepping out tonight, but there's no other way to get what we need. Through a conspiracy of circumstance and intent, Abrini's kept the most critical intel components hidden from me and Gerard. Neither of us have enough information to move forward, even with the vast difference in our objectives and methods.*

To avoid unwanted attention from the staff and local police, Michael had waited to emerge from his room until most guests at The Oremus had turned in for the night. At 1am, he hurried from room 144 and left out the nearest exit. The trains and Metro still ran at that hour, so he easily returned to *Seine-Saint-Denis,* although at a much slower pace than normal to keep himself in character.

By 2:15am, Michael plodded up the steps from a Metro station and meandered toward his nearby targets. Most of the streets were empty, and only a few vehicles and pedestrians were out. As he expected, no one paid attention to another homeless beggar. The handful of people he passed watched him from the corners of their eyes as a personal safety measure, but no one stopped or engaged with him. *Perfect.*

As he trudged along the wide *Boulevard Carnot* toward its intersection with the much narrower and familiar one-way *Rue de Corbillon,* Michael flopped down with his plastic shopping bags and backpack to take up temporary residence in the doorway of a closed business. From that ground level perch on the north side of the street, he watched for movement, security, and pedestrians across the boulevard. The building opposite him, at the southeast corner of the intersection, was his first target that night.

The sign out in front displayed the business name in Arabic and what Michael assumed was French: الاستيلاء على عدن, *Institut Alaistila' Ealaa 'usul Eadn.* He'd spent about an hour researching the business and the building to avoid unexpected danger, but Michael had only learned it was an Islamic school whose name didn't have an obvious, direct translation into English. *Probably local slang or lesser-known vocabulary. Another reason people are always better than computers.*

About a half-hour into his surveillance of the building, Michael's curiosity over the name overcame his countersurveillance concerns. He surreptitiously retrieved his work cell, shielded its screen from the deserted street, and rechecked the name. Once he input the school's name and identified it as Arabic, the translation app converted it to English: "seizing the assets of Eden." That mystery solved, he put the phone away and sought any option other than ascending that particular building. Finding none, he worked to reduce his apprehension. *Ominous phrasing, but I can't disagree with the message.*

Michael waited until after 3:30am to emerge from the shop's doorway with his backpack and plastic bags and approach the first target. *I need to be in-place before the congregation stumbles down to the mosque for the 4:35 prayers.* From the empty segment of boulevard, he cautiously climbed a rickety fire escape on the west side of the building to a small rusty perch on top of the fifth floor. Ignoring Abrini's building for the moment, Michael sat still and watched the surrounding neighborhood. No one reacted to his presence, no audible alarms activated, and no police cars materialized to remove him from the structure.

The cops, he feared, posed a greater risk to him than any of the street ruffians he'd encountered so far. Even a patrol cop might recognize the use and value of the items in his shopping bags and backpack. They'd either assume he stole them, which would end in his arrest for that crime, or they'd realize he was surveilling the Muslim population with high-tech equipment, which would likely result in his arrest for hate crimes under the nefarious and ill-conceived European laws that criminalized free speech and private thought across the continent. *That's the last thing the Church needs right now, to have one of their priests arrested and prosecuted in France for anti-Muslim hate crimes with no record of how or when he got into the country. At least two French churches are desecrated every day, and the anti-Christian reaction would only intensify after that.*

Once satisfied he'd escaped notice, Michael retrieved the first piece of equipment, a set of high-tech mil-spec binoculars that offered both thermal and infrared views. In providing the latest generation mil-spec kit, Jacques had proven the value of his position and access. Michael expected the man had serious connections in the military or criminal underworld. *Maybe both.*

He first activated the binos' thermal function and immediately understood why American cops couldn't use the device on a private residence without a search warrant. The computer-enhanced images showed him the number of people hidden inside the walls and revealed something of their activities at that moment. Movement below his target caught Michael's attention, and he saw the family who lived there was still awake. Two parents and three small children played some unknown game together. *Good to know.* Michael shifted his digital gaze another floor down and saw a couple in that apartment engaged in intercourse. His cheeks flushed hot with embarrassment and Michael cast his binos back to the target. *My bad, sorry about that.*

Abrini's apartment was darker than the others, which meant it was cooler. Some lighter areas emanated near the middle of the space but didn't have a distinct shape. For a long time, he watched nothing change inside the apartment and thought Abrini might have gone out. *If I could trust Gerard enough to have coordinated this with him, he could review the camera feeds and tell me if the man was still inside. Maybe we can get the apartment's floorplan today. It would be helpful to know what the interior layout is supposed to be.*

He considered altering his plan and moving over to Abrini's building now. *There's no one out right now, the target looks empty, and most of the other residents inside the building are staying inside and keeping to themselves.* Michael sighed and weighed his options, given the first optional daily prayer began in less than an hour. The more popular and first *mandated* prayer of started at 6:24, and he intended to use the gap between those to conduct his close surveillance and intel collection at Abrini's windows. He glanced back at his watch and decided he didn't have time to assure his success or protect his escape. *No, I'll just stick with the plan, not enough reason to change it yet.*

Michael switched the binoculars over to the infrared setting, but Abrini's apartment was too far away to see more than the exterior wall. He set them down, retrieved an IR spotlight, and aimed it at the target's windows. With the binoculars in his left hand and the spot-light in his right, Michael manipulated the light on and off every few seconds. The brief view into the suddenly "bright" apartment had at least assured him that no people were visible inside. Because the IR spectrum isn't entirely invisible to the human eye, Michael didn't want to risk leaving the torch on and attracting attention.

He alternated between watching the neighborhood for potential trouble and watching Abrini's apartment through the thermal binos while trying to calm his fears about what the man's absence might mean. The early, optional prayer session came and went with no change to the empty streets. He glanced back at the family's apart-ment below Abrini and found they appeared to be asleep.

He scanned the adjacent buildings in search of a better perch. Michael disliked the idea of again ascending the Muslim-owned school during Ramadan, when much of the neighborhood stayed awake at night and might feel extraordinarily sensitive to perceived slights toward their faith. *It's a religion, a social structure, and polit-ical ideology, after all, not merely their relationship with God.*

brtbrt brtbrt brtbrt

Michael's wristwatch vibrated, and he turned off the alarm notif-ication. He brought the binos back up and gave his target a final, thor-ough look. After nothing moved or changed inside for five minutes, he replaced the device in his backpack and rechecked his watch. 5:06. *It's time.*

Moving as fast as the still quiet morning allowed, Michael descended the fire escape with his bagged belongings, approached

Abrini's building in character, and lumbered around to the southeast corner. He paused outside the closed entrance to the makeshift mosque, confirmed he still appeared to be alone and unobserved, and set about the most difficult work of the morning. He removed the rest of his gear from the few shopping bags, stuffed the devices in his backpack, and cinched it tight against his shoulders.

After its mandated inclusion in his covert training program, Michael had become obsessed with parkour. In his few free hours, he practiced the necessary skills and built additional strength by bouldering and rock climbing, and he needed to be perfect in all of that to succeed this morning. The eastern sky had not yet brightened with the coming sunrise as Michael scaled the building's exterior. His backpack added a measure of difficulty and instability to his ascent. Still, Michael scampered up by the stone structure's small ledges, occasional balconies, and stone windowsills. Although he could have circumnavigated the building to lessen the ascent, Michael had to avoid Gerard's cameras. *I don't want him to know about this, not yet, anyway. I don't mind sharing selected intel with the cop, but I can't divulge our assets and capabilities. I'm already way outside the op-sec protocols just by working with him.* In less than two minutes, he pulled himself up onto the roof.

Once on top, Michael bear-crawled toward the northwest corner to reduce the weight and pressure he put on any one spot. He laid on his stomach over Abrini's apartment, slowly leaned his head and face out over the edge of the roof, and looked down at his target's small balcony. For a long time, Michael stayed still and listened. Curtains rustled in and out of the windows with the light, predawn breeze, but nothing else moved. *He still might be out.*

Michael estimated the top of the windows stood three-to-four feet below the roofline. *Too far to reach a camera over.* Without a way to see inside from there, he shuffled over the edge, legs first, and dangled five stories above a concrete courtyard. *No margin for error, no second chance to get it right.*

USING the narrow stones around Abrini's windows for grip and support beneath his right foot, Michael lowered himself off the five-story roof until his left toes just touched the balcony railing. He had to keep his chest and shoulders on the roof, his fingers clinging like vice grips to the thin ledge to prevent his fall. At that moment, Michael realized his body position prevented him from testing the railing by slowly adding his weight until he knew it would hold him. *This backpack is putting too much weight out over the ledge!*

Michael couldn't look down without leaning out beyond the roof and turning his potential energy into kinetic acceleration. Closing his eyes, he breathed deep and focused on his remaining senses while gravity and his body positioning conspired to shift him clockwise, away from the balcony, and beyond the questionable railing. *I'm too far out to climb back up, so I have to go now, all at once, and pray for the best.*

He inhaled through his nose and let himself down the last relatively stable inches until the ball of his extended left foot touched the scant railing. Before gravity pulled him any farther over the railing to his left, Michael exhaled, slipped his right foot off the narrow windowsill while pushing back off the roof with his hands and then shoved away from the railing with his left foot. The sudden drop surged his adrenaline, even though he expected it, and he landed unsteadily on both feet with a light *thud*. Abrini's balcony flexed beneath the force, and Michael fell back to the outer railing. He collapsed his legs, and the railing struck his backpack before Michael caught himself.

creeeeak

He lunged toward the apartment window, crouched low against the wall, and held onto the bottom of the frame to keep his weight away from the outside of the balcony. Michael realized the window was only open about two inches, and the thin curtains he'd seen blowing in the breeze hung out nearly a foot through the narrow opening. Even though the curtains were parted almost two feet, the apartment's interior was too dark to see inside.

As he clung to the window frame, Michael's fear of waking or seeing Abrini replaced the concern of plunging five stories to his death. He scanned what little he could see inside the apartment and stayed there only long enough to establish faith that the concrete balcony would hold. He still heard and saw no movement, so he pivoted on his feet to the outside of the window, placed himself against the balcony railing, and rushed to gather the intel.

Michael retrieved his binos from the backpack, dialed them to the lowest magnification, and scanned the interior with the thermal. He again saw dark colors and ambiguous shapes near the deep middle of a large open room, and the thermal vision provided no sense of depth. *The bedroom must be on the other side of an interior wall.* Michael recovered the IR torch, switched the binos' viewing function, and examined the interior. He considered pushing the window open farther, but decided the risk was too great without an easy or quick escape route.

A small, two-cushion couch sat ahead of him to his left, most of the middle of the open room was empty, and a small writing desk stood to Michael's far right against the west wall. An interior wall ahead revealed the bedroom's location, and he thought a small kitchen might be near the southwest corner, near the only exterior door. *Not a single picture on the walls. Consistent with Islamic dogma, at least, but it doesn't prove anything.*

A large box on the kitchen floor caught his eye, so Michael zoomed in with the binos and focused the IR torch to illuminate it. Although he didn't have the specific vocabulary to name the glassware he saw, Michael saw enough of the items to understand they were chemical lab equipment. *Never seen those shapes and clear containers in any other setting.* His chest tightened.

Michael reached around to a small outer pocket on the backpack, replaced the binos and spotlight, and retrieved a small Wi-Fi camera. He'd adjusted its settings to maximize the battery life, which should last two or three days if Abrini didn't stand in its field of view and do four hours of jumping jacks. In addition to the cameras and their ancillary equipment, Jacques had provided a gray outdoor spray paint that reasonably matched the stone and concrete throughout much of the city. Michael held the small device in the upper corner of the ornate wrought iron railing, just beneath the top handrail, and secured it with wire coated in gray, nonreflective plastic. *It isn't perfectly camouflaged, but it only has to be 'good enough.' Abrini shouldn't see it unless he's looking for change and anomalies.* He pointed the lens toward the bulk of the living area, and then secured a second camera that looked toward the writing desk from the other side of the balcony.

After ensuring both cameras were powered on, Michael hurried to retrieve another tech device, this one about the size and shape of a gaming console or an iPad, if the Apple product was three inches thick. *Running out of time, need to move soon.*

No longer able to see inside the apartment, Michael hastened his efforts to collect the intel. The boxy device, an all-hazards field detection unit designed for military and law enforcement Hazardous Materials applications, sprung to life, began its internal calibration checks, and cast him in a lime green light. *Nothing to do but hurry now.*

Michael stared into the dark apartment and scanned for movement until he noticed the screen's green lighting dimmed. It displayed a message, *Calibration confirmed. Ready for Use.* He acknowledged the message and scrolled through a menu; based on the alleged delivery of chemical precursors and the lab glassware inside Abrini's kitchen, Michael first pressed an icon to begin a *Chemical Warfare Search.* The device initiated a two-minute collection and test of the air, and Michael held its sensors just inside the window's narrow opening. *Whatever's in there might be heavier or lighter than air, so it might spill out of the top or bottom of the window, and maybe not either.*

chhck

The audible signal announced the end of the test, and Michael read the screen. *No known compounds detected.* Michael hurried to begin the next test sequence, a *Drug-Narcotic Search,* waited for the message to change, and repeated his two-minute hold at the open window slit.

chhck

No known compounds detected.

Michael switched to the last detection function. *Moment of truth.* He pressed the *Explosive Ordinance Search* icon, saw the message change, and moved the sniffer back to the window. Having been out on Abrini's balcony for almost ten minutes now, Michael sensed his increasing vulnerability and exposure. *I can't stay here forever, he'll eventually walk in the front, or out the bedroom door. Nowhere to run but down.*

brrtbrrtbrrt

Unlike the last two searches, the device vibrated in his hands and displayed a new message. *Caution! Suspicious, Unknown Chemical Agents Detected! Evacuate personnel within 100 yards and submit readings for Reachback analysis!*

Michael hadn't expected the message and struggled with how to proceed. Jacques had left a note on the device that explained *Reachback* as a process that submits the sensors' readings to live chemists and physicists at the manufacturer's corporate labs. The note had very explicitly explained that Michael could *not* use that feature under any circumstance. Michael suspected the device's unique identification and ownership data went along with the readings, and he assumed that to be the source of Jacques' concern. *Goddammit.*

Michael cycled a deep, calming breath, and peered back inside the apartment for a few moments. With no movement or imminent threats, he acknowledged the ominous message and scrolled through his other options. An icon appeared below the primary three for an *All-Hazards Search.* Michael pressed that, hoping it would give him something of a second opinion. He again held the sniffer at the window gap for another two minutes and hoped for a definitive outcome.

brrtbrrtbrrt

Michael held his breath and read the screen. *Caution! Suspicious, Unknown Chemical Agents Detected! Immediately evacuate personnel within 300 yards and submit readings for Reachback analysis!* Michael exhaled, pressed the *Submit* icon, locked the touchscreen, and replaced the sniffer in his backpack. *Sorry, Jacques.* He climbed out over the edge of the balcony and began his controlled balcony-to-balcony descent as fast as he dared. *Can't pull the fire alarm and evacuate the building yet, not without knowing what the sensors detected. Could be a false positive, and the alarms might encourage Abrini to run, or blow the place. The neighborhood might be in greater danger from me trying to protect them. No, I have to leave everything as it is for now.*

Michael paused on the outside of the third-floor balcony when he saw a child's stuffed tiger and a small, handmade doll stitched from canvas atop a small bistro table. The sudden, emotional reminders of who shared Abrini's building muddied Michael's evacuation decision.

MAY 9, 7:02AM_

Vatican Housing Complex. Rome, Italy.

BISHOP HAROLD HOFFABURR, Ph.D., knocked lightly on the door of
the luxury apartment assigned to his superior and mentor, Cardinal
Paul Dylan. Regardless of what other tasks, appointment, or meetings
Harold had scheduled on his boss' calendar, the two men met every
morning between 7 and 8 to keep both their primary concerns on
track: directing their covert operatives and managing the cardinal's
political maneuvering inside the modern Holy Roman empire.

Dressed in his usual dark red robe and slippers, Cardinal Dylan
opened the door and smiled at his subordinate. "Good morning,
Harold, please, come in."

Despite the daily ritual, Harold still politely awaited the invitation. He entered, strode to the apartment's opulent rectangular zebra-
wood dining table, and took his normal seat. Steamy gurgling from
the kitchen announced he'd interrupted Dylan's cappuccino
production.

The cardinal strolled through the dining room and disappeared into the kitchen. "Care for a coffee?"

"No, thank you, Your Eminence, I've already moved on for the day."

"How are things in Paris?"

Harold disliked his mentor's lackadaisical attitude toward aspects of their operational security, such as shouting questions pertaining to a covert kill mission between the rooms of his borrowed residence. *The low probability of being overheard doesn't equate to an* impossibility. Unwilling to confront the man and his ego, Harold rose and entered the kitchen to better assure their privacy.

"I've not yet heard anything else this morning, but I know the agent received substantial equipment support in the last two days, and John and the DICE analysts have been diligent about fulfilling his intel requests."

Dylan focused on plunging the cappuccino machine's steam frother in and out of a metal cup of cream. "So, does that mean he'll move on this soon, or does he intend only to keep our resources tied up? He's got more than enough information to move forward, so, what's the problem?"

"I don't disagree with the man's caution, Your Eminence, given the source material and the potential bias from the police--"

"Unless I'm mistaken, the target's received chemical ingredients known to be used in the manufacture of improvised explosive devices, he's taken a fake name, and might have attended terror training camps in Syria. I understand the cops might need more information to arrest and prosecute him, Harold, but our men *are not* the police." Dylan paused and poured the hot milk and froth over his double-espresso. "They're Absolvers, and they aren't bound by the restrictions of mankind's flawed systems of justice. So, again, Harold, what's the problem?"

"I believe John has trained them to be appropriately cautious during the investigation phase, which should ensure their safety and longevity--"

Dylan made eye contact with Harold and uttered a dismissive scoff. "*Safety and longevity?* I don't recall that we asked them to care about either. Their purpose, their *duty,* to us and to the Church, *to God, in fact,* is to remove *by force* the greatest and most dangerous evils that plague mankind. They can't do that without risk, sometimes substantial, and they should have well accepted that reality." He sipped at the hot drink. "In order to carry out their mission and fulfill our needs and purpose for their existence, they must be more aggressive."

Harold followed the cardinal back to the dining table and sat before offering his perspective. "I believe the concern, for them, anyway, is the risk of an insufficient investigation that leads them to an unjustified final absolution. Essentially, they're concerned about the possibility of killing an innocent themselves."

Dylan chuckled, smirked, and sipped his coffee. "Innocent. What a flawed and impossible concept. There's no such thing. These men of yours and John's, it's time they placed greater faith in God. He won't call them to a target unworthy of a final absolution. How many subjects have our men passed up?"

"Well, really only one subject, but we've passed on him several times now, despite the intel analysts' firm confidence that he requires immediate judgement."

"I think those results speak for themselves. Talk to John. Convince him, and then have *him* convince his subordinates. We're wasting precious time and resources needed elsewhere. And, getting back to it, make sure that Paris is resolved quickly."

Harold sat in silence for a moment, aware his cardinal hadn't finished issuing directives.

"Also, while you're speaking with John, remind him that we need his Absolvers to win this battle at all costs. They're expendable assets, and God may very well call for their sacrifice or imprisonment, just as he did for most of the apostles. It's no coincidence most of them are named for men who died in service to God, and they should be proud and honored for the opportunity to martyr themselves for God in the modern era. With the progressive line of thought taking hold over the world, you can't really trust anyone but communists and Islamic radicals to kill their ideological enemies anymore."

Dylan gazed over his coffee cup and Harold followed his stare out to the roofline of Vatican City to their south.

"Reiterate their need to work in isolation from each other, Harold, and their probable need to sacrifice their personal freedoms and lives for God's causes. I'll see it as a blessing when they trust us enough to be jailed or killed fulfilling our orders. Who are we, after all, to deny these men the opportunity to enter heaven as modern-day apostles?"

Harold inhaled and shifted the conversation to something more comfortable to him. "What news of the other project, Your Eminence, has there been any movement there?"

Dylan absentmindedly smiled and kept his visual focus on the interior of the famously walled city, the seat of the Roman Catholic empire, the Holy See. "It's fair to say that great things are just over the horizon for us, Harold. I told you to keep your bags packed when we got here, and I believe we'll soon be taking up residence *inside* the Vatican walls. Perhaps of an even greater office than we expected."

GRATEFUL TO BE SHOWERED and out of the homeless disguise he'd worn since 1am, Michael strode back toward Abrini's apartment building despite his anxiety. He adjusted the yellow-and-blue reflective vest he wore and confirmed the fake employee ID card remained clipped to the left lapel. To show respect for the local culture, he'd donned khaki pants and a black, long-sleeved shirt that he buttoned to its collar. *If Gerard's right, this is a guaranteed confrontation. Hopefully, the same assholes who chased me off a couple days ago live somewhere else.*

He cleared his throat just outside the front door. "I hope you can hear me, Gerard. I'm making entry now, should be on camera for you, too." *Says a lot that it's too dangerous for me to wear an earpiece or carry a weapon.* Michael entered a four-digit code into the keypad that French authorities mandated all such building owners use to grant access to authorities and welfare/aid workers.

Michael stepped back, pulled the door open, and held it for two ten-year-old boys who rushed to leave the building. They both stepped outside and stopped in the door's path before looking up, and their surprise at seeing Michael was obvious. All three looked at each other for a moment as though everyone wondered what to do next.

"Bonjour, buenos dias, good morning!" Michael smiled and hoped to buy himself time.

The taller of the two leaned into the building and shouted. *"Rajul'abyad yati fi alddakhil!"* The boys both waved at Michael, and then ran off the stoop, down the sidewalk, and toward the small bodega he'd first spotted on his nighttime stroll.

Without understanding what the child had just said, Michael could only take solace that the boy's tone didn't convey fear or crisis. *Still, he probably sounded the alarm.* He walked into the dim hallway and hurried to the stairs. The building smelled of mildew, onions, body odor, and curry. Based on Gerard's earlier intrusion efforts, Michael hustled up to five as naturally as possible.

As he passed the third-floor landing, doors opened on the lower floors and several males engaged each other in conversation. *They don't sound agitated yet, so I might have an outside chance of success here.* Michael opened the messenger bag and retrieved a small stack of tri-folded glossy, full-color pamphlets. *I want to avoid opening the bag in front of them if I can, it's just an invitation to ransack it.*

By the time he reached the fifth floor, Michael heard heavy steps ascending the stairs behind him. The target was last seen going into the north apartment, #415, and the camera hadn't shown him leaving. *Unless he went out the window, he's gonna be in there now.* Michael paused near that doorway and stayed there while the footsteps closed in. *I wish I either had blissful ignorance or the Reachback results to tell me what Abrini's hiding on the other side of this door.*

Just before the ascending footfalls reached the landing below him, Michael stepped across the short hallway, stopped in front of the opposing door, and lightly knocked. *This is probably where I get my pockets turned out.*

The door opened and a slight, elderly Middle Eastern man with a trimmed gray and white beard, green gown, and blue skullcap stood before him. A quizzical expression spread over his face.

Two young, angry Middle Eastern men reached the landing and stood behind him, glaring.

Michael turned and stepped to his left to place his back against the wall outside the open doorway. He naively nodded to the two men and turned back to the resident inside the apartment.

The older man's expression had changed to one of concern and fear. *"Bonjour, comment puis-je vous aider?"*

"Bonjour, parlez-vous espagnol ou anglais?"

"Oh, yes," the man quickly admitted and nodded to the two interlopers, "but they do not, and they--"

The smaller of the two MAMs spoke harshly to the elderly man in Arabic, and Michael expected the probable outcome of the debate. He smiled and waited for the decision about what form of violence the younger men wished to attempt. *With luck, the triggerfish will have time to work before they toss me out the front door on my ear.*

The elder raised a finger to draw Michael's attention. "Although I am merely curious, these men are *desperate* to know why you're here and who you are."

Michael smiled, pointed to the displayed ID card with his left thumb, and tried to show his good humor. "I'm Gabriel Desantos, and I'm a volunteer for an aid organization called *Humanitarian Crisis in Motion*. We're in France to assist the U-N Center for Refugees." He handed each of the men a pamphlet that displayed general information about the fictional organization in Arabic, Farsi, Afrikaans, French, and English. The older gentleman accepted and reviewed it. Both of the younger men skimmed it so quickly Michael didn't believe either of them could read any of the languages presented there.

"How can I help you, sir?"

Michael spread his arms out toward the trio. "Actually, that's what I want to ask all of you. We want to know how we can assist anyone new to France with their transition. If anyone needs help to access government serv--"

The shorter MAM spoke over him again, but this time in a much louder, irritate tone. The elder replied in Arabic and referred to portions of the pamphlet as he did so.

Michael kept smiling and tried to stay calm. *Come on triggerfish, don't let this be for nothing.*

"I'm sorry, sir, please forgive my paranoid neighbors," the elder offered. "They proclaim a grave and immediate distrust of you. They have agreed not to resort to violence if you'll permit them to examine the contents of your pack."

Michael let his smile evaporate and slowly raised his hands up in front of his shoulders, in what most people intrinsically recognized as a "surrender position." Those skilled in shooting and combat sports knew it was anything but.

"I don't want trouble," Michael offered while slowly shaking his head, "I just want to help." He stepped toward the aggressors with his left shoulder, leaving his stronger right hand better protected near the wall, and awkwardly pulled the bag's strap off his left shoulder with that same hand.

The bigger man grabbed at the strap and ripped the bag away while his loud-mouthed cohort stepped closer to Michael but didn't yet touch him.

"It's okay," Michael offered, "you can look, it's okay. We're all, okay."

The older man stepped closer to see inside the bag for himself. "They don't speak anything that you do, and we probably can't convince them you're not a threat, Mister Desantos." He looked up at Michael with sincere concern in his eyes. "If there is something in there that will upset them or get you hurt, you should tell me now while I can still intervene on your behalf."

"No, there's nothing dangerous, it's only pamphlets, a computer, and a hard drive."

"I hope you're right. These two have likely only ever attended *madrasas*, so you and I can only guess at how they will interpret your possessions."

Escalating conversation between the younger two drew their attention. The smaller man overturned the bag in frustration and dumped its contents onto the floor. A small laptop fell hard onto the dirty, tiled floor, followed by an apparent hard drive and a hundred more copies of the same pamphlet Michael had handed over.

Michael didn't care about the laptop, but he tried not to react when the triggerfish, disguised as a large external hard drive, struck the computer and the floor. He kept his hands up and stepped back until he contacted the wall.

The smaller man inspected the items on the floor while his muscle stood up and rifled through the bag. Soon bored with that, they looked back to Michael. A quick conversation and pointed fingers made their intent plain before Michael's advocate addressed him.

"They want to search you now. I suggest you do not say 'no,' regardless of how their behavior saddens and offends me."

Michael nodded and raised his hands a little higher but kept them just above his shoulders for power and maneuverability. "I understand."

The muscle ran his hands over Michael and his clothing in a rough, ineffective search. *I'm glad I have nothing to hide, but it'd be damned easy to conceal any of my pistols from him. This guy didn't go anywhere near my crotch.*

Additional footfalls ascended the stairs, and another MAM walked up behind the smaller one. The large mole on the man's left cheek confirmed his identity. *Oh, shit. Unibrow. Hope you can see this, Gerard, because things just went to shit up here.*

All three MAMs engaged in a brief but heated conversation that seemed to involve Michael's groin and some objection from their outnumbered elder. Unibrow didn't seem to recognize him.

They fell silent and the elderly man cleared his throat. "Over my complaint, they insist on examining your genitals, sir. I assure you they're only interested in weapons."

Michael showed some of his fear. *They can't understand me, but facial expressions and behaviors are nearly universal.* He looked at the three impatient men and debated how to proceed. *Could be a ruse to justify beating me up. Could be a legit offer to avoid touching me and degrading themselves. Could just be a bully move to humiliate me. What is most likely to get me and the triggerfish out of here with the least damage?* Michael quelled the rising apprehension in his chest, imperceptibly rotated his hips a little further clockwise, and turned his focus directly toward the elder, who again stood to Michael's left.

"No, please tell them--" *Movement!*

As he hoped the muscle swung a leg up to Michael's groin, and he turned his hips left to deflect the bulk of the impact. The contact retained enough force that he didn't have to add much acting to drop to his knees in pain.

Muscle backed up as though expecting a fight. Seeing no advance from Michael, all three pointed and laughed while the kind elder stepped in to protect him from further assault. He shouted at them while Michael composed himself and exaggerated the not-insignificant pain they'd inflicted. Unibrow and The Loudmouth moved downstairs, still shouting at the old man, but Muscle had to first stomp on Michael's laptop.

After they'd gone, the elderly man knelt next to Michael. "You should leave right away. They claim to have granted you five minutes. Please accept my apologies, as those men do not represent my culture and faith like they believe they do. Unfortunately," he explained and meekly averted his gaze, "I am powerless to stop them without endangering my wife and grandchildren."

"I understand. Did they say when I could come back?" Michael looked up and the man's incredulous expression made him laugh. His insides hurt, which helped to stifle his laughter. "Seriously, can you ask if tomorrow's okay?"

Michael retrieved his messenger bag and the undamaged triggerfish, and then slowly stood.

His advocate gently clapped his left shoulder. "I like you, Mister Desantos. I'm confident you're about to help many people."

"That's the plan."

"Please let me clean this up. Do you want help walking?"

"No, but if you wouldn't mind escorting me out, just in case I need another translator, that'd be great. I'm not sure the next conversation will end this well." Michael moved closer to the door to #415, which also placed him in better view of the camera he saw still concealed in the corner of the stairwell landing below him. *Now Gerard can see I'm upright and vertical. This shit had better be worth it.* He risked a glance toward the target's door. *Not a peep from inside that apartment. He's either paranoid, deaf, or dead.*

Michael and Gerard sat in the leased parking garage office and watched the monitor array before them. Several bags of frozen couscous sat piled on Michael's groin to reduce the pain and swelling. After seeing the confrontation and Michael's relatively peaceful departure, Gerard had stepped out to a local market and purchased the bags. Michael checked his phone, saw he had no updates on the sniffer results, and shifted the makeshift cool-packs. *Priests aren't supposed to father children, anyway.*

Michael focused on three of the ten monitors that best displayed Abrini's apartment, and Gerard watched the overall activity on the other seven. "Are we sure he's still in there?"

"Yes, unless he grew wings and took flight." Gerard sipped at a large takeout coffee. "The first thing I do each morning is to scroll back through the videos to see if anyone entered or left his apartment, and then, the building. The only new item I noted this morning was a beggar, a homeless man, stumbling down the street. He walked off to the south without going into the building, though."

Michael readjusted the frozen bags, sipped from a takeout coffee Gerard had also provided, and tried to keep his tone from betraying his interest. "What time was that?"

"Just before five-a-m." The cop looked at him for a long moment, and Michael stayed focused on the monitors. "You're very concerned this morning about a simple beggar and Abrini's absence. Is there something I should know?"

Michael met Gerard's gaze and allowed no change to his expression, despite the imminent lie. *Gotta be convincing.* "No, no reason. Just haven't seen him in a while."

"That's his normal habit. He stays locked up for days at a time. Most of the neighborhood will be asleep by now, actually." Gerard stretched in his chair. "If only we could get our hands on a telephoto camera, and maybe a helicopter to plant one of my small ones on his balcony."

Michael stared at the monitors and sipped at his coffee. *Is he feeling me out? Does he know?*

Gerard scoffed. "Pointless, anyway, there's no way to get it up there, anyway, right? Even if we did, how would we ever get down?"

Michael risked a glance at him to assess the man's intent and tried to change the subject. "You have access to anything like that, helos or fixed-wing aircraft?"

The French cop dismissively waved his hand without looking over. "Ahh! No use to us, it takes weeks of paperwork. Unless we can manufacture a climate change emergency, then my government will give us all we ask for."

Michael chuckled at the man's antics and returned to the monitors.

"How soon will you have data returns from the triggerfish?"

Michael looked at the device, which rested on the floor beneath the desk, and saw its lights functioned normally. "As long as we leave it running here, it'll keep feeding data to my analysts, so, whenever they find something interesting to pass along, I guess. I'll ask, but they know this is a priority."

Gerard, too, watched the device for a moment. "As long as it's here, mimicking a cell tower and recording electronic data, are you also certain it won't make us a target or give away this location?"

Michael shrugged. "I doubt it. Abrini would require tech beyond most everyone but the government to find us."

Gerard sprung forward in his seat and zoomed one of the camera views in, and Michael looked over to that monitor. Two men came into view, one of whom he recognized as the imam from the mosque in Abrini's building.

"*Ce putain de traître!*"

"What?" Michael looked closer at the two men.

"That, *fucking*, traitor! That man," Gerard fumed and pointed at the second Middle Eastern man on the screen, "*that* is my boss! The esteemed *Lieutenant Algeri*, the very man who closed this investigation! He directed me and my teams out of this neighborhood two days ago, and, now there he is, consorting with *the enemy!*"

Michael grimaced at the cop's choice of words, as well as what his collective suspicions about both men meant now that they were together. *I can't tell Gerard the imam might be on the US Terror Watchlist, that's too inflammatory until we know for sure.* "Do you know something specific about the imam or his mosque?"

"He runs an Islamic school around the corner, a *madrasa*, in addition to the mosque. I don't *have* to know anything specific, I need only know he's flourishing in a garden of snakes without ever having consumed one."

Michael didn't have any intel to dispute Gerard's assessment, but, despite the probable malice, he didn't have irrefutable evidence to damn either man. *I think his job and its inherent biases have got the better of Gerard's judgement.*

"Well, that settles one thing. I'm not walking away from this investigation, no matter what." He looked up at Michael with barely controlled outrage evident on his face. "You'd better be committed to seeing this through, regardless of what it means. If not, I'd rather work alone than count on a man of questionable fortitude." Gerard stood up and shoved his chair back into the wall. "I have to place a few phone calls. Please excuse me."

Michael watched him storm off and considered his position. He had to manage the inspector's actions well enough to prevent his implosion for another few days. His work cell vibrated in his pants pocket. Upon retrieving it, Michael saw John had sent a series of encrypted messages. He opened that specific app and read through them.

Good work, shithead. Jacques is pissed as hell about the Reachback. It's managed though, and well worth it. The HazMat sniffer recorded new compounds similar to those it already knew, and the chemical analysts confirmed the reading: Triacetone-triperoxide $[C_9H_{18}O_6]$

Michael's insides tightened at the acronym. *TATP. Big boom kinda shit, and too damned easy to make at home.*

How soon can you get in there and confirm the air reading? The app's cursor blinked at him and emphasized that John awaited his response, so Michael thumb-typed the answer.

I have to wait until Abrini leaves or I know he's asleep. Apartment's too small to sneak in otherwise. At least one of us will be killed or arrested if he confronts me. I need you to check US Terr WL for name: MAHMOUD ALGERI, approx 40YO, French natl. Connected to imam.

The cursor blinked back at Michael for several seconds.

I'll get to it on my end, you do the same. We're short on time. Be thorough but be damned fast. Stay frosty.

Michael closed the app and tried to imagine any other way into Abrini's apartment without first killing or incapacitating him. *I'll need another night to establish his patterns and come up with a way to get rid of Gerard. He'll ruin everything.*

MAY 9, 10:36PM_

The Oremus hotel. Paris, France.

ONCE LOCKED and secure inside his hotel room, Michael completed his nightly *Compline* prayer ritual and poured another double single-malt from the restocked minibar. The peaty liquor lasted only one gulp before Michael set the rocks glass back on the long dresser above the concealed mini fridge. He'd told Gerard he needed to sleep a few hours before coming back before sunrise, but Michael actually wanted to review the balcony cameras and triggerfish data without the cop looking over his shoulder.

He retrieved the intel packet from the overt safe inside the closet and sat at the desk to find a path forward that didn't force him into the kill mission he still feared he couldn't avoid.

While skimming back through the packet for any data or analysis he'd missed or forgotten, Michael logged into his encrypted Wi-Fi camera feeds, which his triggerfish also helped provide, and reviewed the activity captured there. Seeing the apartment lights out at the moment, Michael scrolled backward and realized Abrini had kept the blinds drawn most of the day. *He doesn't want us to see what he's working on.*

He next opened the secure comms app and texted John. *It's probably early afternoon wherever he is, so the old man should be available to provide some guidance here.*

Mere seconds passed before John called him back. "What's the news, shithead? You finished over there yet? I've been waitin' for your damned call."

Michael wished he could laugh at the dry humor. "Not finished yet. Do you have any intel updates?"

"Yep, lemme see." Papers rustled in the background. "Based on the water usage, it looks like there's four to five people living in 105 and 213, even accounting for all the added bathing and washing that prayer ritual requires of compliant Muslims. Can't find anything that associated them with Abrini, though, so it's probably nothing. Don't go makin' friends with 'em just yet, but there's too many other reasons they might wanna keep their man's names under the government radar for us to worry about."

"What about the watchlist?"

"Nothing yet," John continued, "we still don't know for sure if that imam or that Algeri fella's on there or not. Let's see. No help from the postal records. Wherever you set up the triggerfish, it's still working for ya. The desk nerds are looking into which devices are using V-P-N and privacy software, and they think they can use that to tie traffic to his particular apartment. We won't see exactly what he's saying or doing online, but we might know if he goes dark. Don't ask me how they know that shit, I don't got the comprehension or vocabulary for it. I'm old enough that I hafta believe 'em." John paused. "How did you find the apartment, anyway?"

"I got cameras into the interior stairwells, and just got lucky," Michael lied. "Matched the photo in the intel packet to the man going inside." *John can't ever know that I partnered with an outsider, regardless of how well our interests align for the moment.*

"Those aid worker docs came out alright, then. Must've at least bought you the time you needed."

"They let me get out alive, so, they did their job." Michael didn't want to bother with greater detail on his entry and forced exit.

"So, then, the most important info. We know for a fact that he's makin' explosives, T-A-T-P, specifically, but I ain't lookin' to have you arrest him. It helps us confirm we're on the right track, and the cops can use it later to prove his crimes, but it ain't the absolute proof of his true intent. He could be one-a those environmental whackos from the 80s that's gonna blow up a dam somewhere to protest altering the natural path of rivers. We gotta have more, Andrew, it's just that damned simple."

"That's what I'm looking for. Abrini only leaves every few days, and only for about an hour. I don't think that's enough opportunity to get inside the apartment to investigate this, and I don't want to confront him before I know how to proceed."

"How do you already know he only leaves every few days? You ain't had those cameras up that long."

Michael swallowed hard, knowing he'd just screwed up. "That's, well, I guess it's an assumption I'm making based on what I've seen so far. He hasn't left for work, or school, and doesn't have friends or company over, so I thought--"

"You can't go around presentin' your *assumptions* as *facts*, goddammit! That's how shit goes sideways and people get their heads broke for no good reason. We clear on that?"

"I'm sorry, yes, I'm clear."

"Look, I know what it feels like being on your end-a this." John paused and softened his tone. "I also understand how frustrated Jacques was with the sniffer gettin' burned on that Reachback thing. Don't sweat it. Shit happens, and that was much-needed data. Just means he's gotta go out and find another one, that's all. Nobody we care about got hurt. The sniffer will still function, but you can bet the next time it connects with Reachback, they're gonna ping the location to go out and find it. Until you pushed that button, they thought it was destroyed in a commercial fire last year. If I were you, I'd make sure the device settings don't let it connect to anything else, just to be safe. What else you need right now?"

"I just need suggestions on furthering the investigation. If the cops swoop in to arrest him, things might go very badly, but I also can't risk waiting indefinitely for the perfect opportunity to come along."

"In my former life at the 'old shop,' ya might say, I'd have already put rounds in the man's head, just based on the chemical sniffer returns confirming all the allegations against him. That's enough for me to have taken his life. But, in this role, this *new life* I'm tryin' to carve out here, we don't yet got enough to save his soul. *Ironic, ain't it?*"

Michael smirked at the reality. "Different rules of engagement, that's the problem for both of us."

"The thing you gotta keep in mind, Andrew, is that we're not responsible for preventing Abrini from doin' whatever he's gonna do, even though we sure wanna try. All we can do is to make ourselves available for God to use us as tools, however he sees fit. Maybe He's got another plan in motion and we aren't part of it."

Michael paused before asking a personal question of a generally impersonal man. "How would you sleep at night if we're wrong, either way?"

"Same as I've said before. I'm just a gravedigger. I sleep like a baby most nights, except when I don't." John cleared his throat and returned to business. "So, the way I see it, you just gotta keep up a real tight and close surveillance package until Abrini gives you a chance to slip inside and confirm or dismiss the allegations. Good enough?"

Michael nodded his acceptance. "Yep. I'll be in touch."

"Stay frosty, shithead."

The call ended and Michael set the phone beside him on the desk. *I wish I had another double, and I'm also glad I don't.* He stood up and began prepping his gear for the next day's needs. Now that

Gerard had confirmed he'd climbed onto Abrini's balcony without alerting the cop, Michael thought he might get a chance to resolve this inquiry in the coming days. *Nice to know what both the adversary and the accomplice can and can't do. I might still delay my own death or damnation, after all.*

MAY 9, 6:45PM_
8 RUE DE CORBILLON #415. SEINE-SAINT-DENIS, FRANCE.

ABDEL ABRINI SPREAD his map of metropolitan Paris across his writing desk and reviewed the handwritten notes he'd taped in place. Each note showed, in Arabic, the team and approximate detonation time. He scowled at the thought of "approximate," which was an estimate only because he couldn't yet say whether the bombers would detonate on their own, or if his backup timer would send them on to judgement. *I can only see this through by leaving nothing to chance.*

Abdel had even estimated casualty rates and death tolls based on similar events and expected crowd sizes at each of the sites. He'd used his engineering background to identify sites that offered potential secondary detonations, such as a petrol station near the *Champs Élysées* and its predictable fuel tanker deliveries. Abdel celebrated the grand purpose, and simultaneously feared its necessity.

To distract himself and alleviate his apprehension, Abdel started with the estimated detonations and worked his way backward in time until he reached the appointed hour for him to leave his apartment and deliver the backpacks. *Eleven near-simultaneous detonations across the city, and at very specific targets designed to show the superiority of Mohammed, blessings be unto him, over the Jews and Christians who denied his prophecies and conspired for centuries to*

237

fabricate an alternative existence. God punishes nonbelievers, and that fact will again be plain in less than two days' time.

Abdel took a black permanent marker from the desk's belly drawer. Starting from a common starting point to the south and ending at a common terminus to the north, he drew two curved lines to connect the intended detonation sites. A crescent moon appeared, a symbol that signified to Abdel his submission to one true God, free of equals, partners, or companions. *No son, no father, no associate.*

He focused on the final terminus to the north, which had been a recent addition. Having already cut off all communications with both teams of men, neither of which knew about the other, Abdel had only one choice to ensure this final point completed his statement of absolute and unyielding obedience. *Despite my selfish desire for another path forward, I cannot ask these men to martyr themselves while I fear to do so myself. If I am to snuff out these other lives to fulfill my obligations to Allah, then I must also give up my own, as my final and most confident act of faith.* He encircled that north point and smiled. It stood atop his very building and the mosque that corroded its populace like a cancer.

MAY 10, 4:52PM_
LYCÉE PAUL ELUARD. SEINE-SAINT-
DENIS, FRANCE.

GERARD SAT in front of a small bakery, sipped at a subpar espresso, and let an inferior chocolate croissant dry out on his table in the midday sun. He casually watched five targets, all of whom played on the same team in a spirited pick-up soccer game across the street. As their opposing team celebrated a goal, Gerard snapped off a dozen photos of the momentarily downtrodden men. He checked his watch, knowing the game would soon end. He didn't have the resources to follow them away from the field, but he hoped to photograph them conspiring with Abrini. *Well, that's not exactly possible yet. The analysts tracked a phone that received Abrini's message to the modem tied to the address where these assholes live, and now, I have to hope they use the same phone while I'm watching them. None of this can be used in court yet, and they might be friends or relatives without also being conspirators. We won't know shit until someone can get their actual messages.*

He still didn't understand how Andrew's analysts had identified the phone and the apartment. Gerard expected real bad guys to use VPNs and end-to-end encryption, but he hadn't asked a lot of detailed questions and Andrew hadn't offered detailed explanations.

Hell, he probably doesn't know either, which really *means I have nothing to take before a judge.*

He took several telephoto images of the players on the soccer field at the Paul Eluard High School and glanced around to confirm that no one cared. *Parisians are too accustomed to tourists and their cameras.*

brrtbrrt

Gerard saw Sergeant Le'roux was calling. "Antlé."

"You're fucked."

"Thank you, sergeant, how's your day going?"

"Algeri knows you forged the info on the citations. How stupid are you? You couldn't even pull over--"

beepbeep beepbeep

Gerard glanced at the caller-ID screen. "Sorry, that's Algeri calling on the other line, surely with good tidings. I'll call you back." He inhaled a deep breath, braced himself, and switched calls. "Antlé."

"Yes, I know." Algeri's elation was plain in his tone.

"How can I help you, sir?"

"I fear you misunderstood my directives, Inspector. Is it possible that is the case?"

"I'm sorry, sir, which directives are we discussing?"

"The one where you ended the Saint-Denis investigation and helped Sergeant Le'roux. It's the only things we've discussed for at least a month."

"No, sir, you were clear." Gerard picked up his telephoto camera with one hand and snapped a quick half-dozen images of the soccer players. He resisted the temptation to confront Algeri with his presence in Seine-Saint-Denis and demand to know what he'd said to the suspicious imam yesterday.

"Your actions and your taxi citations suggest otherwise."

"What are you talking about?" Gerard tried to assess the man without directly lying to him. "Is there a problem with the citations?"

"Well, either you had a string of terrible luck, or you're the worst forger in French national history. Every piece of defendant and vehicle information was wrong."

"How can that be?"

"Well, if it was one, I'd suggest that a common street criminal duped you because you're an awful investigator. But, for that to happen to one hundred percent of your citations, twenty-five in all, *that* is something else, is it not?"

"I don't know, lieutenant, I--"

"I'm referring the matter to Internal Affairs, Inspector. You're fortunate the defendants' thumb prints all smudged too badly for a comparison, for I suspect they share the same print, do they not?"

"I've never been good at print collection, sir, you can ask anyone around the unit, they'll agree--"

"What do *you* think, Inspector, is the cause of this? I'm interested to hear your thoughts, just to know how stupid you believe me to be."

Gerard nodded, even though Algeri couldn't see him. "I think you have a lot of circumstance and no real evidence, sir, and I'll just wait for the rat squad to call me at their earliest convenience. My number's still on their speed dial, I'm sure."

"Don't act so smug, Antlé. I don't think you'll walk away from this one, not after you answer for where you've been and why none of your citations appear on a single traffic camera anywhere in the city."

Gerard shrugged. *I forgot about that. The devil really is in the details.* "Peace be with you, lieutenant."

His superior scoffed at the similar well-wish common to both their religions. "And peace be also with your spirit, Inspector."

The call disconnected, and Gerard considered his arrest. *I don't have much time. I hope that Father Andrew, or whoever he is--*

brrtbrrt brrtbrrt

The cell phone's caller ID derailed his thoughts. *Claudette never calls when she knows I'm at work.* He held his breath and answered the call. "Is everything all right?"

"No, not at all! You're nothing but a shitty caricature of a man, an

idealized picture of a poster-boy cop that everyone else knows doesn't exist!"

Gerard grimaced. *Bad news travels fast among the cop sewing circles. My people gossip and peck more than old hens.* "So, how's Marie?"

"What?! When the fuck did you start caring about what happens to your daughter? I just got a call from one of the other wives, *and I'm not going to say who,* but I know you're to be investigated and fired for insubordination."

"Well, if that's the case, you know more than anyone. Are you calling to yell, or does Marie need something?"

His wife's sneer came through in her voice. "I thought you might actually turn this around when you moved out, Gerard, but at least you get that in your favor. You got to prove me wrong, yet again."

Claudette continued to berate him, but Gerard tuned her out and focused on capturing usable images of his five targets. *If she gets this anger out on me, maybe she'll be kinder to Marie tonight, or, perhaps, a little less inclined to call that piece of shit that's willing to fuck another man's wife.* Her voice grew shriller as Claudette worked herself into a frenzy.

The scrimmage ended and Gerard's targets congregated together to change out their shoes, collect their belongings, and leave.

"Are you even listening--"

"I have to go, Claudette, I--"

"What?! You have to--"

Gerard ended the call and silenced his ringer. *Let's see where these guys go, and maybe who else they talk to. If I'm flushing everything down the toilet, I need to turn up something worth my career suicide.*

MICHAEL SAT ALONE in the small parking garage office. He alternated between communicating with John, watching Gerard's ten video feeds, and checking on the two Wi-Fi cameras that broadcasted from Abrini's balcony. Despite his efforts and preparations to move into Abrini's apartment at a moment's notice, nothing had changed throughout the day to give him that opportunity. His cell phone alerted him to a new encrypted message from John. Michael unlocked the phone and opened that app.

No help from the postal records. The building's too transient, more than 30 names tied to each apartment, but no one named ABRINI. No one at Postal updates the records as people move out or get deported. I asked for help with the Terr WL from my old cohorts, but they need a few days, and we may not have that much time...

The familiar blinking cursor showed John typing.

Triggerfish is still active, but suspected target went dark four hours ago. The suspect device has been consistent and active since the triggerfish went live. Could be nothing, could mean he's going hot and protecting his op-sec. You're the one on the ground, so your decision. If you're ready to move, you better find a way in the next 12-24. Copy?

Michael replayed John's words in his head. *I know enough to kill him, but not enough to save his soul.* With nothing else to say, he acknowledged the intel: *Copy. Moving.*

The cursor stopped blinking and Michael closed the app. *All on me now, the full and terrible weight of the whole thing, regardless of how it ends. I have more backup than I've had since Silver City, but I still have to trust my gut and my guns more than anything or anyone else.*

He pulled the balcony cameras up on his smartphone, and saw the curtains still blocked almost all his view into the apartment. With only a little more information, or footage of Abrini building an IED, he'd have to consider passing that on to Gerard and letting him evacuate the neighborhood and isolate Abrini. His soul wouldn't be saved that way, but all the lives around him might. Michael's ever-present inner cop accepted that as a positive outcome, so long as he ignored the history of this conflict. *The last time French authorities moved on that building, more than 5,000 rounds went downrange in the middle of the city. That risks every life and limb within a mile, and Abrini might just detonate, anyway.*

Michael exhaled and considered the benefit of his remaining ignorance. *No, I have to stay at the tip of the spear for now. No one's at certain risk but me, and the police can always step in if I fail.*

The *jingle* of keys fumbling in the outer lock announced Gerard's return. He pushed the metal door open, stepped inside, and secured the door behind him. Gerard raised two large brown paper sacks of takeout to show them off. "It's nights like this that I wish *Férme a Table* was real. No one delivers food to this neighborhood at night."

Michael sat up and made a show of locking his phone. He needed Gerard to believe he'd just been reviewing new data. "What are your thoughts on tomorrow?"

Gerard's expression fluctuated, and Michael thought he held something back. *Looks like we both have our secrets.*

"We're out of time, and I fear we must do something bold and immediate."

"What about the consequences to your career?"

The anti-terror cop set the bags on the folding table in front of Michael. "Fuck the consequences. I'd rather stand trial myself than watch the funerals that follow if we do nothing."

"Our cops back home have a saying about that: 'I'd rather be tried by twelve than carried by six.'"

"You get twelve judges?"

"No, one judge and twelve jurors."

"That's terrifying, but I still agree, my friend." Gerard looked tired, maybe even desperate. "Do you have something specific in mind?"

Michael leaned forward and waved the phone to remind the cop of his background assets. "I got an update on the triggerfish data. I don't know how they established the connections, but Abrini's been communicating with at least one group."

Gerard lowered himself into the chair next to Michael. "That's good, that supports our suspicions, and that he's not yet operational."

"Right. It might be one group. It might be members of different groups. You got photos of the soccer players earlier today, right?"

"Yes. What are you thinking?"

"I'm waiting to get the raw data, but the analysts think Abrini has a meeting at one of several locations around the city tomorrow morning. They don't know if he will attend, maybe, maybe not, but they think the soccer players you saw might be meeting with another conspirator, maybe another group, a cut-out, they can't be sure because of the encoded messages."

"And what will you be doing while I'm driving through the Paris traffic?"

"I thought I would be most useful here, to keep an eye on the cameras and apartment building, but, if you prefer, I can go with you? I don't know the city well enough to drive myself, especially if they're trained to detect surveillance--"

"I understand." Gerard looked down at the takeout packages for a moment and absentmindedly moved them around the table. "Alright.

Yes, that makes the most sense, so long as you're confident the information's legitimate."

"I can't say that, not with absolute confidence, but, based on similar communications over the history of counterterror operations, that's what they're thinking right now."

"Yes, well, get me the places and times, and I'll do my part. Just one question." The cop intently looked into Michael's eyes as though searching for deceit. "If I do this and leave you here, and Abrini comes out of the building in a suicide vest, do you have the means of stopping him?"

Michael mulled the question for a moment before realizing Gerard's intent. *He's had to expect that I'm armed. I've already admitted to running an intel op on his soil as a foreign national, so having a gun should be less important.* "Yes. Yes, I do."

"Good." Gerard turned back to the takeout boxes. "If you need something with a greater reach than whatever's tucked in the front of your pants, I keep a rifle hidden on the underside of the desk. I assume you know how to work one."

Michael chuckled at the unexpected statement. "That is a fair assumption."

"As we agreed two days ago, we must trust one another, especially when we find ourselves alone together, yes?"

Michael nodded and swallowed his guilt. "Yes, absolutely. Thanks for dinner. I'm going back to my hotel for a few hours' sleep." He stood, collected his backpack and immediate needs, and shook Gerard's hand.

"Send me the information. God willing, we'll see one another tomorrow. Peace be with you, Andrew."

Michael fabricated a guilt-free smile. "And also with your spirit." *If everything goes really well, or really badly, we'll never see each other again.*

Rural Training Compound. Esmerelda County, Nevada.

AFTER THE DAY'S end at his clandestine southwestern Nevada training compound, John secluded himself at the desk in his room. He chewed through another handful of Tums Smoothies tablets and read over the most recent intel updates on Andrew's Paris investigation. The triggerfish and IMSI devices had proved only that the area was a haven for anti-Western thought and hatred without uncovering specific evidence of Abrini's intent.

John leaned back in the chair, closed his eyes, and massaged his temples. *I can't let Andrew hang himself so damned far out there, not when there's so much death and devastation guaranteed by his failure. He don't seem to mind risking his own life, but I don't like his odds for success on this one. Time to phone a friend.*

He retrieved his cell phone, ensured the VPN was active and functioning, and routed the call through Japan. A long pause ensued after he dialed the number and pressed *Send*.

mmrtmmrt mmrtmmrt

"*Bonjour.*"

"*Bahn-jewr,* yourself. Can you talk?"

"Of course." The man's heavy French accent and reserved tone never changed.

"You're a man who don't fluster easy, and I got some work that needs tendin' to over in your neck-a the woods. Get your go-bag ready and stand to post, I'mma probly need your help *real bad* in the next day, maybe two."

"Where? In Paris?"

"Yep. One of our own is over there workin' an investigation now, and shit's about to turn ugly for 'im. He can use a friend or two, and I'm hopin' you can be that guy."

The operative's voice grew apprehensive and skeptical. "This is, uh, clearly violates our op-sec. Are you certain it's necessary?"

The aging spymaster scowled. "Let me worry about that shit, just as long as you can keep this between us. No reason for anybody else to know about it. At the end-a the day, if the rules keep you from doin' what's right, then what the hell good are they?"

"I could not agree more. May I know now who I'm helping?"

John paused and considered the risk his answer posed if they didn't need Alpha's help. "Andrew. And you're gonna need to pick up some gear there in town. We got a local quartermaster, which you wasn't ever supposed to know about, seeing as how I try to keep you from workin' in your own backyard. I hope you understand the position I'm in."

"I do, and nothing will ever go beyond the four of us."

John grimaced at the truth Alpha pointed out. *Just adding this one man means four of us will have to keep this secret.* "Something you should understand. Remember the training scenario we discussed at camp that night Bartholomew quit?"

A silent moment ticked by. "Yes. We discussed using a sniper to stop an inbound suicide bomber from driving into a crowd in Saint Peter's Square, and that hypothetical need demanded our competence with that weapon system." Alpha inhaled sharply. "*Is that what's happening in Paris, what Andrew is investigating?*"

"'Fraid so. I ain't got time to deliver the same rifle you used back in camp, but my quartermaster's got one local there that oughta get the job done, if it comes to that."

"You should know, first, that I am not in Paris right now. I'm out of the country, in fact, but I can be back in the city by the end of tomorrow. If Andrew requires more urgent help, I'm no good to him. I will make arrangements for an urgent return, but you may wish to call someone else."

John sighed and shook his head in desperation. *There ain't no one else to call.* "We can only do what's possible. I'll send you a quick intel update on what the hell he's got himself into. Keep an eye on the phone. Haul ass home and be safe if you can." John disconnected the call and ran through the travel calculations in his head. *Shit. I can get to Paris before he can. Desperate times might call for desperate measures.*

SEATED atop one of the couch cushions in the middle of the living
room floor, Abdel put the finishing touches on the last backpack
device. He breathed a sigh of relief, grateful he'd completed that task.
*Even with the delays from my ancillary projects, I'm finished more
than twelve hours before the delivery. I now have time to devote my
final hours on earth to prayer and rest.*

He looked up to the writing desk along the west wall and the
piled-up stacks of items that still demanded his attention. Up to this
very moment, the detailed list of nuisance chores had frustrated and
annoyed him. *I've long heard that depressed humans, once committed
to their own mortal demise, experience euphoria they've never known.
I can now attest to its truth.*

Abdel carried the backpack into his bedroom. The bulk of his
chemical glassware remained in place there, as it offered the only true
privacy in his apartment. His production processes had yielded near-
theoretical volumes of triacetone-triperoxide and produced a kilo-
gram more than expected. Rather than add some additional destruction into each of the eleven backpacks, Abdel had chosen to create a
twelfth device. *When I detonate and make my ascension downstairs*

251

in the mosque, this apartment will explode, as well, and deliver God's wrath to all the deserving imposters.

Abdel set the last backpack on the floor alongside the others. In sequence, he opened each backpack, powered on its backup timer, and initiated a synchronized countdown sequence. *The devices can no longer be stopped. Our objective is now inevitable.* He spread the backpacks out in two long columns at the back corner of the bedroom and gently laid his air mattress over them. With an added blanket, they disappeared from sight. *Only a fool would inspect the bed while a clandestine lab and unknown compounds shared the same room.*

He walked from the room and pulled the door closed behind him. Abdel strode back to the desk, opened the laptop, and brought up his stairwell surveillance camera feeds again. *In another two hours, these will no longer matter, and I can destroy the hard drive to protect my contacts.* Bending down to a red, hand-carried toolbox, he retrieved a handsaw and stepped toward the exterior door to finish protecting his divinely inspired work. *Once the apartment is completely secure, no one but Allah himself may stop us.*

MAY 11, 03:02AM_

The Oremus hotel. Paris, France.

WARM SUNLIGHT SHONE on Michael's face while he sat across the picnic table from Merci Renard, the same one where they'd frequently shared MRE lunches, personal stories, and the roller coaster of triumphs and grief that was international aid work.

Michael didn't feel the warmth on his skin, but, somehow, he knew it was there as he spoke with her. "I think of 'compassion' differently than most priests and Catholics. People are best served with a hand *up* rather than a hand *out*. If I can teach people to make and buy their own bread and soup, then they don't need to return to the soup line every day."

"Don't you think it's futile, that our social problems are too great to overcome?"

Her tone suggested doubt, annoyance maybe. Michael didn't recall ever hearing that from her. "I fear that we perpetuate the need with endless giving. We offer momentary comfort to successive generations without ever creating solutions. I think we can do better, but that means doing things differently."

"There's not enough money for soup, Father Michael, so how we can find money for training? People cannot learn on empty stomachs. The rich must always be forced to give."

Michael feared their differing ideologies would eventually come between them, and he had to prevent that without lying to Merci. "Forced giving isn't giving, it's ransom. We mustn't allow government to rob and murder members of one group for the compulsory benefit of another, despite their round-the-clock efforts to monopolize violence."

Merci's voice became accusatory and hateful. "You know *all* about monopolized violence, committed in the name of *your God*, even."

Michael's chest tightened, even though he still couldn't feel the sunlight or summer breeze he knew were there. "I'm not a serial killer."

"*Not yet*, but you soon will be, and I want *nothing to do with you.*"

Michael awoke from the latest in his diverse series of anxiety dreams and longed for the simple versions that had taunted him as a cop. He glanced around the dark and now-familiar Oremus hotel suite, and his eyes settled on the digital clock near his bed. 3:05. Michael rolled over onto his back and stared into the darkness above him. *Why did I have to bring Merci into this?*

He understood the rhetorical answer, that he'd secretly grown and nurtured an excess of admiration for the woman. *Merci will never accept what I'm doing, and she'll totally reject me when she learns the truth. What does that mean for my conscience? Is she right, and I refuse to admit it now that I'm this far down the road?*

Michael threw back the covers, sat up with his feet on the plush carpeting, and began combat breathing to calm his nerves. *Four count in, hold for four, slow four out. Repeat.*

Within four cycles, Michael had reduced his anxiety and stress, despite having no better understanding of how to someday explain this to Merci. *I, as the compassionate priest, am off to kill evil out of sheer kindness and love. This might be the most morally complicated story since Abraham prepared to sacrifice his son to God.*

He donned a pair of charcoal gray Lycra running pants and a lighter gray long-sleeved running shirt. Over that went his hobo outfit: faded black polyester slacks and a thin green wool sweater with numerous holes and stains. Michael put on a pair of black running shoes that didn't fit the homeless attire, but they also didn't stand out. *I need the agility and foot protection today more than I need to run for my life in a pair of broken-down work boots.*

Knowing that he wouldn't sleep well last night, Michael had stayed up late to prepare all his various kit for the day. After a brief inventory confirmed he hadn't forgotten anything, he donned the military fatigue jacket and his backpack. He double-checked the tranquilizer gun and extra darts. Despite the varied weaponry in the concealed safe, Michael again only took the suppressed .22 and both extra magazines as his lethal cover. *I don't expect high-volume or long-range trouble today. All my problems should be within arm's reach, and plenty close enough to kill me back.*

A light, unexpected knock sounded at the door. He stepped over and peered out the peephole, which revealed Jacques standing across the narrow hallway. Michael racked his brain for anything else he'd asked of the man but came up empty. Jacques had come through with everything he needed, but that didn't equate to absolute trust.

"Yeah?" He watched Jacques lean close to the door to be heard without disturbing the other guests.

"I have a car waiting for you, sir, as this is quite an early start today. You are, of course, welcome to take the Metro after it re-opens at 4:30."

"I'll be right down, thank you."

"Very good, sir." Jacques strode out of sight, and Michael now wished he'd just opened the door and talked with him. *Oh, well. Without paranoia, I might not live long enough to suffer my regrets.*

He walked back toward the bed where his gear sat and stopped midstride when a rhetorical question suddenly emerged. *How did Jacques know I needed a ride, or that I had such an early start?* Michael rescanned the room for surveillance equipment, but soon abandoned the pointless effort in favor of making final preparations. *The room's either bugged or John made some assumptions and called him. I don't have the luxury of being inquisitive right now, so I have to settle for being grateful.*

Within minutes he stepped into the empty hallway and checked his watch. 3:19. *I should just now be rolling out of bed, and I already have a ride. Things are looking up.* Michael hustled away from his room and considered the possibility that he might never again set foot into the hotel. *If things go completely sideways, Jacques can send my stuff to John, but it'll probably just get destroyed or stockpiled for the next guy that needs it. If this is my end, I hope the replacement's blessed with better luck.*

As though accustomed to treating eccentric and unusual guests with non-judgmental discretion, the shuttle driver hadn't appeared to notice Michael's homeless appearance. He'd traded messages with John on the ride over, which revealed the intel analysts had no new information and the electronic devices thought to be associated with Abrini remained dark. The lack of early morning traffic allowed the unmarked hotel shuttle to drop Michael five blocks from his target twenty-four minutes after departing The Oremus.

As Michael plodded along *Boulevard Carnot* in his hobo character, the abandoned street allowed him to stew in his thoughts. He feared that his own assumption of an imminent attack would cloud his judgement, especially if he only uncovered probable cause evidence inside Abrini's apartment but didn't breach the "beyond a reasonable doubt" threshold. *I need irrefutable and absolute, not BARD, anyway.*

He reached the intersection with *Rue de Corbillon* and again trudged toward the Islamic school. *Still no better perch to see Abrini's place, and I can't move onto his roof without first making sure he's not having a slumber party with his conspirators and friends.* Although the cameras still provided a view from Abrini's balcony, their effectiveness had been largely defeated by curtains so Michael couldn't rely on them for such vital intel.

Once he reached the top level of the fire escape, Michael retrieved his binoculars from the gray backpack and scanned the heat signature inside Abrini's apartment. *He's laying by the door. Weird place to sleep, unless you're paranoid about boogeymen coming up the stairs to get you in the middle of the night. That means I don't have a choice. I have to go in through the windows.*

His apprehension again elevated, and Michael lowered the binos and scolded himself. *On its face, this should be the easiest assignment conceivable, from both a logistics and moral perspective. If we could just tell Gerard what I know, he and his goon squad could pull the neighbors out of the building, use a single round to expose Abrini's gray matter to sunlight, and go collect the evidence with a damned robot until they know it's safe to send investigators inside the apartment. I'm tasked with ending the life of a terrorist, and I know he's a terrorist, in my heart and in my head, but I can't prove it in court yet. If putting him down makes me a serial killer, then so be it. I have to get over that arbitrary title.* He sighed and brought the binos back up to his eyes. *Every man's gotta be something, I guess.*

brrtbrrt

Michael retrieved his work cell from the fatigue jacket's internal pocket and saw Gerard had sent a message to his anonymous Google Voice number. The phone's constant VPN ensured the cop had no way to identify him or his actual position despite the communication link between them.

Couldn't sleep. In position early, waiting patiently."

Michael didn't reply. *Not yet. Let him think I'm not yet out and about. He's gotta stay away from here, or the cop will complicate the hell outta this.* A notification at the top of the screen showed he had an unread, encrypted message. *How did I miss that?*

A message from John populated the screen: *Alpha inbound to help. Meet at your hotel in two hours.*

Michael shook his head and typed his response. *Goddammit, John, too little, too late. On the roof, about to make entry. Send him to this area to standby. Give me his app ID so I can make contact if I need him. He should keep a low profile. This neighborhood isn't the welcoming kind.*

Almost a minute passed. *Copy all. Be safe, notify me with progress.*

Michael put the phone away. *Why did John wait until now to send the backup I've spent months begging for?* Returning his focus back to the entry and investigation, he scanned the apartments on the west side of the building and waited until most everyone's heat signatures showed they'd retired for the night. *I still don't understand why the east half of the building is dark. No time to find out.*

Although Michael expected to find a few people out between the two morning prayers, he hoped his hobo-beggar disguise would again repel their potential interest. He descended the fire escape and stayed close to the wall to limit the creaking its rusting metal produced. *I'll be back up on Abrini's roof before sunrise, and sneak in after the morning prayers while all his neighbors are asleep. I still have no idea how I'll get inside to investigate without putting a toe tag on at least one of us.* The unusual lack of operational detail filled his chest with anxiety. *Planning's out the window, so we'll just have to do it live...*

MAY 11, 07:04AM_

Saint Ferdinand Bus Station. Argenteuil, France.

HIDDEN AMONG OTHER PARKED VEHICLES, Gerard sat in one of the unmarked police sedans he'd "borrowed" for his rogue assignment and watched a city bus stop just a few dozen yards away. He sipped coffee from a large paper takeaway cup and tried to set it back in the car's center cupholder. When he felt an obstruction, he glanced down and found the culprit. One quick swat flung the end of the car's unplugged GPS power cable onto the passenger floorboard. *Algeri might be ready to take my job and my badge, but he'll have to find me first. They're not getting their guns or their car back until I say so.*

Pedestrian traffic ebbed and flowed around him. Everything appeared normal, and Gerard didn't recognize anyone. He glanced back at the list of possible locations and times that Andrew's unknown covert organization thought the bombers might meet today. He hadn't offered much context or explanation for the intel, and Andrew had only asked Gerard to devote several hours today to surveilling these spots for Abrini and his known associates.

As the surrounding traffic and crowds thinned again, he retrieved his smartphone and opened his remote access to the ten camera feeds around Abrini's building. He hadn't checked them for the last thirty minutes, so Gerard scrolled backward through two of the interior stairwell feeds to ensure their target still remained inside. *Just the fact that he never leaves should be enough to kick the door and demand some goddamned answers. Who lives like that, other than some kind of psychopath?*

Gerard looked down at the far side of the front passenger seat and the gray nylon rifle case partially hidden there between the seat and the door. He remembered the trouble he and his clandestine teammates had shouldered to sneak his weapon system back into France from the Middle East. The weapon had proved too hard to leave behind when his service ended, so it now lived with a former squad mate on his farm outside Paris. *I may no longer have the support of a wife and daughter, but my military family supports me without question. Even keeping each other's secret treasures hidden is an easy thing to do.* Gerard and his rifle had saved dozens, perhaps hundreds of his countrymen and NATO partners, and he briefly held a longshot record that the American sniper Chris Kyle shattered within days.

His mind wondered back to his only separation from the rifle in the last fifteen years. His squad had run short that day and he'd been on point by himself. The rest of his mates were almost a mile behind him in the Afghan wilderness when eight Taliban soldiers ambushed him just before dawn. *I hadn't given them enough credit, and I paid for it.* With the choice of certain suicide and surrender, he'd chosen the latter. They took everything from him, stripped him naked, bound his wrists, and bagged his head before forcing him to march across the snow, ice, and rocky high-mountain terrain. By the time they stopped and took him into a cave, Gerard knew he approached hypothermia.

Surprisingly, they built him a small dedicated warming fire that his addled mind didn't recognize for the next hour. When the memory returned, Gerard felt like someone had slapped his head from the inside. Several months prior to his capture, another squad had recovered the bodies of three NATO POWs that had been stripped naked and executed next to a small fire. The propaganda video had emerged online a few hours later. *The animals kept me alive to make me productive for their cause.* Gerard had assumed they didn't have stage lighting and electricity in their goddamned cave, which meant they needed bright morning sunlight to showcase their handiwork. With the bag over his head and his wrists still bound together, Gerard huddled naked next to the fire, feigned sleep, and listened for his opportunity. *I might freeze to death out there, and I might be shot in the back running away, but my family won't ever witness my murder.*

The enemy's movement and dialogue established they kept a thin patrol and rotated every few hours. Long after the cave around him fell silent and Gerard had counted to six thousand, he finally risked removing the bag. He looked around for the first time in almost a day. Reduced to embers, the fire still cast a faint red glow onto the nearby rock walls and ceiling. A black abyss stood before him, and faint moonlight called him to climb a steep ascent behind him. He'd been so near death that Gerard had no memory of climbing down into the cave. A bright harvest moon guided him back outside and facilitated his escape through the wilderness. His NATO comrades found him less than a mile away, saved *his* life, and then took those of everyone who'd held him captive. By the time bright sunlight again shone on Afghanistan, his tormenters laid stiff in their own blood and Gerard had both his rifles back.

He chased the memory away and glanced around his present-day environment. Although prepared for whatever lay ahead today, Gerard prayed the need didn't come to pass. *I'll take the shot on Abrini if I must, even with what little I know, and there will be consequences for it. If I only had some objective confirmation of what Abrini is doing inside the apartment, I could again take lifesaving action.* He inhaled a deep breath. *I must choose between facing a trial in the Assize Courts before nine citizens and three judges or watching the hundreds of funerals my* inaction *will bring. That's no choice for any man to make.*

Gerard watched the bus stop until 7:45, when he had to move on to the next location. He drove away more confused by the errand but terrified of missing something developed from data the bombers themselves had unknowingly provided.

MAY 11, 07:37AM_
8 RUE DE CORBILLON. SEINE-SAINT-
DENIS, FRANCE.

BENEATH MICHAEL, the white tar roof of Abrini's building quickly warmed in the morning sun. He laid within six feet of the northern ledge and above Abrini's windows and balcony. Although he'd covered himself and his gear with a white mesh cloth, Michael moved as slow and seldom as he could tolerate to avoid attention from the neighboring buildings. *Only two are tall enough to see me, but I can't afford to get sloppy now.*

A quick check of the Wi-Fi camera feed confirmed the battery in one had died and other had only minutes to live. Michael's only view into Abrini's apartment came from the eastern camera that showed part of the living area, the kitchen, and the back of the front door. *Right where Abrini slept last night.* The target was off camera at the moment. As the device's low battery warning flashed in his screen's upper right corner, Michael prayed it would last long enough.

Abrini, naked and with a bath towel in hand, walked into view from the east, stepped into the bathroom, and closed the door behind him. *I have to go now!*

Michael replaced the work phone in his internal jacket pocket, slid his arms back through his backpack straps, and hurried to the edge of the roof. Just as before, he swung his legs out, lowered himself until he just touched the balcony's railing, and used a barely controlled fall to descend the last four feet. Michael landed with a familiar, soft *thud* and hustled to open the window and sneak inside before Abrini or anyone in the lower apartments came out to investigate.

The bathroom door suddenly opened and Abrini, still naked, stepped out. With nowhere to hide, Michael simply froze. His target took three steps out into the living area before looking up. Abrini's eyes widened in surprise, and both men stared at each other for the full second their respective minds required to identify, decide, and react to the threat before them.

Abrini lunged back toward the kitchen as Michael shoved the vertical windowpane up. It opened only six inches and firmly jammed in the frame. He was stuck outside with no escape, and the sounds of urgent, desperate fumbling came from the kitchen. Michael threw back his outer clothing as Abrini reappeared with an AK-style rifle in his hands. He brought it up to his shoulder and Michael knelt before the window frame and drew his concealed tranquilizer gun from its holster at this right hip.

Time slowed as Michael's brain analyzed the situation in detail only capable when it perceived imminent death. Abrini raised the rifle and Michael struggled to get his inferior darts deployed in time. The AK's barrel leveled at Michael's head from a distance of no more than eight feet. *He can't miss from there!*

click

Michael recognized the rifle's misfire and immediately shot all three tranquilizer darts into Abrini.

thuhthuhthuh

The darts struck his target's center-mass, near the man's lower ribcage and diaphragm. Abrini staggered back a step, likely from the realization he'd been hit, and fear overcame him. While the anesthetic darts dangled from his midsection, he lowered the rifle and frantically worked the bolt carrier to make the gun function. A single round of ammunition ejected from the chamber and *tinked* onto the floor as Abrini's movements grew lethargic. Abrini dropped to one knee but continued to try making the gun work.

Michael had no chance to get inside the window, so he huddled beneath the frame and struggled to retrieve the extra darts from his backpack while begging for divine intervention.

click

A second, much louder misfire.

thuTHUD

Michael glanced over the bottom of the window frame. Abrini and the rifle were both down on the floor. He leapt up, shimmied the jammed window side-to-side until it opened farther, and urgently scampered inside. Bear crawling on all fours, Michael hurried over, took control of the rifle, stood up, and stepped back from the sedated man. He kept the dysfunctional weapon pointed at the outer block walls in case it went off. *I've never had to dart anyone three times, but he should start waking up in about thirty minutes, probably coherent in an hour or so. Gotta keep an eye on his pulse and breathing while I get him restrained.*

thump thump thump

"Hady! 'atfali nayimun!"

Michael didn't understand the man's words shouted up through the floor, but the intent was obvious. He imagined the father standing below him in their kitchen with a broom in his hands and a scowl on his face. *Hopefully, the renewed silence is enough to appease him.*

After setting the rifle across the small stovetop and reloading his tranquilizer gun, Michael took several minutes to assess his most immediate priorities and allowed himself repeated deep breathing cycles. *The neighbors aren't storming up to protest or save Abrini, so I can go hunt the irrefutable evidence I need. Abrini has no reason to tie me to the Church, so, if I don't find what I need to move forward with a clear conscience, I could just open the front door, walk out, and leave everything in Gerard's hands.*

Michael checked his watch and pulled a pair of medical exam

gloves from his pants pocket. Only then did he realize the bedroom door was closed. *First things first. Time to tie up the naked guy.*

AFTER SECURING Abrini in the custom nylon restraints constructed for Michael and his fellow Absolvers, he'd drawn the apartment's curtains closed and conducted a slow, methodical search. Since getting the Reachback return that alleged Abrini had an unknown quantity of the explosive compound triacetone-triperoxide in his apartment, Michael had studied the explosive enough to reduce the probability of initiating an accidental detonation.

A quick, periodic check of Abrini's pulse and breathing again confirmed he remained among the living. Michael has first swept the kitchen and living room with the chemical sniffer, which again directly reported the compound's presence this time. *That's both unsettling and reassuring that the device didn't need secondary confirmation from Reachback. The TATP must be much more prevalent* inside *the apartment than it was at the window two days ago.*

With Abrini and his rifle now incapable of causing harm, Michael devoted his attention to the contents inside the dwelling. Starting in the kitchen, his second sweep was a hand search. He donned medical exam gloves and worked to uncover the source of a light, fruit smell that permeated the space. *Despite my need for irrefutable proof, I'd still rather find overripe plums than a highly volatile explosive.*

The nature of TATP demanded that Michael proceed cautiously and inspect everything by sight before touching or moving it. He reminded himself of what he'd read about the chemical and his need to stay focused and deliberate. *A white crystalline powder that usually smells like bleach when mixed, or fruit when it's nearly pure. Heat, friction, U-V rays, static electricity, or shock all act as a trigger, so yanking open a drawer can detonate any powder caught in the cabinet frame. Slow and steady survives the race today.*

Michael took thirty minutes to examine the living room and kitchen. Moving clockwise inside the small home, he discovered a pistol in a drawer in the writing desk but found nothing else incriminating. Michael stood in front of the closed bedroom door and debated how to proceed. He looked back at Abrini. *Still out. I can either wait until he revives, or risk the door being rigged. That could be why he slept on the kitchen floor last night.* He steeled himself to continue. *No logical reason for him to boobytrap the door while he's still living here. He did just walk out of the bedroom right before he tried to murder me.*

Michael inhaled a deep breath, slowly turned the knob with his gloved hand, and waited. *Nothing.* He moved outside the door frame, next to the handle, and apprehensively pushed it open several inches. Even from his limited view into the darkened room, a dozen dark brown gallon-size glass jugs sat on the floor next to a raised twin mattress. A blue and green quilt neatly covered the bed and fell just above the floor. The jugs' labels had been roughly torn off, and he couldn't read any compound names from the doorway or determine how full the jugs remained. Michael expected that had been Abrini's intent.

As he pushed the door open a little farther and stepped into the doorframe, light from the living room spread further into the bedroom and revealed an elaborate chemistry set along the room's north wall, right in front of the doorway. As the much-feared fruit smell strengthened, every ounce of Michael's apprehension returned.

"What the hell..."

Michael understood Abrini had used the room's long dresser as a laboratory workspace. Light green rubber hoses connected three Bunsen burners to camp stove propane tanks. Tall metal stands elevated several different beakers and a round-bottom flask over the burners. Even though he saw and heard no flames or the hiss of escaping gas, Michael inhaled a deep breath through his nose to deliberately search the air for the rotten egg olfactant routinely mixed with naturally odorless propane. *Nothing but fruit.* A two-liter graduated cylinder sat at the far end of the dresser and white powder filled in its bottom third. *If that's the finished product, that's enough TATP to blow this whole floor apart.* The box of assorted lab equipment he'd previously seen in the kitchen now sat in the back left corner of the bedroom next to the dresser.

Michael remembered enough from his hazardous materials classes with the Silver City Police Department to fear proceeding farther into the room. *The biggest lesson I learned was that my body has natural defense mechanisms to fight radiation exposure, but no such protection against chemical hazards and explosives. One bad whiff, or drop, or granule, and I could end up D-R-T.*

Without knowing what specific dangers he faced, Michael couldn't know if he stood a greater risk in closing the door back and allowing fumes to build inside the room, or leaving it open to risk inhaling greater amounts of whatever remained inside the large beakers and graduated cylinders. *That's definitely the fruit-smell source, and probably the TATP, so I can mitigate that somewhat, but I have no idea what else is in there.*

Although Michael would have preferred to find an assembled and intact IED before proceeding with Abrini's final absolution, he feared intruding into the bedroom put everyone else in the building at risk. *I'll have to go forward with 'good enough.' This is well more than what I'd need to convict the guy in a reasonable court of law, especially when you combine it with what we know of his isolation, the pseudonym, the shipments, and his online and communications behavior. All these straws of information and fact, when taken and considered together, form something far more substantial than their mere sum.*

Placing his faith in Abrini's assumed desire to live through most of the day, Michael carefully closed the door and hoped his target had reasonably done so from greater information than Michael had at the moment. Even though the French police, hazmat, and bomb crews needed to control the apartment building as soon as possible, Michael had to delay his call to Gerard until Abrini chose his eternity. *I don't know French rules of evidence, so if I called the cops in now, Abrini might walk away from the court process and repeat his efforts somewhere else with better op-sec and a different result. At least I got to him before he assembled or dispersed any devices.*

Michael rechecked his watch and stepped over to evaluate Abrini's vitals. The man's pulse and breathing continued to improve on their own. *Once he wakes up and decides on his forever, I can make a better-informed decision. If he refuses to play along, I'll walk away in about an hour and transfer the responsibility of this shit storm to the French police.*

GERARD SAT in his unmarked police sedan and impatiently watched a soccer field in a suburb east of the *Université Paris*. He compared the few men gathered there against the photos of his current suspects, but none of them matched. Only one player on the field even appeared to be Middle Eastern.

Even though Andrew had told him the soccer players he hoped to find were probably cooperating with Abrini, he'd never explained the raw data that supported that conclusion. *He'd only offered that the conclusion came from analyzing the triggerfish data.* Gerard disliked that nothing he knew or suspected could be used as evidence in the French courts, but it did put him in a position to gather evidence he could use. *I don't even have an accusation, really. I've got an unknown form of digital voodoo and nothing more.*

The alleged conspirators and potential bombers played on a soccer team together, and Gerard expected that allowed them a benign reason to meet others and be seen together. *Abrini probably hopes their acquaintance with one another will propel them to success and follow-through. An isolated mind has too much time and space to wander. Teammates, however, can convince you to move forward, even against your own reason and doubt.*

Gerard scanned his surroundings for several minutes, but no one else approached the fields. He rechecked his watch and found he would soon have to move to the next potential meet-up.

Andrew's intel seemed accurate up to this point, so Gerard felt compelled to investigate the leads his impromptu partner's analysts had generated. However, in a few short minutes, this location would become the third miss of the morning. Andrew never explained why his analysts couldn't better define the group's intended meet-up location and time. *Now that I think about it, I'm the one who offered the possible explanation for the uncertainty. Andrew had only agreed with me. Dammit!*

Gerard hammer-fisted the top of the steering wheel and swore at himself. *What the fuck does this mean? Am I chasing bad intel and shitty analysis, or did that asshole send me off on a make-believe assignment?* He hated having been so desperate for help and vindication that he hadn't seriously doubted the plan until this moment. *Something's wrong. I fear I'm out of time to identify the cause, and terrified that I might have allowed myself to become a useful idiot to fulfill another man's ulterior motive.*

He retrieved his cell from the center console, logged into the camera feeds, and urgently scanned the two most relevant views. *Nothing yet. Abrini hasn't left the apartment and he damned sure didn't leap out the window. I have to go back and get to the bottom of this!* Gerard started the sedan, slammed it into drive, and hurried toward the now-distant parking garage.

8 RUE DE CORBILLON #415. SEINE-
SAINT-DENIS, FRANCE.

DRESSED in a black cassock and stark white collarino he'd brought along in his backpack, Michael sat at Abrini's writing desk and watched his laptop force-copy the bomber's computer and external hard drive. He looked the part of a typical parish priest and hoped his subject recognized the authority God had instilled in him to aid the man's transition.

For the moment, Michael focused on collecting electronic evidence while he awaited Abrini's revival. *There's gotta be something in here John's analysts can use to identify and track his conspirators. Even if Abrini defies my expectations, humbles himself before God, and submits to my Catholic dogma, I'd wager there's still no chance he gives up anyone else involved. Whoever he knows on the soccer team are still ghosts, and we need to find them, even if we use the French police to do so.*

"Hhhmmff..."

Michael looked at the kitchen floor to his left where Abrini lightly shifted his limbs against the nylon restraints. A glance at his watch confirmed the third dart had been more effective than Michael expected. *Just glad his vitals stayed up on their own. I'd prefer to avoid tranq'ing another man to death if I can avoid it.*

He rose from the chair, strode quietly into the kitchen, and stood over Abrini, who laid nearly flat on his back in a modified, crab-like position. His eyes remained closed, but the man steadily emerged from sedation. Michael knelt next to him and rechecked the restraints; they had to be tight enough to hold him in a weak position, but loose enough to not restrict circulation or leave bruises that might compel a coroner to label his death as suspicious or, worse, homicide.

Modeled after those used in hospitals and emergency rooms, the restraints confined Abrini by limiting his movement and denying him use of his strongest muscle groups. His arms were bent with his elbows above his head and his hands behind his neck. His legs, also bent, placed his knees above his hips, which were rotated out so that each foot was nearly sideways in front of his groin. Two straps secured Abrini's appendages, crossed his torso behind his back, and tied together there. The strap that secured his right elbow and wrist passed behind his back, over his left outer ribcage, and ended at his right ankle and knee. The other limited use of his left limbs and passed over the man's right outer ribcage.

Not unlike the mechanical principle behind crucifixions, any effort Abrini put into extending one limb collapsed another. Additionally, he could only maneuver smaller, weak muscle groups to prevent circulation loss to his extremities. Abrini could not sit up, roll to one side, or make use of any large movement to escape or resist.

Unlike with his last absolution in Vienna, Michael needed to prevent Abrini from shouting for help which likely stood as close as the next apartment. Now that he began regaining consciousness and easily breathed on his own, Michael stuffed a thick wool sock in Abrini's mouth and pulled a tight balaclava on backwards over his head. He returned to the writing desk and checked on the computer's progress. *Now we just wait until he's coherent.*

Michael had completed everything he thought possible to help Abrini ascend to judgement with a clear conscience. With most of the building's occupants asleep, little noise invaded the apartment beyond the light traffic from *Boulevard Carnot* to the north. Left idle in the quiet with his thoughts, especially his fear and dread at what Abrini's expected reaction meant for his soul, Michael again pondered his purpose. *Am I here to save men from themselves, or to confirm the choice that God already believes they've made about where to spend their eternity?*

Despite his rational understanding that God may have known he couldn't save either of his previous targets from damnation, Michael considered a darker paradigm: a vengeful God who denied His own children the potential to live at his side. *No, that isn't possible. Only Abrini can save himself, and I wouldn't ever be sent on a kill mission. I have to believe that.* With no ability to collect further evidence, Michael bowed his head and prayed his morning liturgy recitation.

A half-hour passed before Abrini's muffled voice and attempted movements became continuous and indicated his coherence. Michael stood up from the desk chair and paused. *Did John or the intel say anything about him speaking English? This might be more difficult and desperate than I've even imagined.* He took in a deep breath and reminded himself of Saint Francis of Assisi's long-ago advice to his friars. *Preach the Gospel with all your might. If necessary, use words.*

Michael retrieved and donned a pair of medical exam gloves from the desktop and walked back over to Abrini. He knelt beside him, and the man struggled against the restraints. Michael carefully removed the balaclava and sock, which had been Abrini's only clothing.

Abrini blinked hard several times at the sudden light, and he stared at Michael with an even mix of fear and rage. *"Min 'ant?"*

Michael could only infer the context of his question. "I'm Father Andrew. Do you speak English?"

Abrini's eyes shifted to Michael's garb for several long seconds before returning to his face. "Of course. Who are you?"

"I'm here because God sent me to absolve your soul of its sins. I understand that you wish to ascend to heaven, and I intend to help you do that."

His eyes narrowed with anger. "Release me, and I'll do it myself. I can even make you the same offer, priest."

Michael smirked at the man's dark rhetoric. "No, thank you, our methods might be too different. Do you believe in fate, Abdel?"

Abrini's eyes widened at his first name, but only for a moment. "If you know anything of Islam, you know fate is a core foundation of my faith and obedience. Why are you here? What do you want?"

Michael ignored the questions for a moment. "I, too, believe in something akin to fate, but tempered with free will. Catholicism and Islam have much in common, and the Catechism of my religion specifically acknowledges the importance of Muslims. The Qur'an acknowledges the importance of Jesus Christ as a prophet of God, and that his return to earth is a vital and assured eventuality.

"I am here, Abdel, because our fates and free will are entwined. We depend on one another for salvation. You cannot ascend to heaven without my help to absolve your sins, and I will likely not ascend there myself if I do not secure your absolution. What I mean is that your body *will* die today, but not of your own direct hand. I offer to help you save your soul from the same fate."

"You are here to murder me."

Michael shook his head and smiled pleasantly. "No, I am here to *save* you. If you *want* to be saved. That choice is yours alone, however, and no one else can make it for you. Your physical death is imminent, therefore, so is your judgement. Do you wish me to take your confession and deliver Reconciliation and Last Rites, or do you wish to make this spiritual transition without my help?"

Abrini looked past Michael and stared at the ceiling. Several long minutes silently passed between them before the subject spoke. "I fear you are right. God must have willed this. There is no other reason you, a nonbeliever, could have bested and humiliated me in such a manner. For Allah to allow you to do so, it can only be that I have done wrong, and am no longer in His graces. What is your intent, priest?"

Michael consciously closed his mouth and shook off his surprise. "I, uh, *intend* to lead you through the Reconciliation ritual, hear your confession, absolve your soul, and send you on to your judgement while your spirit remains free and clear of its mortal sins."

"'Nothing shall ever happen to us except what Allah has ordained. He is our *Maula*. And in Allah let the believers put their trust.' If He's presented you and your rituals in this manner, then I must acknowledge this, too, is God's will for me to comply. Or, perhaps," Abrini paused and nodded, "it could be a final test of my dedication.

"It is His divine right to be inconsistent," Abrini continued, "for absolute consistency limits His divine and limitless power and authority over us, his devoted and loyal subjects. Even without known cause or reason, he can say or do the complete opposite of anything else He's done or decreed. Allah explained this himself, by the gift of allowing us to understand his nullifications."

Michael sat by and watched Abrini work through his intrinsic philosophical debate.

"The *qadar* dictated by the Qur'an, the destiny that Allah has laid before each of us, my faith in that flawless, divine fate compels me to accept that this moment, our interaction, and even our relative positions of power and leverage are meant to be."

Michael couldn't allow Abrini's rigid understanding of fate to stand unchallenged, as it negated free will and the responsibility or rejoicing that followed mankind's actions and decisions. *This isn't the time for a theological debate, but there's no point if Abrini feels compelled to go along with the rituals.* "You do understand, Abdel, that your fate isn't predetermined, and you *do* have a choice in absolving your soul of its sins?"

"History shows that Mohammed, peace be upon him, initially feared the revelations Allah sent him through the angel Gabriel, and that his first wife's cousin, named *Waraqa*, a Christian, confirmed the authenticity of his prophecies. Without that Christian, Mohammed might never have fulfilled his divine purpose. Likewise, I must then concede the irony that Allah chose you and your faith to help me fulfill mine." A wide smile spread across Abrini's face. "It is most pleasing to consider that I will have direct commonality with Allah's last prophet."

Michael responded by reciting section 841 of the Catechism of the Catholic Church from memory. "The plan of salvation also includes those who acknowledge the Creator, in the first place among them are the Muslims, who profess to hold the faith of Abraham; together with us they adore the one, merciful God, mankind's judge on the last day.'

"As such," Michael continued, "I want to be very clear. I'm not asking you to denounce your faith. We both believe in the one, merciful, and loving God."

Abrini wryly smiled and nodded toward the nylon restraints. "The death sentence demanded for abandoning my faith does not concern me at this moment, Father Andrew. I am concerned only with assuring my salvation. The pleasures of heaven await me, and it's imperative I accept this opportunity to avoid the horrific, torturous dungeon that is hell."

Michael nodded at the man's gallows humor. "I appreciate your candor."

"I choose to believe God does not doubt my dedication and faith, so, it must be that my mind has gone astray of where my heart would have led it. Proceed with your absolution, Father Andrew. Help restore me to my righteous place in God's kingdom."

Despite his elation at the man's potential salvation, Michael had to confirm his genuine intent. "What's in the bedroom, Abdel?"

"You must know."

"I know you acquired the precursors for T-A-T-P. Is that the final product, there in the bedroom?"

"Yes."

"Is that everything you produced?"

A curious grin crossed his lips for a moment. "Yes. All the explosive I made is now in the bedroom, that is true."

Tremendous relief washed over Michael and calmed his fears. *I worried so much about absolving this man, and wrongly assumed that guiding him through Reconciliation would be pointless and, ironically, fated to fail.* Michael bowed his head and closed his eyes to begin the ritual of hearing Abrini's confession and reconciling his sins.

"How different are we, you and I," Abrini interrupted, "both of us willing to kill for our faith, for our beliefs, and for the God we serve? You're here to punish me for the way I've lived my life, and I came here to punish hundreds and influence millions for the same end. Please, proceed, Father, but take your time. This is our only chance to get this right."

Michael crossed himself as he again bowed his head, grateful to have the man's unexpected compliance. *This should be the most impossible sell I've ever made, but his acceptance and paradigm guide him to absolve himself of his wrongs.* An unsettling question appeared before him. *What if Abdel submits to Reconciliation, converts, and expresses his heart's desire to live a peaceful life as a disciple of Christ? How can I then possibly deny him the rebirth assured us through baptism?*

MAY 11, 10:14AM_

Jamaeat min Al-khadam Mosque. Paris, France.

IMAM ABDUL SIDDIQI had spent the last week preparing his humble re-purposed mosque to welcome today's guests. Although he always strove to make sure the small former halal market pleasantly welcomed all who entered, guest and flock alike, Abdul had devoted much of his recent time and effort to that purpose. Today was that important, not just to him and his neighborhood, but to the whole of Muslims throughout France, and, really, all of Europe. *The flyer I sent the neighborhood drew quite a crowd. I am blessed and humbled to lead such a devoted and faithful congregation.*

Abdul and his local elders greeted their guests, which included another twenty-nine imams from across France. The call to *dhuhr,* the second mandated prayer of the day, sounded through the tinny loudspeaker above the mosque's entrance. With only five minutes left, Abdul merged in with his flock, ritualistically washed himself, and entered his tiny prayer hall as the projected recitation ended.

Today's short prayer and unusual Saturday sermon were intended to begin the great and difficult work that lay ahead of everyone.

After reaching the pulpit, Abdul turned to face his audience, which now spilled well outside the prayer space, into the narrow hall, and beyond the entrance. Where dozens normally stood, even for Friday prayers, hundreds now squeezed together. Their quiet energy and optimism electrified Abdul, and he prayed for words to explain the moment before them.

"My brothers and sisters," he announced in Arabic. "I cannot possibly overstate the significance of why we've gathered here today, and what we wish God to accomplish through us." Abdul stopped every few sentences and repeated his words in French.

"Today, through our collective and individual efforts, we will publicly, loudly, and adamantly proclaim for all to hear that our faith, the beauty and tolerance of Islam, has been hijacked. We denounce the violent few who degrade our faith to advance terror and the subjugation of other peoples and cultures. We pray for the global reformation of God's word and our faith and service to Him.

"The imams gathered among us today have all signed an open letter that I delivered yesterday to our national newspaper, *Le Monde*. It bore thirty signatures, and we invite anyone else to add theirs, regardless of your position in our community. We pray to establish secularism alongside Islam in France, and throughout Europe with the rest of our faithful. No longer will we sit idle while barbarians murder under the guise of our faith. No longer will we ignore the necessary reformation of the early suras of the Qur'an."

Abdul paused and stretched his arms out toward his audience. "First, let us pray together."

MAY 11, 10:14AM_

Cluny La Sorbonne Metro Station. Paris, France.

ASAD MAH'MOUD ALI had stopped pacing. His comrades leaned against the handrailing just outside the Metro subway station stairs and waited. Unlike most everyone their age, none of them held smartphones. In fact, none of them had a phone, identification, or personal effects of any kind.

Just as Imam Abrini had ordered, the five men wore soccer jerseys to impersonate supporters of the Paris-Saint-Germain Football Club, a team scheduled to compete against another *Liga 1* rival, FC Toulouse, at 3:00pm. Asad pointlessly rechecked his watch. Their group should have arrived at the *Porte d'Auteuil* station and mingled among the crowds walking to the nearby soccer stadium hours before the game began.

The blessed attacks in November 2015 had included the *Stade de France*, and their particular target today was the 45,000-capacity crowd at *Parc de Princes* and the surrounding crowds, vendors, and the footie-loving public. Each of the aspiring martyrs had grown up with soccer, some in their home countries in the Middle East, and two of them in Paris enclaves. To a man, they all regretted that Allah had chosen to target their sport and its fans, but theirs was not to question the all-knowing and merciful God. They asked only to have fulfilled their duties to enter Paradise and live out eternity among the pleasures and indulgences denied throughout their lifetime on earth.

"He will be here, do not concern yourself," Omar counseled with a weak, nervous smile. "There is still time. Just ten more minutes. Anything could have delayed him, and we have no means to contact him."

"He wrote the security protocols," Mohammed objected, "and we agreed to follow them, regardless of whatever happened. We should have separated and fled by now."

Asad rechecked his watch. "Five minutes. I will give him no longer."

"Asad. He's *not* coming," Mohammed whispered, even though he was sure no one around them spoke Arabic. "You know the protocol. We were to leave by 10 o'clock. He's caught or dead, and we can no longer risk staying here."

"You're right." Asad looked around once more and then stepped in close to his men, his soldiers. "We are to go our separate ways, flee this nation, and live to fight another day. Stay prepared and vigilant, the fight may still come to us this day. Escape so that God may again use us to His purpose. Peace be with you."

MAY 11, 10:14AM_

La Courneuve Aubervilliers Metro Station. *La Courneuve, France.*

KAREEM MUSTAFA WAS IRATE. His simmering rage at this missed opportunity threatened to boil over. He scanned the slow single-file line of cars approaching the Metro station, none of which matched the sedan he so needed to see. The imam was to have driven there in a dark blue Renault coupe to pass off Kareem's backpack, and had been due no later than 10am. Kareem had been ordered to flee by 10:15 if the imam didn't arrive but refused to believe they'd failed.

Rechecking his watch only further elevated Kareem's anger. *Imam Abrini has never been late! How could he have been betrayed when our path has been so plain and well-lit! God ordained this to be, and now it's been stopped!*

Kareem searched the crowds ebbing and flowing around the station and the surrounding neighborhood. *The imam must be dead. The police will question me if I remain here much longer.* He no longer had any communication with the imam or other members of his group, all of whom had spread out to various locations around the city.

Frustrated, Kareem glared at the skyline to his south and the spires of the *Saint-Denis Cathedral* rising in defiance against his very soul. He eyed those pieces of his intended target, just visible over the few kilometers of rooflines that stood between them. In one obliterating moment, he could have struck a terrifying blow to the French nation and Rome *and* denigrated the insidious history of both blasphemous institutions. *First, their beloved Notre Dame burns only weeks ago, and then ten centuries of French and Christian arrogance suffer the violent end they deserve.*

A single realization calmed Kareem's stewing animosity. *I could follow the protocols, or I could take matters into my own hands. Opportunity remains for me to enter Paradise today with the fresh blood of Allah's enemies on my hands.*

rrrrrrrrrr tck

Michael's head snapped up, and he stared at the apartment's only door, the source of the unknown mechanical noise. He glanced back at the man who called himself Abdel Abrini. Despite still being restrained on the apartment floor in a modified crab position by Michael's soft nylon straps, he wore a terrifying, Cheshire-cat smile.

"Time's up, priest." The call to *dhuhr,* the second mandated prayer of the day, sounded outside over a tinny loudspeaker from the mosque four floors below. "The door is permanently locked, and its shell conceals enough explosive to kill everything on this floor if anyone tries to force it open. God inspired me to guarantee the success of His plan regardless of what the world might do to stop me, so we are now held captive *inside* with my devices while the police and military bomb crews are locked *out.*"

"Abdel, you can't be serious!" Michael hurried over to the door and realized for the first time that both it and the surrounding door-frame were metal. *It opens in, so I can't kick it open, and that much force might set off the I-E-Ds. Goddammit!*

"As you first offered, priest, our fates are entwined, but not in the way you had hoped! Time draws near, and eleven explosive-laden

287

backpacks await their impending destiny only a few yards from us. I had hoped to spread them all across the city, but Allah had a better plan for their usefulness. Today, I will ascend to Paradise from here, and you and all the imposters gathered in the false mosque below us will fall into your own eternal hells. It *must* be His plan for this to have come to fruition, yes?"

Incredulous to the sudden and unexpected turn of events, Michael stood in place while his brain spun like a Rolodex in search of a solution that wouldn't present itself. *He's been playing me the whole time, and I fell for his lies.* "What, why, why go through this--"

"Now," Abrini called out, "I will give *you* the chance to humble yourself before Allah in the final moments of *your* life! It is the same blasphemous choice you offered me, is it not? You should have known better, priest, than to waste time converting a soldier of Allah at the very *moment* of his ascension to Paradise! Your mysticism is nothing but heresy! This moment, the culmination of my lesser *jihad* against you unbelievers and Crusaders, it is the one missing piece I needed to make amends for the failings in my life. I've paid my *zakat*, I've made my pilgrimage, I've prayed beyond the mandate, and I've adhered to the words of Allah. It brings me no pleasure to send you and the others to hell, but it does bring me undeniable joy to have completed everything Allah demands to secure *my* place in Paradise."

Michael stepped closer to his subject. *"Abdel, tell me how to stop the devices."*

"You *can't*." The bomb maker shook his head despite the restraints. "They're active, and there is *no* kill-switch. I set them to detonate by phone, but I also installed and activated backup timers. No matter what happens today, I have guaranteed my bombs *will* detonate and target the greatest heretics, even if no one else. Our physical destruction is as divinely inevitable as tomorrow's sunrise."

Unexpected grief contorted Abrini's face before he continued. "I wish there was another way, I do, priest, but unfortunately for all of us, there is not. This is not what I want, but I have no choice as a slave to Allah. It is what He ordained, and I am powerless to question it, I can only choose between my eternity and yours. Perhaps now, the remaining believers will see the promised One Great Day and establish the final caliphate on earth. If you blasphemers would only submit, then none of this violence would any longer be necessary." Tears streamed down the sides of his face. "*Allah Akbar!*"

Michael stepped closer and feared he had no time left to alter Abrini's engineered outcome. *I have to appeal to his humanity!* "No, Abdel. There *is* another way. You're a *good man* at your core, in your heart, and you can't want to *murder* these peop--"

"*People?* If we're the same, priest, why does Allah specifically proclaim Jews and Christians are *cursed swine and apes*, that only a few of you are not filled with deceit and can be trusted?"

The fear and guilt Michael saw wash over him moments ago disappeared as easily as they'd arrived.

"He foretold us," Abrini loudly professed, "'The hour of the end times will not be established until you *fight* with the Jews, and the stone behind which a Jew is hiding will call out, 'O, Muslim! There is a Jew hiding behind me, so kill him!' When judgement day arrives, Allah will provide every Muslim a Jew or Christian to kill so *none* of us enters into hellfire." He paused and raised his voice as though reassuring himself. "And so, Allah has given me you. *You,* priest, by your mere proximity, you will have the honor of being my *first* kill!"

Michael swallowed hard and spoke through his fearful uncertainty of which moment would be his last. "Your text is *wrong*, Abdel. We're *not* slaves, and we aren't commanded to kill for our own salvation."

Abrini spat at him. "'Allah is an *enemy* to those who reject faith in him. Make war on them until idolatry shall cease and Allah's religion shall reign supreme.'" He looked away, and Michael heard reluctance and hesitation in his voice. "Prepare thyself, priest, your judgment is imminent."

Michael fought to suppress his rage over Abdel's murderous treachery and refused his impulse to kill him. His breath came in short, panicked gasps as he kneeled next to the man and desperately pleaded his case. *God, give me the words!* "What of free will, Abdel? If you have no choice in anything that happens, or that you do, then some portion of humanity is *fated* to go to hell. How can that be the intent and desire of a merciful and loving God?"

"Allah has granted us your precious *free will,* with the conditions that we accept Islam and praise Him alone, subjugate yourselves to the Muslims, or die upon our blades for your refusal. There is no fourth option, but humanity remains free to choose from among those three." His tone confirmed Abdel's increasing arrogance. "I hold out faith for your salvation, priest. You think you failed, but you have proved Allah's superiority over the Christian and Jewish abominations!"

Michael abandoned his futile efforts and focused on escaping and evacuating the building. *I can't stop Abrini from killing himself and dying a mass murderer, but I might limit his victims.*

Abrini followed Michael's scan of the room. "You can't get out, priest. We will meet our fated judgements together. Mohammed ordered the deaths of Jewish leaders for the blasphemy of writing verses that mocked him, and he rejoiced in their deaths. Now, I will get to rejoice in yours for your attempted interference with Allah's wishes!"

Michael stepped into Abrini's bedroom and found a butane torch on the far side of the dresser. He picked it up and shook the bottle to confirm it still held liquid gas. After retrieving a nearby lighter, Michael ran over to a fire suppression sprinkler near the front door, opened the butane valve, and ignited the fuel vapor.

hhsssssssssss

He reached up and held the flame on the system's heat sensor. Tense seconds passed with no result. An alarm sounded in the hallway outside the door, and a deluge of dirty, rust-colored water sprayed from the overhead sprinkler, doused Michael in its metallic slime, and extinguished the torch. *Everyone else gets the head start I don't deserve!*

"*Are you ready to die, priest?*" Abrini looked especially pleased with himself. "Are you ready to meet Allah and face the conse-quences of your failed and arrogant life leading believers away from Him?!"

Michael stepped out from under the spray and relit the torch. A short, blue flame resurrected itself from the spout.

hssssssss

He adjusted a knob on top of the regulator to increase the fuel output. The flame extended a foot beyond the spout and turned yellow-and-white as its temperature increased.

shhhhhhhhhhh

"God and I are good, Abdel, but I'm worried about you."

"There's now no escape for you, just as you said there wouldn't be for me!"

Michael left the torch on, its flame hissing as he crossed the room toward his restrained subject. "You bombers are all the same. There's always a failsafe, always a bypass. You're gonna help me stop it. No one but you has to die today."

"That's where you're wrong! I *added* detonation triggers to fulfill my obligations!" The man's eyes widened, and he squirmed in vain to back away from the flame. *"What are you doing?!* You'll only add to your conscience in your final minutes on earth!"

Michael shook his head as he reached Abdel and waved the flame toward his chest. "You might be ready to die, but you planned for a quick and painless end. One way or another, you'll tell me how to stop the timers."

"I'm sorry, priest, do what you will in the next five minutes, but you're only leaving here in painless, high-velocity pieces. You may, of course, go out the window, although I believe you'll dislike the landing."

FIVE MINUTES, Michael told himself as he climbed out onto the small balcony, leaped up, and pulled himself back up onto the roof. *Abrini gave up intel he didn't intend. The devices detonate at 1055. Four minutes to be safe. I can do a lot in four minutes!*

Michael sprinted across to the south side of the roof and dropped to the narrow concrete balcony below.

THUD

Despite landing on the balls of his feet and fingertips, the balcony flexed with the sudden application and force, and Michael jumped into the open doorway.

With the klaxon siren barely audible in the background, a cacophony of urgent, frightened shouts erupted, and Michael looked around as he rose from the floor. The elderly Muslim grandfather who'd likely saved his life two days ago struggled to get up from a couch while his wife and grandchildren fled Michael's intrusion. Their apartment was dry, and the fire alarm outside hadn't encouraged them to leave. *It didn't trigger the whole system!*

"*I'm sorry, but there's no time,*" Michael shouted at the man. "*Get your family and leave the building, right now, there's a bomb in your neighbor's apartment!*"

"What, a what, bomb, wh--"

Michael grabbed the grandfather's left arm and guided him toward the door. *"No time! Take your family out and tell the others on your way! Go! Now!"*

Michael recognized Abrini's voice shouting through the closed and booby-trapped door across the small landing.

"Allah yil'anek! God damn your devil, priest! God damn you!"

The grandfather and his family hurried by, and the old man looked up at Michael after hearing Abrini's curse. Michael descended the stairs behind them and wished the vulnerable group had someone sturdier to cling to. *I can't leave anyone behind. I have to be the last one out of the building, no matter what that means! If I would've called Gerard when I first got into the apartment, this might not be happening, so I have to make it right!*

Michael's heart leapt when he saw a red fire alarm on the wall. Even if not for the familiar design, *FEU-FIRE* displayed on the top of its frame with *TIREZ-PULL* on the handle. He yanked on the white handle and continued downstairs.

WE-AHH-WE-AHH-WE-AHH-WE-AHH

The immediate, deafening alarm made the grandparents jump and their grandkids flee much faster. Michael stepped out onto the fourth-floor landing while the group continued toward the exits. He slammed several hammer-fists into each of the opposing doors to ensure he could be heard over the alarm.

WE-AHH-WE-AHH-WE-AHH-WE-AHH

Critical seconds passed with no reaction, so Michael reared back and kicked open the closest door.

BOOM

The cheap wood doorframe gave way and shattered into splinters, and the door slammed back against an interior wall. Michael rushed inside. *"Get out! Get out! Everyone out!"* He cleared each room and found no one. A quick sprint back out to the landing and another heavy boot opened the opposing door.

BOOM

Michael found that apartment empty, as well, and realized he couldn't access the structure's eastern apartments. He had to go to the ground floor hallway and find another set of stairs that would return him close to the devices he sought to escape. As he fled down to the third floor, Michael accepted the likelihood of his death. *I want only to avoid damnation for failing the prevent the murder of anyone else! I WILL BE THE LAST ONE OUT!*

The doors to both apartments on three were open and curious children and parents stood nearby. Michael's desperate descent convinced them of the legitimate urgency, and he soon followed their escape.

Michael found one of those apartments open and empty, the other door had to be kicked open.

BOOM

Empty! Move!

He again descended the stairs, taking three and four at a time in a barely controlled fall to move as fast as he could. *I have to get everyone out and they need time to get behind some kind of hardened shielding! Dammit! I'm too close to the epicenter to survive the initial blast, much less the shrapnel and fragmentation. Just one more floor to go.* He raced down the final flight of stairs toward bright daylight and an open doorway. Michael found both ground floor apartments open and empty, so he sprinted toward the east side of the building as the elderly grandfather emerged from a doorway ahead of him. *"Hey! You have to go!"*

"So do you! Come with me! Now!"

"I have to evacuate the other side, there's--"

"Stop! Those apartments are empty, no one lives there! The city condemned them because of flooding last winter!"

Michael paused, unsure if he could wager his salvation on the man's word.

"Now! I don't want to die here with you, but I will if you insist!"

Michael looked deeper into the hall, and a sheet of plywood covered the east stairwell entrance. He turned, grabbed the man's upper right arm, and they fled the building together. While half-carrying the smaller man's weight, Michael rushed across the interior concrete walkway and feared the overhead building was as fragile as its balconies. He pushed harder to get them to salvation on the other side of the doorway. *Just another three--*

IMMERSED IN A STRANGE, black silence, Michael fought to regain his senses. Absent any sound, he experienced only suffocation. The once-familiar feeling resurrected the sheer terror of his near-drowning. His body's chemoreceptors screamed at him to breathe and oxygenate his blood, but Michael couldn't take in air. His lungs didn't move, and the desperation of imminent death overwhelmed him.

Michael's eyes popped open, and he gasped in a deep lungful of chalky, debris-filled air. Blurry, indiscernible shapes and various colors moved about to his far left, and relative darkness remained over the rest of his consciousness.

He blinked hard once, and then repeatedly did so. Michael's visual focus returned, along with increasing control of his limbs and dexterity. Realizing he laid on his right side, he pushed up onto his right elbow and found himself in a gutter. With some pain, he could wiggle all his fingers and toes. A bloody gash poked through his torn left shirt sleeve, but he didn't see the white of fatty tissue or bone.

Michael's back bumped up against a dirty white car, and he looked forward, back at the building he'd exited. Now broken and damaged, it no longer appeared to be the same structure. Thick gray dust filled the air. *Where's grandad? He was with me, wasn't he?*

Several people walked around, closer to the building, but no one stepped inside. Although they appeared to cry and wail, Michael heard nothing. *Have to find grandad and get the hell outta here. The place's gonna blow any second, no time. No time.* Michael stood up and leaned on the car for support. *No. Time. Wait...it already, blew up.*

Michael gazed up at the building's missing roofline and saw the whole west side of the top floor had vanished into a smoky, concrete-dust cloud that slowly descended toward the ground. He blinked hard again and felt tiny scratches in his eyes. Leaning more heavily on the car, Michael scanned his surroundings. Chunks of concrete, debris, furniture, and glass lay strewn across the sidewalk. A slight layer of thick gray dust covered everything in the immediate vicinity. *People, but no bodies. No blood on anyone but me. Maybe we made it.*

His hearing slowly returned like his brain cautiously increased the allowed volume input from zero. A muffled wail from his right drew Michael's attention, and he saw the grandfather's wife holding him eight or ten feet away, right next to the gutter. She sat in an unnatural position as though she'd collapsed there, and their grand-children were nowhere around. Michael stumbled over to offer help, but his heart sank when he saw a thin trail of blood from both the man's ears.

His brain increased the volume, but at an infuriatingly slow pace. Michael dropped next to the woman, afraid for a moment to touch the man and risk making things worse for him. *"Ma'am!"* He felt himself shouting, but Michael sounded as if he'd managed only a hoarse whisper. *"You have to let him lay flat!"* No change, more wail-ing. *"Ma'am!"* Michael touched her right shoulder, and she reacted with frightened surprise. Her eyes changed to angry, hateful slits just before she slapped his face.

Already unstable and caught off-guard, Michael fell into the gutter and landed on his back against a parked car. He looked back at the grandmother, shocked that she'd struck him for trying to help, and noticed the growing crowd behind and around her. Through his muffled hearing, Michael could only pick up on the emotion in their voices and the body language, both of which conveyed belief in his involvement with the bombing.

Michael struggled to rise from his vulnerable position and stand to defend himself.

The first injection of pain shot through his right knee when he put weight on that leg, and a warm, liquid sensation descended from his left temple. Michael wiped at it with his hand, which returned the expected confirmation. *Blood. No time to triage that right now.*

Still dazed, Michael knew he had to get away from the scene before the cops and medics arrived, and before the frightened crowd devolved into an angry mob. A flat, hard piece of metal caught his right elbow at his waist, and Michael realized he still had the suppressed pistol inside his beltline. He tugged the front of his dusty shirt down to keep it concealed. *These people don't deserve to be shot, probably not even if they resort to violence against me or--*

Michael's thoughts stopped cold when Imam Siddiqi appeared in front of him. Much of the crowd then pointed at Michael and shouted at them both, alternately pleading for the imam's blessing of their bloodlust and calling for Michael's damnation. As the crowd encroached closer, Michael scanned for an escape route to the north. *I have to get--*

poppop pop pop poppoppop

At the first sound of the nearby gunfire, Michael dropped to the ground. Both he and the imam covered the grandparents, while everyone else around them scattered, desperate for their own protection.

poppop pop pop poppoppop

The gunshots continued to ring out, and Michael found he and the imam both tried to cover the other three, while Michael also sought to keep the pistol concealed and out of reach and notice of the other cleric.

While the fleeing crowd thinned and ran, Michael rose up to look around during a lull in the gunfire. A hand grabbed and pulled at his left shoulder of his shirt.

"Get down!"

Michael looked toward the unexpected voice as he fell, and the imam focused on his wounded left arm. *"We have to get you out of here! Help me move them!"*

Michael shook off the man's grasp and rose back up to see across the hood of an adjacent parked car. Several panicked people ran north toward him, and Michael saw the top of a black pistol bouncing up over the roofline of the parked cars two dozen yards away.

poppop

The muzzle flashes and cordite smoke accentuated the gunfire, and Michael knew the unknown gunman was running toward the apartment building as he held the weapon up. *Toward me, clearing the street of innocents as he moves!* Michael needed to be close to disarm the gunman and fleeing with the imam would only get him shot in the back or beaten to death when the mob resurrected its anger. He looked back at the imam, who ushered the grandmother to her feet.

"*Come this way,*" he shouted at Michael, "*help me get her out of here!*"

"*Someone has to stop the shooter, no one's safe until that happens! Take her now and come back for him!*"

"*You'll die out there!*"

Michael turned toward the oncoming threat. "I'd rather be shot in the face than beaten to death from behind." He crept forward to the next car as more panicked victims rushed past. The suppressed barrel of his still-concealed pistol pressed into the inside of his right thigh. After withdrawing the gun from its holster, Michael grasped it tight in both his hands and pointed the barrel to the ground. A quick glance around confirmed no one had noticed.

Distant *we-ahh we-ahh* police sirens echoed off the tall, closed-in buildings and announced the imminent arrival of authority. Michael put that problem aside for the moment. Watching the street on the other side of his cover car, he waited until a shadow hurried toward him. He inhaled a deep breath, brought the gun up, and slid his right index finger toward the trigger. Michael stood up in a solid combat stance, and squarely aimed the assassin's pistol at the center mass of his target. Catching the glint of steel, he began pressing the trigger but suddenly recognized the source was a police badge and not a weapon. He yanked his finger from the trigger guard and plunged the weapon's barrel toward the asphalt at his feet.

Gerard shuddered in surprise and briefly began to bring his pistol down before realizing Michael had already lowered his gun. A *Police Judiciaire – SDAT* badge hung from a metal dogtag chain around his neck and glowed in the sunlight, despite the dusty haze that still permeated the air.

Michael struggled to understand the cop's presence and actions. "You're supposed to be--"

"*I know, you asshole! You sent me away, and now I have to clean this up!*" Gerard hadn't yet holstered his semi-auto. "Am I now to arrest you, shoot you, or die here in the gutter beside you?"

"What do you think?" Michael held his breath and waited.

"I think we have to get you off this street if either of us wish to understand what happened. Follow me! Now!" Gerard held his pistol in a low-ready position near the center of his torso and pointed it at the ground in front of his feet. He turned and jogged southwest toward the back entrance to the parking garage.

Michael did the same, and hoped that keeping his pistol out would lead everyone around to believe he, too, was a cop. He glanced back at the sidewalk, and the imam and both grandparents had disappeared.

MAY 11, 11:05AM_

13 RUE DE CORBILLON. SEINE-SAINT-
DENIS, FRANCE.

MICHAEL RAN behind Gerard toward the parking garage office He remained unsteady on his feet. No one else was inside the structure, but dozens of people flowed by on the adjacent sidewalks. Michael glanced around, thankful that no one challenged him or showed interest in their escape.

Gerard led him back into the small office and locked the door behind them. "*What the fuck happened over there, Father Andrew?!*"

Michael shuffled to a desk chair and plopped in it. "I never told you I was a priest."

"And *that's* the most important thing to discuss right now?! *How do I know that?!* You go first, and tell me how the goddamned building blew up, and I'll--"

"Abrini. He used the chemicals to make T-A-T-P, it's an explosive--"

"I know what it is! How do *you* know that?!"

"I confirmed the explosive presence in his apartment two days ago, and I found his lab this morning. I didn't know he packed eleven backpacks full of the stuff. He intended to hit eleven targets in the city today, probably all at once, and I expect that's where his soccer players came into the picture. We contained him to one building and a pretty small number of casualties."

"Where is he now?"

"Dead, I guess. He was still tied up in the apartment when I climbed out the window, and I don't think he cared to even *try* escaping. This was his last checkbox to get into his fucked-up idea of heaven."

Gerard paused and stared at him a moment. "Are you sure you're a priest?"

Michael grimaced as increasing pain set in. "What happens now, between us, I mean?"

"I have to go back out there and help anyone I can. I want you to stay here and answer every goddamned question when I get back."

"Are you willing to make me?"

Gerard stared at him a moment. "No. I hoped for what I think you American cops call 'professional courtesy.' If you're not here when I get back, good luck, Father Andrew. Peace be with you."

"And also with your spirit." Michael watched him leave, and the door lock *clicked* shut behind him. He wanted to follow Gerard out to the rubble pile and help where he could, but the increasing pain and dizziness convinced him he would soon be a casualty himself.

bangbangbang

Michael sat up and looked to the noise coming from the outer office door.

bangbangbang

"*Andrew! Are you in there?! Open up!*"

Michael thought he knew the heavily French-accented voice, so he stood on unsteady legs and stumbled over to the door. "Who is it?"

"Alpha."

He unlocked the deadbolt, pulled the heavy metal door open, and Alpha stepped in just in time to help keep him upright. This was the first time Michael remembered seeing the black Frenchman without a bright white smile on his face. His friend and former training partner wore a gray tracksuit that would easily blend into most crowds, and Michael felt a pistol concealed at his right hip when Alpha propped him up. He reflexively checked to make sure his own suppressed .22 remained in place inside his right front waistband. "How did you find me?"

"Later. Can you move?"

Michael pondered the question for a moment. "Yes, but I might need a steady shoulder."

"I can be that, but we have to leave. Emergency services are closing the area, and the street is filling with a mob. The Saint Denis Cathedral is an eight-minute walk from here, and we should try to get you inside that sanctuary in no more than five. Moving."

Michael stepped forward in response to the common team-movement vocabulary they'd used at John's training camp. "Move!"

MAY 11, 11:13AM_
13 RUE DE CORBILLON. SEINE-SAINT-
DENIS, FRANCE.

MICHAEL LEANED on Alpha's right shoulder, and they scanned the garage and rushed to avoid the growing crowds.

"We could boost a car."

Michael weighed the option and its potential success, given their training in the art of theft and evasive driving. "No, it'll connect the bombing with the cathedral. We have to go on foot. I wish I could change clothes, though, I can't deny being close to the building when it blew." He tried to wipe concrete dust and soot from his clothing as he fled.

"Your clothes won't matter as much as your white face. I can blend in anywhere and hide in plain sight in this neighborhood, but your best hope is that they only assume you're French."

"That's ironic, coming from a Frenchman, and more than a little racist."

Alpha scoffed. "Call it what you like, but it's our present reality."

They soon emerged onto the sidewalk at the south end of *Rue du Corbillon*, just a few dozen yards below the epicenter. Gray concrete dust still hung in the air and continued to fall on everything in the vicinity. The approaching sirens grew louder, but Michael didn't see any emergency vehicles on the street itself. Everyone around them was fixated on the demolished building, and Michael thought few took notice of them. *How long can a tall white guy lean on a short black guy and run away from a crime scene?*

As they hurried east, the crowds inbound to the site grew denser and slowed their progress. Alpha moved over to walk in front of Michael. So far, no one had challenged them.

"*Tawaquf! Arrêtez!*"

The shouted Arabic and French words halted the crowd in front of them and prevented further escape. Imam Siddiqi appeared to the immediate left, and Alpha swung around to put himself between the cleric and Michael. *Everyone's suddenly realized we don't belong here, and they're waiting for his command.*

Siddiqi pointed his thick right index finger at Michael. "*What were you doing in the building?*"

Michael swallowed hard and chose his words. "Trying to talk someone out of doing exactly what they did."

"Abrini?"

He had no real choice but to be honest. *No more than a few around us understand what we're saying.* "Yes."

"I *knew* that man was a *snake* from the moment he walked into my mosque and pretended to accept my message of reformation and tolerance!"

Michael breathed out his relief and leaned close to Siddiqi despite fearing his answer. "Are the *grandparents* okay? The ones from the sidewalk where I last saw you?"

"They are, thanks to you. His recovery is now in God's hands, but he owes his life to you. They both told me you saved everyone in the building. Ali, the grandfather, he said you tried to evacuate the deserted apartments, and he had to convince you to leave with him."

"That was the second time he saved me. How many are hurt?" Michael looked around and felt the immediate crowd grow less tense as they spoke. *The still-inbound sirens can't be more than a few blocks away.*

"Very few, and no one is yet missing or killed. You saved much of my congregation today. What of *Abrini?* Where is *he* now?"

Michael smiled. "Judgement."

"I don't think it will be what he expected." Siddiqi looked around as though having just noticed the sirens himself. "You must go and let Abrini alone answer for his crimes, yes?"

"We agree," Alpha injected.

Siddiqi pointed to the closest four men to Michael's right and spoke to them in Arabic. All four nodded, exchanged a glance with Michael and Alpha and then turned east as the crowd parted before them.

"They will get you beyond the crowds," Siddiqi explained. "These men are all imams who believe as I do. Thirty of us gathered today to begin a great schism, for all the reasons that Abrini made this happen above and around us at that very moment. They will escort you to sanctuary. There is a cathedral nearby that will allow you to rest and acquire whatever aid you need."

Michael didn't have the mental capacity to come up with a believable lie. "Yes, that will be helpful." *The best un-truth I can manage at this moment.*

"You have will have no troubles from my congregation. I fear there are more Abrinis, though, who may want to hold any outsider responsible. Peace be with your spirit."

"And with your spirit, as well." Michael and Alpha both offered the common reply, and then pressed on behind their four appointed guardians. A police car turned onto the street and moved toward them with its European *whee-aww* siren blaring. Michael ducked his head behind their Sherpas and picked up his pace. *The whole area will be cordoned off soon, and we still have a half-mile to go.*

MICHAEL AND ALPHA continued east toward the historic cathedral when their escorts stopped two blocks back at *Rue de la République* and *Place Jean Jaurés*, the same intersection from which Michael had fled north only a few nights ago.

He followed Alpha into an unmarked entrance where he used an old iron key to unlock a heavy door. Alpha led Michael into the rectory's living area, the same place where he'd heard Father Luc's confession only days before. Michael reclaimed the same seat and exhaled a portion of his stress. *I'm away from the epicenter, but I still have to escape the neighborhood and the country.*

"I'll let my friend know we're here," Alpha offered. "Can I get you water while we wait, or anything else you need?"

"Yeah, maybe water will help, unless there's whiskey handy."

"I don't recall seeing a bottle here, but I'll keep a lookout." Alpha stepped into the kitchen, retrieved a glass from the first cabinet he opened, and poured water from a pitcher in the refrigerator. He handed Michael the glass and frowned at his injured partner's suspicion. "What?"

The door behind him opened before Michael could answer, and Father Luc burst inside. His surprise at their presence was obvious.

"Oh, merci mon Dieu!" He rushed forward, grabbed Alpha in a tight hug, and quickly released him. Luc saw Michael and his relief turned to concern. "Oh, my God! Father Andrew! How did you, I mean—"

Alpha answered first. "He's with me, Luc."

Luc rattled off something in French, but Alpha insisted they use English in front of their guest. "Wait. With you, Chasseur, how can that be? Did you also know he was here, and what about—"

"There is much that I *cannot* discuss, but Andrew and I are old friends."

Luc nodded his acceptance but remained exasperated. "I was so worried when I heard it, and then news came in from the street, and now, you are here and injured! What kind of help do you require? A doctor, yes?! Oh, no, what of Gerard?!"

Michael shook his head. "He's fine, Luc, and I don't need a doctor yet. We do have to discuss a few things."

"Of course, I expected you might return for me to hear your confession, and then the explosion hap--"

"How do you know Gerard?"

Luc's expression showed deception and nervousness. "He's a friend, a parishioner."

"I assume you told your *friend,* about me and that we had discussed his case, because he knew too much about me, including that I'm a priest."

Alpha's mouth fell agape, and he stared at the parish priest. "Luc, what have you done?"

"Rien, peut-être quelque chose." He shook his head. "Sorry, I mean, perhaps nothing. It is possible, maybe--"

"You told him about me. You gave him my name, Luc."

Luc bowed his head and closed his eyes. "Perhaps we both have things to confess to each other, Father Andrew."

Michael stood and stepped in front of Luc until he'd deeply invaded the priest's personal space. "Bullshit. I have nothing to confess to you, and I can't trust you with it, anyway. I didn't do a damned thing to that guy back there. I didn't even make him suffer when I probably should have."

"Please," Luc's voice trembled, "please forgive me, I--"

A distant scream from inside the massive cathedral grabbed Michael's attention and all three men briefly stood in place. He and Alpha glanced at one another, and Michael realized his training partner had heard the same thing.

"Allah Akbar!"

"On me!" Alpha leapt toward a second scream and Michael sprinted right behind him.

His pain and suffering now made a distant memory by the magic of renewed adrenaline, Michael waited to draw his pistol until he could move more cautiously. Alpha led him through the sacristy and to a small doorway that required him to simultaneously step up and duck down to quickly pass through it. An explosion of panic and mayhem echoed through the massive central corridor of the cathedral, and Michael now led Alpha toward it. He didn't understand what the victims and civilians shouted around them, but the repeated frantic shouts of *Allah Akbar* propelled him on faster.

Alpha shouted at him as they ran. *"They are yelling about a knife, a man with a knife that's cutting people!"*

The two-man team moved in concert and shouted at bystanders to flee as they rushed through the long nave. Up ahead near the entrance to the cathedral, a young man stepped in front of a woman and a child who had fallen to the floor. Michael lost sight of him while the mother and child frantically crawled away, but the man quickly re-emerged with fresh cuts on his forearms and dark red blood streaming to the stone beneath him. The Good Samaritan slipped and fell backward, and, in a panic, flailed his arms and kicked out with his legs to keep the unseen attacker at bay.

Alpha ran along Michael's right side, and everyone now moved themselves from the priests' obvious path. To their right, an elderly man struggled to get his wife out of a pew and made eye contact with Michael. He shuffled closer to their vector and held his cane out for them like a relay baton. Alpha veered right and accepted the tool without slowing. Michael wondered if his French colleague had ever before swung a baseball bat with precision at a dead run. An early twenties, able-bodied tourist stood near the end of a pew on Michael's left and recorded the horror with his cellphone. Michael swatted the device away as they sprinted past, and it shattered on the stone floor behind him.

As they closed in on the chaos, a Middle Eastern man emerged from the far side of a pillar two dozen yards in front of them near the left side of the narthex, the long entryway at the back of the structure. Two men, each of whom had found a folding chair, tried to keep him at bay like a trained lion, but one slipped in a blood pool and awkwardly fell onto his knee. The assailant struck out and cut the man's arm. As the latest victim shrieked in pain and terror, the aspiring murderer shoved him down to the floor and dropped on top of the victim's waist in one swift and practiced motion. His eyes widened with bloodlust, and he continued his frenzied shouts of *Allah Akbar*.

Michael leaned forward and sprinted toward the attacker's left chest and shoulder. *No time to stop, draw, and shoot!* He watched the assailant raise the bloody knife in his right hand and hold it over his head for a moment to further terrify his panicked and pleading victim. Michael lowered his body and lunged forward as the aggressor's hips and shoulder collapsed down for the kill. Contacting the man's upper left torso, Michael propelled himself through the tackle.

whuh

Michael felt the man's lungs collapse, and the tremendous force cast the smaller and lighter assailant back and to his right. The open field hit freed the victim, redirected the knife's downward stroke, and plunged the long blade deep into the attacker's left abdomen.

thock

The attacker's skull struck the ancient stone floor and sounded like a ripe, wet watermelon breaking open on concrete.

Michael's momentum carried him up and over the lighter man,

and he crashed hard onto his knees and right shoulder. He leapt up and prepared to defend himself, but the unconscious aggressor laid in an awkward heap on his right side where he'd struck the stone floor. The man's own knife had buried deep into his spleen and intestines. Only his left eye was open but unfocused, and it endlessly stared at the floor as a growing blood pool emanated from an unseen injury on the right side of his head.

The parishioners all backed away from the sudden corpse.

Without a further fight before him, Michael doubled over at the waist, put his hands on his hips, and gasped for each breath. Alpha lowered the borrowed cane he'd had no opportunity to use. Luc finally arrived and fell to his knees next to the decedent and crossed himself.

"What, are you doing," Michael asked him between gasps.

"Leading by example," Luc offered, out of breath himself. "We must pray for this man's soul and his forgiveness."

Michael resisted the urge to spit at the corpse and stood upright. "He can go to hell. You do what you want. I'm gonna help his victims."

San Miguel Chapel. Santa Fe, New Mexico.

MICHAEL SHUFFLED into the small rectory, the parish priests' shared living space in his historic home chapel. He closed the door behind him and found his mentor, Monsignor Eduardo Hernandez, sitting on the small living room's threadbare couch. *He'll always remind me of Jerry Garcia.*

"*Woof!*"

Ira, the border collie-heeler mix Michael rescued from Wyoming last February, barked once and rushed to greet him. Despite his aches and pains, Michael knelt and petted his beloved dog. Hernandez looked up, smiled, and folded the afternoon newspaper.

"You look a damned sight better than the last time you came home." H stood and walked over, grabbing a letter-sized envelope from the kitchen countertop as he did so. "Apparently, your dog isn't the only one that misses you." He presented the envelope to Michael.

Curious, Michael stopped petting Ira, stood with some effort, and accepted the envelope. It had been addressed to him, for delivery simply to "San Miguel Chapel, Santa Fe, New Mexico." The return information showed only an address and didn't identify its sender. *Who do I know in Switzerland?* Michael roughly tore open the glued, back flap and pulled out a heavy-stock card. The front displayed a high-resolution photograph of the Alps. Michael opened the card, skipped the handwritten paragraphs, and looked to the bottom for a signature. *Merci. She must have moved her research facility.*

"So, who's it from?" Hernandez sounded both curious and accusatory.

"The doctor I met in Columbia last year, Merci Renard." Suddenly self-conscious about the woman's attention, Michael blushed.

"I remember telling you to be careful with her. She called here, you know, after you came back from Bogotá, and she sounded very much like a woman in love."

Ira nudged Michael for attention, so he scratched the dog's head while he read the card. "I don't know about that, H," Michael weakly replied as he read the doctor's beautiful cursive.

"Dearest Father Michael—

I am incredibly grateful to have met you. I've thought of you often since our last conversation, every day, in fact, and I don't know why. I can't imagine what might come out of our friendship, as our lives are so very different and separated by so much distance. Despite the effort and rational thought I've put into leaving you in my past, your memory refuses to allow it.

I cannot explain why, but I believe God does not yet intend for us to part ways. I hope this isn't too brash or assuming, and, selfishly, I need to know that you feel the same way. Please know that I'm sending this without a specific hope or agenda, and I do not wish to ever ask you to leave your work with the Church. I only wish for you to know that you remain important to me, and that I do hope we can one day meet again. Love & Light, Merci"

Michael looked up from the note and blushed again.

"That's the first time you've smiled in several months. There's gotta be a reason for it."

"I don't know, H, I really don't. Doctor Renard is an incredible person, with this amazing, compassionate heart of action and selflessness, but I don't know what to do with that."

"What would Michael the Episcopal priest do?"

"You mean, if things were different and I could marry and not have to maintain my vow of celibacy? I'd probably pursue her. I loved Catherine, back when we were together in Silver City, but I didn't hold the same esteem for her." Michael leaned back against the small kitchen counter and looked at the floor. "It would be cruel enough for a parish priest to let a woman hope for a relationship with him, even more so with what I'm actually doing for the Church. It's guaranteed heartbreak when one of the investigations spins out of control."

"I think 'guarantee' is a little harsh--"

"No, really, H, I think this assignment will be what ends this life for me. I've almost been killed, several times now, and, just for bonus points, I'm now..."

"Hang on, it sounds like you have something to confess." Hernandez's tone was more direction than observation.

Michael nodded and both men moved to the rickety bistro-sized table next to the kitchen and sat in its unstable chairs. Michael crossed himself, and H did the same. "Bless me, Father, for I have sinned. It's been six days since my last confession, and I have grief and sorrow in my heart."

"Go on," Hernandez offered as he rose and walked to the small refrigerator. "Just gonna make this official." The aging monsignor pulled out two bottles of Trappist ale and opened them while Michael spoke.

"I feel guilty, H, but not for what I've done, directly, I mean. I feel guilty for not feeling guilty. I had a hand in ending the lives of two men yesterday. Two. Both intended to die in a mass suicide bombing plot all across Paris, and one of them did just that, so I'm not even sure that I get credit or blame for him. The other one, though, I gave him the shove that ended his life. He was trying to carve up and murder a bunch of innocents, and I had to stop him from killing another man he had pinned on the floor.

"The worst part is, the local parish priest, he showed up right after I killed the second guy, and his knee-jerk response was to drop to the deck and pray for that asshole's soul, beg God to forgive him."

H set their beers on the bistro table, sipped from his own, and sat back at the table. "What was your knee-jerk response?"

"To stop myself from spitting on the corpse." Michael paused after his sheepish admission. "I think I said something about hoping the guy went to hell, and I was gonna triage his victims instead. Something like that."

"Who's to say either of you are wrong?"

"I get that both things have to be done, and we should have that much capacity for forgiveness and compassion in our hearts, H, but I wasn't there. At all. I'm still not. Maybe, after every single victim was treated, then I might consider praying for his soul. Which, of course now means that I feel guilty for not feeling guilty. Not for either of them."

"Alright. What else is eating you? I can see you got something else."

"It's an arbitrary definition, H, and it's tied up in my gut with this Doctor Renard thing..."

"And?"

Michael hung his head and forced his words. "I'm a, uh, I'm a serial killer, H. A damned serial killer, at least by F-B-I standards."

"Why?"

Michael looked up at his mentor's obvious surprise and ignorance. "Well, so, after a man kills three people in a similar manner and for similar reasons--"

"Bullshit! If you're gonna look at it that way, almost every soldier that came home from the fields in Europe, a lotta troops comin' outta the sandbox and the 'Stan, they're serial killers, too. All the pilots who've seen combat and dusted at least three other pilots. You'd call them serial killers, too, right?"

Michael felt even more sheepish. "No, of course not."

"How many men have you sent for judgement now, Michael?"

"Five, including Bogotá."

"You're at *war*, Michael. A foot soldier combating the greatest evils that walk the face of the earth. You're no serial killer, son. Hell, if anything, you're a goddamned *ace!*"

Later that night, Michael sat alone at the petite writing desk in his bedroom. A single bulb desk lamp illuminated his work surface, and Ira had curled up by his feet. Michael donned medical exam gloves and carefully removed a Ziploc bag concealed inside his backpack. Pulling a manila envelope from inside the plastic, Michael retrieved its contents and cast the envelope aside. Reading back over the two pages in his gloved hands, he considered whether he wanted to proceed. *Once I do this, there's no going back.*

Michael pondered the possible outcomes for what felt like a long time. *I want to know who the hell I'm working for. Tired of finding my ass in a sling for people who don't trust me with their name.* He retrieved a Silver City Police Department latent fingerprint kit from the bottom desk drawer and used its magnetic brush to apply black print powder to John's memo explaining the new operational security arrangements with the Oremus hotels. Six viable fingerprints appeared along the edges. *Might be his prints, might be Jacques', might be someone else I don't know.*

After he collected the black fingerprint images on his old department's print tape, Michael packaged them for delivery in tomorrow's mail. He waited to address the envelope from sheer paranoia that its contents might be discovered before morning. *A man has to protect his sources.*

That task completed, he pulled a yellow legal pad from the desk's top drawer and grabbed the first working pen he found. After a moment's hesitation, Michael began the letter he'd feared writing.

Doctor Renard--

He stared at the title, and then tore that page out and crumpled it. *I need to say everything I want her to know and understand, even if it's from the grave because H sends it after my burial.*

Dear Merci, I just got

knockknock

"Michael!"

At the urgent sound of his mentor's voice, Michael turned the legal pad over and shoved the bottom desk drawer closed to conceal the print kit and the sealed envelope of print tapes. "Come in."

Hernandez stepped into the room, his face ashen with worry. "The bishop just called. The pope, he's, uh, he just *resigned.*"

EPILOGUE_

May 13, 7:45am local.
Vatican Housing Complex. Rome, Italy.

Bishop Harold Hoffaburr and Cardinal Paul Dylan sat in the cardinal's furnished luxury residence. As usual, Dylan's open window blinds allowed his view over the Vatican City wall to dominate the apartment's living area. Saint Peter's Basilica glowed under the warmth of the rising, late spring sun. Despite the early hour, both men smoked rich, dark Cuban cigars and sipped Italian liqueur while they relished their view and the morning's news.

Harold had never seen his mentor so jubilant, and he hesitated from directly asking how the resignation impacted them. He took another pull from his snifter of *Centerba*, a traditional Italian liqueur made from herbs and medicinal spices in the Abruzzo region. Despite his lack of detail, Dylan gloated over his future while fielding dozens of phone calls from other cardinals and bishops, several of which came from Cornelius' innermost council. As he'd done throughout their relationship, Dylan obviously withheld information and wanted to ensure Harold knew he did so. Harold, meanwhile, strove to merely ensure he stayed in the best of his cardinal's graces. *His future is mine, just as I've long professed.*

The Italian CNN broadcast played with English subtitles. Dylan claimed it helped him brush up on the language, but Harold found the delay between the audio and inaccurate transcript frustrating. A passionate local Roman anchor discussed the sudden and unexpected resignation of His Holiness, Pope Cornelius II.

Harold thought the announcement shocked everyone but Dylan. *And yet, we're suffering through the local info-tainment as though we might learn something through public information channels.*

Dylan pointed his smoldering cigar at the screen and its rolling transcript. "I have sacrificed so much over the past two decades to be in this moment, in this position." His words slurred a bit, and he took another pull from both the cigar and his drink. "We're standing at the precipice of success and vindication, Harold. Everyone who shunned us and our traditional views of Saint Peter's church and its rightful place in the human experience. Our sacrifices and persecution will have all been made worthwhile after the conclave convenes, I assure you."

"Notizie Urgenti" flashed across the screen, and the anchor broke into their nonstop wailing and pontificating. Harold had to wait for the transcript to catch up.

After Saturday's bombing in the suburbs outside Paris, a local anti-terror cop has been hailed as a hero, while an immediate inquiry into his supervisor's possible complicity has begun.

In London, Scotland Yard inspectors have launched an investigation into a murder there reminiscent of 'Jack The Ripper.'

beepbeep beepbeep beepbeep

Harold retrieved his cell phone from a nearby glass-and-wood end table. The caller ID confirmed his educated guess, and he accepted the call. "Good afternoon, there, I suppose. What may I help with today?"

Anger saturated John's voice. "I assume you've seen this business in London?"

"We're only just hearing of it now."

"We need to get our boys back over there, on the first available plane. This shoulda been resolved months ago, and now another body's stacked up over it!"

"We, err, I couldn't agree more, John. What's the hang-up?"

"The *hang-up* is that one man'll never succeed on this one. We gotta send a team, or we're never gonna catch this guy. The boys have been very lucky so far, except on this one, but it's too big a thing for one man."

Harold frowned and sipped at his drink. He watched Dylan in his peripheral vision for any reaction to the phone call. "We've been over this so many times I'm growing concerned about your ability to take orders. No teams."

"I get the reluctance, I do, but--"

"No. Teams. Ever."

Dylan looked over and showed interest in the conversation, so Harold hoped John didn't press the issue while he sat next to the cardinal. He feared upsetting both men, but for very different reasons.

The line went dead, and Harold looked at his phone to confirm it had disconnected.

"Does John already see a problem with the London fiasco?"

"Other than the serial killer they can't stop?" Harold gulped at the remains of his liqueur. "Do you think John and his men have begun to outlive their usefulness?"

"I hadn't looked at that possibility, Harold. How do you mean that?"

"Just, that, well, quite frankly, Your Eminence, with everything that seems so imminent before us, and the sudden spotlight and global publicity that success will cast on you and your associations, I wonder if their continued existence isn't too dangerous for you and the longevity of your papacy."

Dylan sat back and considered his subordinate's thoughts. "I suppose you might be right, Harold. If we make that decision, how should we, *errr, disband* the group?"

"First, in this interim, I will keep closer tabs on John. Nothing too risky, just a few simple surveillance operations."

"Do you know someone who can tail a man of his training and capabilities?"

Harold rose to refill his glass. "John keeps saying he's nothing but a gravedigger, Your Eminence, so I expect that's what we need. A *better* gravedigger, certainly, but thousands of men with John's skills and experiences retire from the world's preeminent spy agencies every year. We need only one of them."

Dylan scoffed in agreement. "We found him, so we *can* find one better, especially for a few simple contracts. I didn't expect the conclave vote to come so soon on the heels of creating this organization, Harold. From a psychological standpoint, are your soldiers and assassins prepared to follow through on orders, even if they doubt their complete accuracy?"

"Rather than my opinion, let me instead offer you the facts." Harold sat back in his chair and leaned forward. He spoke in a hushed tone despite their absolute privacy. "As of this morning, we've sent the operatives on twenty-two assignments, and they've absolved fifteen of those subjects."

"I had hoped for much higher follow-through."

"The context may help, Your Eminence. Five assignments revolve around the same subject, the new Ripper in London. Two revealed no evidence, *and* we later learned originated from false allegations."

Dylan smiled as he considered the information. "As soon as they put that London monster down, they'll be perfect."

"And," Harold beamed, "most of those fifteen subjects were delivered to God within forty-eight hours of the assignment."

Dylan turned back to the television, which had returned to its pontifications from Saint Peter's Square. Growing throngs of the faithful poured into the square as they did for every major event in the Catholic world. "It appears our secret weapon, this clandestine cabal, *is* in place and ready to remove those who place themselves squarely against God's intended plan by opposing our upcoming vote."

Harold refused to show his discomfort with the unexpected turn. *If the cardinal's willing to send assassins after church officials for merely voting against him, what will he do if he believes I've betrayed him?* He leaned back and spoke toward the television and the news anchor now shown there. "We need only give them a target and a reason. If need be, they'll find all the evidence they need. I'll make certain of it."

Dylan again pulled in sequence from both his drink and his Cuban. "And, only after the vote's assured, we can hire enough of those *better gravediggers* to remove ours from the field. Some secrets just can't be trusted to lesser men, Harold."

Continue reading for a sample of *The Copycat*, the third novel in *The Michael Thomas* series. You can also purchase using the link below:

The Copycat: Https::/amazon.com/dp/B09FTHDN2T

MICHAEL THOMAS SERIES_

The Absolver
The Trafficker
The Bombmaker
The Copycat

THE COPYCAT: PROLOGUE_

May 14, 07:32am.
San Miguel Chapel. Santa Fe, New Mexico.

Father Michael Andrew Thomas knelt next to his bed in the private living quarters of the chapel where he'd worshiped as a child and now served as a part-time parish priest. Dense foam kneepads dulled the sacrificial ache that emanated up from the cold stone floor as he recited his daily morning prayer. Having returned from his assignment in Paris less than two days ago, he hoped to stay in the parish long enough to recover and heal from his injuries.

brrtbrrtbrrt brrtbrrtbrrt

Although he normally ignored his personal cell phone during the time he devoted to prayer, the early morning hour compelled him to retrieve it. Unknown caller. Michael silenced the ringer, returned it to the top of the nightstand, and knelt back on the floor. He closed his eyes, deeply inhaled, and—

brrtbrrtbrrt brrtbrrtbrrt

The skittering phone demanded his attention, so Michael rose and answered the call. "Hello?"

"What the hell did you get me into, Mikey?"

He recognized Brandon's voice, but he hadn't heard simmering rage in the man for years. "What do you mean?"

"Those fingerprints, dipshit. The ones you sent over and had me run through the national databases." Brandon paused and sighed. "What the hell are you doing?"

Michael stood and considered how to protect his friend from the unintended consequences of having involved him in the first place. "I'm sorry, man, but you have to give me context more than that."

His former shift partner and current Patrol Sergeant for the Silver City Police Department scoffed. "Alright. I'll play your stupid little game for a minute, but I will run out of patience real soon." He took a deep breath and exhaled. "I ran them through the national print databases, and they didn't match anything. Turns out, they actually got two matches, but they weren't in the databases us lowly street cops can access."

Michael's chest and throat tightened, so he fought back the stress reaction and continued to play dumb for the moment. "So, what did you get back?"

"I have no idea. They didn't tell me, so all I know is how I found out," Brandon shot back. "I'm working nights right now, so I just got off-shift about ten minutes ago. You know who was waiting for me when I walked back into the station house at 0-500 this morning? Some fuckin' clown in a suit from the State Department, and you know why, Mikey? Because he wanted to know where I got the prints and why I was looking into their owner."

"State Department? Did he give you a name?"

"Yeah, 'Special Agent Black,' but that was a blatant lie. He said, 'State Department,' but what he meant was 'O-G-A,' which is just spook-speak for—"

"C-I-A." Michael finished the sentence and held his breath. A pregnant pause passed between them.

"Yeah, Mikey. The first thing I'm struggling with is how you know that. I ran into a bunch of those guys over in the Sandbox and the 'Stan. I know exactly who and what 'Special Agent Black' was, but you were a small-town cop from New Mexico. Now I think you're a parish priest. I mean, that's the only thing you've told me about what you're doing, but what the hell do I know?" Brandon let silence chew on Michael, but he didn't take the tacit invite to explain himself. "So, after I finish my story, I need to know how you know what you know, Mikey."

Michael ignored the challenge for the moment. "What did you say about the prints?"

"Exactly what I wrote in the report. I pulled 'em off a stolen high-end mountain bike because I wanted to nab the thief for a solid felony. He didn't buy it, but no one can prove any different. I answered your questions, so, it's your turn to answer mine." Brandon's anger and fear infiltrated his voice and slapped Michael through the phone. "What is a Catholic priest doing with fingerprints from a goddamned spy?"

Michael shook his head again. *I never should have put Brandon in this position. John's contacts in the Agency will call him about this if they haven't already.* He took a deep breath in through his nose and exhaled. "What do you want to hear, B?"

His friend scoffed again. "At least give me something, even if it's a *lie* so I can pretend that we don't have targets on our backs right now." Brandon's normal sarcasm returned. "I already miss my life from last week, you know? Back when all my phone calls, and emails, and Internet search history were getting scraped and saved by the N-S-A, but nobody was really looking through them? You remember that, right, the good times that I didn't know ended a couple days ago? After that fun little meeting this morning, every federal intelligence agency is busy assigning about a dozen digital proctologists to work me over, so that's the kind of news you can use." He paused and exuded anxiety. "Did you know there are *sixteen* federal intelligence agencies, at least that they acknowledge publicly? Sixteen, Mikey, and I'm now known to every one of 'em, even the ones that aren't supposed to look at Americans. That's why I had to get this burner phone. If I dump my cell phone, they'll know something's up, so I have to leave it in the truck to make sure nobody's listening in. Probably doesn't matter, anyway, because they would have already found your phone number in my call records, and they can prove I lied to them now...goddammit..."

"They might get this cell number shut down, but they can't record it. The cell number you've had for me for since I got back from Columbia is an Internet number, and the phone never connects to cell towers. It only ever works through Wi-Fi, so no one can record the calls or find the phone."

"How, what, how?? *Who the hell are you, Mikey?!*"

"I'm still one of the good guys, Brandon, and I hope you still believe that. If you don't change your behavior and they don't dig up anything else, you'll be okay. The proctologists will get bored in a couple weeks and move on to something new and shiny." Michael couldn't read Brandon's silence across the phone. "If it's any consolation, they've been reading your shit all along. It's just a real file now and someone at N-S-A's hitting 'forward-all' to Langley."

"Alright. We can't undo any of this. Can you tell me a little bit about what the hell's on my shoes? What am I stepping in here?"

Michael sighed. He hoped Brandon could one day understand what his life had become. "It's best you don't know. I'm sorry this happened to you, I just didn't imagine it would go this far."

"Yeah, well, you don't sound surprised. Don't call me for any more favors, and don't forget about this one. If C-I-A operatives are leaving fingerprints on your whiskey glasses, I can't tell if that's real trouble for me or a massive Get Out of Jail Free card." Silence ground on them both for a moment. "I guess that depends on who you're working for these days and what you're really up to, eh?"

Michael's work cell rang, and he picked it up from the top of his desk. *Speak of the devil and he appears.* "Listen, I gotta go. The guy with those fingerprints might be calling."

"If you need help, Mikey, call me, or just show up on my doorstep but, at the same time, please don't need my help for a while."

"Be safe out there, B, and I'm sorry." He ended the call on his personal phone before accepting the one from his boss. "John, what can I do for you?"

The aging spy master scoffed before anger filled his gruff baritone voice. "You can start by explaining yourself, shithead, and then we'll see what happens from there."

THE COPYCAT: CHAPTER ONE_

May 14, 07:34am.
Rural Training Compound. Esmeralda County, Nevada.

With his cellphone to his ear, John stood looking out his bedroom window. He watched the current class of trainees run disciplinary wind sprints up a steep and rugged hill just west of the clandestine facility in the dusty Nevada desert. John showed his concern for those who reported to him by trying to ensure they suffered as much or more in his training program than most of them ever would in the real world. I can push 'em to succeed or ease 'em into failure.

"John?"

His focus snapped back to the phone call, and he strode away from the window. "How's the aches and pains, Andrew? You gonna live?"

"I've been worse, and I'll get better."

He let silence grind on his subordinate as he watched the struggling recruits. "I don't like the way Paris turned out. Nobody we care about got disabled or dead, but you're damned lucky no good guys got killed. Far as I can tell, the press and the French government don't know about you, so all the blame's goin' to the terrorist and all the

credit's landing on some local cop that was lookin' into the same guy."
John paused and let suspicion replace the disappointment in his
voice. "How do you figure you two managed not to run into each
other, two white faces investigatin' the same suspect in an enclave of
Middle Eastern Muslims?"

Andrew audibly exhaled before answering, but his voice stayed
measured and consistent. "I don't know, John. We must have crossed
paths at some point."

"Uh-huh." More silence that might inspire a confession or excuse.
Every operative in every covert organization has secrets and resources
he doesn't disclose to anyone, and this guy's apparently no different.
He knows better than to admit to anything. John nodded to himself
and adopted a factual tone. "I know you just landed back at the
parish and you're a little banged up, but duty calls. When can you get
yourself back on a plane?"

"A few hours. I have some things to tend to here, but I can hustle.
Where to?"

John scowled. "You must be the only one not watching the news.
Jack's back, at least that's what Scotland Yard and the British press
think. You're gonna wrap up this London thing, once and for all."

"It's a waste of time without the resources. One investigator can't
cover everything we need to absolve this guy—"

"That's why you're not going alone, shithead. I'm callin' in the
cavalry this time. Because of your previous cop work and your talent
for snatchin' victory from the jaws of defeat, you're gonna run the
team that puts this thing to rest."

Andrew took an audible breath, and John sensed surprise and
suspicion seeping through the phone. He stared out the window and
evaluated his current recruits, the *aspiring* Andrews, two of which
crawled up the rocky hill. *Too little gas, too little quit. We'll see about
that.* Another stopped only long enough to project his breakfast into a
small patch of scrub bush. John smirked. *Somebody's gotta make 'em
question their decisions.*

"Thank you for trusting me with this, John."

The hesitant comment drew him back into the conversation. "I'll trust you with my life, until you give me a reason *not to*." John eyed the leading recruit as she began another uphill lap and chugged past her suffering classmates. "You got about three hours to get your shit together and show up at your home airstrip." He let a pause grow back into palpable tension. "It's time to re-up your dues with the Merry Union of Snake Hunters and Gravediggers."

John disconnected the call and checked his watch. *My plane takes off in thirty minutes, and that only gives me about five hours to get everything set-up before Andrew's plane lands. No rest for the weary...or the wicked.*

Enjoying The Copycat? Click here to pre-purchase now!

www.amazon.com/dp/B09FTHDN2T

AFTERWORD_

AUTHOR'S NOTE

I must first thank Mrs. Reese for her creative inspiration, perseverance, and support during the last year that I wrote the first three
installments of this series. *Mo Anam Cara. You have always been and
will always be my everything.* L&T, you remain my biggest fans and
your encouragement and criticism have made the difference I
needed. BL, your technical advice continues to save my bacon, and
your kind words mean more than you know. Grandad, your research
added significant depth to this project. Thank you for your time and
effort, and I hope you enjoy our family's part in this story. My beta
readers devoted substantial time and effort to this project, and have
again applied the edge, polish, and shine required to help my uncut
draft evolve into a glistening manuscript. Thank you!

To my readers: I humbly appreciate the time and treasure you've
traded for a few hours' enjoyment. I strive to ensure you always come
out ahead in our transaction, and I hope that you always feel I've
succeeded in that. Thank you for your support and reviews, and for
telling your friends about this new, emerging author.

Research for this novel, much like its predecessor, *The Trafficker,* shocked, disappointed, and surprised me. The culture clash between violent, literal Islam and the West hasn't been news since 624 AD, but the extent of the current no-go zones and enforced sharia across Europe, for me, was. I fear that global apologists seriously delay the reformation so desperately needed within the Islamic religion, and, by their efforts to deny the creation of sharia-controlled neighborhoods and enclaves across Europe, they invite vigilantism, civil war, and even a modern Crusade. Political correctness and alternate realities seriously harm the hundreds of millions of moderate Muslims who live every day in peace and harmony with their non-Muslim neighbors.

Sweden recently convicted a retiree of a hate crime for an online post and fined her in excess of her monthly income. England, as of this writing, is investigating a mother for a hate crime after she misidentified the assumed gender of another woman's transgender child on a news broadcast. On 15-Jan-2019, the Sweden's Security Service (*Säpo*) declared a terror attack remains "likely to occur" on their soil. On 24-Mar-2019, *Säpo* released a report that identified radical Islamic terrorism as the nation's greatest security threat.

The descriptions of the no-go enclaves in this book are based on or taken directly from news reports, first-hand accounts, and verifiable sources. My references, among others, included articles published by the **British Broadcasting Corporation, jihadwatch.org, the Associated Press, Newsweek, New York Times, the Washington Post, Breitbart News,** and **Gatestone Institute,** as well as French publications *L'Obs* and *Valeurs Actuelles,* along with a report entitled **"No-Go Zones in the French Republic: Myth or Reality,"** and a 2,200-page report entitled *Banlieue de la République* (**Suburbs of the Republic),** which found Seine-Saint-Denis and other French suburbs are becoming "separate Islamic societies" where sharia law supplants French law and inhabitants are openly immersed in violent, literal Islam.

On 24-April-2018, thirty imams from around France sent an

open letter to the French daily, *Le Monde,* a strongly worded condemnation of antisemitism and Islamist terrorism that stressed remaining silent "would make us complicit and therefore culpable." The signatories described themselves as "indignant" — both as French citizens and as faithful Muslims — "at the confiscation of our religion by criminals." **God bless those brave men, their families, and the work ahead of them. Their success is also our success.**

The ***Seine-Saint-Denis*** neighborhood and the apartment building in which Abrini lived at ***8 Rue de Corbillon*** are those used by some of the terrorists who conspired to commit the November 2015 attacks in Paris. Paris police and French military assaulted that building on 18-Nov-2015, three days after the Paris attacks.

Finally, the Notre Dame Cathedral. I'm grateful to have seen it several times in my life, saddened by the heartbreaking tragedy, and terrified of how the French government may handle its reconstruction. As of 1905, France confiscated all Catholic churches in their nation and has allowed many of them to fall into substantial disrepair. The 15-April fire that destroyed the cathedral's roof and weakened much of the structure remains under investigation at the time of this publication. According to research from **Gatestone Institute** and its contributors, more than 800 French churches are damaged, attacked, and desecrated each year, and the suspects are often followers of literal, fundamental Islam.

"If the fire really was an accident, it is almost impossible to explain how it started. Benjamin Mouton, Notre Dame's former chief architect, explained that the rules were exceptionally strict and that no electric cable or appliance, and no source of heat, could be placed in the attic. He added that an extremely sophisticated alarm system was in place. The company that installed the scaffolding did not use any welding and specialized in this type of work. The fire broke out more than an hour after the workers' departure and none of them was present. It spread so quickly that the firefighters who rushed to the spot as soon as they could get there were shocked. Remi Fromont, the chief architect of the French Historical Monuments said: "The fire could not start from any element present where it started. A real calorific load is necessary to launch such a disaster"." – *The Burning of Notre Dame and the Destruction of Christian Europe, by Dr. Guy Millière, a professor at the University of Paris and author of 27 books on France and Europe for Gatestone Institute.*

As with the first two books in this series, all the characters are entirely figments of my imagination. **Gerard Antlé**, however, shares the background and experiences of one of my paternal relatives who emigrated to the US in the 18th century and became a sniper in the Continental Army's Swamp Foxes. Gerard's fictional escape from Taliban captivity is based on one of his Revolutionary War experiences. Any other references to actual persons are used fictionally and have been clearly identified. Most locations are real and used fictionally or based on actual locales. I relied equally on my own travel, photographs, and open sources like Google Maps to assure accuracy when required. The list of completely fictional locations will be much shorter:

Although the **Hotel Grimod de la Reynière** previously existed at the corner of *Avenue Gabriel* and *Rue Boissy d'Anglas*, it was destroyed to make way for the US Embassy building that stands there today. The fictional location in this book is at the northwest corner of *Place de la Concorde,* which is currently occupied by another, real-life hotel. My technical adviser, BL, gets credit for naming **The Oremus** hotel chain, which translates to "Let us pray." Even though it's a figment of my imagination, I believe a well-funded clandestine organization would do well to run such an overt operation. It would offer tremendous operational flexibility if they could keep it secret. That's always the hang-up, right? At any rate, the **Greenwich** location stands at the site of an **ibis** hotel near the National Maritime Museum. As of this publication, **The Oremus - Paris** stands at the modern-day location of *Theatre de la Ville* at 3 *Avenue Gabriel.*

The aid organization Michael used as a cover to enter Abrini's building, **Humanitarian Crisis in Motion,** is also a figment of my imagination. The underlying political philosophies, however, are not. *Férme A Table*, the grocery delivery service Gerard used for the same purpose, is also fictitious.

ABSOLVERS_

- Michael Thomas: Priest, AKA "Andrew"
  - Sergio Guzman: Priest, AKA "Jude"
  - John: Supervisor and Trainer
  - Chasseur Antlé: Priest, AKA "Alpha"
  - James The Lesser: Fixer and Quartermaster

CHURCH OFFICIALS_

□ His Holiness Cornelius II: Current, Sitting Pope

□ Cardinal Paul Dylan: Under-Secretariat of the Economy, Vatican City

□ Harold Hoffaburr: Assistant to Cardinal Dylan

□ Eduardo Hernandez: Monsignor, San Miguel Chapel, Santa Fe

□ Luc Devoux: Priest, Saint Denis Cathedral, Paris

THE REST OF GOD'S CHILDREN_

◻ Shawn Moore: Fallen Priest, AKA "Thomas"

   ◻ Frank Thomas: Michael's Father

   ◻ Mary Thomas: Michael's Mother

   ◻ Gerard Antlé: Counter-Terrorism Inspector, French National Police

   ◻ Mahmoud Algeri: Lieutenant, French National Police

   ◻ Claudette Antlé: Gerard's separated wife

   ◻ Marie Antlé: Gerard's teenage daughter

   ◻ Abdul Siddiqi: Self-proclaimed imam, Seine-Saint-Denis

   ◻ Abdel Abdullah Abrini: Syrian refugee, electrical engineer

GAVIN REESE_

Gavin answered his call to service by working as a professional cop, spent many weekends and holidays in a cop car of one kind or another, and is honored to have protected and served the public in this manner. His training and experience in areas such as Patrol, Narcotics, Undercover Operations, Counterterrorism, Sex and Human Trafficking, S.W.A.T., and Dark Web Investigations provide an ever-growing queue of ideas and stories for his fact-based fiction. Gavin currently works on advanced academic degrees that he hopes improve the public good.

Gavin's rare free time is devoted to family, travel, martial arts, SCUBA diving, mountaineering, and pursuing the perfect ice cream. Never all in the same day.

A portion of all Gavin's sales is donated to crime victims, as well as charities that serve law enforcement professionals and veterans, their families and heirs, and honor the memory of our Fallen Heroes.